Praise for What We Give Away

"Enlightening, thought-provoking and heartwarming. Perfect for book clubs!"
—Barbara Bos, Managing Editor, Women Writers, Women's Books

"Paulette Stout once again creates a powerful inspection of life... raising important questions about body image. Libraries will want to recommend *What We Give Away* to book clubs."
—D. Donovan, Senior Reviewer, Midwest Book Review

"This book is a must-read for any woman. It's a heartwarming and thought-provoking journey of self-discovery with a touch of romance that will leave you thinking long after the final page."
—Amanda Speights, Author, Love's Arrival

"A delicious love story, but way more. As someone who fought weight all my life, it took me decades to give up on the weight-loss merry-go-round. Thank you, Ms. Stout, for the great story, and I hope it will help others on the weight-loss road. Highly recommend."
—Laura Drake, Award-Winning Author

"Stout's strong women characters make big changes in their worlds, and this one is no exception."
—Annie M. Ballard, Author

Also by Paulette Stout

Love, Only Better: Bold Journeys Book 1

What We Never Say: Bold Journeys Book 2

What Eyes Can't See: Bold Journeys Book 3

What We Give Away: Bold Journeys Book 4 (February 2025)

A Million Ways: Stories of Motherhood (Anthology)

Short Stories

All About Kyle

Ho Ho Hanukkah: A Kyle and Rebecca Holiday Story

The Breakup: A Barbara and Joe Prequel

What We Give Away

A Delicious Standalone Novel |
Bold Journeys Book 4

Paulette Stout

Media Goddess Inc.

First Edition

Edited by Miranda Darrow.

Cover Design by Rena Violet

Interior Design by Rena Violet.

ISBN 979-8-9890239-1-2 (eBook Edition)

ISBN 979-8-9890239-3-6 (Paperback Edition)

Library of Congress Control Number: 2024920851

Published by Media Goddess Inc.,

241 Arlington Street #814, Acton, MA 01720

Visit **paulettestout.com** for author information.

For everyone who has wondered if they're good enough.
Know you are.

Author's Note

I can't remember a time when I didn't think I was too fat. From an early age, friends, family, doctors, teachers, and more made it quite clear that trim was the only way to live. Larger kids were teased and treated badly, as were any large adults I encountered. Including those in my family, who genetically tended toward larger sizes on both my mother's and father's sides.

And so began my lifetime of yo-yo dieting, constantly chasing the elusive "perfect weight," so I could avoid being on the wrong end of the scale. The pressure to conform to the socially accepted standard was both overwhelming—and single-minded. For example, I was once in a doctor's appointment discussing a tragic family incident of attempted suicide. Instead of comforting me, the provider ignored my tears and redirected the conversation to the diet app she wanted me to use. True story. Snide comments and other hurtful experiences left me avoiding checkups and hating myself for not being the right size.

It wasn't until I discovered the anti-diet movement that I learned why my diets always failed.

They're designed to.

That's a bold statement, but the contrary views included in this book are based on sound research from reputable sources, including the CDC and NIH, that I have included in the back as additional reading.

My research also included *The F*ck It Diet* by Caroline Dooner, *Fearing the Black Body: The Racial Origins of Fat Phobia* by Sabrina

Strings, *Intuitive Eating* by Evelyn Tribole and Elyse Resch, and *Health at Every Size* by Linda/o Bacon. To that I added learnings about anorexia nervosa, including *Life Hurts* by Dr. Elizabeth McNaught.

I also engaged experts to read and give feedback on my manuscript, including Sydney Gatward, MS RD LDN, who was once my registered dietitian, and Jaimie (OJ) Bushell from MEDA Inc., a Multi-Service Eating Disorder Association, who both read and gave valuable input to help me more accurately bring Leslie's journey to life.

Many of you may doubt these experts, thinking I've abandoned the diet chase simply because I'm undisciplined or lazy. If so, I once thought like you. And my personal journey to body acceptance made writing this book essential.

I've since found it takes way more discipline to step away from the failed reality of dieting when doctors, the media, governments, big pharma, food manufacturers, and academia all financially gain from us endlessly trying to lose. It sounds like a conspiracy theory but read on. There's way more to food, bodies, and dieting than meets the eye.

Paulette

A Note About the Word "FAT"

In everyday conversation, the word FAT is typically avoided or considered an insult. If someone says they look fat, witnesses rush in to say, "No! You don't look fat. You're beautiful." By implication, fat is the opposite of beautiful.

Many in the body liberation movement have reclaimed the word FAT and use it as intended: a neutral word to describe someone's larger size.

You will see the word FAT used in this book in this respectful context.

Chapter 1

LESLIE

My four-inch heels echoed off the shadowy Manhattan sidewalk, the lonely sound reverberating off the glassy skyscraper ahead. Tugging down the miniskirt barely covering my ass sent my handbag sliding off my shoulder. The bag too small for my laptop. Hence my 11:00 p.m. detour to our co-working space in my streetwalker garb.

How do women wear these?

Every muscle in my weary body ached from hours of standing, especially the balls of my feet. But blending in was the only way to get close to informants at the heart of my sex trade articles without raising suspicion.

After following their lives for nearly a year, I'd grown attached to these women. Online commenters cried for updates. So I allowed myself one last check-in to say goodbye before putting this story behind me. Being a journalist meant there was always another story waiting, all impatient, and tapping her foot. But no such story had inspired me, and sitting in my empty apartment got old fast.

I pushed through the building's revolving door, the lobby warmth chasing away late May's chill. I rubbed my arms as my shoes clacked on the marble floors.

Chuck, the night security guard, glanced up from where he sat reading the *New York Daily News*. He smirked, shaking his head. "Evening, Miss Allen."

"Chuck." I nodded hello. He'd long since gotten used to the crazy getups I wore to chase stories. Besides hooker garb, there were the tight dresses and wig disguises essential for getting close to organized crime bosses. Sometimes tattered jeans and vests, a bandanna, and fake tattoos for biker gangs. Even a suit and skirt when skulking around City Hall. The guard rarely stopped me, except when I disguised myself as a man and he didn't recognize me. Tonight I sailed through to the waiting elevator and pressed 47.

When the doors closed, the car's polished chrome interior left me alone with my reflection. Ignoring the microscopic miniskirt, halter top, and fishnets, my eyes sought that stubborn bulge of skin where my waistband pinched. The bump of flesh marred the otherwise smooth contour from my abdomen to my ribcage. No matter how I sacrificed, skipped meals, and suffered through juice cleanses and sit-ups, that annoying mound reappeared above every waistband without fail. It tormented me almost as much as the loudmouthed reporters upstairs were about to.

I sucked in my gut as the pressure from the slowing elevator forced my legs to flex. The balls of my feet screamed bloody murder, but I slapped on a game face to run the heckle gauntlet ahead.

Showtime.

The doors opened into our co-working space, a huge bullpen of desks separated by cubicle dividers, barely high enough to prevent people from seeing their neighbor's keyboard. Everything else stared back at you. The shitty seating plan forced many of us to stalk the office at night for privacy. Though all journalists, we worked at a menagerie of publications. Lucky me sat next to the poor slobs writing for tawdry men's magazines. Their patrons were the ones keeping the women I just visited selling their bodies on dark street corners.

"Yo, yo, yo! Check out what Allen's got on tonight!" Tony, the loudmouth, clapped, rubbing his palms together with eager anticipation.

Justin clawed at the air like a cat. "Rawrah! You're one tasty piece of—"

"Watch it!" I yelled back.

"I'm on deadline," he continued. "But can definitely squeeze you into my calendar!"

As if he had the stones...

I made my way to my desk, ignoring their hoots and whistles. Unlocking the drawer, I grabbed my sweatshirt and slid it over my head to a chorus of boos.

"Now why'd you go do that?" Tony yelled. "Ruined my view!"

"I can't believe you wear that out in public, but thank you!" Justin slapped his palms together, praying to whatever god would have a brute like him.

"Hey," Vince said. "Imagine that tub of lard, Victoria, in a getup like that?"

Vince laughed so hard his own rolls jiggled. The other two joined in an escalating round of insults at Victoria's expense.

What idiots.

Victoria Cooper Rawley had more reporter chops than the three of them put together. While they wrote about bustlines, Victoria made headlines. She was the reason two corrupt New York City mayors had to resign. Once exposed, they had no choice. She owned politics in this town and had for decades. Victoria had a steady gig at a local TV network and published noteworthy articles on the side. It was a career path I emulated. As I surveyed my fishnet-clad legs, ripples of shame washed over me. She would never be caught dead in the outfits I wore chasing stories.

But my approach helped me get close to sources others wouldn't attempt and invest fully in the people at the heart of my stories. Walking in their shoes helped me better empathize with their struggles. I infused that passion into my writing. It was a delicious high that kept me going all day. Exposing ugly truths alongside the despicable people who lined their pockets by letting corruption flourish. Meanwhile, innocents suffered. While I wasn't at Victoria's level, my trophy case proved I was doing something right. Unlike the hyenas, who continued catcalling me over my head.

I slammed my desk drawer and stood up to block their line of sight. "Will you jokers fucking shut up? Christ, if one of you got laid once in a while, you might have a whiff of self-control. God, you're pathetic."

Vince's face fell. "No need to get bitchy, Allen. We're just appreciating your... ASS-ets."

They broke into rolling laughter.

"Is that what you call it? Appreciation? It's as lame as your circulation."

"Ding!" Tony yelled between gulps of air. "You've been KO'd by a skinny broad dressed as a hooker!"

"Dumb cow," Vince muttered under his breath, tossing a half-eaten sandwich into the trash can we shared.

Turkey, cheese, lettuce, tomato, loosely wrapped in white wax paper. My stomach knotted at the sight. The tang of the vinegar dressing assaulted my senses, causing my stomach to churn. I grabbed a bottle of water out of my desk drawer, chugging it until familiar fullness quieted my hunger pangs. I then dropped into my chair and swiveled away to swap shoes. My feet moaned in relief. The faster I slipped on my sneakers, the quicker I'd escape these assholes.

My phone chirped from within my purse as it came off Do Not Disturb mode.

Fishing for it, I found a series of text notifications on my lock screen. A message from my editor, Viraj, and another from the host of *The Kaelen Reed Show*. Reed was number one in prime time news and an insufferable jackass. You'd never know it to look at him, and I certainly hadn't before we'd briefly dated. The man's ego could barely fit in the enormous studio where we taped his nightly show. My recurring panelist spot meant I got to see the real man up close, usually at least once a week. A glutton for punishment, he still harbored hopes we'd be a "we." But I had no intention of letting that happen.

I tapped open my messages.

> Viraj: Reed's team called. He wants more eye candy tomorrow night. Suggested you wear your hooker garb. I told him to stuff it.

Gotta love Viraj. He'd really come into his own partnering to run the online publication *Dear Diary* with my best friend, Rebecca. I first freelanced for him when he worked at the world's top fashion magazine, but he left it all behind to be his own boss. A passion to which I could totally relate.

I texted back three laughing/crying emojis before tapping open Reed's message.

> Kaelen Reed: Your editor has zero eye for TV. Ditch the white blouse and show some skin for once.

I could screenshot that text and blast it on a digital billboard in Times Square and nothing would happen to him. No one would believe America's darling would say such a thing. Must be awesome to live a life without consequences. The rest of us didn't have that privilege. And I had no intention of showing up on network television in clothing that'd undermine the credibility I'd worked over 15 years to earn. Even longer if you counted my college newspaper stint. No. The best answer for a narcissist like Reed was silence. I stuffed my torture shoes into my computer bag and locked my desk.

I started to say goodbye to the clown squad before realizing they didn't deserve it. Besides, they were already back at work. Absorbed, their fingers flew as fast as their mouths had moments earlier. Now clothed, I no longer held interest. As if my only value was as a body exposed for their amusement. But that left me wondering who the true jester was between us.

Chapter 2

LESLIE

On set the next night at NewsOne, Reed rapped on my open dressing room door.

"Knock, knock!" he said, checking to be sure we were alone.

I removed the makeup shield from the collar of my white blouse, tucking the fabric tight into my dark-wash jeans. I looked into his exasperated face. "What?" I asked.

"God, Allen. You've got so much potential and you're wasting it."

"Enlighten me." I slipped an arm into my caramel-colored blazer, less than enthusiastic for the mansplaining about to head my way. This from a man who used so many note pages during shows that I wondered whether he was more actor than journalist.

I crossed my arms as he sauntered close.

"You're like a fucking blank page. A muse. You're hiding that knockout body of yours under all that fabric. Remember, I know you. *Intimately.*"

"Don't remind me." I focused on the ceiling, waiting for his mating dance to end.

"Dark curly hair, half-Latina. All your awards and the gritty underworld bullshit you're in. It's so hot."

I allowed myself a hard eye roll.

He halted his inspection, standing before me. "I've got to compete with the sexpots across the dial, and you're doing me no favors."

I'd had all the sexpot ogling I could handle last night. I didn't need every man watching to think I was a bimbo prancing for their amusement. Why did women reporters have to accept this shit? Older, balding, lumpy men graced the screen 24/7.

"Are you asking Stan to show more skin, too?" I asked.

"God, no." He reflexively shivered, cleansing his tongue. "His chunky body and bald head are all I can take. I will never unsee that image. Thanks for that."

I smiled, bending to push my computer bag out of the way. When I rose, he remained leaned over to get a better view.

"You're a pig."

I brushed by him and out the door, but he followed, whispering in my ear. "We'll be working more closely once you take over the Saturday host role. When is that?"

"I start in late September. Playing dumb is beneath you."

"Okay then, have dinner with me? The two of us out? We'd make Page Six."

Kaelen Reed was the worst hound dog in network news. I had no intention of going for a double-dip now that I'd finally scored a solo hosting spot. Working every Saturday night meant no weekends off work for the foreseeable future. But the opportunity could be a launchpad for something greater.

Lost in my head, I forgot Kaelen still awaited an answer.

Did he just lick his lips?

Eww.

"That's probably a bad idea. Besides, you forget I write for the *Post* sometimes. Why should I settle for Page Six when I can appear on page one all by myself?"

I chuckled, thinking it an amusing line, but he smarted, releasing my elbow.

"Don't bite the hand that feeds you. I got you that hosting gig. It can be gone like that." He snapped his fingers.

"I have a contract." I lifted my chin.

"Funny thing about contracts. The good stuff is in the fine print."

Checking for eavesdroppers, he stepped back from me with a repulsed look on his face. Muttering what I thought was "bitch" under his breath, he stormed toward his anchor chair. The stage manager intercepted him with two children in tow, all polished for what looked to be a special visit. Kaelen's frown vanished, replaced by a smile I knew to be genuine as he tousled the hair of the little boy and gave the girl a high five.

How was this the same guy who had threatened me moments before? My contract was far from tissue paper. I'd read that damn contract backward and forward before signing. Barbara, my other best friend and attorney, did too. I exhaled, clearing the knot in my chest. Kaelen was being a blowhard. Besides, my dig about Page Six served him right. Here he was, the biggest thing going in network news, someone covering presidential elections and breaking events, chasing tail. It should be beneath him. Though he probably didn't view anyone as his equal. The great Kaelen Reed, floating in a solar system all his own.

Crazy to think I used to have a crush on him. His on-screen caring and empathy were so convincing. His dark hair, brooding eyes, and deep-bronze skin reminded me so much of my ex. But two seconds in bed with Reed only made me crave the original. I missed Risto every damn day. I'd never been able to replicate what we had with anyone else, so I gave up trying. But my asshole colleague was the closest stand-in I got to the man who broke my heart.

I shook off the nagging longing for Risto and made my way to the panelist seat nearest to Reed. The chair of honor. When the camera pulled out for a two-person angle, Reed only wanted to share the frame with someone "lean and attractive." His words, not mine. With such an egotistical attitude, it was a wonder he allowed any guests on the show at all. Tonight, panelists included reporters from two news organizations who, like me, recently ran articles on the sex trade. Both supremely accomplished and entertaining, their physical appearance must have launched our esteemed host into panic mode.

Victoria was full-bodied and fabulous, impeccably dressed as always in a formfitting cobalt blue dress, with shiny black braids coiled in a knot on top of her head. Meanwhile, Stan's pasty baldness took a triple coat of translucent powder to keep from blinding us with the reflection of overhead studio lights. A last-minute stand-in for a canceled panelist, Stan wore a suit that somehow got wrinkled in the thirty feet between his dressing room and the set.

I rubbed the chill out of my arms. Despite the layers that my host abhorred, I could never get warm in the studio. Hell, I couldn't get warm outside the studio, either, one of the few traits I had in common with my mother. Even if I wanted to, I'd freeze in a tiny dress on set.

I stole a glance at Reed, who sat shuffling papers, his head bowed as if listening. I glanced over to the control room's soundproof window.

Maureen, the show's producer, stood talking to her host.

"Everyone ready?"

Reed finally saw fit to acknowledge we existed. He smiled at me as if we hadn't just squabbled, but the harmony didn't last.

"Stan, you're a fucking mess, man," Reed yelled. "And you two are dressed for a fucking church luncheon. Do we have no stylist around here?"

"You're lucky I'm dressed for church," Victoria said. "That sewer you call a mouth needs all the prayers it can get. Can I get an 'Amen!'?"

"Amen!" I cried but was the only one.

Reed's crew muffled snickers, knowing better than to mock their boss. Stan stood to let the stylist do a quick jacket steam, leaving me and Victoria to savor our moment of rebellion.

"Why do we come here again?" I asked her.

"It pays well, and Reed's easy on the eyes?" Victoria answered.

"Oh, yeah."

"I can hear you, you know?" Reed said, eyes glued to the papers scattered on the desk in front of him.

A less-rumpled Stan hopped back into his chair.

"Quiet! We're live in three, two..." The stage manager's dramatic double-arm flourish pointed to us as the "On Air" light glowed white from the wall just as the red bulb atop Camera A switched on.

Showtime.

"Welcome to Kaelen Reed Tonight. This evening, we've assembled a power panel to dive into the issue of sex trafficking in America. We often think of sex trafficking as limited to movies or border drug cartels. But crime syndicates freely operate here in New York City, a subject our three guests know intimately. Let's meet them…"

Kaelen guided the panel through intros and a discussion with his usual grace and charm. He struck concerned expressions at the right moments, making me forget he gave two shits about the harrowing stories he covered. He played worried anchorman to perfection for the entire hour, ignoring us during the commercial breaks, as always.

Small blessings.

When the "all clear" signal sounded, we breathed a sigh of relief. My show appearance would send countless readers to my article on *Dear Diary*'s website. That not only amplified the stories we covered, but I also enjoyed it tremendously. So much so, I'd started my own YouTube channel to get my fix in between appearances. The extra exposure left Viraj smiling at the magazine's web traffic data.

"Great job everyone," Reed barked. "Vicki, sit forward a bit more next time. We need more cleavage and fewer chins. Do something about that, will you? It's like a fucking goiter's on your throat. Stan, you best stick to print."

He flashed us a Cheshire Cat grin. His wordless challenge said, *Yes, I'm an asshole. What are you going to do about it?*

Reed strode off set.

Stan wandered off muttering, so I stood up, expecting Victoria to follow. But she sat, dumbstruck, her effervescence gone flat. She swallowed hard as tears flowed around the sideways fingers, struggling to dab them dry.

"Hey," I whispered. "Let's get you out of here."

I hug-lifted her, guided us back to our shared dressing room, and closed the door.

"He's an asshole. Don't listen to him." I grabbed the nearby tissue box and aimed it in her direction. She snatched two.

Victoria blotted her eyes, trying to talk around her choked sobs as she gestured toward the set. "He's got all the power and privilege. Yet he insists on belittling us. I don't need this shit! We're the ones doing him a favor."

I understood what she meant. His ability to ask questions of hardcore journalists made him appear to be an empathetic "everyman." Reality was the exact opposite, though he seemed to have a soft spot for children.

Victoria sniffled, calmer now. "I'm a big girl, I know it. I've struggled with my weight my whole life. But shit like that? It hurts. Calling my neck a goiter? I thought after what he said in that interview, it'd be different..."

In Reed's recent cover story with *Esquire*, the magazine praised his show and impact as a leading Black newsman. They asked about his commitment to showcasing women of color on the show, mentioning Victoria by name. Reed hailed her as one of the most accomplished Black journalists in America, saying he was proud to have her on set. That context must have made today's rant sting all the worse.

I had no clue what Victoria was going through or how it hurt to be shamed that way. Every time I heard someone insulted for their weight, I died for them inside. But it also jolted me back in line should I ever stray from the acceptable thin standard. Not that I needed a reminder.

At 37, I'd long since surrendered to my mom's dietary guidelines. Few meals, fewer calories, and lots of water to fill the emptiness. Hard as it was to manage the hunger sometimes, insults like Victoria endured made me fear ever gaining an ounce. Strong as I tried to be, I could never withstand the disgusting abuse hurled Victoria's way. But she shouldn't have to. No person should.

She squeezed my arm in thanks and turned to gather her things.

Someone had to hold Reed accountable.

Maybe one day I would.

Chapter 3

RISTO

"Risto, look who's a panelist on *Chopped*," Jose said, staring at the small, ceiling-mounted television I had installed in the restaurant's kitchen. My executive sous-chef had apparently taken a break from one of his telenovelas to gawk at the Food Network.

"Not interested," I yelled through my open office door. If I didn't complete our product order soon, I'd miss the deadline for tomorrow's delivery.

"It's Chase. Dude must have a hell of an agent," Jose called.

Seriously?

I pushed away from my desk and stepped into the bustling kitchen prep for dinner service. Sure enough, Chase Patel's smug face sat alongside two other chefs.

One of these things is not like the others.

I shook my head. "He spends more time on TV than cooking, and his skills are sketchy to begin with."

Dot, my restaurant partner and the closest thing I had to a mother, pumped my shoulder as she passed. "That's probably smart."

I chuckled at her dig. "Oh, good point."

When I was home from culinary school one weekend, Chase tagged along and insisted on preparing dinner. Dot rarely shared her kitchen but relented to Chase, who whipped up a batch of ceviche that gave us all food poisoning. She hadn't eaten it since, despite me adding the dish to our seasonal menu two years ago.

"Turn it off, will you?" I called to Jose, who silenced the TV.

"That should be you," Dot said.

Of course, she'd think I should be on television. The woman was a dreamer, like my parents before her. While former classmates like Chase pursued fame, my grandparents' lessons about staying humble guided my path. My restaurant, Boricua, was thriving. Our recent addition had barely dented our reservation wait list, with tables still booked solid two weeks out.

When I'd opened my Puerto Rican eatery six years earlier, I hoped for a more casual experience where last-minute diners could find a table. But we'd grown too popular. I hated the idea of dinner crowds waiting for hours, clutching their cell phones while waiting for a "your table's ready" text. Or worse, those annoying squares of plastic that vibrated and blinked.

I once ate at a seafood restaurant in Boston with a lobster-shaped buzzer. As if that made waiting outside for an hour in the scorching sun more enjoyable.

Not my style.

I wiped my brow with my forearm before stepping out the side door of the restaurant's kitchen to get a breath of fresh air in our herb garden. I snapped a few leaves of oregano and rubbed them between my fingers to enjoy the pungent, earthy fragrance. The breeze swayed the trees overhead, casting afternoon shadows on the white house my business called home.

My restaurant.

Even years on, I still pinched myself to confirm it was real. Me, the orphaned brown boy from small-town Pennsylvania, owner of a thriving restaurant. I fed people so well they devoured my food, then returned with friends. The local radio station had approached me, asking about running advertising. But I saw no point, given how busy we already were.

I lowered myself onto the bench, the wooden boards creaking under my weight. I'd have to talk to Dot about getting a sturdier one. When my silent partner planted the small kitchen garden, she'd skimped on the outdoor furniture. This Home Depot special wouldn't cut it. In the rare moments I had to relax outdoors, I didn't want to worry about the damn seat cracking under me.

I closed my eyes, letting an herbal bouquet fill my senses. Birds chirped from the oak tree overhead.

This was happiness.

Or would be if Leslie were here. Thoughts of her invaded my every waking moment. The forever love that wasn't. Whenever I strained to remember why I broke up with her, the memories of her rejection came flooding back. All the times she refused to support my culinary career and dreams of opening Boricua. She looked devastated when I got the bank loan and told her it was happening. She had passions of her own, always chasing news stories. Why was my goal less valid? Ending our relationship was painful, but how could I be with someone who couldn't believe in me as much as I did her?

The one thing I hadn't considered was how hard it'd be to cut ties. Her aunt was my business partner and neighbor, which meant pictures and news of Leslie were all around me. Hell, I had to stop watching my favorite news channel because *The Kaelen Reed Show* promos too often featured Leslie. By contrast, she likely had no trouble forgetting me. Out here in Pennsylvania, I felt like a love-lost clod, pining over someone who so clearly had no interest in me, my life, or...

"No, I will not! I must speak to him!" a man yelled from the kitchen.

"Whoa, buddy. Can't be back here. Just turn around and—" Jose said.

"Take your hands off me!"

"Sir, sir?" Dot pleaded.

"Risto! Need a hand in here!" Freddie hollered.

What the hell was going on?

I crossed to the door in three long strides, flipping it open with such force it banged on the wall before slamming behind me.

A tiny man in black slacks and a blue-and-white striped shirt stood arguing with Freddie and Dot. He turned my way, tilting his head to scan up my 6'4" frame. His throat bobbed as he swallowed, but he quickly recovered.

"Ahhh, Chef Zaldo! Please, you must help." The curious intruder shuffled over to me.

Once my eyes adjusted to the inside lighting, it was my turn to be stunned. Before me stood Silas Greene, the lead restaurant critic for *Philadelphia Metro* magazine. But why had he stormed my kitchen?

"I'll handle this. Back to work, everyone," I said. "Mr. Greene? Why don't we step outside for a word?"

I gestured the way I'd come, and he followed me out the screen door.

He smoothed his dark hair back, glistening with so much styling product I wouldn't be shaking hands with him.

"Chef Zaldo, you must excuse the interruption. I've been trying to secure a reservation for weeks, and my impatience got the better of me."

He unfurled a printed page from his pocket. "Everyone is crowing over your food in the *Philadelphia Metro* chat rooms, and I can't get a table. This article wasn't even about you, but it was overrun with diner comments singing your praises. I rarely pull the 'do you know who I am?' line. But in this case I will. You must find a seating for me. Please."

Dot heard what happened from a few of the gals in her women's group. It was pretty comical that passionate diners were having throwdowns over my mofongo with shrimp.

"I'd be honored to serve you, if you don't mind dining in my office. I can't put out my guests and have no available tables tonight."

"Splendid! Yes, absolutely!" He clapped. "Put me in a corner and you won't even know I'm here. You're brave to let me into your kitchen like this."

"Anyone this desperate for my food is always welcome. I'm proud of my team and our attention to detail. We keep things immaculate and have nothing to hide."

Greene settled into my office, but like a little mouse, he nosed out the door moments later to watch us in the kitchen. I eyed him but returned to my meal preparations. There were rice and beans to make, chicken to roast, plantains to peel and ready for frying, onions, peppers, and mounds of garlic to prep.

Periodically, I looked up to see him whispering into the voice memo on his phone. I removed a pernil from the oven and sliced him a portion of succulent roast pork. He moved to clap, but before his hands collided, he pocketed them. I smiled as I mounded his plate with a side of rice and beans, sweet fried plantains, and accepted a wooden bowl of shrimp mofongo from Jose.

Silas' face lit up as he saw me approach, and he darted back into my office.

Armed with a bundle of cutlery wrapped in a green cloth napkin, he dove into his meal.

"Mmm, oh my Lord, this is..." Greene's eyes reflexively closed while he chewed. "Outstanding. I... um..." He interrupted himself for another forkful. He savored each bite, his body going limp. It was such an intimate experience, I questioned whether to leave him be. But the theater of it all was utterly fascinating. It was precisely the ego boost I needed to evaporate visions of my classmate on the Food Network.

Once Silas swallowed, he glanced my way through heavy lids. "You, my friend, are a talent."

"Thank you. That means a lot coming from you."

"The world needs this food." He gestured to his plate with his fork. "And the world is bigger than Easton, Pennsylvania. I drove two hours to get here."

"You're too kind, Mr. Greene—"

"Silas. Call me Silas."

"I have my hands full here. We've just expanded..."

He waved my concerns away. "Pish, posh. You're thinking too small. A man with your talent is a rare gift. You mustn't deny your adoring public!"

Silas wasn't the first person to comment about my location being a problem. I'd resisted the call to bigger markets. Philadelphia. New York. Someone visiting from Puerto Rico once offered to make connections for me in San Juan. But Easton was home. Whenever I visited Leslie in Manhattan as a teen, and later, when we dated, it'd taken me days to recover from the sensory overload. The people, the noise, the concrete. I couldn't imagine living there. But I'd be lying to myself if I denied the temptation to grow my career. Former classmates appearing on TV made it hard not to wonder about the possibility.

Yet every time I allowed myself to dream, my grandparents' voices would break through and urge caution. Just as they were doing now.

I blinked away starry visions to focus on dinner service. "Enjoy your meal. There's some flan with your name on it when you're ready."

I turned to leave, but my guest had more to say.

"I've seen your type before. The bashful genius. You think Bobby Flay became a global star by being humble? Please. Give it some serious thought." Silas bent to his plate, so I left him to it and returned to the kitchen.

"Everything okay with Lord Helmet?" Jose joked as he sautéed a pan of vegetables.

"Shhh!" I gestured a slicing motion across my neck. "Don't offend the man who could tank our restaurant with a pen stroke."

"Start a fan club is more like it. We heard what he said." Freddie stopped chopping to hold eye contact.

"What do you want me to do? We just expanded. We're up to our necks in business already."

Jose shook his head. "Camarón que se duerme, se lo lleva la corriente."

A shrimp that sleeps gets carried away by the current.

It was an old Puerto Rican saying, but how did me being a respected restaurant owner in my hometown equate to me getting pushed along? Our staff had solid jobs. Diners praised us in chat rooms. Life looked pretty good right now from where I was sitting.

I returned to the chef's knife I'd abandoned before my break, taking my frustration out on a fillet of beef. My attention drifted back to my open office door, where gleeful chirps periodically floated over as Silas savored his meal.

Something told me I hadn't seen the last of my newest culinary fan.

Chapter 4

LESLIE

The next morning, sunlight streamed through my apartment's large windows. From my lower Greenwich Village vantage point, all of Manhattan sprawled out before me. Stillness hung in the air as I stared across the open-concept space to the kitchen beyond. It beckoned in a hopeless way, distracting me from the tall glass of water in my hand. Even the berry-lemonade electrolyte packet I added did nothing to make the drink more exciting.

"Fine. You win," I answered, the echo of my mother's voice whispering in my ear. I called her Little Diana. While Mom was clear across the country and mostly out of my life at this point, her proxy remained frustratingly close at all times. Like a prison guard keeping inmates in line.

I gulped the water down, my tension easing as the liquid filled my stomach and settled the hunger pangs I'd had since my last meal. Whenever that was. Tracking meals wasted brain space better focused on my work.

My cousin Gabby's ringtone sounded from my jeans pocket.

"¡Hola, chica!" she said.

"¿Que tal?" I asked, dropping one of the few Spanish phrases I knew despite years of language classes. As a child, Mom banned me from speaking Spanish at home with my dad. She feared if I picked up his Puerto Rican accent, my future job prospects would evaporate. Ironically, adopting Mom's heavy New York accent likely dampened my opportunities far worse than Dad's accent would. I still resented him for caving to her ridiculous demand. It was another of the many battles we lost to my mother. When emotional wounds and diverging priorities became too much, they divorced. Growing up, I spent every free moment with Dad's family in Pennsylvania. My cousin Gabby and I had been close ever since.

"Great show last night," she said. "I don't know how you do all that undercover work. It sounds risky."

"Not usually. Guys have gotten rough a few times, but I scrape by. I get my revenge in published words."

I plopped onto my sectional sofa, curling my legs up underneath me. I expected my cousin to continue talking. Chatty as an informant, Gabby typically held up both sides of our conversations. I once timed her at 17 minutes straight without a pause. But not today.

"Is something wrong?" I asked.

"There's no good way to ask, so I'm just going to say it. My mom's having surgery this week, and I wondered if you'd be open to coming out to stay with her."

"I thought it wasn't for a month?"

"It got moved up since the doctor is going on vacation. That's put me in a bind since I'm flying out for a trade show in Japan. I'll be there for the procedure but need to leave immediately after. I can't cancel, and David will have his hands full with the baby."

"It's no trouble. I'm happy to come."

She sighed in relief. "I hoped you'd say that."

"Of course, anything for her."

"Sure it's not a bother? You can work from anywhere, right? I mean, when you're not dressed up as a mob slut at some seedy bar…"

I laughed at that. She wasn't wrong. "Gabs, take a breath. I'll be there."

"It might cause trouble with Aunt Diana."

"Let's focus on your mom, not mine."

I hadn't heard my take-charge cousin this worked up since her mom caught us playing spin the bottle in the basement with a couple of neighborhood boys. That was before Risto's family moved in. There was a lot of smooching in the dark after my ex arrived. But I better get my mind right. Risto and I hadn't spoken in ages, and he was no doubt dating someone.

"Mom won't be able to bend or lift heavy things for a month. She'll need help with laundry, groceries, stairs. Which means she can't teach her yoga class, lead her women's group, or work at the restaurant. She'll be miserable."

My Aunt Dot—short for Dorothea—had always been a force of nature and a superstar in my eyes, ever since my summer stays at her house. Full of love and mischief, watching Dot fearlessly navigate life was likely where I inherited my daring tendencies. No way those came from my mother. My dad's only sister held a special place in my heart.

Running around the countryside as a teen, exploring creeks and fields and junkyards was as exciting to me as visiting Manhattan was for Gabby. My parents savored uninterrupted creative time, and I got a two-month break from my mom's helicopter parenting. Guess Dot's surgery gave me an opportunity to show my enduring appreciation.

"I'll try to keep her distracted. When do you need me there?"

"Is tomorrow too soon? You can get settled before her surgery on Wednesday. You haven't been out here in a while, so it'll be good to see you."

"Sorry about that. Work has been nuts."

"This work trip couldn't be happening at a worse time. But if you're around when she gets home, I'm way more comfortable going."

Gabby muffled the phone with her hand while she talked to someone. "I have to go."

After hanging up, my Spidey senses tingled. Gabby said Auntie's surgery wasn't serious, but my cousin definitely had an optimistic streak. I was glad to have a few hours to research her condition so I could enter the situation informed. Not all doctors got As in medical school, so I hoped hers was good. Sometimes I wished my Pennsylvania family would choose an A+ New York hospital for treatment, but the distance made that impractical.

I logged in to check email. With nothing pressing, I emailed the editors managing my many freelance projects and TV appearances to tell them I'd be working remotely for a while. No biggie, given that every one of them did too. And after Reed's antics last night, I could use a break from his toxic ego. Frankly, Pennsylvania might not be far enough. If they needed me, I could always join via satellite from a n affiliate or drive in for the show.

I shuffled over to the fridge, full-well knowing the bare shelves within made the trip fruitless. A small part of me hoped a grocery fairy would deposit delectable nibbles and save me the harrowing trip to the market. One step inside any supermarket, and my senses ignited. Colorful veggies, flaky baguettes. It took all my strength not to break off and devour the crispy loaves on sight. I did it once and was forced to pay for the bread with its empty wrapper. That's how out of control I was around food and why it was better for me not to eat at all.

I bowed my head until it connected with the refrigerator's glossy black surface. I pressed harder, pain registering, as what would soon be a red splotch formed on my forehead. Even that was preferable to hunger. Plus the sensation made me feel alive. Like the adrenaline hit of danger I got while snooping around New York's underbelly to uncover secrets. The thrill of tight deadlines. The rush of live podcasts and TV interviews.

Yeah, being between stories was a problem.

An issue I'd better rectify.

Fast.

I grasped the refrigerator handle in rebellion, a dizzy faintness taking hold.

When did I last eat?

Oh, right. The granola bar one of my streetwalker sources forced on me two nights ago. She said my hungry look was bad for business. The comment triggered every neural pathway hardwired to resist food and anyone trying to fatten me up. Little Diana's mantra echoed in my ears.

Nothing tastes as good as thin feels.

Fine, Mom. You win.

I tugged the refrigerator door open, substituting a chilly blast from the empty fridge for a meal. Once sufficiently chilled, I strolled down the loft's long hallway to my bedroom, stripped off my clothes, and jumped into a scalding shower.

Afterward, dampness clung to my skin as I slipped jeans over my stubbornly curvy hips. All the women on my dad's side had curves, a fact my mother never accepted. To her, a pear shape was a sign of weakness. Evidence that you'd yet to master your body and wrestle it into submission.

My thoughts must have summoned Mom, as moments later she called my cell phone. Either that, or some mutual friend squawked about Dot's surgery on Facebook.

"You're up early," I said, doing mental calculations for her New Mexico time zone. Mom painted wild, colorful desert scenes with haunting figures, and she often slept in after overnight painting sessions. People called her a poor-man's Georgia O'Keeffe, but Mom's disturbing work had earned her some hefty commissions recently. A fact she never failed to mention.

"You're going to stay at Dot's, I hear?" Her voice dripped with accusation. I never expected a "hello," given her passion for beginning phone calls mid-fight.

"Is that a problem?" I asked.

"You tell me. Sounds like you're going to be there a while? Weeks, even. What will that do to your waistline?"

"Can you stop? I'm a grown-ass woman. If I want to eat a few fried plantains, the world won't end."

"Every time you go there you gain weight. Every. Time. It took months to get back to your normal size each fall. By the time you were trim, the winter clothes were already in stores. You'll need to be strong. Think before every bite. How will this impact you? What is this food doing to your body? How will this impact your career?"

My first thought was to make my current body less hungry, but I mustn't exhale that in her presence. Besides, I knew better than to listen to my body's signals. If I did, I'd eat and eat until I exploded into a million pieces. The idea was too terrifying.

"They eat so unhealthy," she continued. "Well, at least if you're in charge of the menu, you can keep it lean and nutritious. Maybe Dot will lose a few pounds."

Mom paused her tirade to think, and I let her. Nothing I said now would register, anyway. My opinions never counted. I'd become an award-winning journalist who was about to have my own Saturday spot on cable's leading network news show. Yet my mother still treated me like I was nine.

"Actually, this is wonderful." Mom's voice grew light and cheery. "If Dot can't shop, she can't buy all those nasty foods she usually does. I'm coming around to the idea now. This is probably the opportunity she needs to save her life."

Dot seemed pretty fine, as far as I could tell. True, she carried more weight than was likely healthy. But she was committed to her path and had been teaching body acceptance classes to others. That blossomed into leading body-inclusive yoga at a local studio. Mom would no sooner change Dot's diet than Dot would Mom's.

By contrast, my mother had long followed a low-carb, low-sugar diet. Drinking nearly two gallons of water a day, she also religiously practiced meditative yoga. She controlled her regimen as strictly as her paint strokes. Her mania kept her thin as a rail and chasing the "health" she preached about but could never attain for herself. Each new medical condition that popped up, from the osteoporosis to the irregular heartbeat and digestive problems, deepened her fervor to get her diet right.

Lacking deep conviction on the matter, I'd only partially adopted her routine. Half-assing the diet and the water and skipping the exercise bit altogether. I managed my intake and walked to appointments when I could instead of taking the subway. Besides, Dad's sturdy genetics would likely spare me from her fate. He had fewer chronic conditions than her by a long shot.

"Stop worrying and go back to bed. I'll have my hands full tending to Dot. Shouldn't our focus be on helping her heal?"

"That's what I'm doing. Thinking of her health, now and in the future."

Really?

"Should I come help?"

"No. Please. You two are like oil and water. I'll be fine."

As I wrangled free from Mom to pack my bags, a pit formed in my stomach. When Gabby called, I longed to go visit, see my family, and reconnect. One hug transformed my street-hardened soul into a molten pool of gooey love. Mom's bucket of cold water swamped all that, a stark reminder that while Dot was the one having surgery, staying with her meant I'd have some struggles of my own.

Chapter 5

RISTO

Before Silas left the day before, he insisted I program his number into my phone. As I entered my house from my morning walk, his name lit up my device screen.

"We meet again," I said, dropping my keys in the bowl by the door.

"Forgive me, but I made a few calls on your behalf to some investors—"

"Whoa, now. Didn't you hear me yesterday? I'm not looking to move."

I'd just met the man and had no intention of letting him stampede through my life in the same way he'd ambushed my kitchen. But I had to hand it to him. The dude was persistent.

"Not move, expand," Silas said. "Spread your wings and fly to Manhattan."

After one meal, he presumed to know me and my life's goals? Nobody knew that, not even me. But maybe that was his point. I should want more.

Besides Dot, there was no wise elder guiding my life. My grandparents had passed away, and they did their best raising me after my parents died. I was six when it happened. Mom and Dad were on their way back from a date night when the sleeping driver of a semi-tractor trailer crossed into their lane. The collision forced their car over an embankment and out of my life. I awoke the next morning at my grandparents' house into a world forever altered. All the sparkle gone, save for a single glimmer.

Cooking.

The kitchen had been the center of our happy home. I helped Mom prepare family favorites, standing on a stool at her side. My dad, a cook at a restaurant, taught me how to dice an onion so every square was the same size. It only took a few well-placed slices, and that technique served me until culinary school upped my game. But back then I'd beg to tag along with Dad. He'd arrive at work and sit me in a corner, warning me to stay out of the way. He never fully understood how fascinated I was by it all. In minutes, skillful hands transformed ordinary ingredients—meats, onions, plantains, rice, and more—into the savory dishes I loved.

Comforting arroz con pollo.

Garlicky mofongo con camarones.

Golden maduros, fried until the plantains caramelized to perfection.

It was nothing short of magic, and I wanted in. Part of that came from my mom, always at the ready with a smile and a storybook full of wizards. She helped Dad keep the faith that he'd soon have a business of his own. Tragically, he never did. Every day I worked for myself, I honored his memory and his passion for cooking. Would my parents have been like Silas and encourage me to stretch myself?

Of course they would.

"Sueña en grande," they'd say each night with a kiss. Dream big.

"Why me, Silas?"

"Why not you? Top marks in culinary school. Impressive stints in several excellent Philly restaurants until you opened Boricua. You're a proven restaurateur. And from what I can tell, an honorable man."

My little pest had done his homework. I sighed into the phone. "Okay. Fill me in."

Silas had spoken to three different restaurant groups interested in meeting with me. Each had ideas for bringing Boricua to New York. Puerto Ricans were no longer the dominant Hispanic group they once were within the city's diverse Hispanic population. This created a prime opportunity to celebrate the pride many Puerto Ricans held for their culture. Each investor thought the time was right to innovate the culinary game in this space, with some suggesting locations along the Fifth Avenue route of the Puerto Rican Day Parade. A spot like that would build instant awareness for the restaurant and definitely got my attention.

I strolled to my kitchen counter and poured a mug from my waiting coffee maker. I took a fiery sip, dabbing my mouth with my hand.

This was more than I expected. Smart investors were giving this serious consideration. But did I really want to open another location just as Boricua was settling back to normal post-construction? Plus, I'd never had a partner who wasn't family. Well, technically, Dot wasn't family. But she was to me. And I knew our patrons felt likewise. As hostess, Dot remembered guests by name and was the driving force behind the homey vibe that kept diners hooked. How would it work partnering with investors who only cared about the money?

It was a lot to consider, and I had to talk to Dot. She had a financial stake in Boricua too.

"I'm blown away."

"Well, you deserve it. New York is the right move for you."

"And this from a Philadelphia guy," I teased.

"Give it some serious thought."

"I will. But I also have to discuss it with my business partner."

"Yes, yes. But take the meetings. You'd be a fool not to."

I hung up with Silas, a stupid grin taking over my face. While I'd been happy owning a restaurant and living my life, every time I saw a culinary school classmate make it big, I wondered if I could too.

Mind buzzing with possibilities, I cooked a poached egg, fried plantains, and made a small salad. Fork poised before my mouth, I caught a flash of movement out of the corner of my eye. Dot knocked at my sliding back door and I waved her in.

"I'm out of coffee and sniffed yours..." She stepped in and made a beeline to the cabinet for the sparkly blue mug I brought back for her from San Juan.

"You eat yet?" I asked.

"I'm good. Thanks." She faced away from me as she poured her mug full, but something was up. Board-stiff, she paced a room she'd seen a thousand times, inspecting every corner to avoid looking at me.

"Everything set with the surgery for tomorrow? Gabby taking you?"

"About that." She turned to face me. "Gabby has a business trip, so Leslie is coming to stay for a while. She'll help me with my surgery and the recovery for a while afterward."

"What!?"

"I'll be out of commission for several weeks and need the help. And so will you at the restaurant. You'll be down a hostess, and I figured she could fill in."

I slammed my mug down harder than intended, sloshing coffee over the lip and all over my hand. "That's not happening."

"Don't be stubborn. You're short-staffed, and she can help. She'll arrive in a few hours."

"Anyone but her. No. It's out of the question. You couldn't have given me more warning?" I dried my hands on a dish towel.

"What was I supposed to do after the hospital moved the surgery date? Anyway, we're down two servers and everyone else is needed in the kitchen. We don't have a choice."

I grumbled, knowing she was right. But instead of ramming my fist through a wall, I aggressively stabbed at my breakfast, not eating. The food had lost all appeal.

"I was afraid you'd react this way. Honestly, you two are so silly. Can't you work this out? You still love each other." She clutched her chest with both hands as if the memory of our breakup four years ago gave her heart palpitations.

But indulging my feelings wasn't the answer. I'd only end up wrecked and crying in my office. Too many people depended on me now to risk another emotional meltdown. To stay strong, I had to distance myself from Leslie.

I slouched in my chair. "Can't Ava come instead? She lives closer and only works part-time."

Dot crossed her arms. "Ava's filling in for me at yoga. Besides, I can visit with my favorite niece if I want."

"She's your only niece."

"All the better." Dot tilted her chin up, her tell for when she was up to mischief. She only got stubborn when she knew she was wrong. Like when she confused the paint colors for the restaurant's interior remodel, and we ended up with psychedelic purple walls.

"Please give up this fantasy of yours. It didn't work between us."

"Neither of you has moved on. She's miserable and you're miserable and I'm tired of it. I won't live forever, and I'll see you both settled and happy so I can enjoy it."

I ignored her, aggressively scraping my breakfast into the compost bucket. But Dot wasn't done.

"I'll eat my sofa if you two don't end up together. There. I said it. Sue me." She crossed her arms in defiance.

Of course, I still loved Leslie. But that didn't matter. Try as I might, I failed to get past the wall she erected between us. Shit, the woman couldn't even make it through a meal without hopping up to clean or leave. An endless string of nonsensical excuses prevented her from helping me when I was short-staffed at the restaurant. On vacation, she'd abandon me at a table or before planned excursions while she took naps or disappeared for some alone time. The way I saw it, I put us both out of our misery.

Or at least one of us, given my lovesick limbo.

Hearing she was single left me perplexed. Dot tried to hide it, but I'd heard Leslie dated that anchorman of hers for a while. Thought they were still an item. Had Leslie dropped him because she had lingering feelings for me? Despite Leslie's odd behavior at times, I missed her terribly. I'd thought we were forever, until we weren't. All this time,

I assumed the pining went one way: me regretting letting her go with every fiber of my being, despite knowing I had to. My hurt cut too deep, and I could only stand being rejected for so long. I chewed my lip, thinking, before spitting it out. But not fast enough.

"Aha! That's what I thought." Dot sipped her brew with a wide smile.

I washed my breakfast dishes before anything stupid flew out of my mouth. Guess today was the day to pile on Risto before 9 a.m.

Actually...

"I've got news for you too," I said.

Her eyebrows shot up.

"Silas Greene called me this morning."

"Is he giving us a good review?" She clasped her hands in anticipation.

It was the first time I realized I had no answer to the most obvious question. Silas and I were so engaged with investor talk I'd forgotten to ask. But given the ecstasy on his face when eating, I expected nothing less than a stellar review.

"He loved the food, so don't worry. He'll probably get to the write-up after he finishes rounding up investors for our expansion to Manhattan."

I filled her in on our odd visit and even odder business proposal from our new guardian angel.

"Please tell me you're joking," Dot said when I finished.

"Not interested?"

"Exhausted is more like it." She hopped onto a chair at the counter and swiveled to face me. "I'm sorry. With my surgery tomorrow, and being told to take it easy, the timing just seems bad. I won't be at the restaurant or at my yoga class for at least a month. Do you mind running with it and filling me in after?"

"You sure?" My burst of excitement was a surprise, even to me.

"Yes, absolutely. I trust you."

An hour ago, I crapped all over the idea. But now that Dot was hesitant, my emotional investment was obvious. Starry visions of flickering candles, clinking glasses, and soft murmurs of New York diners danced before my eyes. Christ, I could already smell the garlic. Philadelphia's top food critic had me excited about a future I'd thought impossible.

Since opening Boricua, my life followed an easy routine. The renovations were exciting, but part of me was restless for another challenge. A move to New York might be it.

But before that happened, I'd have to survive a few weeks without my partner.

She sat brooding, so I reached over to rub her shoulder.

"Hey, no matter what happens, it's still you and me. This is your baby too. But you're right to focus on getting healthy. Deal with your surgery and I'll handle any meetings Silas cooks up. We can talk after we see how serious they are."

She stood, cupping my face. "You're a talented chef. I'm sure they'll love our food as much as we do."

Dot washed her cup, then slipped out the back door. She crossed the patch of grass between our homes. That was how close I'd be to Leslie when she arrived. I shook off the idea and headed upstairs to take a shower. I had to get out of the house before Leslie got here.

Before long, my ex-girlfriend would invade that space too. And not just any ex. THE ex. The one I still dreamed about every damn night.

Not every night.

Often enough.

Fine.

I'd head to work, prep for lunch, and make a few calls. Then I'd rip the Band-Aid off when she arrived.

Liar.

I laced my fingers behind my neck, sighing.

I'm screwed.

But I had to keep reminding myself why Leslie and I could never be. She doesn't love me like I love her, and never will.

What am I going to do?

Dot had made avoiding Leslie nearly impossible.

Guess I was about to find out.

Chapter 6

LESLIE

I tossed my leather messenger bag on top of my suitcase in the hatchback of my rental car. The car's make was my favorite kind: cheap and small. I drove so seldom luxury would be wasted on me. However, they'd handed me keys to a clown car barely big enough to hold my luggage. I pressed firmly on the trunk's hatch until I heard a confidence-inducing click, then shot it a mean stare for good measure.

One could never be too careful.

The retelling of my parents' luggage tragedy was seared into my brain. They were newlyweds, on their way back to the City from Aunt Dot's house in Pennsylvania. Each thought the other had closed the trunk, and their poor communication left a trail of underwear, pants, and bras scattered across Interstate 78. That experience made my mother maniacal about closing car doors and trunks. One of the many questionable habits she passed along to me that now had me doing an about-face for a final trunk check.

Gassed up and ready to go, I navigated down the West Side Highway to the Holland Tunnel and was zipping across New Jersey in no time. My rusty driving skills left me hunched over the wheel, gripping it for dear life. I typically stayed that way until the nasty stares from fellow motorists shamed me to relax. Cars would pull alongside and startle when spying me, expecting to find a gray-haired old lady. Risto once joked about me being terrified of driving, yet not thinking twice about rubbing elbows with organized crime bosses.

Risto.

I gulped hard at the idea of seeing him. That delicious man was mostly why I'd been scarce at Aunt Dot's. After meeting him during my high school summer visits, we dated for years. I thought we had a future together, but Risto and I could never get on the same page. He was all food all the time, and his total obsession made me suffocate like a fish gasping for air. I'd used every excuse in the book to avoid hanging with him at the restaurant. Risto became convinced I didn't love him, and I was unable to persuade him otherwise.

He'd called me a hypocrite. I was an extrovert with a star personality who lived in Manhattan yet complained about the crowds at Boricua. Unlike the restaurant, random New Yorkers didn't comment on my appearance or expect me to sit down and eat every two seconds. The whole vibe felt like a garlic-scented jail cell. He wanted me to love his career as much as he did. But I didn't like it any more than he'd enjoy chasing stories around New York City. Despite my misery, I would never have left him. There was too much goodness between us to let our career paths get in the way.

But Risto saw things differently.

He broke up with me over four years ago, but neither of us moved on. Besides Kaelen Reed, I rarely dated. From the sounds of it, Risto hadn't either. Or at least, my family made him sound perpetually available. That almost stung worse because it meant he'd rather be alone than be with me. Our scorching chemistry between the sheets, snuffed out.

A pleasure memory rippled up my spine, making me grip the wheel tighter.

Focus on the road.

Why did he still impact me this way?

Because you know how good he feels.

Felt. It was in the past.

You sure?

Yes. Definitely.

The idea of "us" was a silly childhood fantasy. I lived in Manhattan. He was a pillar of his cozy community, a restaurant owner and talented chef, turning heads. I was a city girl through and through, chasing stories and building a fierce reputation. A star-crossed lovers' plotline was hard to justify.

Frankly, it pissed me off that I couldn't get over the guy.

I cracked my neck and concentrated on the road, hitting the accelerator a little too aggressively for my driving ability.

Driving *was* cool, though. Coming and going as I pleased, free from bus and subway schedules. It was how everyone not from New York City got around, but to me, it was a revelation. I could get used to it, for sure. I wouldn't even need lessons like Mom did when she moved to Albuquerque. She once confused the brake pedal with the gas and nearly crashed through a restaurant window. My teasing hadn't gone over well.

While I loved my mom, having her several time zones away suited me just fine. Bad enough her words reverberated in my skull, critiquing what I did, wore, and ate. Her years of nagging mirrored back, unbidden. I did the job so thoroughly I should invoice her for my efforts. I would've flung myself in the Hudson River had it not been for my summer breaks at Dot's.

I missed my aunt desperately and was happy for the opportunity to take care of her for once.

Which meant cooking.

Dot was a wizard in the kitchen, and I'd be a lousy substitute post-surgery. I made a mental note to swing by the store to pick up ingredients for the few dishes that I knew how to cook: omelets, chef's salad, and a poor imitation of her rice and beans. Oh, and grilled cheese sandwiches. It had been so long since I had eaten one, and I was looking forward to the cheesy goodness I never allowed myself at home. Mostly because of the debilitating guilt that accompanied each bite.

About two hours after starting my drive, I pulled up next to Dot's car in her double-wide driveway. She had downsized to a new development since I'd last visited, so I still imagined her living in her old place. The five-bedroom home she once shared with my uncle Arty. After he passed away, it became too much to manage. So she sold it and bought what looked to be a charming home not far from Risto's restaurant. Scratch that. With Dot's recent investment, Boricua was now partially hers too. The cash infusion helped the restaurant expand to better handle its growing popularity. Between hostess duties, teaching yoga, and her food-coaching work, keeping Dot off her feet wouldn't be easy.

I slammed my car door, the intense sun searing the chill off my air-conditioned skin. I tilted my sunglasses to take in Dot's two-story house, which had a sandy stone exterior and a cute front porch. Like her old home had shrunk in the dryer. Leaving my luggage for later, I rounded the car and ascended the front porch steps, entering without knocking.

"I'm here! Hello?" The cool central air welcomed me as I closed the door. "Auntie?"

All was quiet. I crossed her great room, which directly connected to a gourmet kitchen via a two-seater island made of rosy marbled quartz. It had to be quartz and not granite, the counter surface she preferred because of its non-porous food safety benefits over granite. Her obsession with it made me dig into it for an article I'd never finished writing. If I wasn't passionate about a topic, it showed on the page, and food safety left me flat.

"You got your dream kitchen at last," I whispered.

Moving through it, I saw Aunt Dot through the glass sliding doors to her deck. She sat in a lounge chair, talking aloud. But to whom?

I stepped out and shielded my eyes from the sun with my hand. "There you are."

She jumped up. "You're here! I didn't hear you pull up."

Dot grabbed me into a vice squeeze, her hands linking around my back to hug a smile onto my face. I buried my face in her shoulder to inhale her floral perfume. Memories flooded back, all happy, but too many for any of them to step forward. I'd been here nanoseconds and already floated on a cloud of love.

She pulled back, gripping me on both shoulders. "You are a sight for sore eyes."

Next, she plastered kisses on both cheeks, leaving what I knew to be perfect red lipstick smacks behind. She blended them into my cheeks with her thumbs.

"There, good as new," she said, looking satisfied.

"Hey, Leslie." Risto's resonant voice vibrated to my core. And in that instant, my pep talks in the car evaporated.

I whipped around to find him standing on the deck of the house next door.

I shot daggers at my aunt. "Neighbors? Seriously? Why didn't you warn me?"

"You wouldn't have come."

She wasn't wrong.

"What do you care, anyway?" Dot asked. "You haven't visited in ages, and he's my business partner. It's easier this way."

Auntie's terrier, Pepper, wiggled between my legs. I crouched to pet him, fluffing his fur with both hands while avoiding eye contact with my ex.

"Hey, Risto. Been awhile." I hid behind my wall of curls. After blow-drying them straight for so long, I'd forgotten how handy the volume was. They were the only shield between me and the man who made my pulse race like I was on deadline. I peeked up to find his longing eyes seeking mine from Auntie's porch steps.

Holy shit. Get a grip.

But that was futile when it came to Risto. An oversized teddy bear, Risto's largeness felt like home. I used to snuggle in, my head resting on his chest while he played with my hair. Our cocoon of safety kept the world at bay. Until it didn't. Yet it was useless to deny the sexual tension zinging between us. The bedroom had never been our problem.

Risto swallowed hard. "I better head back to the restaurant. See you there for lunch?"

Dot said "absolutely" at the same time I glared in her direction. The moment Risto disappeared through his sliding door, I slapped Auntie's shoulder.

"We can't eat there for lunch!" I yelled.

"You love his cooking. Don't deny it. And he's been a wreck all morning. They tossed him from the kitchen earlier because he kept burning onions."

"You're lying. He never burns anything."

She shrugged.

"They ejected the owner and head chef?"

"Jose called and begged me to distract him at home for a few hours so they could prep for lunch. I called and told him he might have left the stove on at his house."

I shook my head. "You probably have a key to his place."

"Of course I do, but he was so wound up, he never asked." She touched my cheek. "There's love between you two. Always has been."

Anything that left my lips now would get me into trouble, so I said nothing. The hardest, and wisest, of all choices.

"Let's get you settled, then head over to the restaurant."

I grabbed my suitcase out of the car, but Dot insisted on carrying my overflow duffel. I marched behind her up to the second floor, struggling to keep up with her ample frame. Dot's energetic movements made me realize I should probably hit the gym more than never. Exercising had long been an agonizing chore, considering my perennial tiredness. It didn't matter how much I slept. My leaden legs wanted no part of working out. However, the ragged breath huffing out of my lungs from lugging my suitcase up a single flight of stairs spoke volumes. I forced my lips closed so Dot wouldn't notice.

"I put you in the guest room. The bathroom is down the hall, and it's all yours. I have my own, and there's another one on the first floor. Shall we eat? I'm starved."

The moment the words left her lips, her face froze in shock. "I'm sorry. I didn't mean…"

I shrugged. "It's fine. I'm used to it by now."

Being the sole trim person in a family of larger bodies meant a lot of teasing came my way. Mostly comments about me needing a sandwich or looking like I'd starved myself while marooned on a tropical island. The small portions I served myself at mealtimes became a battle, with relatives insisting I eat more. The unwanted attention made me more likely to skip a meal than sit down and chow. A choice they'd never understand.

Dot shook her head. "No, it's not alright. As someone routinely shamed for my large body size, it's wrong of me to do the same to you. I'm sorry."

"Really, it's not a problem."

"It is, and I'll tell you why." Dot went first down the stairs and grabbed her handbag near the door. "It's taken me a long time to accept who I am, and my group work has been focused on helping people with larger bodies navigate the hostile world we face every day and get to a place where we can love ourselves. But I know you have your own set of challenges...”

Like what? nearly flew out of my mouth, but that would have only prolonged the conversation. I let it go, and we endured a silent drive to the restaurant.

Dot rarely ate anywhere besides her baby, Boricua. And who would blame her? One step through the back door, and the scent of garlic, oregano, peppers, and onions flushed my senses alert. Whiffing the air nearly made me die of happiness. Like I'd already nibbled on crispy roast pork, tender chicken, and golden sweet fried plantains. Savored black beans and white rice cooked just right. It was surprisingly easy to ruin white rice, but no one in my Puerto Rican circles had mastered the embarrassing skill. Except me.

A stomach growl vibrated deep within me, but the boisterous kitchen yells and pot clanks drowned it out. Risto's back was to us as he talked to one of his chefs on the far side of the kitchen. They hovered over a mammoth tray of eight pork shoulder roasts wrapped in plastic. From the looks of it, the meat was still marinating and wouldn't be cooked for several more days. Once done, a crispy layer of skin would cover succulent meat, blooming with flavor perfection.

Dot nodded to her staff while walking us through to the dining room. The navy interior was new. Tasteful gold sconces dotted the walls, casting arcs of light over painted canvases from local Puerto Rican artists. Each splashed its own brand of framed creativity in bright colors, from idyllic rural scenes to abstract faces screaming in agony. Between them, tall, paned windows stood sentry as the only reminders that we were in a former residence and not in a white-tableclothed dining mecca.

By now, the restaurant was halfway through the lunch rush. After checking that the servers had their tables under control, we sat at a round high-top table for two near the bar. A heated soccer match between Brazil and Argentina played on the screen over the bar. The action captivated the bartender's attention while he dried glasses with a dishtowel before stacking each on the shelf behind him.

Dot leaned in to whisper, "Felipe must be on pins and needles. Brazil is ahead. Notice not a soul dare talk to him right now."

Funny thing about eating in your own restaurant. No one brings you a menu. Least of all your co-owner. But here, wearing his black chef's coat, Risto came trotting over to our table, looking more tempting than the food.

"What can I get you?" he asked Aunt Dot.

"Bring some arroz con gandules with that lovely pernil you must have just taken out of the roaster."

My eyes met his, which held a special sadness reserved for me.

"I'll have my usual," I said, looking at my lap.

I caught him shooting a questioning glance at Auntie, who threw up her hands.

"It's what she wants. But you know..." Dot said, arching her eyebrows in some silent language only they understood.

Risto nodded and left without saying a word.

What was that about?

Our server brought us water and cutlery. Risto returned barely five minutes later with our order. Golden seasoned rice with green peas alongside succulent slices of roast pork. A separate plate held glistening plantains, sliced on the bias and caramelized to perfection. Dot's eyes closed to savor the aroma, scooping vapor to her face with a cupped hand.

"Nothing better," she said.

A brawny arm entered my field of vision to set a salad plate in front of me. Arugula, field greens, mushroom slices, and a lemon wedge. Risto knew better than to put carrots on my plate. After decades of my mother complaining about the high sugar content, I'd banned them from my diet completely.

"Thanks," I said. "It's lovely."

Risto said, "Enjoy," and was gone in an instant. Almost like he couldn't bear to be in my vicinity for one second longer than necessary.

Living next door to him was going to be torture.

Chapter 7

Risto

Leslie ordering that salad was a gut punch. Stubborn as ever, she refused to give me the satisfaction of having her eat my cooking. Time and again, she preferred cold, tasteless food to the dishes people waited weeks to try and drove hours to reach. But apparently that meant nothing. I kept flunking a test I wasn't allowed to take.

I smashed through the swinging door to the kitchen, turning the heads of my staff hard at work feeding the lunch rush.

"You okay?" Jose asked, but I waved him off and stormed to my office. Best for everyone if I was alone right now.

The leather squeaked as I dropped into my desk chair, my elbows slack on the armrests in defeat.

Leslie eating lettuce and lemon stung like she squirted the citrus in my eyes. It was an insult to who I was and all I'd overcome to achieve my dream. The few times I smuggled bites of food past her lips, she loved it. Dot always took a to-go box for her to enjoy at home. So why didn't Leslie sit and eat like everyone else? Was rejecting my cooking some twisted form of revenge?

You're the one who broke up with her.

Yeah, but she rejected me first. Leslie's nonexistent support for my culinary career spoke volumes. As if she thought me becoming a chef was an embarrassment. She manufactured excuses to discourage me from opening a restaurant. It was too expensive. Too competitive. I didn't have enough experience. All that made it too risky. I laughed at the "risk" line, given her brazen investigative methods.

Me starting Boricua was the first of many "restaurant" disagreements. After I bought the place, she moped around the dining room or got lost in her phone until I stole it away and gave her work to keep her busy. After a while, she got better at helping me prep ingredients or set tables. But once guests arrived, she left. I longed for her to see the place in action, but she insisted she'd be in the way. She only returned later after the kitchen was cleaned up.

The one time Leslie stayed, I caught her playing hostess. She tended to diners, refilling water glasses and shuttling drink orders to the bar. Her bright eyes, wide smile, and lean but curvy hips sold more booze that evening than I could remember.

I swiped my face with my hands.

Shit.

Dot knew we needed help, but having Leslie near was already tying me up in knots.

From the looks of it, Dot hadn't shared her "filling in at Boricua" bombshell. I bet Leslie wouldn't like it any better than I did, but we'd have to make the best of it. I had a busy restaurant to run and patrons lined up at the door.

I sat forward in my chair to head back to the kitchen when an idea hit me. Jose, my chef de cuisine, ran the operations so well, he barely needed my supervision these days. Realistically, I could manage a second location. It'd give Jose space to grow and allow me to launch another restaurant.

It could work.

But there I was, getting ahead of myself. I hadn't even contacted the potential investors Silas emailed over, and I'd already begun a staffing plan. My heart swelled at the idea, just as it had with Leslie. Building an imaginary future only I wanted.

Jose appeared at the office door. "Can I have a word?"

"Yeah, of course."

Jose closed the door behind him. "You're a wreck, mijo. What's going on?" He sat on my desk, facing me with crossed arms.

"That obvious?" I said, but Jose settled in for a wait. He expected an explanation. The man had been with me long enough to know every intimate detail of my business and life. He wanted some tea.

I sighed in defeat. "Leslie is staying with Dot while she recovers from the surgery. I only found out this morning. Now she's sitting in my dining room, eating lettuce, and making me wish I was anywhere but here." I pointed at my office wall, knowing the bar—and Leslie—sat on the other side. This was fucking torture, and it'd only been a few hours.

"First, maybe she doesn't like your food," Jose said. "There are worse things in the world, like murder and that asshole who scratched your car last week after he showed up with no reservation and had to wait. Second, make up with the woman and be happy. Or get your head out of your ass and find someone else. You choose, but you're useless to me right now."

Jose had a point. And I was in no mind space to have this conversation. I'd yet to speak to Leslie. Until I did, my head would likely remain up my ass. I had to drop all visions of us getting back together. While I'm sure Jose would love to get me out of his hair, it was too early for me to mention the idea of a second location. First, I had to find investors and make a deal stick. While I told him everything, I skipped mentioning my contact with Silas about the investor interest. No sense raising his hope about becoming executive chef here before it was real.

"It gets worse. Dot wants her to fill in while she's laid up after surgery," I said.

Jose whistled, long and low. "Sucks to be you."

"Tell me about it."

"Hey, it might not be so bad. Leslie's a looker. It'll be good for business." Jose laughed, playfully slapped my shoulder, and rose to leave. "Plus, you never know..."

Jose rounded out of sight, but that last barb spoke volumes. Jose, like Dot, presumed I'd end up back with Leslie. But neither grasped how little the woman sitting out there eating lettuce wanted any kind of future with me. I did the right thing breaking up with her.

I swiveled to the desk and pulled up the contacts Silas sent me via email.

At least there was one future I had the power to control.

Chapter 8

LESLIE

"You want me to work here?" My jaw dropped clear to the floor as I glanced around the restaurant interior. The patron at the next table gave me a quieting stare.

"Just for a few weeks." Dot took a sip of her ice water. "I play hostess a few days a week and help around the restaurant during the day, doing whatever's needed. There's no sense hiring anyone. It's only until I recover."

My head dropped back in frustration. I had no good reason to refuse, except the petulant *I don't wanna.* I was in town for the foreseeable future with no articles to write or TV commitments. But when I agreed to come, the last place I wanted to be was stuck with Risto.

I stared her dead in the eye. "If I didn't know better, I'd say you cooked up this surgery to get us back together."

She patted my hand across the table. "Glad you're beginning to see things my way."

"Dream on..." I stopped as a server appeared and dropped a white shopping bag in front of me.

"Rice, beans, and pork chops. With utensils."

"I didn't—"

"Thanks, dear." Dot nodded, and the woman left. "It's for you when I'm in the hospital. Shall we?"

She gestured toward the door, leaving me to pick up the take-out bag holding my favorite meal. Dot knew it, and so did Risto. Though suspicious as hell, I swallowed my pride—and my words. Instead of marching through the kitchen, we left via the front of the oversized house Boricua called home. With a red roof, white clapboard siding, and blue shutters—each with a single white star—it screamed Puerto Rico. Patio diners chatted merrily as we passed.

I had to stop and catch my breath, still stunned I was expected to work here with Risto on a regular basis. But the chirping birds and meticulous landscaping made my dour mood seem out of place. My aunt was having surgery and didn't need me acting selfish. It was bad enough that I hadn't visited in so long. The least I could do was accommodate one small favor. She bent to deadhead a few flowers.

"Your doing?" I asked.

"Yes. It makes up for losing my flowers at the old house." Dot buried her nose in a rosebush. "It's good to have less home to maintain, but I still miss my gardens. Lots of memories there."

I kissed her cheek. "I miss the old place too."

Dot made her way to a bench surrounded by pink impatiens. "Then why have you stayed away for so long? I know you're busy, but it's been years since you've been out to visit. If we didn't come to you, we wouldn't have seen you at all."

This conversation was overdue, but that didn't make it any easier.

She slid aside and patted the space beside her. I sulked over and plopped down on the bench, stretching my legs out in front of me. I wasn't sure how far to go with my confession. She had surgery the next day, and the last thing she needed on her mind was my sticky love life.

"I'm sorry. Really, I am. I get so heads-down with work and only surface briefly in between assignments."

"That's not a healthy way to live."

"I can't say. I never think about my life like that."

"I don't believe you."

"It's true. As soon as I finish one story, another scoundrel surfaces. My skin crawls at the idea of wrongdoing going unpunished. But there's been so much downsizing in news divisions most big investigations are ignored. The work I do is desperately needed, and I have trouble saying no."

"You'll land in an early grave at this rate." Dot's eyes bored into me, forcing me to look away. Deep down I knew she was right, but was I supposed to refuse when opportunities came knocking?

"I'm up for a few big awards this year because of my series on sex trafficking in Manhattan. I also landed the permanent Saturday host spot for *The Kaelen Reed Show*."

I expected elated congratulations, but Dot's face wore a pitying expression.

What was I missing?

She, more than anyone, understood how hard it was for me to succeed in journalism. Newsrooms weren't exactly breaking down my door when I started out. I'd pitch articles under the name Leslie

Molina and rarely heard back. When Dot suggested I try using my mom's last name, I thought she was joking. But sure enough, after I switched to Leslie Allen, my words suddenly became worth paying for. I got steady freelance jobs and hitched myself to leading news outlets, building a fearless reputation for pursuing stories most journalists ignored.

Gangs.

Organized crime.

Prostitution.

Slum landlords.

Crooked politicians, police officers, business moguls, and appointed bureaucrats.

With no man and no children, my career was my sole focus for over a decade. I was approaching the pinnacle of my profession on the largest stage. Yet Dot's pained expression made me feel like a pathetic loser.

"Bola…" she said, using the pet name my dad's side of the family favored. Apparently, I was so chubby as a baby they all took to calling me "ball." My mom hated it but couldn't get folks to stop. Drenched in so much affection, it was hard for me not to appreciate the sentiment.

"Do you work because you love it, or do you work to fill an emptiness?"

"Of course, I—"

"Think before you answer. I see you working and achieving, but are you happy? Do you ever pause long enough to find out?"

My instinctive response was I didn't want to know. What good was learning if you were happy or not? What if I wasn't? Learning I was miserable was worse than not knowing in my book. Sure, that was a cowardly answer for a journalist. Someone trained to dig in and uncover the truth. But my personal truth was far uglier than I'd wanted to admit.

What did she want me to say? That I was addicted to work and put it first? That stories mattered more than my safety or needs? That was all obvious. What good would come from saying it aloud?

Besides, without work, what else did I have? I had no desire to date anyone who wasn't Risto. And Risto made it very clear he wanted nothing to do with me. Kids weren't a huge draw, and my intermittent menstrual cycle gave me zero confidence I'd ever carry a baby if I tried. So where did this leave me?

I met Dot's waiting stare. "Am I happy? No, I can't say I am. But maybe not everyone is meant to be happy. Maybe people like me have to settle for being okay."

My answer landed like lead, leaving her head shaking in disapproval. "I never thought I'd see the day... I've finally realized the one person you're afraid of."

"Who?" I asked.

"Yourself."

I stewed in indignation as Dot drove us back to the house after doing some errands.

Me?

Afraid of myself?

How did that even compute?

So what if I wasn't squishy like some people who wanted to dig into the dark recesses of their souls? That wasn't my temperament. Anyway, wasn't that narcissistic? To only worry about one's self? The City needed a few people who put others first, true journalists who acted as instruments of public service. Our stories aimed a disinfecting light on the underbelly of New York City corruption. That got my pulse racing. When there were bad guys to chase down, who had time to be happy?

"So, what's your next story?" Dot asked, glancing at me briefly before refocusing on the road.

"Not sure yet. I just finished my last sex-trafficking installment, a 'where are we now?' update. I have a few ideas, but nothing concrete has surfaced."

She nodded, but I could tell she had something else to say.

"I've been on this body journey for a while. I've learned so much about the falsehoods of the diet industry. It might make for a good story," she said.

Whenever someone suggested an article topic, I typically listened and stayed noncommittal. Sometimes the idea panned out, but more often, suggestions fell into two categories. Either the person felt wronged and sought justice (mostly for themselves), or they had a nagging inconvenience they wanted me to rectify.

The subways take too long after midnight. We stand around for a half hour before a train comes and then they only make local stops.

How do they choose the lights for the Empire State Building? There's got to be a corporate fix in.

The potholes on my street broke a second axle on my car. Something has to be done.

But diets?

"Why should I investigate dieting? What's controversial about them?"

"For starters, dieting has tentacles in every major institution, from medicine, to education, to the food industry, fashion, religion, government. Not only that, it also has roots in the subjugation of women and marginalized peoples."

"Oh, come on..."

"Don't take my word for it. Dig around. You're the big-time reporter."

I sighed and stared out the window. Few people were as wise and respected as my Aunt Dot. Yet the words flowing from her lips sounded like conspiracy theories and excuses. Ever since I was a kid, Dot had battled with her weight, trying one diet after another. Each would work for a while and she'd lose a few pounds, only to have them creep back on. That history made me wonder if this new vendetta against dieting wasn't part of a surrender strategy. If the whole industry was a scam, didn't that give everyone a huge reason to step off the treadmill?

Says the girl who wouldn't recognize a treadmill if it bit her in the ass...

"I'm having one of my body group meetings this evening," Dot said at last. "I moved it up from next week because of the surgery. Spend the afternoon doing some research on the topic. If you're curious, sit in and listen. You might be surprised."

I loved my aunt, but the last thing I wanted to do was to dive into a story about body positivity. It always struck me as misguided. More of a celebration of being unhealthy. I could be wrong, but I didn't think so. Yet Aunt Dot had never once led me astray. I owed her a few hours' time to hear her out so she could go into her surgery tomorrow with a good frame of mind.

"No promises, but I'll give you the afternoon."

While Dot packed an overnight bag for the hospital and set up for the meeting, I sat at the kitchen island perusing my laptop.

"What study did you want me to look up?" I asked while she fluffed her sofa cushions.

"Ancel Keys' work at the University of Minnesota on starvation. Researchers wanted to figure out how to help people recovering from severe malnutrition after World War II. But the findings shocked everyone."

I turned to her, more interested in the oral history than the computer screen in front of me. "Tell me about it. I'll verify everything later."

She shared how the 39 men who volunteered for the study were followed for three months on a normal diet, then were gradually starved over a period of six months on a 1,600 calorie meal plan.

"Wait! They starved the participants on a 1,600 calorie diet? That's barely less than the 2,000 calories the US government recommends now."

We exchanged stares while she allowed me to process the information. Dot never forced her ideas on anyone. She wisely presented details and let people draw their own conclusions. My astonished expression likely signaled I was ready for her to continue.

"The extreme calorie restriction led the men in the study to experience severe psychological trauma. They began thinking of food all the time and found it difficult to focus on anything else. They also became depressed, listless, lost interest in sex, and were socially withdrawn."

Sounds like me.

"A few of the men even attempted bodily harm. After food was restored at normal levels, most subjects kept the same food-obsessive behaviors as they did when starving. They were forever fearful food would disappear again, many bingeing when food was present. Others stashed food away to hide it from others and eat alone, later."

"How sad."

"I agree. But that's essentially what we do to ourselves when we diet."

Mic drop.

There was no sense arguing.

Restricting food, then becoming mentally obsessed with food and eating?

That was the definition of a diet.

Or a lifestyle.

Our eyes met. "You've got my attention."

Dot smiled. "Good."

Chapter 9

LESLIE

The first guest arrived promptly at 7:00 p.m. And a steady flow continued until eight people gathered in my aunt's living room. Dot's Healthy Bodies meeting mostly attracted larger-bodied women, but there were two that most would label as thin.

Before our conversation about the Minnesota study hours earlier, I would surely have harbored a shameful attitude about her group members. Like the soldiers in the study, I was taught to view food as the enemy. Hunger was a base instinct to be suppressed. At least, that's what Mom raised me to believe, and the world's experts seemed to agree. Were these women living free lives, or putting their health at risk? Guess I'd soon find out.

Dot clapped her hands. "It's seven-thirty, so if folks want to grab a plate of whatever and snag a seat, we can get started. Don't forget your name tag stickers, please."

Guests helped themselves to cheese cubes, crackers, and fruit, or a glass of wine before settling into the sofas and folding chairs arranged into a circle. I sat outside the group on a bar-height stool against the wall to better observe the room.

"Before we begin, I want to introduce my niece, Leslie Molina Allen, visiting from New York for a few weeks while I recover from surgery. She's also a journalist who might write about toxic diet culture if she finds there's a big enough story there."

Everyone erupted in laughter, but Dot hushed them. "Be kind, folks. She just learned about the Minnesota study an hour ago."

All kinds of gasps and ahs sounded, which made me feel like an ignorant clod. But that was why I attended. To begin my education about the food industry.

"Alyx? How did your month go? Want to kick us off?" Dot asked.

"Do I ever!" The woman laughed, and her flawless mahogany skin shone bright. Alyx likely came from work, wearing a flouncy cream blouse and black skirt. "It was the oddest sensation in the world to crave something and eat it. Scary really. What would happen if I didn't debate for hours about should I eat it, shouldn't I eat it, before eating it, plus more?"

"Preach!" a woman yelled.

"If I wanted something, I ate it. As much as I desired. At first, it was like I'd never seen food before. Like one of those men from the study, I ate myself sick. The difference was I didn't shame myself. After a couple of weeks, my cravings shifted. Sometimes I'd crave fruit or protein instead of sweets. One day at dinner, I prepared a lovely stir-fry with broccoli, with a little lean beef, and some brown rice. I normally would have eaten the whole thing, but I stopped when I was full and had leftovers for a few days."

Wow. What a great way to control what you ate. Eat everything until you don't want it. I made a mental note to dig into the psychology of that.

"Everyone, let's not forget that the broccoli isn't the goal. It's no better than a cookie. Yes, it's more nutrient-dense. But you are not a better person the day you eat broccoli than the day you eat a bowl of ice cream. Right? There are no good foods and bad foods. Only food," Dot said to a room full of nodding heads.

I made a second mental note never to say that in front of my dear mother. She'd have a coronary on the spot, and I'd be arrested for attempted murder.

"Intellectually, I get that's true. But I spent my entire life grading my self-worth based on my food choices. 'Did I cheat today?'" Another woman, Inez, made air-quotes with her fingers. "It's hard to deprogram."

"Don't I know it!" said a woman with a Nadia nametag. "I'm forever having to remind myself that. It's almost like I need a new way to think about myself. Besides my weight, I mean."

Nadia wore a low-cut hot-pink wrap top that knotted under her bust. Her makeup was impeccable, making me wonder if she worked in fashion or beauty.

Nadia continued, "I'm finally happy with who I am in the body I have. But my family isn't. Thanks to you all, I recognize it's a 'them' problem, not a 'me' problem."

As the meeting wore on, it was impossible not to get distracted by thoughts of my own body image and eating history. Could I model Alyx and eat whatever I wanted? Try living in a larger body, loving myself, and telling the haters to go screw, like Nadia? Dot's world sounded like a dream. But people like my mother and Kaelen Reed had their thumbs firmly pressed on their side of the scale. Fat was to be feared. It remained the only truth accepted by all in an otherwise polarized country.

Scanning the chatting faces in the room, I saw these women for what they were: a rebel alliance fighting overwhelming odds. There was so much legitimacy underpinning their way of thinking, and I yearned to learn more. This new radical approach to food and self-care made me both excited and entirely uncomfortable.

The last guest said her goodbyes as I gathered the glasses scattered around the living room to stack in the dishwasher. It was nearly 10:00 p.m. and Dot was due at the hospital by 7:30 a.m. the next morning for check-in. We'd barely talked about her procedure since I arrived. I couldn't tell if she genuinely wasn't concerned, or if she was so troubled she sought distraction.

"Auntie, I'll get the rest. Why don't you settle in? You'll have a long day tomorrow."

"No chance." She scooped the remains of the guacamole into the trash. "I'll be laid up for weeks. I want to move as much as I can, while I can."

She buzzed around the living room, humming to herself. Her contentment was so palpable, I wondered if that was what happiness looked like. Lightness in your chest and confidence in your heart. Her question from earlier in the day nagged at me like a lash stuck in my eye. You could feel it but not see it. Crazy how in a few hours' time

I was reevaluating a cultural mindset I'd taken for granted. Dot was right. There was a story here, a big one.

After Dot went to bed, I started down a rabbit hole, researching the Minnesota study. The details were just as gruesome as Dot mentioned. Reading the information left me haunted by the spirits of men who became so obsessed by food it drove them into deep mental distress.

Were they dieters, we'd tell them to suck it up.

What a cruel irony. Telling starving people to do without. Be stronger. Be more disciplined. I then learned that you could be biologically starving and malnourished at any size. Fat people could have anorexia, but there was next to no research on it that I could find. Larger-bodied people with eating disorders were praised for the exact behavior that undermined their health. Hungry? Starve yourself more.

On cue, my stomach growled. Ignoring it, I clicked into my next browser window to launch a new search.

Then sat up straight.

Huh.

Unlike the starving men in the study, I could do something about it. I rounded the kitchen island to stand before the refrigerator.

Shadows draped the room, save for the under-cabinet lights and the warm glow filtering over from a table lamp in the living room. Usually, when I raided Auntie's kitchen at night, I did so in pitch dark. A stealth operation where I finally gave into the cries from my hungry stomach. Typically, I'd indulge, beat myself up, then not eat for days as penance. That behavior sounded like the men in the study.

But that wasn't me.

Prove it.

I opened the fridge, coolness prickling my skin to attention. Unlike my fridge at home, Dot's was packed with food. Baggies of snacks from the meeting. Fruit, veggies, milk, and cheese. Yogurt, prepared macaroni salad, and a red-topped storage container full of her famous curried chicken salad. Cooked farfalle pasta with a tub of basil pesto nearby in its usual spot: opposite the cardboard carton of eggs.

Then I saw it. The takeout bag Risto sent home from Boricua.

Sure, it was late. But every fiber of my being wanted to answer my body's call.

Eat something.

Why was it so hard for me to open a fucking plastic container of food? Millions of people did it every day. Some, multiple times per day.

Without thinking, I wrestled the white bag from the back of the first shelf and spied the black plastic containers with clear lids within. Even in the dim light, there was no mistaking that Risto had packed each one to bulging. *God bless that man.* I removed the four boxes, their savory scents inviting me to dig in. Chilled sweetness from the once-crispy fried plantains. Garlic and oregano from the black beans and pork chops. The promise of fluffy rice. I kicked myself for not ordering them myself. I'd wanted to, but my robotic instincts took over. How pathetic that I limited myself to inhaling the delicious vapors as we walked through the kitchen.

If I didn't have an issue with food, I could just dig in. In my mind, Little Diana berated me for being weak, but I ignored her.

Holding a wide bowl from the cupboard, I layered in rice, beans, and two pork cubes. Risto's idea to cut pork into bite-sized squares was new. That man was a constant evolution. Then I added three slices of plantain and covered it all in plastic wrap and heated it in the microwave. My skin danced in excitement as the dish rotated, popping and hissing as steam escaped the gap I left in the plastic.

Despite being hungry—and filling my bowl—I hadn't fully committed to eating. There would be stages. Staring at the food came first, breathing in the luscious aroma of garlic and herbs through the warm plastic. Then I'd peel it back and hover a fork over the mound, my arm stiff from the strain of holding back. If I speared the meat, I had one last chance to resist. Sometimes the mere mechanics of eating were enough to satisfy the urge, without food ever crossing my lips. I'd dump it all in the trash and consider myself lucky for avoiding a catastrophe.

This time was different, though.

I had something to prove. I wasn't like the emaciated men I'd seen on my computer screen. I intended to eat clear down to the bottom. The wavy blue design of its interior would whisper hello, and hopefully stop there. Sometimes, empty dishes shouted back. They'd castigate me for being weak and launch me into punishment planning. Eating had long since become a battle zone.

The women in the living room hours earlier talked about their liberation from the expectations society stacked on them to look a certain way and be ashamed of who they were. I wanted to stand up and cheer, "You go girl! You do you."

So why couldn't I do me?

Why was it so hard to stuff food in my mouth, chew, and swallow?

As the microwave timer counted down, Mom's voice invaded my thoughts.

People are only fat because they're lazy.

Don't be one of them. Don't give in.

She'd wrinkle her nose in disgust when hearing about what I ate at Dot's. The car door had barely closed, and her inquisition would start. Not, "Did you have fun?" Her first question was always, "What did you eat?" Followed by, "Did she buy you ice cream from the neighborhood truck? Did you politely decline?"

When she'd pick me up after I'd visited for weeks at a time, Mom would stew in silence looking at a fatter me like I was the hugest possible disappointment. While I hated her lectures, her brooding was worse. As was readjusting to mouse-sized portions, fasts, and juice cleanses after getting free rein in Dot's kitchen.

The same fat disapproval was echoed by every movie, song, TV show, and social influencer I swiped past in my Instagram feed. A tsunami of opinions that all rushed in one direction. I'd never thought to question whether those opinions were right. Didn't they have to be? The consensus was clear.

The microwave beeped, and I used a potholder to remove the steaming ceramic dish.

With both hands on the counter, I leaned my nose over the food to start my ritual.

I warred with myself.

Who was right? Dot or the rest of the planet?

Fuck it.

I ripped off the plastic and jabbed my fork in, scooping a mouthful of rice, beans, and pork in my mouth.

Mmm! Oh, my good gracious.

The pork was tender as anything, melting as I chewed. Tastes spread around my tongue, flavors arriving and receding. The tang of the cider vinegar, the savoriness of the meat, the herbaceous lift of the fresh oregano, picked from their garden. Happiness raced through me, knowing Risto's hands had prepared something that brought me so much joy.

I swallowed, then went for more. Twice, three times, four times, chewing and swallowing each bite. A plantain called me, soft now from the steam rather than golden and crispy as it'd been earlier when glistening from the fryer. I slipped a slice into my mouth, licking my fingers.

Sweetness from the caramelized sugars hit first, then a starchy delight only plantains delivered. But it was so much more. It tasted like home, family, and love. It comforted me like love in a dish.

I paused for a sip of water from the fridge door dispenser, and an unfamiliar sensation of fullness registered. Nearby, the half-empty bowl cried for attention. My stop instinct kicked in, this time well-placed. Better I walked away before I felt so sick my meal ended up down a toilet. That'd disrespect the skillful hands who created it.

I lifted the bowl. But instead of scraping the remainder into the trash and burying it beneath other refuse to hide the evidence, I did something new. I covered it with fresh plastic and slipped it into the fridge. I'd eat it another day. Maybe even tomorrow. There would be no purgatory for this kitchen raid. Further proof I was fine.

Silence descended on the house once more, the sole sound the fridge compressor humming its approval.

This was good.

I'd eaten.

My body's frenzy quieted, at least for a time. Nagging regret would soon pound on my psyche, begging for entrance. But not if I fell asleep first. Force Little Diana into the oblivion of dreams where she'd lose her way in the mist. I cracked a smile at that thought. A night of peace.

I would deal with the angry voices tomorrow. Perhaps by then I'd decide whether I wanted them to win.

Chapter 10

RISTO

Dot's surgery was today, and I needed a distraction. I tapped my desk, staring at my cell phone like it was the problem and not me. I'd tried dialing the investors three times in the last day, but each time I hung up in defeat before the first ring. Starting down the "expand to New York City" path had me cooking a mystery dish.

No recipe.

No ability to taste the ingredients.

Only vague confidence that I had what it took to get it right.

But exploring had consequences too. I knew myself that well. Starry visions would blind me to all else. I'd start yessing over nos, and before long, my life would swirl in utter chaos.

But wasn't that how my success started?

When I abandoned college to go to culinary school?

When I rented a beat-up house to open a restaurant?

When I took a chance and asked Leslie out on a date after being "just a friend" for 11 years?

And we saw how well that ended.

I'd long since convinced myself I made the right choice. That it'd never work out between us. She dedicated her life to one just cause after another, never considering her own needs or mine. Leslie's allergy to me being a chef made matters worse. When we broke up, her complete shock surprised me. Leslie never shared my misgivings. Tears streamed down her face as she pleaded, of course, she supported my career and was proud of me. But how could that be true when every action she took said otherwise?

Leslie did everything in her power to avoid the restaurant. She'd promise to come, then last-minute deadlines would surface and drag her away. A few times, I watched her approach the restaurant's rear screen door. My heart would swell in anticipation until her hand landed on the doorknob. That's when Leslie froze, sighed, and fled back to her car, only to call me and say she wouldn't make it. I never mentioned I'd seen her, and why would I? Anyone could see she hated being around me. She rarely ate at Boricua—hell, she'd have to enter when it was open to do that. None of it made any sense. Even when we were alone together, something unspoken lingered between us. Driving us apart. I thought breaking up would come as a welcome relief, but her reaction said otherwise.

Was my choice a terrible mistake? Leslie looked stunned to see me that first day, then avoided all my attempted chance meetings.

Walking by Dot's house when they were on the porch. Dropping by to say "good luck" this morning before they headed out to the hospital.

Each time, Leslie scurried away before I had a chance to speak.

You hurt her.

Yeah, I know.

I sighed, scratching my beard. Leslie being near made me feel that much more alone. Jose was my best friend, but I tried not to be a burden, being his boss and all. Soon, I'd be her boss too, and I didn't need Jose and Freddie teasing me every damn second, though they probably would.

Beyond my closed office door, grinding sounds filtered through from the kitchen as the team readied marinades for the trays of chicken, pork, and beef waiting in the fridge. Prep time at Boricua was joyous. Everyone had their tasks, working with purpose, and of course, a healthy dose of playful ribbing.

Found brothers, we became a family with a shared passion for making magic with raw ingredients. Our common heritage sizzled to life on the plate for diners to enjoy. The investors craved a piece of what we had. But could I replicate this success without Jose and Freddie? As good as we had it now, the competitor in me itched to try. Like an acclaimed coach wanting to win without his star players. Thrilling, yes. But it still sent icy chills down my back at the thought of doing it all over again, from scratch.

The investors would have to fill the void, but their intentions would always be suspect. They would be in it for the money and would expect me to deliver, likely not caring much for how the sausage was made.

Fuck me.

I lifted my cell and dialed. The phone rang three times before he picked up.

"Chef Zaldo! I was wondering when you'd call," said investor number one, Ruben Santiago from the Pibb Equity Group.

He must have programmed me into his cell.

I relaxed into my chair, my shoulders easing. That tiny gesture made his inquiry feel genuine. Like he planned to be around for a while.

"I'm honored by your interest in Boricua. Expansion to another city wasn't something I entertained before Silas raised the idea."

"Silas has been a great scout for us, and he rarely misses." I'd never seen Ruben before but could hear his broad smile. Like the one he wore on the firm's leadership page, his dark, tanned skin and black, spiky hair silhouetted against a blue sky. The headshot oozed confidence. As if only success lay ahead for him and anything he touched.

"I've never worked with outside investors, so don't know how this all works."

"If you're open to it, we'd love to swing by and see your operation. Sample your food and talk in person. Then we'll hang around to witness the restaurant in action. Observe how you operate at peak capacity. If all goes well, we'll schedule a time to sit down to review financials. When are you busiest?"

I chuckled. "When isn't it busy? We started taking reservations because I hated to keep people waiting outside like cattle."

"For lunch too?"

"Yes, we had no choice. But we hold a few tables for walk-ins. Hate to turn guests away."

We agreed that he and two partners would visit on a Tuesday, in between lunch and dinner. A test to be sure. With most restaurants closed on Mondays, Tuesdays were crammed with food deliveries, stocking, and inventory. It meant he was trying to catch us at our absolute best. Fresh ingredients. Rested staff. Game on.

I called the other two groups and made similar plans, each stopping by for a weekday dinner to check out our operations and sample the menu. After hanging up, I crossed my arms, satisfied. There were worse things than having three top restaurant investors vying to give me a bigger platform.

I could do this. I would even whip up some of those conceptual dishes I'd been wanting to try. They'd either love us and want in or walk away.

I didn't care which.

Liar.

Sadness fluttered across my mind at the prospect of all three taking a pass.

Shit. I was already emotionally invested. I hated placing all the power in someone else's hands, but that was how it worked. Those with cash got to decide where to put it.

I slipped into my chef's coat and opened my office door. In the kitchen, Freddie's favorite music mix blared as he sang along. Jose danced a salsa in front of the stove while Freddie looked up from the butcher block.

"¡Jefe! Where you been?" Freddie deveined shrimp at a furious pace. Damn, that boy was good. How would I ever find his equal?

"We need to talk. Turn that down, please," I said.

Jose flipped the switch, and the room went silent, except for the comforting gurgle of sauce simmering on the gas range and the whoosh of the hood vent.

"What's up?" Jose asked.

"Remember that *Philadelphia Metro* critic who barged in the other day?" I asked.

"Hard to forget our Lord Dark Helmet!" Jose said with a laugh.

"The Force is strong in him," Freddie said in his best Yoda voice.

As tall men, it was easy to be entertained by folks a foot shy of our chins. Toylike, they instantly amused, especially when agitated. The Silas Greene episode was epic.

"Well, he crowed to a bunch of New York City restaurateurs and three different outfits are interested in helping us expand to Manhattan."

Freddie laid down his paring knife. "No joke?"

"Yeah, no joke."

Jose and Freddie exchanged glances before landing on me, speechless. This wasn't the reaction I'd expected when breaking news that had me stupidly giddy.

"What's the matter?" I asked.

Jose spoke for them both. "We have our hands full here. How are we supposed to run two restaurants? Would we need to move? And if you're gone, what happens to us here?"

"Let's not get ahead of ourselves. They'll be stopping in like any other guest to taste our food. If they're interested, we'll see where it goes. The point of them being involved is so we won't be alone. No decisions have been made on either side. For now, these people are just another reservation."

"I can handle that," Jose said.

"Are you doing this because that douche, Chase, is on TV all the time?" Freddie asked.

That had bothered me, but no. I wanted this because it was stupid to ignore signs blinking brightly in one direction. Success.

"My grandparents were humble people and taught me to be grateful for what I have. But everything I have would never have happened if I hadn't put myself out there and taken a chance. We have a huge opportunity to partner with world-class restaurateurs. We'd be stupid not to try. My gut says there's more out there for me. For all of us. I'm committed to making this happen."

"Okay. I'm in," Freddie said.

"Me too." Jose reached over and switched the music back on. Just like that, prep resumed as if I hadn't just broken life-changing news.

I'd be lying if I said I wasn't disappointed by their reaction. If this New York thing was going to work, I needed them on my side. But I'd also be lying if I said my interest in opening a New York location had nothing to do with getting closer to Leslie.

Chapter 11

LESLIE

"Do you think Mom will be all right?" my cousin Gabby asked, hugging herself as we walked the long hospital corridor toward the family waiting room.

I stopped to hug her. "She'll do great."

Last we saw Aunt Dot, she was talking the ear off her anesthesiologist. Meanwhile, the nurse inserted an IV port into her arm, then flushed the line. Super-chipper since we arrived, you'd never guess Dot was about to have a major procedure.

Gabby pulled away. "I know the adrenal tumor is supposed to be benign, but what if they find something serious when it's sent for testing?"

"Let's get her through the surgery and deal with the next steps as they come. I'll be here to help, even after you return from Japan."

"Thanks. I'm sorry you had to upend your life to be here." Gabby's cell rang. "It's David. I'll take it out here in the hall."

I walked into the waiting area to give her some privacy, surveying the other families sharing the space. An older couple whispered in Spanish as they checked the wall clock every two seconds. A blond woman with thick, curly hair bounced a sleeping infant in her arms as she nervously paced the room. The baby was zonked out and the mom probably wished she was too, given the bags under her eyes.

Poor thing.

A single fact kept me from worrying about Dot. It wasn't yet her time. I could feel it in my bones. She'd recover and be back to her hectic life before we knew it. Trusting my instincts had saved me more times than I could count. It's what made me a good reporter. I chased off fear at the sharp end of a pitchfork, refusing to accept any alternative. Sure, I'd probably get jabbed in the ass one day, but not today.

Craving distraction, I checked my phone and saw a text from Dad, so I called him back from my sculpted plastic chair.

"They just took her in," I said when he answered.

"How did she seem?" Dad asked.

"Lively as always, you know her."

Normally, he would've laughed in reply. That he didn't showed the depth of his worry. "Dot said you planned to stay awhile. Thanks for being there. I wasn't sure you'd be comfortable operating from Pennsylvania for that long."

I wondered the same thing, but more because of the complicated situation with Risto. And my mom's nagging. But nothing would keep me away from helping one of my favorite people in the world. Who knew? Maybe it was the overdue break I needed to reset and start something new. Which reminded me of my article topic.

"Did you ever say anything to Mom when she'd talk so negatively about Dot? About her size and all?"

He sighed. "You think I didn't try? She did the same damn thing to me. Her constant nagging was one of the things that drove me out the door. Food is central to our culture, and she sucked the fun dry."

Dad chuckled.

"Remember the time I made pigs' feet when she went out of town for the weekend? She got home early from her spa trip to find the two of us standing over the pot, sucking on hooves. You were on a stool, if I recall."

I was about eight years old and felt like a badass eating dinner straight from the stove. No plates. Just us devouring succulent meat, then scooping tender rice into our waiting mouths with oversized serving spoons. I bet Mom wanted to divorce him on the spot. She threw a fit, complaining that he was setting a terrible example for me. To his credit, he shooed her out of the kitchen and told her to chill out. She ran to the neighbor's apartment, and we didn't see her for hours.

"That was one of the best days of my life," I said—and meant it. Just me and Dad doing what we wanted in the kitchen. I think we baked cookies too, eating them while dinner cooked. Backward, forbidden, and delicious.

"We did have fun. Okay, call me later and let me know how it all goes. Tell Gabby I can pass the update along to our cousins. Save her a few calls."

I hung up, but my mind remained back with him in that kitchen. Was that when Mom went nuclear about my eating habits? I couldn't remember when the pivot point happened. But something triggered my descent into what I was beginning to recognize as a strong aversion to food. If I dissected it, Mom's intensity focused on not just avoiding eating but on discouraging the *enjoyment* of it. To her, eating was a necessary ritual to be dispensed with as quickly as possible. She hated long holiday meals with Dad's family. We'd sit around for multiple courses, laughing and talking—but only when we left Mom home. It was impossible to enjoy myself with Mom brooding in the corner, asking why we hadn't finished yet. A couple times Dot asked her to fold laundry, just to get her out of the room.

By contrast, when we visited Mom's side of the family, they swept plates away so fast you were practically mid-chew when your plate disappeared. To dull my hunger, I'd wander into the kitchen on the pretense of being helpful so I could swipe a few morsels of food off serving platters.

Gabby returned and took a seat next to me. "I'm calmer now that my beloved husband talked me off the ledge. Want to grab some breakfast at the café downstairs?"

I did.

My 1:00 a.m. refrigerator raid had worn off.

We trotted downstairs, changing elevators twice and ending up on level D. Whoever designed this hospital layout must have expected visitors to have tour guides. We followed the crossed fork and spoon signs and found the end of our treasure map, a basement cafeteria with bright refrigerated cases and several steaming stations with chefs working magic. A far cry from where Risto worked these days, but I blinked away memories of him to focus on my task at hand.

Gabby handed me a tray and set off, holding one of her own. The concept of filling an entire cafeteria tray sent joy fizzing to my fingertips. Suddenly I was eight years old, standing over the pot with no rules. Actually, I had lots of rules, but what would happen if I ignored them? Leaned into the pleasure of food?

Across the space, Gabby surveyed the hot breakfast options. By any measure, she was beautiful. Her heart-shaped face had full lips and striking cheekbones. Her full body had breasts to die for, paired with curvy hips and a plump ass that had her swatting away her husband's pinching fingers when he was near. By anyone's standards, Gabby dressed flawlessly. In a few hours, she'd board a long flight to Japan and would likely be one of the very few plus-sized brown women strutting around the trade show floor in Tokyo.

When we were kids, our similar coloring and looks made people mistake us for sisters. As we developed into our teen years, Gabby's body filled out as a woman's should, while mine resembled a deflated boy. I had curvy hips, given my pear shape, but lacked the meat needed to soften my edges and cover protruding bones. How would life be for me if I let my body decide what to weigh, like they talked about at the Healthy Bodies meeting? The idea was equal parts terrifying and exhilarating.

I sidled up to Gabby just as hot plates were handed to her across the stainless steel counter. She glanced at me and my empty tray, expecting nothing else. But she'd get a surprise today. As would I.

I loaded up on eggs, toast, fruit, and coffee at the self-service breakfast bar and joined my cousin—and her bulging eyes—at checkout.

"We're together." I handed my card to the cashier.

Once seated at a booth in the rear of the cafeteria, she couldn't contain herself.

"What gives?" she asked before spearing a sausage link and biting off the end.

I could pretend that I had no clue what she was talking about, but Gabby and I had our own special language. We rarely miscommunicated, so there was no need to play coy about the world-shattering revelations pinging around my brain.

"I went to your mom's meeting last night. Let's say I'm curious to learn more." I slipped a forkful of scrambled eggs in my mouth and let the long-forgotten egginess nurture me from within.

Were eggs always this good? I took another bite.

"Let me guess. You're going undercover as a fat person?" She snorted a laugh, chuckling to herself as she buttered her toast.

I dropped my fork. "That's a fantastic idea."

"Sweetheart, I was joking."

The thought filled me with more delight than I had a right to muster. Why not go on a food journey and see where it took me? I wouldn't commit to becoming a specific size, but eating more than nothing could be an interesting experiment. For all I knew, my body wanted to curve and be voluptuous like Gabby's, but I'd denied it the opportunity. My dad, aunt, and cousins had larger bodies. Why wouldn't mine be the same?

"After last night's meeting, it's hard not to wonder about my relationship with food."

"It makes sense that you'd be off-kilter, given how your mom raised you. Why would you be any different?"

"Because I'm a grown-ass woman now?"

"And?"

"I sometimes wonder how it'd feel to not be ravenous all the time. But I've never had the courage to find out."

"You're scaring me. What are you saying?" Worry clouded Gabby's face.

I closed my eyes, unable to watch her watch me as we had this conversation.

"It's not that I don't like food or don't get hungry. I'm hungry every damn minute of every day—"

"So why do you never eat?"

"I'm more afraid of eating than not eating? Mom's wrath, combined with society's doomsday expectations, made hunger seem like the admission ticket for staying small. From my initial article research, I'm learning there are a lot of negative health consequences to skipping meals. Ones I never considered."

"Les, you haven't just skipped *A* meal. You've skipped damn near every meal for years. That's probably why you're always so worn out, can't keep up when walking, and have zero energy to do anything but work. Did that never occur to you?"

I sat back, taking large bites of my toast and enjoying the mouthfeel as the apricot jam worked its way around my tongue. Sweet, then tart. *Interesting...*

Gabby's question triggered more of my own. Did I avoid socializing and dating because I was just too wiped out? Did I instinctively save up what little energy I had to fuel undercover investigations? Maybe. Was I addicted to the adrenaline because it drowned out all else? The thrill erased the hollow pit in my stomach and gave me purpose.

When I became Leslie Allen, I mattered. She was an award-winning reporter who made headlines and sat on cable TV news panels. Meanwhile, Leslie Molina was a starving woman, more afraid of a breakfast buffet than a mob boss. I missed out on companionship, family, relaxing, free time. Did I avoid all these because they involved eating? Did I so fear the judgment of others that I avoided them altogether? Or was my life so full of work and accumulating accolades from strangers that I forgot what and who should be a priority?

I wasn't sure.

Gabby's eyes grew dewy, so I took her hand.

"I feel like I failed you, Les. I wondered about it but was too afraid to ask. I'm so sorry. I should have done something—"

"Listen to me. I'm fine, a little hungry, but okay. I've been this way for years. Once I get some questions answered, we'll see where it all leads. I've started thinking about eating more. But either way, it's nothing you need to worry about."

Gabby didn't look convinced, but she resumed her breakfast, shooting me the stink eye.

"Stop staring at me. Give me some time to dig into the industry data and health research about weight and body size. This is all new to me, but not for long. I'm a damn good reporter."

I picked up my fork, but lost interest after a few bites. My mind was too distracted with article planning. I told Gabby I was full when she asked, rather than tell her the truth. Little Diana had whispered that I'd eaten enough.

Unlike last night, the desire to stop eating was impossible to resist.

Too many social cues flagging me to zip my lips.

Ironically, it was the same tact I'd have to take when I headed over to Risto's restaurant later for my first fill-in shift for Dot. With all the surgery worries, I hadn't had the bandwidth to sufficiently freak out and was making up for lost time.

I'd be stuck in the same building as Risto for hours.

His dark dreamy eyes penetrated the deepest recesses of my soul. Just thinking of them made me melt into my hospital chair.

How would I survive this?

I cared for someone who wanted nothing to do with me.

Get a grip.

His entire staff would be there working. And if it was as busy as it was at lunch yesterday, I might not have to see Risto at all. Like a good hostess, I'd stay up front and pretend I was somewhere he wasn't.

Maybe it could work?

Chapter 12

RISTO

The bracing chill of the walk-in fridge did nothing to dull my nerves. I topped off a stainless steel tray of produce, pretending the tropical salad I was testing for tonight's menu would distract me from the inevitable.

Leslie would be here any minute.

The good news was that Dot was safe. I heard a few hours ago that the surgery went well, and she was resting comfortably in a private room. But that meant the woman I was trying desperately to avoid would arrive at the last place on Earth she wanted to be: Boricua. When it was open. My dream was about to happen. Leslie would be in front, not watching but participating in the action. I couldn't lie. The idea kind of thrilled me.

Back before we broke up, I'd hoped that if she could just engage with diners and learn why my food was so special to them, she'd fall in love with it. And me by extension. A barrier easily climbed, but she never tried. It felt like she wanted me to choose between my career and our love. Food and air. But life required both, and I'd only be half living without Leslie.

As much as I loved Leslie, no one had the right to dictate my passions. Never in a million years would I do that to her. It'd be unthinkable for me to demand she abandon her life's work to be with me. That was akin to telling someone not to dream. Not to strive for better or want more for themselves. It shocked me to my core that she seemed to be demanding that of me.

She never said that.

She didn't have to.

Where's your proof?

I supported her work, but she refused to support mine.

Guess you have a point.

Ya think?

Ironic, now, that the very thing that drove us apart was about to force us back together. At least, in the closest proximity for the longest time we'd experienced for years. Her volunteer shift would last hours. Leslie would be the face of Boricua, greeting diners as Dot did. She'd play a special role in making sure every dining experience was stellar. While she hated the restaurant herself, this was business. I damn well expected her to do her part to make customers happy.

My lead server, Kayla, stuck her head into the fridge. "Boss? There's a lady here to see you. Says her name is Leslie?"

"Very funny."

Kayla knew exactly who Leslie was and wasn't anymore. The first server I hired after opening the restaurant, Kayla had witnessed my love struggles firsthand.

"You okay?" she asked, stepping into the fridge with me.

"Guess I have to be."

"I'll keep her up front. You won't even know she's here."

I seriously doubt that.

"Thanks, but she's going to be with us for a while and needs to feel welcome. She'll be a part of the team, and we owe it to our customers to help her be successful."

I strolled out of the fridge and dropped my tray of ingredients on the kitchen's butcher block. Kayla followed, but I stopped her.

"I'll train her myself."

Her eyebrows shot up. "Can you even teach front of house?"

Freddie overheard and busted a gut holding back his snickers.

"I can do every job in this restaurant myself. Including onboarding—and firing." I said the last part loud enough for everyone to hear. Freddie's head snapped around to refocus on his work.

"Oooh, she's under your skin already. This is going to be good." Kayla winked, then headed toward the dining room. "I'll tell her you'll be right out."

I steeled myself, took a breath, and pushed through the swinging door moments later.

Leslie stood surrounded by empty tables. Soft daylight from the windows caressed her features. She glowed like the angel she was. When her dark eyes met mine, a snap of electricity pierced me through.

Fuck me.

I am so dead.

"Hey, I'm here," Leslie said, her voice uncertain.

"So you are." I was so distracted by her lips that I stopped way too close, forcing me to take a corrective step back.

"I can see the space better without all the people. It's great. So much bigger than before the construction."

The restaurant.

Follow the conversation.

"Yes, it's been packed to the gills. The investment will pay for itself in no time. Let me show you around."

I paced over to the hostess stand to demonstrate the point-of-sale system Boricua used. "You'll be stationed here to greet customers. After checking their reservations, you'll get them settled. There may be a few takeout orders, so you can cash those out here."

Breathe, Risto. You've got this.

"On this monitor, you can see the layout of the restaurant. You toggle between screens by swiping or using these little arrows. If a guest has been here before and has preferences for seating or meals, that'll appear in this field here." I looked up from the screen to find her examining my face.

We stared at each other, neither of us blinking or talking for an eternity. We stood close enough for her intoxicating scent to make me dizzy. I braced myself on the podium, pretending it was a suave move of indifference instead of a wilting man barely able to hold his shit together.

"Do you have any questions?"

"Too many. But not about this POS system. I've worked in bars before, undercover, so I've used something similar before."

Bubble burst.

Her career.

She always found a way to elevate her job over mine. Like what I did was so unimportant she could master it with zero effort.

"Every system is different. Every system has nuances that you need to understand, so the network doesn't crash. If you're confused, ask." My sharp tone a surprise.

"Sorry, yes. I won't guess at anything."

I nodded and finished my computer tour, then showed her the bar and how our table numbers were situated around the restaurant. Being in a former private home, Boricua had multiple rooms and outdoor spaces. After we rounded the last dining area, we toured the kitchen, stockroom, and the laundry area where she'd assist with sorting and pretreating, if needed. The lunch linens had already been readied for pickup, and empty bins awaited dinner service.

"Risto, I mean, wow." Leslie looked amazed. "This is so impressive. I had no idea there were so many moving parts in running a restaurant. Your parents would be so proud."

Leslie stepped forward, spreading her arms as if to hug me, but stopped before making contact, hugging herself instead. "Um. Sorry. I'm not sure how to act around you."

I sighed, pocketing my hands. "Me neither."

"What do we do? We're not together, but I still care about you. Can we go back to being friends? At least while I'm here?"

I didn't want to be friends.

I wanted to hate her for rejecting me. For forcing me to end us and leave me pining after her every damn night. For making other women look like overcooked rice by comparison. She ruined me. Asking to be friends was only slightly less offensive than my ridiculous longing to take her back.

Not that she was asking.

Looking at her now, all sexy and hopeful, I'd be a major jerk to turn her down.

My gaze rose from the floor, scanning her body, up her long legs to the white T-shirt hugging her breasts under a black blazer. Her earnest face awaited my reply. My last decision about our relationship left her in tears. I could already tell I'd be the one needing Kleenex before this was all over.

I extended my hand to shake. "Friends."

"Great." Leslie curled her fingers around mine to seal our pact, her skin surprisingly cool to the touch. Maybe the restaurant's climate control settings were too low. Dot liked it chilly, and sometimes guests complained. I'd have to go check.

We exited the laundry area, and I shut the accordion doors behind us. "So, you landed the Saturday host spot on *The Kaelen Reed Show.* Congratulations. That's a big deal."

"Yeah, it's pretty cool. I'm excited to see how it goes."

Leslie gathered her curls in her fist, shifting them over one shoulder. As she did, her diamond stud earrings sparkled in the overhead lights. The ones I bought for her. I wonder if she remembered?

"We shot some promos the other day. I stood around looking all serious." She waved the idea away. "So silly, but I guess they'll help get the word out. Hopefully, someone watches besides Dot."

"Stop worrying, you'll be great. You always are," I said, immediately kicking myself for the admission.

Her eyebrows shot up. "You watch?"

"Some," I lied. I watched every damn episode she was on. My DVR made sure of it. Reed was an insufferable blowhard, though, so I fast-forwarded over his parts. I never much liked the guy to begin with, and my dislike only worsened once I determined he'd likely been in her pants. A place I was dying to revisit. But that wasn't what "friends" did.

Shit. I'd been in the friend zone for all of three minutes and already hated it. I wondered which zone Mr. Slick Newscaster parked in?

"How is Reed in person? You two friends?" I asked.

She smirked at my prying question. But if we were supposed to be friends, this was a totally legit conversation. Plus, I had to know if there was competition. You know, in case the platonic thing didn't stick.

"Not really. He's a bit much to take and refuses to stop flirting with me."

"He probably can't help himself."

"When I want his attention, I'll ask for it. Till then, he can keep his hands to himself."

That's my girl.

I filed that tidbit away as the familiar snap of sexual tension zinged between us. My breath grew ragged as I struggled to fight the longing. Her body tensed, nostrils flared, in an apparent struggle of her own.

Weren't we a pair?

Leslie spoke first. "Risto, I—"

"Why don't you go find Kayla up front and help get the tables set? I'm needed in the kitchen."

She nodded and walked off toward the dining room. I stormed past dinner prep to my office and slammed the door.

Having Leslie this close was fast becoming my personal nightmare.

Chapter 13

Leslie

When I arrived at the hospital the day after Dot's surgery, she was fast asleep. I took it as a good sign and I huddled on the window seat. I'd been chewing on my pen ever since.

My shift at Risto's restaurant the night before was an unbridled disaster.

I messed up guest seating, spilled water on tables as I tried to refill glasses from a carafe, and left diners waiting to be greeted while I broke down crying in the linen closet.

It was all too much. The sights and aromas of the food made me want to throw up and devour it all at the same time. All the people looking at me. Whenever I looked up, I swore Risto's face was plastered in that stupid porthole window in the swinging door to the kitchen.

Casting judgment from afar.

Probably calculating how much money I was costing him. And Dot.

I looked up to find my aunt watching me.

"Hey, you're up. How do you feel?" I slipped the pen behind my ear to hide the gnawed end.

"I've been better." Dot flinched. The simple act of speaking took effort, and my heart ached for her.

"Mind getting me some water?" she asked.

"Yeah, sure. It's cold. They just brought a new pitcher."

Crushed ice sloshed in the pint-sized pink container as I poured. Her unsteady hands almost spilled the water, so I grabbed the cup back. After slipping the straw between her waiting lips, she took a sip. When done, she gave me a weary glance.

"I feel the fool. Laying in this bed with you serving me." Dot grimaced as she attempted to sit more upright. Her stink eye stilling me as I moved to help.

"I have to do this myself if they're going to let me out of this place."

"They also said to take it easy for the first 24 hours."

"Well, I've given them that, plus some. Time for me to get up." She pressed the bed controller to lift her head and flatten her bent legs so she could more easily stand.

I bolted around, but she was already standing by the time I grabbed her arm to steady her wobble. A wide gap in her hospital gown exposed her bare butt.

"Um..." A laugh gurgled up my throat.

She tossed a glance over her right shoulder. "Thought I felt a draft."

"Let me tie those strings for you."

We rotated her gingerly in her yellow, rubberized socks so her back faced me. But it was no use. The hospital gown was too small for her, and there was no way the strings would connect and not leave Dot mooning the ward. Seemed cruel to give her an ill-fitting gown.

I covered the upholstered recliner chair with a towel from the bathroom and got her settled, tossing a blanket over her legs. "Let me check with the nurse about getting you a fresh gown that fits."

She nodded, eyes drooping closed as she nestled into her new resting spot.

As I stepped into the hall, the chaos of the central nursing station assaulted my senses. Two staffers talked loudly on phones cradled in their necks, computer keys clacking under their brutal assault. A doctor whisper-screamed in the corner, disagreeing over a chart he held. A gaggle of laughing voices burst through the open door of a kitchenette nearby. With everyone occupied, I meandered over to a navy roller cart where the rounded edges of basil-green paisley gowns peeked through the canvas flap. While clean, the frayed necklines betrayed their age.

God, they're ugly.

I searched each gown for sizing, finding only smalls and mediums before the pile lurched forward against my chest. I tried to balance the stack and shift it into place, but the tower of cloth toppled sideways.

Shit.

"Hey!" a husky voice yelled as a nurse rushed to steady the falling gowns before they fell to the floor. Her skilled hands rescued me from catastrophe.

"Thanks. Are there any larger gowns? The one my aunt's wearing leaves her exposed." I stepped aside to clear the way.

"What color does she have now?"

"Like these. Green."

She flipped the cart flap closed. "I have a stash in the back of larger sizes."

"Contraband?" I joked.

"They go fast. Hold on." She walked through a nearby door while I waited next to the gowns no one needed.

Why make folks jump through hoops to find the right size? Seemed unfair to keep some up front while forcing others to ask. Or maybe we were supposed to ask in the first place?

The nurse returned and handed me a version with a maroon color palette. "What room are you in?"

"232-A," I said, hugging the prize to my chest.

"I'll make a note on her record so we provide the right size."

"Thank you."

When I reentered the room, Auntie was dozing in her chair. I let her be and sat down to my computer, noticing an email from my editor, Viraj:

Strong ratings from the other night on The Kaelen Reed Show. *He's pissed you won't be available for weeks. LMK if you're open to trudging back for an appearance or two before you start in September.*

The thought of my creepy colleague sent my anger boiling. But Viraj had a point about me not being invisible for so long. And it'd give me a reason to avoid the restaurant. Definitely something to consider. I replied, telling him I was open to the idea but would just need enough notice to get back and ready. Once again, I was using work to escape Risto, but he was the one who walked away, not me. Christ, being at his restaurant last night was misery.

Except for that moment in the hall.

Pleasure rippled through me at the thought of Risto's earthy, musky scent. I caught a whiff when his hot breath caressed my face. It took me back to all the nights we'd laze tangled and boneless in bed after making love. My head on his chest, his heart pounding fiercely at first, then gradually settling down as sleep took hold. I'd often awake to a kiss being planted on my neck and his hand rounding the curve of my ass. Good God, that man made me feel some kinda way. And I craved it like air. Resisting that temptation was hard as hell, especially since I never wanted us apart to begin with.

His hungry look the other day left me wondering if he still had feelings for me. It'd be too much to hope. I hated myself for missing his scent, his deep brown eyes, and his rugged shoulders... Damn him and his gorgeousness. Another zing caught my breath, forcing my eyes closed to savor it. Remembering I wasn't alone, I popped them back open. But not soon enough.

"So...?" Dot asked with a crooked grin. "How'd it go last night at Boricua?"

"Tragic. If I wasn't volunteering, they would have fired me." I rose to retrieve the new gown from the foot of her bed.

"You're exaggerating."

"If anything, I'm being generous. It's just not my favorite place to be."

"Why is that?" An unmistakable challenge tinged her voice.

"You know very well."

Dot rubbed her temples. "I'm groggy from the anesthesia. Remind me."

Why was she doing this?

"I don't want to be around a man who doesn't want to be around me."

"You've never enjoyed being there, even before you broke up. What is it about that place that makes you so uncomfortable?"

Oh, I don't know? Being around food all the time and knowing I can't eat any of it?

I unfolded the gown. "Let's get you into this so we can stroll a little."

"You're changing the subject."

"Yes, I am."

After swapping gowns, I tied the strings at her back. This time, they closed easily, with lots of room for her to move comfortably.

"Much better. Thank you," she said.

Dot shuffled toward the door, unsteady in her slip-resistant hospital socks. "You'd never know I taught yoga by the look of me."

"You'll be yogaing again, soon." I kept a firm grip on her waist and arm as we trudged along.

"Did you walk Pepper before you came over?" she asked, pausing to rest.

"Yes, and it nearly killed me. I didn't realize it was over three miles."

She stopped to glare. "How do you live in New York and not walk? It's impossible."

"I walk. There's just a lot of buses, cabs, and subways in between. I have a busy life and need to put my energy where it matters."

"Did you eat anything today?" she asked, already knowing the answer. "I left the fridge stocked."

I meant to eat. I really did. But it wasn't part of my daily routine. I was so wound up about Risto, the last thing I wanted to think about was food. Hunger had become the background music of my life. Present, but never fully registering enough to prompt action. I promised to change, but I felt so full after breakfast with Gabby yesterday. I now realized I hadn't eaten since.

"If you don't want to end up in this place, you must remember to feed your body. It's not the enemy. You live in it. It's what keeps you breathing. You're so up in your head all the time that you forget 98 percent of you is below your neck. Your body is part of you too, and it's screaming for help. You've got to listen."

Her face carried so much worry, I hated to disappoint her. Ashamed, I eyed the gray floor tiles, saying nothing. Better to not make promises I couldn't keep. Though I would try to change. The hours I'd spent reading articles over the last few days left me more confused. Every article I read about the wrongs of dieting was countered by ten elevating lean living as the best lifestyle.

Dot resumed walking, now with more purpose. *Wow*. If my post-surgical aunt had more stamina than me, the anti-diet position might have merit.

"Talk to me about the idea of 'diet culture.' It's a phrase I'd never heard before but am seeing all over the materials I've been reading."

She looked at me sideways, a knowing smile on her lips. "Diet culture is the societal concept that prizes thinness above all else. It becomes the holy grail and leaves people thinking that there's something wrong with them if they don't shrink down."

Made sense. I found a study of Miss America contestants and *Playboy* models that documented how their weights and sizes plummeted between 1959 and 1988. So much so that the newest contestants met the criteria for anorexia nervosa. If *Playboy* models and pageant queens were starving themselves sick, what did that mean for the rest of us?

We reached the end of the hall and sat on a window bench to rest.

"This diet industry data is the biggest shock I've had in years," I said. "And I've seen dead people."

Dot laughed, flinching as she pressed a hand against her stitches.

"Hey, girl!" a cheery voice said.

I looked up to find a Black woman with lovely goddess braids. Cornrows tight to her scalp that collected into a high ponytail of thick braids that cascaded down her back. Gold beads dotted throughout, matching the hoops she wore in her ears. A black pencil skirt hugged her thick curves, topped by a turquoise-and-black flowered blouse beneath her hospital ID badge.

"Tasha!" My aunt's face glowed into a smile.

Tasha leaned in to whisper, "The surgery go okay?"

"Yes, but I've still a ways to go. Tasha, this is my niece, Leslie. She's out to stay with me awhile from New York. Leslie, Tasha is my dietitian."

Shame bubbled in me for thinking a larger-bodied nutritionist was a misnomer. I had so much to learn. My aunt often mentioned the rude women in her yoga class who were offended by having an instructor of her size. Here I was doing the same thing to Tasha.

"I've been telling Leslie about the truth behind diet culture. You'd be a great person for her to speak with. What do you think?"

"Yes, if you have time?" I said, trying to recover.

"I had a client cancel, so I can talk to you at 3:00 p.m. That work?" Tasha told me where to find her office and was off.

I sat biting my lip, but then just spat it out. "Forgive me, because I'm learning and I'm probably going to ask stupid questions. Maybe even insulting ones."

Dot stood. "I'll need to move for this."

We shuffled back toward her room, and I spoke low to avoid sounding like the bigot I knew myself to be. "Talk to me about being a nutritionist at a larger size. I thought the whole point of going to one was to stay at a healthy weight."

"That's been the current standard, but there is a new generation of nutrition professionals who realize that their obsession with weight is wrong. These folks help people make lifestyle changes. Yes, to what they eat, but more about how they think about food and movement. It frees people to live their best life in the bodies they have."

"It sorta makes sense, but it sounds weird. Like you're only going partway to deal with our health."

She shook her head. "If you live a healthy way, move as you're able and enjoy, and get the nourishment your body needs, your weight will land where it's supposed to. That could be large, it could be small. The idea is to decouple the concepts of weight and health. They're not the same thing. Just because you're fat doesn't mean you're unhealthy or have no endurance, and just because you're thin doesn't mean you're healthy or fit."

Those last words were a gut punch.

Just because you're thin doesn't mean you're healthy or fit.

Shit.

I was a living example of that.

Dread clung to me like wet jeans.

What the hell was I supposed to say to Tasha at 3:00 p.m.?

Or worse, what would she say to me?

Chapter 14

LESLIE

Three o'clock rolled around.

While Dot rested in her room, I navigated through the hospital to my appointment.

Tasha's interior office had no windows. Instead, an overhead skylight flooded the space. The sun's warmth a welcome relief after the hospital's frigid AC. Vivid, poster-sized dioramas of vineyards, beaches, and forests gave me an eerie sensation of stepping through a fairy portal. It was all I could do to not touch the plants extending past the frames to see if they were alive.

"I'm sorry, but this is a really cool office." My face dipped close to the garden boxes and detected both humidity and a subtle floral fragrance. "These are real?"

"No, but they remind me of the beauty beyond my four walls." Tasha gestured to one of the two chairs nestled against a small, round table under the beach scene. We both sat.

"Many of my clients live in larger bodies, and they feel the outdoors are reserved for those who are trim. But nature is open to us all. There is no litmus test of worthiness to enjoy it, least of all weight."

Tasha was right. Images depicting outdoor activities were anchored in a specific body type: Slim, young, usually white people. That stereotype relegated everyone else to intruder status. It might be unintentional, but it had the same chilling effect. It was so easy to internalize these messages and use them to fuel limiting beliefs. Which brought me back to why I was in Tasha's office.

"I've been digging into a lot of information about diet culture." I laid my phone on the table between us. "Okay if I record this interview?"

"Sure," Tasha said.

I tapped my voice memo app and opened a new recording file. "Your hospital profile described you as a Healthy Bodies practitioner. Can you explain what that is?"

"The medical and dietitian fields have been huge contributors to the negative culture around body size. We are trained to look at fat as a disease, instead of treating clients equally, regardless of the package they come in. Too often, this leads to poor health outcomes and misdiagnoses because we're focusing on the wrong thing."

"You're saying that fat isn't a problem?" I hated the disbelieving tone of my voice, but this was all so mind-boggling.

Tasha reached into a nearby drawer to pull out a glossy flyer with bar graphs and pie charts. "This study by the US Department of Agriculture followed a group of obese women for two years. Half dieted, half were encouraged to follow a Healthy Bodies approach. They ate when hungry, learned to appreciate fullness, were encouraged to choose nutrient-dense foods and find a way to move that they enjoyed."

I shifted in my seat. "No dieting? Sounds like a dream."

Tasha pulsed an eyebrow in amusement. "At the end of the study, the participants all weighed about the same. The dieters had lost weight, but then gained it all back. The Healthy Bodies group had healthier blood pressure, lower cholesterol, and were more physically active than the dieting group. Other studies show the significant metabolic harm caused by yo-yo dieting. Over time, dieters routinely get less healthy than those who adopt more positive lifestyle behaviors, not focused on getting smaller."

"What about all the studies that show obesity causes death? I think I read something about an American Medical Association study?" After finding that, my enthusiasm for my aunt's approach flatlined. Based on Centers for Disease Control data, the study found that nearly 400,000 people a year died from obesity. If that was true, then everything I was hearing was as much a fairytale as Tasha's wall art.

"You've done homework. That's good. Let's correct the record, because those rarely make headlines. When the CDC learned its methods were faulty, it redid the study. The corrected methods found that only 26,000 overweight and obese people died. The same data set showed overweight people lived longer than those with normal weights. Underweight people fared the worst, dying more often than overweight or obese people. Experts decry the 'obesity epidemic.'" Tasha air-quoted. "But as our weights have increased, so has our life expectancy. And what is the end goal of dieting, if not to live longer, healthier lives?"

I'd landed in upside-down world. Fat people lived longer? How did that compute?

"Can you share the studies with me so I can verify all this?"

She scribbled a few study names on the pamphlet between us, having memorized the details and researchers. She slid it in front of me. My eye landed on the chart about the better health outcomes for the non-dieters.

I knew where I fell on the continuum. Based on what I learned, I'd been starving myself for decades. And according to the CDC, I would die sooner than the full-figured woman across from me. Suddenly, this investigation wasn't only about humoring my aunt. It was about saving lives. Maybe even my own.

I'd never made the connection between my meager food intake and my overall health. Yet food was fuel. Denying this truth was kidding myself that I didn't have a serious problem with how I thought about my body. I tapped the voice recorder off.

We sat in silence. Tasha, being a trained professional, graciously allowed me to gather my thoughts.

"I'm going to be in town for a while. Would you mind if I made an appointment? I've got some questions. Personal ones."

"My door is always open. Happy to talk."

After Dot ate her dinner at the hospital, I headed back to her house. I'd been reeling ever since my meeting with Tasha. Now I found myself curled up on the sofa, glued to my computer screen, confirming every damn thing the nutritionist said. And then some. Study after study disproved the connections between weight and health. It led me to a professor at a college nearby, whom I emailed for an appointment. That left me simmering in misery about my own circumstances.

How could I have been so impossibly wrong about nearly everything to do with weight and food? I'd suffered for so long, and in the process, I'd become my fucking mother. A joyless woman so petrified of getting fat that she'd pushed away everyone in her life. That realization chilled me. After struggling to have a relationship with Mom, I turned around and did the same damn thing. How many family holidays had I skipped? How many dinners had Risto made me, preparing my favorite dishes with love, only to have me eat two bites? The hurt in his eyes seared into my memory. In rejecting his passion, I rejected him.

Is that why we broke up?

Had I left him long before he left me?

The rattle of Risto's garage door opening launched me pin-straight where I sat.

He's home. Oh my God, he's home.

My heart throbbed in my chest. Then sank.

We weren't a couple. I'd rushed out after my shift at the restaurant, too embarrassed to speak to anyone. Neither of us called or texted, and why would we? There was no reason to talk and certainly less reason for him to come over. But I needed to see him. He had to know how sorry I was for screwing up yesterday. And for not being more supportive of his career. For letting my stupid food hang-ups drive a wedge between us.

Leave the man be. He's had a long day and probably wants to be alone.

Maybe? Maybe not.

I tiptoed to the rear sliding doors to peer out between the vertical blinds. Visibility hampered, I moved to the far end, pressing my face against the glass.

Bingo. A clear view of his dark, empty deck.

Would he step out for a nightcap?

Then what?

I could go apologize?

If I went out, he might see me and follow?

I rested my hand on the door handle just as Risto emerged on his deck, triggering his motion light. He sipped from a green bottle of beer.

Shit.

I jumped back, sending the blinds swaying wildly. He turned my way, a smile erupting on his face as he brought the beer to his lips.

Fuck. He absolutely saw me spying on him.

I bit the bullet and stepped out into the crisp evening air. Cricket chirps brought me back to the last time the two of us were together on a night like this. A clear evening with warm breezes and mesmerizing stars. Hopefully, tonight would end better than that one had.

"Hey," I said, slipping my hands into my jeans pockets as I leaned against the deck rail.

"I saw the light on." He brought a second bottle of beer out from behind him and wiggled it. "Care to join me?"

Of course. Risto knew me better than I knew myself. He probably also knew I wanted to knock him over and smash lips. But my poor showing at his restaurant meant that might not go over too well.

Yet we had a passionate history between us. A lot of love and amazing memories. That had to count for something.

I stepped down my aunt's steps and padded barefoot across the cool grass to where he stood.

He handed me the dewy bottle, his finger grazing electricity up my arm.

My eyes shot to his. Dark brown, purposeful, and sexy as hell. Just as they'd always been.

Damn him and his gorgeousness.

He'd ruined me for anyone else.

"You were a train wreck last night." He chuckled. "Haven't you ever worked in a restaurant before?"

"I barely eat in restaurants. Why would I work in one?" I swigged my beer, then wiped sticky foam off my lip with the back of my hand.

"Fair enough. I appreciate the effort, though. Dot's shoes are hard to fill."

There was the understatement of the century. Trying to be helpful, she'd programmed in customer preferences, anniversaries, kids' names, travel plans, and more. I couldn't keep it straight, but all the other servers knew it cold. Kayla rescued me from placing a dish with almonds in front of someone with a nut allergy. They hadn't mentioned it because Dot always got it right. I drowned memories of my pathetic performance with another swig.

"Back to the hospital tomorrow?" he asked through wet, glistening lips. Not that I noticed.

"Yeah, I'll hang there and keep her company. If we're lucky, they'll let her come home soon. She's doing great already."

"What do you think of her new place?" Risto gestured to Dot's house with his bottle. "It's a lot smaller."

"Seems perfect for her. Less work and closer to the restaurant. Congrats again on the expansion. You're absolutely killing it."

His mouth curled up on one side. A proud papa, unable to contain his joy.

"It's a dream. As many tables as we add, guests fill them. A restaurant critic from Philadelphia was so pissed that he couldn't get a reservation that he stormed my kitchen, unannounced, demanding to eat."

"Seriously?!"

"Yeah. I swept him into my office, sat him at my desk, and let him eat his fill."

"That's ballsy," I said. "What if he saw a mouse or something?"

"In MY kitchen?" He waved me off.

Risto had always been neat as a pin. At home and everywhere else. We'd watch that show called *Kitchen Nightmares*, and he'd leave the room in a fit of rage. A bit triggering for a professional neatnik.

"Did the critic like the food?"

He tilted his head toward the house. "I'll show you."

I followed him inside, which was the mirror image of Dot's place. But that was where the similarity ended. We passed through his top-shelf kitchen into his sleek living room. Black leather sofas curved around a circular smoked glass coffee table at the center. Framed family pictures hung in a perfectly aligned display on the wall above. An enlarged color picture of the two of us featured prominently among them. Our teen selves squished into an amusement car ride meant for smaller children. Risto had just put his arm around me and planted a kiss on my cheek as our car swung past my dad's camera lens. We were in focus, but the rest of the image blurred into a carnival kaleidoscope of perfection.

I set my beer down to stare at our former selves.

"I love that one," he said. "But this is what I wanted to show you."

He put down his beer and lifted a printed email off his coffee table with the upcoming issue of *Philadelphia Metro* magazine. Risto would be on the cover. The headline read, "The Chef that Put PR Cuisine Back on the Map."

Chills ran down my spine.

He'd done it.

He fulfilled his ambition of becoming the celebrated chef he used to dream about.

"Oh, Risto!" Unlike yesterday, I flung my arms around his neck and drew him into a tight hug. "That's incredible!"

As I hugged him, drinking in his scent, I noticed he wasn't returning my embrace.

Shit.

I stepped back. "I'm sorry, I didn't mean to... It's exciting, that's all."

His broad chest stretched his T-shirt as his arms hung tense at his sides. Twitching muscles betrayed that his desire was the same as mine.

"Ah, fuck it." He wrapped me in his arms and planted a longing kiss on my hungry mouth.

His earthy scent filled every void in my body. The hands he used to work culinary magic were now tangled in my curls, tinged with lingering wisps of the garlic and herbs forever mashed into his fingertips. Our mouths melted together, every moment of loneliness and wanting from the last many years healed in an instant. Risto cupped my head like a delicate flower as he pulled away. But instead of the expression of love I expected in his eyes, his face morphed from ecstasy, to recognition, to horror. He jumped away.

"I'm so sorry. I... shit."

"No, really. It's okay..." I pleaded, hating the desperation in my voice.

God, I'm pathetic around this man.

Risto folded his arms across his chest defensively as he leaned against the top of his sofa. His expression shifted again, sadness taking over where joy had been seconds before. His eyes searched mine.

What do you want? Just tell me.

Was he sorry he kissed me because he regretted it or because he thought I did? For the record—holy shit—I did not regret it. It took all my restraint not to club him over the head and drag him upstairs myself.

Chest still heaving, I feared that saying anything now would drive him away. But it didn't matter. The passion evaporated, awkwardness growing in its place. And not in a good way.

Risto scratched his neck. "So, I..."

So, I what? I love you? I'm sorry? I want you back? I waited for a pledge of enduring love, but all I got was silence. I debated letting it linger long enough for him to realize how much he wanted me back, but pride got the better of me.

"It's late. I should be going." I hiked a thumb over my shoulder.

"Sure. See you tomorrow? At the restaurant?"

I headed toward the door, glancing back at him sitting alone in his living room. Once again, Risto chose to be alone over being with me.

Chapter 15

RISTO

I blinked into the blue morning light of my bedroom. Last night, the dreams about Leslie were so vivid, her scent lingered on my skin. This time they almost broke me after a kiss for the ages that should never have happened. Only a fucking brute took a woman without permission. After she left, I took the coldest shower I could stand and remained hard with want. Just like now.

She wanted me as much as I wanted her.

Dream on.

You were friends, remember? You shook on it.

That's the last thing I wanted, but what choice did I have?

Try as I might, I repeatedly drifted over to watch Leslie during her shift at Boricua. I expected her to own the dining room. Instead, she was distracted and confused, spilling water on guests and mixing up orders. She either wasn't trying or didn't want to bother.

She had an off night. She'd get better.

For all our sakes, I hoped so.

I flung the covers back and scratched my head en route to the bathroom. After splashing my face, I blotted it dry and wrapped myself in a navy robe I rarely wore. The terry cloth caressed my skin as I made my way to the kitchen. Jamaican Blue Mountain coffee called to me, so I ground enough for a pot and set it to brew.

The fridge's vegetable drawer held a vivid spectrum of bell peppers—red, yellow, orange, and green, along with bundles of herbs. Snatching a few culantro leaves and a red pepper, I shut the fridge. I plucked a few slices of tomato out of my dehydrator and mashed them into a powder in my wooden mortar and pestle.

What else?

I snapped my fingers and knew the perfect cheese to add. Sourcing authentic Puerto Rican cheese had been hard. But on a recent trip to the island, I'd visited an artisan cheese maker and begun ordering wheels of his nutty montebello. I retrieved it from the fridge and sliced a wafer-thin piece, then speared it with the knife tip.

Overhead lights barely pierced the translucent slice, whose rich, tangy notes sent my nostrils quivering. I slid it into my mouth and let the pungent sensations smooth around my tongue before they mellowed into a bold, yet familiar finish.

Bold and familiar?

My eyes wandered to the stairs that led up to where Leslie should have slept before refocusing on the ingredients before me. I craved them both—Leslie and cooking—but Leslie had been downright hostile to my career as a chef. She complained about the hours I spent tinkering with recipes and made snarky remarks about the demands of my job. After I opened Boricua, the tension only escalated. I tried to involve her, but she flat refused.

No tasting my new dishes to give feedback.

Rarely coming round the restaurant and eating plain salad when she did.

Her behavior mirrored that of a jealous rival.

But what did she have to be jealous of? Did she think I loved cooking more than her?

Don't you?

You chose it over the relationship.

No, I abandoned the toxic squabbles that turned us into our worst selves. As much as we loved each other, I made the choice we both wanted to make. Neither would admit we'd grown into people who sought different things. I didn't fit into her life any better than she fit into mine.

And yet.

Love, lust, or sheer stubbornness kept us magnetically anchored in the other's orbit. We'd pass so close, the mere potential prickled gooseflesh. *She'll be here today at the baby shower? What do you mean, I just missed her?!* Countless near misses made it impossible to make a clean break. I suspected Dot's investment in my restaurant was actually a secret ploy to get me and Leslie back together. Force proximity and let nature take its course. *Like it almost did last night.*

Despite our flammable chemistry, Leslie hated that I was a chef, and I hated how she disregarded her personal safety to chase stories. That painful truth remained unchanged.

My palms pressed into the counter to brace myself against the cold reality. She was here, but she wasn't mine and would never be.

Thoughts clogged my mind, none making sense. I flushed them away to focus on the ingredients glaring at me from the cutting board. What I was going to make.

Breakfast?

Yes. I had to perfect this recipe. I planned to include it on the tasting menu I was prepping for the investors. Boricua wasn't open for brunch, but a New York City location might need a brunch menu.

I pictured a sunny sidewalk with outdoor seating. We'd have glass tables under umbrellas, customized to resemble the Puerto Rican flag. Diners would sip mimosas and comment on how clever it was to make home fries out of plantains. They'd wonder how the chef made the eggs taste so delicious. Servers dressed in black with slicked-back hair would glide between tables, attending to guests. Meanwhile, our gem of a host would have the sad job of ushering people without reservations to the bar for their 40-minute wait.

Scenes like these haunted me daily. I went from dismissing Silas for suggesting I expand, to becoming petrified at the idea that none of the investors would come through.

I was content, happy even, with our successful expansion in Easton. Silas ruined it all.

The article printout on the coffee table caught my eye. How he'd managed a cover story on me was a jaw-dropper. I sidled over to read it again. There I was. Me. A small-town orphan from Pennsylvania featured on the front of a magazine. I'd received good press before, but nothing on a scale like this. Mostly good restaurant reviews from local papers or food blogs no one read. Any press was good press, and I soaked it all in, grateful but never ambitious enough to aim higher. I'd been too busy loving food and pouring myself into every bite. Yet Silas was right. I could be a brand that celebrated the food and culture of Puerto Rico in a new and exciting way. Explore the flavors and recipes people loved but add a modern twist for sophisticated urban palates.

Now that would be worthy of a magazine cover.

Demand was there. Countless diners who visited Boricua from New York City wished we had a closer location. Was I a raving egomaniac to believe I lived up to Silas' headline? The chef who put Puerto Rican food back on the map? Glossy covers featuring me, like I was some tech tycoon who transformed their passion into a multi-billion-dollar business.

That could be me.

I could be the next face gracing cooking shows like *Chopped* and *Beat Bobby Flay*. Replace fraud chefs like Chase Patel, who hadn't worked in a kitchen in ages.

I'd start with restaurants, then add a cookbook, cooking tools, and packaged goods. Maybe appear at culinary events or food festivals?

Head down, working tirelessly, I forgot to step back and think about my future. In a matter of moments, I put it all together. All I had to do was become the next big celebrity chef.

No biggie.

I fired off an email to Silas, asking if he knew any culinary agents, and pressed Send before I could change my mind. He was correct. I'd been thinking too small. And for a guy my size, you'd think that'd be a hard thing to do. But this suddenly felt so right. Like my dad's dreams were channeling through me. I pictured my parents, proud, looking down on me from heaven.

It wouldn't be easy and might never happen. But I had to try.

I glanced toward my empty bedroom. Becoming a famous chef might just be easier than resisting the woman I loved.

Chapter 16

Leslie

Over the next four days, my shifts at the restaurant went slightly better. I barely saw Risto except through the porthole in the kitchen door. I wondered if spying was his typical MO, or if he was keeping tabs on me. I pretended it was the latter, though settling Dot at home after her hospital stay left scant time for my imaginary love connection.

Auntie gingerly moved about the house, delighting in the silence and absence of electronic blood pressure cuffs and IV tubes. She waved off my offers to cook (likely a good idea) in favor of the massive containers of leftovers she'd prepared beforehand. To her, they looked untouched. But I had eaten while she was away. Mostly grazing out of the fridge when hunger pangs stirred. But she was lucky I got that far. Every bite launched an exhausting psychological battle with Little Diana screaming bloody murder in my head. It sucked the joy dry and made me question the wisdom of the whole chewing and swallowing thing.

"I think I'll go lie down," Dot said as she put her lunch plate in the kitchen sink.

"You should let me help more. I feel so useless."

"I'll recover faster if I stay active. I'm not used to sitting around, so the quicker I get back to my walks, the better."

"Once you're steadier on your feet, we can give it a go. I'm here to help—"

"You are. You're doing laundry and running to the pharmacy. You're helping at the restaurant. Having you here is a blessing." She cruised around the counter, using it for support, and kissed my forehead.

"I don't want you to overdo it," I said.

She cupped my chin. "Believe me, if I've learned anything, it's how to listen to my body. And right now, it wants to go upstairs and sleep. You've got work to do, anyway."

Dot wasn't wrong. While not helping my powerhouse aunt, I had time to research her contentions about the food industry. Big Diet evidence was mounting to support her case, but I didn't build a solid reputation as a journalist by blindly accepting information as true without fact-checking it backward and forward. Anything I put my name on had to be bulletproof.

The more I read, the more I drowned in implications for my life. Instead of inspiring further investigation pathways, I got mired in distraction. How would these factoids change how I lived? What new habits must I adopt? Then there were the mounting grievances against my mother. Shocking truisms sent me running to my phone to shame her for all the lies. Only sober reality stilled my hand. I shared the blame. Despite being a fucking reporter, I never once questioned the cage I'd woven for myself. Realization left me pissed off and confused. I rarely leaned on anyone, but it'd become painfully obvious that I needed a sherpa to guide me toward whomever I was supposed to be. And if I couldn't find her, I'd need instructions for building a new one. My next session with Tasha was still three days away, giving me no choice but to wade deeper into my work.

After Dot went upstairs for a nap, I hopped in the car to drive over to my appointment with a professor I'd discovered at a local university. Her research debunked the notion that weight management led to healthier outcomes. The CDC study findings were convincing, but I yearned to learn more.

During my ride, questions pinged around my brain. Between my mother's dictates, health establishment decrees, news coverage, and entertainment industry stereotypes, it was impossible not to question how a scientific truth this easy to find received no media attention. There were scores of studies for decades all over the world, all pointing to the same conclusion: you didn't need to be thin to be healthy.

Why had I never learned any of this before?

Every popular information source parroted the same message, like magnets drawn true north. The uniformity should have attracted my suspicion. But it never did. Instead, I marched blindly along, ignoring my inner compass, trying to divert me from heading over a cliff. If someone presented me with a story this one-sided, I'd cross my arms and demand to hear the other side.

But not about fatness.

And not about food.

Since my cafeteria breakfast with Gabby, I'd eaten more than usual. Not full meals by my family's standards, but better than nothing. The few times I tried to walk away, Aunt Dot made me share my hesitations aloud.

"I'll eat later," I'd said.

"Why not now? Talk me through it," Dot said.

"Well, I just ate an hour ago and shouldn't be hungry."

"But are you? Hungry?"

"Yes."

"So what happens if you eat?"

Thoughts had collided around my mind, but only one emerged from my mouth. "I get fat."

My reply stunned me. In my head, eating had no other purpose than to make me fat. It had nothing to do with nourishing my body with the nutrients it needed to function. Thinking. Breathing. Sleeping. Moving. Meals became warped into gateways to fatness. Giving into hunger showed I was weak and undisciplined. Deprivation was the only legitimate path to be healthy, pure, and worthy. Or so my mother t aught me.

But there was no sense denying that since I'd begun eating more, I felt better. I had more energy and mental focus. I could walk the dog twice daily without my legs going to jelly. Analyzing my thoughts about food led to one inescapable conclusion: they were all rooted in fear.

Fear of ridicule.

Fear of poor treatment by colleagues.

Fear of not fitting in.

Fear of not being loved.

Fear of people pointing at me, repulsed, on the street.

Fear of receiving second-rate service in stores and restaurants.

Little Diana lived rent-free in my head, promising to descend with every worst-case scenario I could imagine simply because I ate a meal.

That was a hard pill to swallow, and it only unleashed a barrage of additional questions. If, as my aunt contended, there were no good foods and no bad foods, then food was just... what? Food?

I drove past a dairy pasture dotted with cows while imagining my mom's head blowing clear off. Besides being an artist, my Mom's entire persona revolved around the near-religious dogma of her dining regimen.

Mom's way of eating was the one true way.

Eating freely was weak, immoral, and should be rejected.

Following my mother's clean-living path would make me healthy and protect me from harm.

Only the righteous eater will be rewarded with a long, healthy life.

If you slip, you must repent, make restitution in the form of skipped meals or additional movement, and promise to do better.

Holy shit.

I swerved to the side of the road and cut the engine, my pulse throbbing my ears.

How had I never noticed?

My mom was a fucking cult leader.

My shaky hands gripped the steering wheel for dear life, aching for something solid. Something reliable and true. Never had a story contorted my worldview as much as this one. Revelations jolted my body with electric current as if a sadistic executioner helmed the switch. It hurt. So much so that I battled an overwhelming instinct to turn away from the story. Past critics of my investigations complained I was a pest, needlessly unearthing secrets best left hidden. Being on the receiving end made me realize they might have a point. But I refused to succumb to personal fears.

Yet I couldn't deny the risk. My approach to reporting required me to be fully invested. Not just observe events dispassionately from afar, but dive in up to my neck. From living the sex trade to drinking with gangsters, I was part of the story. How would that work this time, and where the fuck would it leave me?

Victoria flashed to mind.

One of the most accomplished journalists today was reduced to tears by disgusting anti-fat bigotry.

Did I want that?

Not in the slightest.

Did I want to change the culture that tolerated that behavior?

Abso-fucking-lutely.

I turned over the car's engine and pulled back onto the road.

Time to meet the good professor.

After parking, I crunched down a gravel path and across a lovely campus quad. Red brick buildings bordered an impeccably mowed lawn, like chess pieces on a green checkerboard. A pang of longing surged through me. College held amazing memories. It was where I'd met my best friends Barbara and Rebecca, two women who'd been by my side ever since. Funny how my family noticed my eating challenges, but neither of my girlfriends had. Or at least, they never mentioned it. In their defense, though, our time together was one of the few instances when I allowed myself to eat more normally. Our Central Park picnics, Sunday brunches, and girls'-night-ins were full of laughter and fun—and food.

Why did I eat with my girls but rarely anywhere else?

I'd have to ponder that question another time, since I'd arrived at my destination.

I climbed the stone steps of Jonston Hall, yanking open a two-ton wooden door on whiny hinges. Lights flickered on as I passed into the cool interior, goosebumps erupting on my skin. I rubbed my arms as I searched for stairs to Professor Hawley's second-floor office, huffing more than I wanted to admit as I ascended the grand staircase.

A pool of light splashed into the hallway ahead from her open door.

She muttered under her breath while wrestling a filing cabinet drawer closed. It slammed, then she startled when seeing me.

"Oh! Are you Miss Allen?"

"Yes, Leslie Allen. Thanks for meeting with me, Professor."

She gestured for me to sit. Her pale cheeks had a natural rosiness to them that complemented her dark bangs and blunt shoulder cut. I wasn't sure what to expect from a woman advocating for fat acceptance. Professor Hawley was a larger-bodied person, which sent Little Diana into a tizzy.

Of course she's heavy. Fat acceptance is an excuse not to control oneself.

I shook off the toxic thoughts, but shuddered, knowing I'd have to interview a skeptic who would gleefully articulate the same position. Sometimes journalistic balance sucked.

Scores of articles recounted the prevalence of anti-fat bias in the workplace and the world at large. This led to a host of unfair practices, such as fewer job opportunities and promotions and unequal treatment from doctors, leading to missed diagnoses and poorer health outcomes. Then there was ridicule from the media. Navigating life in a larger body was hard all around, and I was glad to have access to Professor Hawley so I could learn more.

Professor Hawley explained that countless studies about weight and diet were funded by those advocating for strict calorie control. Companies depended on people buying products, supplements, and meal plans to manage their weight, with profits tallying into the billions. "Big Diet is just as toxic and dangerous as any interest group. Big Pharma, Big Oil, Big Tobacco. Anything too big gets corrupt."

She took me through the data. Like the CDC study, Professor Hawley's work showed overweight people lived longer. But not all overweight and obese people were necessarily healthier than those of normal weight. It was about lifestyle, which was why the professor advocated for people to avoid getting weighed at the doctor.

"It forces medical professionals to treat their health indicators instead of making assumptions based on a patient's body size," she said.

I sat back, thinking.

Just the other day at the hospital, the doctor on rounds nearly fell over when hearing that my full-and-fabulous aunt taught yoga. By the end of their conversation, the trim doctor was doing a standing eagle pose, modified for larger-bodied people, that still stretched the shoulders and upper back and relieved his back pain. Dot was the living personification of what Professor Hawley was describing.

"Are you aware of the origins of the BMI?" the professor asked. "I sometimes hesitate to quote studies founded on that data because it's such a bogus measure. It was developed using data sets containing only white men, yet it's used as a standard across races and cultures who were never included in the data collection."

"Yes, I hear it's badly flawed," I said as an idea formed. "But surely you agree that there is a limit to weight beyond which it's unhealthy?"

"The data sets in this area are so flawed I can't scientifically give you an answer. There is so much variability from person to person, and ultimately, I question what the purpose is of declaring right and wrong weights. Why not engage with medical conditions and health factors and take weight out of the equation altogether?"

I opened my mouth to protest, but stopped. She had a point. What benefit was there in categorizing people into arbitrary weight groupings? If there was no right or wrong height and no right or wrong shoe size, why had weight assumed such importance in determining health? I needed to investigate further to find out.

But first, food. Suddenly I felt very hungry.

Chapter 17

Risto

Four nights after "the kiss," I was once again neck deep in disappointment. Conversations with two more restaurant groups left me sitting at my desk at Boricua, deeply unsettled.

The first investors had no footprint in Manhattan, and I had no intention of being their guinea pig. There was too much at stake, and I'd have one chance to get this right.

The second investment group was top-shelf in the culinary industry. They'd successfully launched twelve properties, five of which expanded to multiple cities. My hopes were sky-high until I met the clueless scouting team. They toured Boricua, making snide comments about the decor and how the restaurant wasn't likely a good fit before they'd even tasted my food. Once they began eating, their condescending attitude and banal scoring sheets left me fuming.

They checked boxes and whispered, commenting like I wasn't there.

This simple fare won't do.

New Yorkers are too discerning.

He's a big guy. Will diners relate to food prepared by someone like him?

I interrupted at this point.

Someone like him?

What did my size have to do with my cooking? Most diners would never see me. It made no sense.

Their comments about the menu were equally worthless.

I'm not sure Puerto Rican food is the right fit for us. It's so basic, but that's to be expected given the limited ingredients they have to work with.

Such a poor country.

They bristled when I reminded them Puerto Rico was part of the US and got Goya shipments from New Jersey, like the rest of us. They blinked at me as if I were insane.

Would all the investors be this ignorant?

I regretted planning a tasting menu with the third group. The expansion would be toast if I had to partner with people like them. Sure, it included Ruben Santiago, a Puerto Rican restaurateur. If not for that, I might have canceled. At least he wouldn't look at me crosswise and ask me why so many dishes had bananas.

I was nanoseconds from yelling, *They're called plantains, you idiots. Do you know nothing about Puerto Rican cuisine?*

Lucky for us all, Freddie was nearby. He saw my reddening face and dragged me to the kitchen for a question. That turned out to be, "How quickly can we get these morons out of our restaurant?" We cut down the menu and sent them packing. We had a special early dinner for ourselves and used the rest of the ingredients as daily specials.

Those investors didn't deserve me.

The concept of who did and didn't deserve me led me straight back to Leslie. My feelings for her had never wavered. The moment she'd hugged me and I'd landed face-deep in her curls and intoxicating scent,

I'd almost let myself slip. Days later, I'd barely seen her during her shifts and now wish I jumped at the chance when I had it.

Leslie had an appointment this afternoon, so I gave her the night off. Instead of being relieved, not having her at the restaurant tonight left me listless.

Dot kept her busy during the day, but my business partner went to bed early. When I drove home each night, her living room light glowed bright, the blue glow of Leslie's laptop lighting up her face. Not that I was spying. On her list of priorities, I didn't register, though I'd hoped things might change for us.

I passed through the kitchen where dinner service wound down and cleaning had begun. No one paid me any mind as I strolled out the door to the garden, the sounds of evening enveloping me.

Frogs croaking

Crickets chirping.

Breeze rustling the walnut tree leaves overhead.

I shared countless stolen moments with Leslie outdoors in the summer. Evenings like this that ended with us tangled in each other's arms.

Through the restaurant window, patrons chatted merrily, their faces lit by flickering candlelight.

A woman with dark, curly hair leaned forward to feed her dinner mate, who nodded appreciatively before puckering for a kiss.

I wiped my face in frustration.

Love was everywhere.

But not for me.

Why did she have to come back? I'd finally patched my broken heart, a sloppy job to be sure with duct tape and gum. But good enough to function. Now I'd devolved into a tormented mess, pining for a woman who didn't want me.

"Risto!" Jose called from the kitchen.

I sighed, heading inside, but not before glancing once more at the woman with dark hair.

Chapter 18

LESLIE

Nagging doubt kept me up half the night. I sat up in bed to untangle my limbs from the sheets, physical evidence of my endless tossing. After my conversation with the professor, I eagerly grabbed a soup and salad for lunch at Panera while digging into more research on my phone. That's when my mouth turned to paste. For every assertion Professor Hawley made, I found twenty sources claiming the polar opposite.

Reputable studies.

Prestigious universities.

That led me to have an unfortunate video conference with a passionate professor at Princeton University. The dude was thin as a rail after losing a ton of weight and had published multiple books with step-by-step plans for how the rest of the world could be just like him. Anyone could do it. It only took the right balance of discipline, determination, and commitment to living a healthy life.

Where had I heard that before?

He'd had a health scare and had become a fervent advocate for clean living. Twenty years later, he was still at it. Had I interviewed him first, I never would have entertained Aunt Dot's point of view. The man was that convincing. If my crazy mother wanted a boyfriend, I'd have sent him her way. Our conversation took a tense turn when I brought up contrasting data.

"You can get numbers to say anything you want," he said.

"What motivation would the CDC have to falsify data to contradict its previously published findings?"

"It wouldn't, but one study doesn't disprove a mountain of established standard."

"What about other studies showing the positive correlation between longevity and high body weights?"

"The only reasonable explanation is that the study used flawed methodology."

"So you're not the slightest bit open to understanding new information?"

"I'm living proof that my way works. If I can change, anyone can."

Sitting in bed reflecting on the conversation made me regret swallowing my retort. That it was unscientific to ignore research simply because we didn't like the findings. While extreme dieting worked for some, overwhelming stats showed it wasn't sustainable. That left overweight people chasing an impossibly thin standard. Perhaps those of us fearing fat were the ones who needed to change.

Two additional facts further confused me about the contrasting worldviews on body size. First, since eating more, I'd lost that hollowed-out sensation I'd grown so accustomed to. Second, the Healthy Bodies advocates had studies too. Plus, they had logic on their side. Normal variation would suggest that some people would be thin, some fat, and many ranging in between. Somewhere along the line, a value judgment got placed on bodies, labeling thin ones better than fat o nes.

When did that happen and why?

I slid out of bed and meandered across the hall to the bathroom. When washing my hands, I caught my reflection in the mirror.

Ten days after arriving at Dot's, my cheeks were slightly fuller and the hollows under my eyes had faded. Not fully gone, but less noticeable after I began focusing on sleep. I hated mirrors, so seldom looked at myself. When I did, I avoided eye contact. Now I knew why. I hadn't wanted to see the gaunt woman staring back. People I encountered routinely approved of my appearance, which made it all the worse.

Had I always known?

That my thinness was a lie? That I loathed myself and my inability to shake the constant thoughts of food? Little Diana's voice would invade, scolding me for failing to control the vessel of a body I inhabited. Like the Princeton professor, Mom was supposed to be my living example. My beacon. Meanwhile, Dad never saw the point in all the rigidity. I'd always held that against him. Now I wondered if I was a disappointment to him. After all, I stripped myself bare of his lineage. My work name: Allen instead of Molina. Flat ironing my naturally curly hair. Siding against him in the divorce. Starving myself.

I stood back to better see my hips in the mirror over the sink. My hip bones protruded over the top of my pajama bottoms, but my nemesis bulge looked fleshier. Was I getting soft, healthy, or both? What would happen when I returned to Manhattan and my life? The world's best culinary delights would be at my fingertips.

Including Risto's. No way investors would pass him up.

Nor should I.

It was stupid for me to ignore the longing I felt for the man. Avoiding the issue wasn't doing either of us any favors, and it was driving me batty having him so close without seeing him. I'd text him to see if I could come by the restaurant later. For now, I splashed my face with cold water and dabbed it dry with a fluffy towel to join my aunt, who was clanking pans in the kitchen.

When I reached her, she stood at the stove, cooking.

"Hey! I'm supposed to be doing that for you," I said, kissing her extended cheek.

"Your cooking is worse than the hospital's," Dot said with a *that's obvious* lilt in her voice.

"I ate at the cafeteria and have had worse..."

Damn. Point taken.

I went to make coffee, but the pot was already full. I chose a glossy yellow mug from the cabinet and filled it with the aromatic brew. Topping it with cream and sugar, I ignored the guilty voice in my head shrieking not to indulge.

Auntie took a sip of her own coffee, then refocused on the onions and lox in her pan. If I'd known she was making us lox, eggs, and onions, I'd have bolted downstairs sooner. It was my favorite, and I kissed her again on the cheek.

"Let's split a bagel. That, I'll let you do." Dot gestured to the bread drawer.

I opened the bag from the bagel shop that we'd gotten the day before and sliced a sesame bagel in half to drop into the wide-mouthed toaster.

"How do you feel about seeing Tasha today? As a client?" she asked.

"I was chomping at the bit initially, but now I'm petrified." I stopped my task to face her. "Do you think I have an eating disorder? That there's something wrong with me?"

Dot slid the pan off the burner and turned off the flame. She opened her arms, and I nestled in as she stroked my hair. "It's not for me to say. You'll talk to Tasha, and she'll guide you. I've worried you don't eat enough for a long time. If the professionals say you have an eating disorder, at least we'll know, and we can get you the help you need. Let's see how it goes."

The toaster popped. Yeasty steam drifted over from the crisp, golden bagel. I drifted over to it while Dot divided the scrambled eggs between two plates. My fingers hovered, tense, the toaster's heat near searing my fingers. I wanted to eat it, yet couldn't ignore the jumble of consequences colliding around my brain.

Why can't I be like everyone else?

Find joy in food instead of fear?

"Coming?" Dot yelled from the kitchen nook.

I'm trying.

I plucked the bagel halves out of the toaster and dropped them onto the waiting plate. One more neurosis to discuss this afternoon with Tasha.

"Why did you want to see me today?" Tasha asked as we sat once again at the small table in her office.

Could I say it?

The question that'd been plaguing me ever since I heard about the Minnesota study?

Normally bold, I found it impossible to make eye contact, focusing instead on my fidgeting fingers. Worry swirled around me. Aggressive and unrelenting.

As a professional interviewer, I sensed Tasha wouldn't speak until I did.

Tears streamed out of my eyes from the strain, so I squeezed them shut.

"I think I have an eating disorder. Anorexia. I'm researching this stupid article, and I can't help but see myself on every fucking page. It's all there in black and white. Like someone has been stalking me for years and taking notes. I'm so confused. I'm a journalist. Why don't I even know myself?"

Tasha nudged the tissue box on the table closer to me.

Frustrated, I aggressively snatched two out, like the Kleenex was to blame. I blotted my tear-stained face.

"Let me put the question back to you. Why should you have thought there was anything wrong with how you were approaching food?"

"Oh, I don't know. I'm scared shitless at mealtimes. I avoid family and friends when there's a meal involved. I keep an empty fridge to reduce temptation. Shop online to spare myself the sensory assault of the grocery store. I haven't had a regular period since I was sixteen. Oh yeah, how about the nagging thoughts of food but the inability to eat? Zero desire for sex and the constant tiredness in my bones?"

It all sounded so obvious when I said it aloud. So why was I just fitting the puzzle pieces together?

"Normally when clients come to me, we need to deconstruct their lives and arrive to where you already seem to be. You've done a lot of great work, Leslie. You should be proud of yourself."

"What good is knowing if I can't make the problem go away?" Breakfast leapt to mind. I'd forced myself to choke down the first few bites of bagel, then I couldn't stop until my plate was empty of eggs, bagel, and fruit, and I sat stuffed and withering under a barrage of Little Diana's insults. "I'm not strong enough to win an epic battle every time I get hungry. It's just too hard."

Tasha leaned forward, her arms crossed. "So quit fighting. Throw your weapons down and make peace with yourself. It'll take time, but it's the only way to develop a more healthy relationship with food and your body."

"Don't fight?"

"No."

"Then what do I do instead?"

"Well, that's where your treatment team comes in. We'll schedule an appointment with a doctor and run some tests. Based on what we find, we'll put a care plan together for you. If you've been underfeeding yourself, hunger cues will not function as they should. Following a carefully designed eating schedule will be very important to restore the weight more appropriate for your body size and lifestyle."

A meal plan? "What if I'm not hungry?"

"Odd as it may sound, you've forgotten what hunger means. As treatment proceeds, you'll be able to eat when you're hungry and trust yourself. But that takes both time and counseling."

"Therapy?"

"Yes. Anorexia nervosa is classified as a psychological disorder, so the treatment plan includes therapy."

Tasha clarified how I'd been ignoring my body signals for decades, in deference to an artificial, external standard projected on us by others. They didn't know us, our bodies, our lifestyle, genetic history, or needs. Yet they presumed to dictate when and how we should eat.

Based on their arbitrary rules for living right, we'd concoct rules and regulations for ourselves and sentence ourselves to a lifetime of hard labor for any transgressions.

Crawling under the table sounded splendid, but I was only minutes into a session I desperately needed.

Tasha slid a reading list in front of me. "Here are some books and podcasts worth checking out to help you understand the condition, but you can read that later. Let's discuss what happens now."

While still in her office, she arranged for me to visit the lab for some blood tests. I'd see the doctor the next day, and then we'd decide next steps based on the results. When I walked in today, I expected some light admonitions and a diet program. Knowing there was a team heading my way took the control out of my hands.

And that wasn't my way.

"Tasha," I said as she navigated the scheduling system on her computer.

"Yes?"

"What if I don't want all this? The doctors and the therapy?"

"Let's talk about it. Dot mentioned that you have a rising career. You're a respected journalist who's passionate about many causes. Is that right?

"I guess."

"Untreated anorexia nervosa has the highest mortality rate of any mental illness. If you want to live, I recommend you take this treatment plan very seriously."

A nervous laugh rippled through me. "You make it sound like a death sentence."

"It could be. The patient suicide risk is 11 to 18 times higher."

A boulder formed in my throat. I wasn't laughing any more.

"Let me ask you something." Tasha sat back, steepling her fingers. "Are you prone to any risky behaviors, or have ever tried to hurt yourself?"

"Don't be—" I stopped mid-sentence. I was about to say *no*, but the answer was unequivocally *yes*. My work involved such high risk my family cringed, accusing me of having a death wish. But surely that wasn't the same thing. Being an adrenaline junkie didn't mean I wanted to be dead.

Did it?

Harsh truths overloaded my synapses, escaping as tears. "I've... yes. I routinely ignore threats to my personal safety. But it's my job. That's not the same as trying to end my life?"

Tasha sat watching me, her face a mirror of my own concern.

"I don't want to die. I promise."

"Good. Knowing that makes all the difference." She smiled, and I breathed easier. I'd earned a small measure of her approval, which eased the knot in my chest enough to let air pass through.

"How concerned should I be?" I asked in a whisper.

Tasha folded her hands. "We'll take everything step by step. You're not alone, and that's important. You'll have a team here, and of course, I know Dot thinks the world of you. She'll be in your corner."

I sniffled, nodding, knowing I'd failed at the one task on my plate for my visit to Dot's: Help her recover from surgery. Besides her refusing to let me help as much as I'd like, this bombshell would now make me a burden to her. That mustn't happen. There had to be a way for me to get well without hampering her recovery. Gabby had her hands full with work and life. Dad was too far away, and Mom would make everything worse. If I was sick, that meant Mom was too.

No. There was only one person I could talk to. And his name was Risto.

Chapter 19

Risto

"Yo, Risto! You have a visitor!" Jose yelled from the kitchen.

I checked the time. Three o'clock, smack in the middle of our downtime transition between lunch and dinner service. With no appointments on my calendar, I wondered if Silas had sent another potential investor my way.

I pushed back from my desk and abandoned the relative peace of my office to find Freddie's salsa music blaring in the kitchen, while an uncomfortable Leslie shrank in the corner, hugging herself. I waved her over, and she wiggled away from her would-be dance partner.

I led her to my office and closed the door.

"Sorry to arrive unannounced."

"I'm surprised to see you here. It's your least favorite place." I slipped the pen from behind my ear and slotted it into the breast pocket of my black chef's jacket while she sank onto my sofa. Leslie navigated life big, loud, and took up a full measure of space. Not today. She shrank small, occupying as little real estate as possible, looking like a tiny child who wanted to disappear.

Something was very wrong.

"Are you okay?" Worry soaked those three words.

Leslie's eyes welled with tears. "No. But before I tell you what it is and ask you a favor I have no right to ask, I need to know one thing."

She smashed her lips together as if fighting to keep the words from spilling out.

"Anything."

"Do you love me?"

Emotion clenched in my chest. I wanted Leslie more than I felt comfortable sharing. But this sudden outpouring of vulnerability felt wrong. Diving in without thinking would leave us both drowned. We'd been there before, and I'd be an idiot to forget how wrecked it left us when I walked away. But that didn't mean I couldn't be there for her in other ways. As a friend.

"I think you need to tell me what's going on."

"Fuck, Risto. Why do you always have to make everything so difficult? I need help. I can't do this alone... But if you don't love me, then it's wrong for me to ask... I just... I need. Oh, God, what am I doing here?" Overcome, Leslie dissolved into mournful sobs, her body heaving as she hid her face in her hands.

I'd never seen her like this, and it scared me.

"Please. What's going on? Help me understand." I dropped to kneel before her, hugging her close.

She shifted to my shoulder, where her warm tears soaked my coat through. I waited as she expelled whatever pain had her tied in knots. Squeezing tighter, I pressed strength into her while drawing out the hurt. She was always so strong—it killed me to see her in distress. Once settled, she leaned back, and I kissed her nose.

"Better?" I asked.

"Yeah." She sniffled, wiping her eyes with her palms.

"Can we start over?"

"Yes, of course. So. Have you ever noticed I don't eat much?"

It had to be a trick question, and the mild sarcasm in her tone made me wonder why she was asking and what flavor response she expected.

"What about it?"

"That article I told you about led me to ask some questions about myself. I came straight from the hospital, where they're beginning a treatment plan for me. I have anorexia nervosa. I've been starving myself."

I wrapped her tight in my arms and she wept, silently this time. At last, she resumed talking, her head still resting on my shoulder.

"I didn't realize that my eating habits were caused by a mental illness. They're doing a battery of tests and may admit me for treatment depending on how sick I am. How am I supposed to support Dot if I can't even help myself?"

I pulled back to look her in the eyes. "It's not a choice. You both deserve love and support."

We locked eyes.

"So you do love me," Leslie said. She didn't ask. We both knew it was true, but knowing wasn't enough. She needed to hear it.

"Yes. I still love you."

I pulled her close, rocking her in my arms before kissing the top of her head.

Leslie had been rail-thin since we were teens. I saw how often she ate, which was never. But I'd never put a name to it. I assumed it was how she was. Like her mom.

"How can I help?" I asked.

"Just be here for me, if you're open to it. I don't want to overtax Dot, and it sounds like I might be seriously sick from not eating enough for so long. It's a lot to ask, but is it okay if I lean on you a bit? I'm scared."

I never imagined hearing those two words cross her lips. *I'm scared.* That she admitted that to me showed how serious the situation was. I'd be there for her, now and always, if she'd have me. This conversation wasn't about us, but maybe it was. Maybe her resistance had never been about me at all. My life centered on the thing she feared most.

Food.

Rejecting me was the only logical solution. I'd pushed her away because I thought she didn't love me. It seemed the grownup choice to voice what I thought to be the truth. Her coming here today showed there was only one adult between us, and it wasn't me.

I held her face in my hands. "I will be here, by your side, for as long as you want me. I'll do anything for you."

"Anything?" She asked.

"Name it."

"Would you mind making me something to eat?" Her mouth curled up in a tentative smile. As if asking a chef to cook was a huge inconvenience.

I pulled her up, and we walked hand in hand back to a now spotless kitchen. Dinner prep was done, and the boys typically took a quick break in the afternoons before diving into the evening service. Living so close, they sometimes ran home for showers or chill time alone.

Leslie trailed behind me as I entered our walk-in fridge. The wet spot on my shoulder instantly chilled, sending a shudder down my back. Leslie stood in the doorway, rubbing her cooling arms.

I grabbed an empty stainless steel tray to fill with ingredients. "Let me guess. Pork chops, rice, and beans?"

"And maduros," she added.

"Ahh, how silly of me to forget your beloved plantains. I'll get the fryer on." I strode past her with my bounty, and she snapped the door handle locked behind us.

Leslie leaned her elbows on the counter, sniffing and savoring the oregano and garlic as I chopped. Our eyes met, and she cracked a closemouthed grin. I loved that I was able to be here for her and help her heal. Her request for my cooking was a dream come true. It gave me hope that we might have a lasting future together.

But first, we had to get her well.

The plantains crackled as I dropped them into the fryer, which would caramelize the surface into a golden brown. After a few minutes, I lifted the basket, shook it, and toppled the crispy slices into a stainless warming tray. I tossed them with sea salt, then dumped them into a black metal stand lined with white parchment paper. Ready for prime time, I slid it across to her on the counter.

Now came the moment of truth. I'd cooked for Leslie many times, but getting her to eat and enjoy meals was a struggle. Why hadn't I realized something was wrong?

Our deep history together made it easy to forget we'd been apart for years. That made her personal life a mystery, though I had more than a passing interest and tracked what I could from afar. From her guest spots on TV, to her articles and updates from Dot, I knew enough to keep me on edge and yearning. But that was about to change.

Without hesitating, Leslie picked up a fork and speared a steaming plantain. She blew it briefly, then took a tentative bite. "It's not as hot as I thought."

She slid the rest into her mouth, moaning as she chewed. "It's so good. I can't believe I get to eat these."

"Whenever you want. Just ask," I said.

Watching diners enjoy my food never got old. Watching Leslie eat my food was borderline erotic. I couldn't tear myself away from the sight.

She ate two more hunks before pausing to give me a stink eye. "Um. Shouldn't you be cooking?"

"Yeah, probably."

I turned back to my work, emerging with her favorite dish within 25 minutes. Crispy pork chop cubes with rice and black beans. I put the plate in front of her, sprinkling chopped parsley across the top with pinpoint precision.

The dish steamed with anticipation. But, as she'd done with the now-devoured maduros, she dug in, savoring each bite. I let her eat in peace while I cleaned up. The staff would be returning soon. When drying my hands, my cell phone vibrated in my pocket.

"This is Risto," I answered.

"Chef Zaldo, hello! This is Brock Benson. I got your name from Silas Greene. I hope this is a good time?" the man said. "I hear you're in the market for a culinary agent, and I'd very much like to be your man."

Leslie looked to be in a blissful dream state, her eyes dropping closed with each mouthful.

"Okay if I take this call?" I asked, but Leslie shooed me away.

I meandered into my office to talk in private. "Silas has become my guardian angel. The dude's pretty relentless."

Brock chuckled. "That's Silas. He's sent many clients my way. But I'm the reason the famous chefs you know are names you know. I'm good at what I do, just as you are."

He explained how his firm represented some of the most celebrated culinary talent, food writers, and kitchen personalities in the industry. His client list was a Who's Who on the Food Network. Rapt, I hung on every word, forgetting his goal was to make me a star like they were.

"I get all that, but why me?" I asked. "There are thousands of chefs across the country."

"Two reasons: the cover of *Philadelphia Metro* and the rabid fans warring about you in chat rooms. That, my friend, has sent people chattering from coast to coast. If we can tap that energy and use it to build momentum, it will work to your financial advantage with your expansion to New York."

"How do you—"

"Oh, come now. Do you think this industry has ANY secrets?" Brock chuckled.

Apparently not.

"I only have one question for you. Do you want to be famous? Be on more covers? Judge on TV shows and appear at food festivals?" he asked.

Up until now, I lived a quiet life. But I'd be lying if I said I didn't crave more. The success of Boricua made me a big fish in a small pond. Brock could make me a bigger fish in a gigantic ocean, which both thrilled me and triggered queasiness. Ambition was for other people, or so my grandparents preached. A long shot reserved for a rare few. The likelihood of success was so remote it was a waste to try. But they were wrong. It was time for me to step out of the shadows and own what I wanted.

Did I want to be famous?

Hell, yes.

But if I was going to sign on with Brock—after confirming that he wasn't lying about his abilities and client list—I needed to be all-in about being in the spotlight. If I could pull it off, it just might get me enough success in New York to fulfill two dreams. Being a celebrated chef and building a life with Leslie.

"Okay, Brock. If you're as good as you say, make me the next big thing in food."

He whooped into the phone. "Buckle up, Chef Zaldo! You're about to be a star."

Chapter 20

LESLIE

I arrived at the hospital the next day, Dot frustratingly in tow, to begin my treatment. Tasha mobilized a care team, which now included a doctor and a psychiatrist. They ordered extensive blood and urine tests and took my vitals—standing me backward on the scale so I wouldn't see my weight. The nurse quickly entered the figure on her tablet, hiding the screen from view.

I was relieved not to have a number to obsess over. But it irked me that I had an identified condition with predictable behaviors. The doctors understood me better than I did myself, and that pissed me off to no end.

I shifted on the exam table, the white paper crinkling under me. "I shouldn't be here and neither should you. You're supposed to be home resting, not here playing nursemaid."

"We're both exactly where we need to be. Try to relax. The test results should be back soon." Dot's reassurance meant everything. Intellectually, I understood I was sick. Emotionally, the exam room felt like a cage, and I wanted out.

"It's ridiculous that some numbers on a piece of paper can make them keep me here. I feel fine." I swung my legs, my heels rattling the metal exam table drawers as if they were to blame for my health predicament.

I knew better.

But didn't want to know.

Not knowing had kept me functioning for decades in an unpredictable world. My intake was the only thing I could control. But these experts were about to swoop in and tell me what to eat and when. The situation launched Little Diana into panic mode. She said I'd suffocate, gagging on food being force-fed down my throat. That I'd balloon so huge I'd burst. That people would point at me and laugh in the street. The chaos in my head triggered nausea, and I imagined myself hurling my light breakfast all over the floor.

"I don't think I can do this," I said, twisting the hem of my hospital gown into a cloth spike.

"You can and will get well. These are talented medical professionals, and they only want the best for you." Dot reached over from her chair and squeezed my hand. "You're not alone. I'm here for you. Gabby is here for you, and so is Risto. Give yourself some grace."

The door opened and Dr. Alexandria Wheaton walked in. She was a slim white woman with long blond hair pulled into a ponytail at the nape of her neck. I learned earlier today that she'd once been anorexic herself. After recovery, she went to medical school to help others in the same way she had been helped. Knowing that healing was possible gave me a glimmer of hope.

"Okay, some initial results are in. The good news is that you're eligible for outpatient care. We don't have to admit you."

"That's great! See, Bola." Dot hopped up and planted a squeaky kiss on my cheek, making me smile.

"But—it was very close. Your tests are worrying, and we still have to assess potential organ damage. If you take this treatment plan seriously, you can hopefully avoid being admitted. It's up to you, but we're here to support you every step of the way."

I blanked on everything she said after "organ damage" and asked for clarification.

"We look for arrhythmia and heart muscle wasting. We screen for thyroid function and kidney damage as well. Unfortunately, there is no body system immune from the damaging effects of this condition. While that sounds dire, with proper care, most complications are reversible," Dr. Wheaton said.

Dot's face fell. "Most?"

"Yes, well. Osteoporosis is not reversible, nor is cerebral atrophy. Some cognitive deficits and impacts to taste and smell can be permanent. But that's not anything to worry about now. We'll cover all that once we've completed the testing. The task ahead of us is to keep you stable and moving in the right direction so we can avoid hospitalization."

Numbness took over. Brain and bone damage could be permanent? Kidneys? Heart? And I'd done all this to myself. I covered my face and wept, the shame too overwhelming.

I had no idea the harm I was doing to myself. And even knowing, I still dreaded the eating to come. How twisted was that?

Dr. Wheaton described my home meal plan, which focused on eating five times a day—three meals and two snacks.

The concept was unthinkable. I had proof that eating made me sick. After I ate big at Risto's, I got ill later at home. But the doctor explained that was normal. The food shocked my system. But instead of resisting eating like I had been, my goal now was to eat small portions spread throughout the day to retrain my body to receive food. Over time, I could work up to more.

Thank goodness for Dot. She scribbled notes and collected everything in the folder Dr. Wheaton left behind. I then dressed, and the two of us slowly walked back to Dot's car.

After I buckled in, the enormity of it all finally hit me. "I'm really sick, aren't I?"

"Yes, I'm afraid so."

The next morning, my nostrils reflexively twitched as coffee aromas registered. My initial instinct was sadness, knowing I couldn't have the sugar and cream I craved. As my sleep faded, the day before came flooding back. Not only could I eat, my treatment plan demanded it. Maybe it could be an adventure, as I discussed with Gabby back at the hospital. I could pretend I was going undercover in a new body. As someone who liked food more than she feared it.

I huffed a laugh at that impossible dream.

But guess I had to start somewhere.

Besides coffee, the spicy, smoky scent of what was undoubtedly top-shelf chorizo registered. I pictured it alongside eggs and fruit. I sat up, leaning back on my hands as I squinted to adjust to the morning light.

Dot was a quiet cook, especially when I slept. The clanking sounds from the kitchen sounded like a man.

I scrambled into clothes, detangled my curls using my fingers, and ran down the stairs.

Bowls, cutting boards, and knives cluttered the counter. An All-Clad stock pot with a colander insert sat in the sink filled with soapy water. Earbuds in, Risto worked the handle of his sauté pan, flipping his concoction of onions and peppers without losing a single piece on the burner surface below.

I brushed his back to get his attention.

"Hey, what are you doing here?" I asked.

He took both earpieces out. "I wanted to see you. Hear how it went yesterday. Figured I'd make you some breakfast."

My heart swelled, knowing he cared. I hoped he would, even after I strolled into his office and broke the hell down.

"It smells great. Thanks for doing this."

"Don't thank me yet. I'm trying out a new brunch menu. You'll have to let me know what you think."

I made my way to the coffee maker and fixed myself a cup. Cream, sugar, a mug, and spoon awaited me. I ignored Little Diana.

Risto's focus mesmerized me. His hand hovered a foot over the pan, sprinkling salt into his sauté. A few turns of the pepper mill followed before he lifted silver tongs to add bright green spinach from a bowl on the counter. No frozen greens for Risto. He'd cooked it ahead of time. Warming it all, he poured the eggs into the pan, nudging the mixture gently with a rubber spatula while the yellow liquid solidified. He folded the omelet into thirds and slid it onto a plate. It glistened like golden sunshine, without a hint of the brown scorching I associated with cooked eggs. At least mine. Over the top, he shredded a pale cheese from a golden rind.

That got my attention. "What's that?"

"My new favorite cheese." He set the plate on the counter between us and handed me a fork. Not waiting, he dug in and closed his eyes to dissect the flavors. He chewed, thinking, then rushed to a notepad to scribble thoughts down.

Meanwhile, I held my utensil, unsure what to do.

He walked back for another bite. "I love it. Needs some acid, but otherwise is close to balanced. What do you think?"

My tongue tied as panic sprang to life, turning my stomach. Why did this always happen? I felt like a fool.

I dipped my fork but paused before contacting the egg's surface. *What's wrong with me?*

Risto nodded toward the plate. "Running through scenarios?"

"Kinda."

"Talk me through it. I'd love to understand." He took another bite, avoiding eye contact.

I hated being forced into sharing. After conversations with the doctor and therapist, and reading all the materials they sent home, I expected the rational part of my brain to kick in. The one that knew I had to eat and that every caution my care team shared was deadly serious.

Decades of restricting food would take time to change. I had to be patient with myself, but I wasn't built for it. Hard-wired to be impatient, I plowed ahead into everything. If only my stupid psyche would comply.

I looked up to find Risto's tender brown eyes waiting for me to answer. Giving me space to come to the words myself.

"You'll think I'm weird."

"Too late for that."

I playfully shouldered his chest, then lowered my face closer to the plate. Spicy vapors pierced my outer defenses. "It looks delicious. I want to eat it, but alone in a dark room. It's somehow safer that way."

"Huh," Risto said, like something occurred to him. "You crave darkness. Why is that?"

Good question.

"When it's dark, I'm less on display and prone to commentary about whether and how much I'm eating. There's less pressure."

He kissed my forehead. "People don't pay nearly as much attention to you as you think. And so what if they did?"

"There's one person who cares."

"Ahh. The mighty Diana."

"Mom skewered me on the drive over here about what to eat, and I hadn't even arrived yet. She's the best appetite suppressant going. She makes it impossible to, God forbid, actually enjoy a meal. Easier for me to skip food entirely."

That's what got me into this mess. It seemed more trouble to eat than not. Now the doctors told me the exact opposite was true. They didn't come out and say it, but if I didn't eat, I'd die. And even with that most dire of threats hanging over my head, I couldn't get myself to bite into this fucking egg.

"You realize your mom is over the top with the food stuff, right? It's wrong and always has been. But that can't be what's stopping you. She's clear across the country."

God, I was fucked up.

Why was this egg different from the ones I had chowed down at the hospital cafeteria with Gabby?

Risto slid the plate toward me. "What's going through your head? This instant. Say it out loud."

"Is it worth the price?" burst out of my mouth. "Is it worth the price of eating until it's gone? What if I can't stop? What if I keep eating and eating and become..."

"Fat?" Risto patted his belly, smiling. "Would that be so bad?"

I choked on his words.

Would that be so bad? To be fat?

I'd never contemplated the rightness or wrongness of being fat. After a lifetime of successful conditioning to revile it, it never occurred to me to question an alternative perspective.

According to my mother, fat was bad. Fat was ugly and unhealthy and signaled an undisciplined and lazy work ethic. Being fat would hamper job prospects and lead to misery, loneliness, and death. Fat was the culmination of all things wrong in the world. Like a dutiful soldier, I believed it all, brainlessly following the mantra like a zombie. And yet... My father's side of the family all had larger bodies. Dot, Gabby, and most of my adult cousins. Risto was a large man, and I craved him like air.

When I looked at them, I saw the impressive, smart, vibrant people I loved. Gabby had a soaring career, and so did Risto. Dot was the most active person I knew. Christ, she taught yoga.

If that was all possible, was being fat really so bad?

And if not, why was our society so singularly aligned against it?

To understand myself and get back on track with my article, I had to dig in and unearth how we'd gotten here. When did we start persecuting fat people? And why did we still do it? Solving that puzzle might be the medicine I needed to heal myself.

But that wouldn't happen if I was a dizzy, starving mess.

I repositioned the fork in my hand and cut a bite-sized piece of the omelet. "Here's to a new beginning."

I forked the egg into my mouth and let the magic take hold.

Chapter 21

LESLIE

When the battery of test results came in, they showed minimal heart and organ damage. By following a tightly controlled meal plan, together with daily check-ins and therapy, the team seemed optimistic about my chances for a full recovery.

A week into treatment, my energy and mindset were both improving. So much, Dot had agreed to let me drive myself back and forth to the hospital unsupervised. I pulled into her driveway and cut the engine, proud of how far I'd already come.

Eating still triggered me, but I started stuffing a cork in Little Diana's mouth so I could feed mine. The first few days were rough. Two minutes after I finished a meal, the next one arrived. Or so it seemed. The perpetual fullness spiked my anxiety, but therapy provided new coping skills. Those helped me stick to the dining plan when every brain cell screamed, *Resist!* the moment food arrived.

The doctors said my hunger cues would return once I healed from malnourishment. But hunger was normal for me, though I never recognized it as anything but the undercurrent of my life. Losing that anchor left me floating untethered in murky waters. My longtime friend and protector had vanished, with no one to replace her.

A tap on the driver's window jarred me back to the present.

"What are you doing in there? You'll fry." Dot pulled my car door open, and a floral breeze blew in from her gardenia bushes. Their sweet scent, clean and unapologetic, lifted my spirits.

"Sorry. Lost in a daydream." I grabbed my handbag and slammed the car door firmly behind me.

But Dot hadn't moved. She stood assessing me, and I'd forgotten I now lived around people who both knew me and cared about my well-being. At home, I was typically alone. That made it easy to mask low moods for a few hours while visiting with friends. They'd be there for me if I asked for help, but it pissed me off to be on the needy end. Weakness had never been my strong suit.

"Let's go sit on the porch." She walked gingerly, using the handrail to support her as she took the stairs. "I want to hear how it went today. If you're comfortable sharing, that is."

With all my personal drama, I'd forgotten that Dot was still recovering from surgery. Her stitches had to hurt. If not, she'd already be back to her yoga class.

She noticed me staring.

"I've overdone it the last few days. Everything hurts, and my incision yanks whenever I move." She dropped onto the swing, lifting her feet to the ottoman with a sigh. "Okay, out with it."

I sank into one of her white wicker chairs nearby, leaning forward to rub my hands. There were too many contradictions running through my brain to form a coherent thought.

"Everything the care team says makes sense to me. But at the cellular level, I'm struggling. Every bite feels wrong. Negative thoughts bombard me while I'm chewing, telling me embracing food is a huge mistake. I wish I could flip a switch and make it all go away."

"You're a person, not a lamp. It'll take time."

I huffed a laugh. My aunt had a habit of stating the obvious in an instructive way. Mom's rules were no longer my guidebook, and I was still getting oriented to my new North Star. That had me defining my worth by something other than my weight. If you'd asked me two weeks ago what I thought of myself, I'd have told you I was proud of my career accomplishments. Being a journalist defined me. In reality, work kept my mind occupied so I didn't have to examine the tough questions about my life and relationships. It also helped me avoid a shallow truth: my lean physical appearance factored heavily into how I navigated the world. I wanted people to think well of me, beginning with how I looked. But would they approve if I showed up in a different-sized body than they were used to?

I tuned back into my conversation with Dot, who I now realized had been talking.

"Deprogramming from the diet culture is hard because the messages are all around us. Even more so for someone like you who has basically been in your personal Minnesota experiment since you were a kid. I swear, your Uncle Arty had to hold me back a few times with your mom. I had words on more than one occasion with my beloved brother. He should have done better by you, but he was too busy trying to keep the peace in the house at your expense."

It was hard to picture her and Dad arguing about my health. I thought I had slipped through life, unobserved. That was the farthest thing from the truth. Dot noticed things I didn't notice myself, and that kind of love and attention were priceless right now.

"Would it be okay if I stayed here for a while? I'm going to need all the help I can get with all this."

"Of course, sweetie. You stay as long as you like. You're always welcome here."

"Thanks." I stood. "Want anything from the kitchen? I'm thirsty."

"I'd love a big glass of water with lots of ice. There's lemonade in there, if you're interested."

My first instinct was to decline the sugary drink. Wasted, empty calories. But if I was to truly embrace this journey and remove the power food held over me, I had to take the process seriously.

"One water and one lemonade coming up." I said and went into the house.

Later that evening, Dot and I sat together in the living room watching a reality show where people were doing risky challenges. A contestant had just crawled into a box full of big, hairy tarantulas.

"I can't believe she'd do that. They're venomous. She could die!"

I swiveled to see my aunt's skeptical face smirking at me.

"What?" I asked.

"Says the person who has literally slept in the same bed with a gang leader who had a loaded gun under his pillow."

I sighed. "Only once. And we had our clothes on the whole time. What did you expect me to do? I was trying to blend in. If I made a big stink about it, he'd know I was faking my identity and would never have spilled the location of the kidnapped woman."

She slow-blinked at me to show she wasn't having it. In Dot's world, what I'd done for stories was just as crazy as lying in a box with spiders. Right now, the gal was smashing her lips together to keep hairy legs from crawling in her mouth.

Not the same thing at all.

"What I do saves lives."

"Not yours."

"Pardon?"

"You might be helping other people, but your whole life is a frantic marathon. Chasing stories. Running after fame. Getting that network job. Doesn't it ever seem like too much?" The smooth skin of Dot's age-defying face crinkled in worry.

Since arriving here, a peace had settled over me that I'd not had in ages. The ravages of hunger had lessened. Instead of keeping busy and pouring my soul into my next story, my mind between meals was surprisingly quiet. It wandered while I walked Pepper in the morning. Images of Risto cooking for me in the kitchen, then the bedroom, danced across my field of vision. We hadn't yet kissed beyond his brotherly pecks to my forehead. But even those shot pangs of longing to body parts I'd long since forgotten. Another benefit to my new dining regimen. One walk, the sensations were so real, memories of his tender touch rippled across my skin. So much so I nearly smashed my face into a telephone pole.

That peace could very well evaporate once I left this idyllic bubble. But I couldn't stay here forever. Could I? Besides my show-prep meetings in Manhattan and the Saturday night tapings, I could work anywhere. And that included right here with Dot and Risto. I selfishly dreaded the outcome of Risto's investor visit. I wanted him to be happy, fulfilled, and successful. But in my head, our future was here in Pennsylvania. I liked myself here so much more than the person I became in the City. Shouldn't I be the same me everywhere? Had I worn character disguises for so long chasing stories that I'd forgotten who I was?

Dot still waited for an answer. *Doesn't it ever seem like too much?* Of course, my life was a lot, but there was too much clanging around in my brain to formulate existential answers. Luckily, a call from Viraj buzzed through, rescuing the day once again.

"I gotta take this." I lifted the cell to my ear, plugging the other with my finger as my aunt turned up the TV volume to show her displeasure.

"Hey, what's up?" I unfolded my legs to walk to the quieter breakfast nook.

"The Saturday night gig is technically locked up, but I fear you being out of sight all summer will somehow prompt them to shift priorities," Viraj said.

My stomach dropped. Having a permanent host spot on a cable news program was a tremendous honor. I didn't want my break at Dot's to jeopardize the opportunity.

"What do I need to do?" I asked, ready to do near anything he mentioned.

"Post videos to that YouTube channel of yours. It's been awhile, but you have a decent following. I can redirect traffic there from the *Dear Diary* website. It might be enough to keep your name circulating while you're out there."

My last series of videos focused on the behind-the-scenes dirt of my streetwalker investigation. That exposure and the resulting buzz was partly what prompted the network to add me as the Saturday host. He was right to fall back on proven methods to ensure the network suits didn't forget why they hired me. Plus, it helped raise the profile of *Dear Diary*. With Viraj coming from fashion publishing, my articles stretched the online magazine beyond lifestyle coverage into investigative news.

"Have I mentioned my next story to you?"

"I don't think so," he answered.

I relayed my plan to expose the colossal lie behind the diet industry. How mounting research showed that dieting didn't work and made us less healthy. I also shared that I was going through eating disorder recovery myself.

"Are you okay doing videos? Why not take time off?" Viraj asked.

"Nah, I need the distraction. I've had entirely too much 'me' lately. I know that's part of the process, but I'm at my best when working. The restlessness is way too overwhelming."

He was leery but dropped the issue, too lost in excitement about the new article.

"Being in the fashion industry for as long as I was, I contributed to the diet culture you're talking about. I'm eager to correct the record."

Before co-founding *Dear Diary* with Rebecca, Viraj was a senior editor at the world's top fashion magazine. He was, quite literally, at the epicenter of setting beauty standards. But Viraj wasn't alone. There was a gigantic machine from publishers to design houses to retailers that were all major contributors. Together, they amplified the anti-fat bias that surrounded us. The more I learned, the more absurd it all seemed. Like the world had gotten swept up in a Salem-like witch trial, with fat people on the losing end.

Repent or perish.

I shuddered, hugging myself as Viraj talked on.

We discussed how to shape each article in the series, since there was too much information to cram into one installment. Sidebars would share the progress of my recovery. Mixing personal takes with news set our coverage apart from other outlets. Our competitors professed to be fact-based and non-biased, but that didn't stop them from presenting their opinions as straight news. Our savvy readers knew the difference and appreciated the raw passion reflected on our digital pages.

"Okay, the first article installment will hit in early August, but since you're comfortable sharing, you should begin posting this week about your personal food journey."

This week? My blood drained. What the hell was I supposed to say? Suddenly the big, bold, mob reporter fled the building, replaced by a scared-shitless woman about to tell her 44,000 YouTube followers that she had an eating disorder.

"You there?" Viraj asked.

"Yeah."

"If you don't want to post about your personal stuff, that's fine. Focus on the industry story."

"No. I'll do it. It'll be a way to hold myself accountable."

"It's your private medical information. Please, I don't expect you to share. I'm sorry if I misunderstood, but I thought you'd already decided to chronicle it."

His ears worked fine. But now that I had a deadline, it felt too real. A clock began ticking, and soon my personal story would be splashed across screens worldwide. No more hiding in dark corners. I had to face my fears. Sharing it with my fans might provide the encouragement I needed to stay focused. I'd claim my truth and let the chips fall where they may. I liked the sound of that.

"Count me in. I'll start tomorrow."

Chapter 22

Risto

I ladled the carne guisada onto a mound of rice, topping the stew with a crispy piece of grouper, lightly breaded and fried in garlic oil. I slid the plate across the kitchen island, enjoying a late-night cook with my potential new agent. After dodging Brock's calls for a week, he badgered me until I agreed to cook for him.

"Fish? Doesn't carne mean meat?" He picked up his fork with a raised eyebrow.

"I'm surprised you know. This is typically a beef stew, but I removed the meat after the stew cooked, so you get the beefy flavor with a lighter protein. It's crispy and flakey, with a light crunch, but bathed in the sauce. The combination is unexpected."

Brock took a bite, his eyelids drooping. "Oh, yes."

My chest swelled beneath my crossed arms. "Even without the beef, it's got that homey goodness you want in carne guisada."

"What happens to the beef? Sounds a little wasteful, and the investors will count every penny once they sign on."

I was ready for this question. "I always serve ropa vieja on the same night. After shredding and bathing in the wine sauce, the beef adds another dimension to that dish that diners can't quite place. They say my ropa vieja is their favorite, and the cross-recipe pollination is probably why."

His grin looked slightly menacing, just like the rest of him. When my potential new agent first arrived at Boricua, I was shocked to find he towered over my 6'4" frame. That rarely happens. But unlike me, Brock was a lean guy reminiscent of the beanpoles in my abuela's garden. My grandmother had insisted on growing, drying, and soaking her own beans. Said they tasted far better—and she was right. Once you ate them side by side, it was impossible to go back to the bland pallor of bagged beans. I locally sourced mine, given the volume we used at the restaurant. But all those little touches, like with the ropa vieja, made diners' palates explode with pleasure the moment my food hit their mouths.

Brock took a few more bites, then pushed his mostly full plate away. "I hope that's the last dish. I can't remember when I've been this stuffed."

While he'd sampled four appetizers, two soups, and six entrées, my stomach churned with anticipation. And hunger. I had a small snack when the crew left at 10:00 p.m., and the aromatic fragrance of onions, garlic, cilantro, and oregano finally registered. That's how it was for me when I cooked. My complete focus was on food someone else would enjoy. Many days, I forgot to eat until Jose or Freddie shoved a bowl in my hands. Who would do that if I moved to New York? Friendships like ours would be hard to replace. A pang of doubt crept across my psyche.

"Your food is amazing and totally earns all the raves in the online chat rooms. Puerto Rican cuisine is humble, made of simple ingredients, but I wonder if it's too basic."

That got my attention.

"There's nothing about my food that's basic. It takes time, care, special sourcing of fine ingredients, and a shit-ton of creativity to put those flavors together. No other chef in the world makes these dishes in this way. Not. One."

While speaking, I leaned onto the counter in an aggressive display that usually made my opponents wither. But not Brock. He refolded his napkin and placed it on the butcher block island where we sat.

"That'll do. Remember that answer when this question comes up at dinner."

I bolted upright. "Wait?! That was a test?"

"You're green, Chef. Not in the kitchen, in the boardroom. The investors are money people. Sure, they like food, but they open their wallets for the right combination of food, passion, and personality. They covet chefs bold enough to think what they cook has never been tasted before in the history of planet earth. THAT generates reservations. THAT makes foodies fear they're going to miss out on the next big thing. And oh, foodies want their bragging rights. They crave early access so they can boast about having eaten a chef's food BEFORE they made headlines. Never forget, we're not just selling food. We're selling you."

My blood drained, leaving me lightheaded and grateful to be leaning on the counter for support. Until Brock mentioned it, I forgot the chat room posts didn't simply talk about the food. They talked about me by name. In my heart, Boricua was an embodiment of me. It held my dreams and all the staff who'd become family. It was how I built my reputation as a solid community member. It provided a pathway to financial freedom. My restaurant was everything to me. But I was fast learning I was getting noticed too. And because of that, a seasoned agent like Brock was sitting in my rural Pennsylvania restaurant instead of off with one of his famous clients.

He had faith that the next star would be me.

"So I take it you're impressed enough to represent me?" I asked.

Brock slipped a folder out of the black canvas backpack at his feet, sliding it across the butcher block to me.

The first page had "Contract of Representation" printed up top. I flipped the pages with my thumb. Despite being bleary-eyed, I was sufficiently savvy not to sign on the spot.

"I'll have my lawyer review it and ping you with any questions." I closed the folder.

"You do that. But I'll still be here when the investors come. To advise. To support. You want them to see me here, so they know they're dealing with someone of consequence."

"This all started before you called, so you don't get a cut of my restaurant deal," I said as Brock stood to gather his things.

"That's true. But not to worry. I'll sink my hooks into you just the same." He winked and headed out the side door into the humid evening.

Boxes crowded every surface in the kitchen as our Tuesday food deliveries arrived. This week they included a few extra seafood items I ordered to experiment with for recipes for the tasting menu. Despite being said as a test, Brock's comment about my food being "basic" kept me up the last four nights. It led me to completely reconceive the meal I planned for the investors into one that would have New York diners buzzing with delight.

Modern.

Complex.

My food would have their eyes and taste buds whirling in delicious confusion.

The investor dinner couldn't arrive fast enough.

A feisty lobster arched in my gloved hand, its blue and brown mottled legs crawling in protest when my attorney walked in. I returned the critter to its crate of mates and wiped the lingering dampness off my chef's jacket.

"Hola, Maria." I kissed both her cheeks, being careful to keep my briny mitt away from her tailored gray suit and tightly bunned hair.

"In your office?" she asked, not waiting for me.

"Sure," I replied as she strode off.

Freddie sidled over. "What's she doing here?"

"I need her to review a contract. Brock offered to represent me."

"The agent?" Jose yelled from the refrigerator, his arms full of cellophane-wrapped packages of pork chops.

"Yeah. Sounds like he wants to make me famous. Book me on Food Network panels and food festivals. Could be good for the restaurant. Especially if we expand to New York."

The two exchanged glances, shrugging and saying nothing. No lit-up faces. No "attaboys" or back slaps at this tremendous news. Something smelled fishy, and it wasn't the lobster.

"Out with it," I said.

Freddie flipped his chin at Jose to start.

"Why always me?"

Freddie shrugged.

"Fine." Jose turned to face me. "Ever since that food critic showed up, you've been chasing your tail, talking about investors and expansion. Bra, we just expanded here. I've never heard about you wanting any of this. And suddenly Maria is looking at contracts and blancos are cruising in from New York to whisper in your ear? You've never once asked what we think or mentioned how this will impact what we have here. What happens to us?"

Damn it. They were absolutely right. Every spare moment, I'd sneak over into a corner to work on recipes. Food service swirled around me while I tinkered and made notes, never stopping to tell them why—or as Jose said—ask for their opinions or blessing. I hadn't signed one deal and was already taking them for granted.

Was this who I'd become if I got famous? A douchey egomaniac?

My arms dangled at my sides in defeat. "You're right. And I'm so sorry. Come here."

They finished their immediate tasks and gathered next to me by the island. It reminded me of talks with my grandparents around our kitchen table. When they told me harsh truths I'd rather not hear.

Mom and Dad aren't coming back.

We can't afford to send you to culinary school.

Grandma has cancer, but she'll be okay.

We've left everything to you in our will.

Freddie, Jose, and I had been through a lot. I owed them a solid explanation for where my head was at and where I saw the restaurant's future headed. Without them, none of it would be possible.

Their hurt brown eyes awaited answers.

"When Silas showed up, he mentioned I was thinking too small about my career. It got me to wondering whether I was."

Jose stiffened in offense, so I squeezed his shoulder. "Not that what we have here isn't amazing, but that it's so special that we should bring our vision of Puerto Rican food to more people. Celebrate the cuisine and take pride in the flavors that give us such joy. Food traditions have held us close as a community since coming to the United States. When I named this place Boricua, it was because I was proud to be Puerto Rican and wanted the world to know. Now I'm obsessed about the opportunity to gain a broader platform to serve our food. Forgive me for not discussing it sooner, but I think it can be good for all of us."

"Go on," Freddie said.

"If we open a New York location, everyone here gets a promotion. Jose, you'd become executive chef. Freddie, you'd become chef de cuisine, and so on."

Jose scratched his head, a smile erupting before he tamped it down. But it beamed through anyway. "Executive chef, huh?"

"Yeah, and while you two are running things here, I'd work on opening the new place in New York. I'm thinking of overhauling the menu, which means Boricua stays unique. If you want these dishes, you have to come here. It gives each of us a chance to stretch our skills and grow. Then who knows? Maybe there's a Boricua empire in our future with more locations!"

My enthusiasm for the idea was impossible to hide, so I stopped trying.

"Sueña en grande." I quoted my mom, the rightness of it all falling into place.

Jose nodded. He'd heard me say it often enough as I tried to get Boricua off the ground. He, more than anyone, even my late grandparents, knew how driven I was to make my parents proud. To live the dream they were robbed of achieving for themselves.

"Okay, I'm in." Freddie extended his hand to shake, his firm grip pressing his approval into mine.

I turned to Jose. "It's a lot for you. But I know you can do it. Give it some thought?"

"No worries. I'm good. Who knows? I might even toss a few of my grandma's dishes on the menu to test them out." Jose stuck his arm out to shake, but I knocked it aside for a hug, which I wrapped around Freddie too. We huddled, knocking heads like we did when we played soccer in our restaurant league.

I sniffed tears back, breaking our circle. "Okay, I better go talk to Maria. She looked pissed."

I entered my office to find Maria sitting behind my desk, marking up what I knew to be Brock's contract.

"Have you read this?" she asked, leveling me with her stare.

"No, you have the only copy."

She reclined, lacing her fingers in her lap. "According to this, you may need to drop everything to pounce on media opportunities. It's going to stretch you thin. We can work some language in about remote versus in-person options and put some scope to the requests that require travel. You're not hopping on a plane to speak at a library in the middle of nowhere."

"I think Brock is aiming bigger." I took a seat opposite her at my desk.

"Yeah, well, the contract has to specify that. And we need to insert a more favorable 'out' clause, plus adjust the fee structure. Looks like he's making a grab for a percentage of restaurant expansion beyond Manhattan."

What a shady move! We talked about him not getting New York revenue, but it didn't stop him from clawing into me thereafter. From what I could tell, Brock was the best agent going. But I'd have to keep a tight watch on him. I could easily picture him agreeing to deals before asking me. While a big guy, I had softy plastered across my forehead. He'd called me "green" himself.

"There's also a physical appearance clause. He wants you to maintain a certain BMI, and you are way over what he's suggesting. If you sign this, you'd need to lose weight."

A weight clause?

"Let me see." I reached for the contract, and Maria pointed to the section she'd circled in red ink. Sure enough, I would be expected to drop down to what BMI charts called "overweight." Currently, I was considered obese, though the stupid charts had no accommodation for muscle mass, bone structure, or genetics.

My grandmother detested dieting, saying it was all gringo bunk. That our people—even the big ones—lived to a ripe old age, and forbade me to diet. I had tried a few times in high school. The teasing got to me, and my trim friends already had girlfriends. It certainly seemed like you had to be thin to make it in life. But when abuela found out, she grounded me. I missed a road soccer game, and everyone blamed me for the loss.

I never dieted again.

"Give me your pen," I said. She handed it over, and I crossed the section out. "No fucking way. That has to come out. What else did you find?"

Maria showed me the sections in question, and I gave her Brock's contact information to sort it out. By then I had more important things to think about. In two days, the investors would arrive for a meal.

It had to be the best one of my life.

Chapter 23

Leslie

The day after Viraj's call, I hopped in the car and drove home to Manhattan. After shouldering the apartment door open, I stepped in and let it slam behind me. It'd been three weeks, and the eerie silence and stale air made me glad I wouldn't be staying long. I only needed to pack up the camera, lighting, and sound equipment for shooting my YouTube videos.

I also owed my best friends an update. Try as I might, I couldn't tell them about what was going on over the phone. The doctors. The tests. And my new awareness that I had an eating disorder. They deserved a face-to-face conversation, and I couldn't wait to see them.

I kicked off my shoes and juggled the two paper shopping bags I hauled from the bagel shop around the corner. Garlicky goodness drifted over from the everything bagels I picked up for today. The second bag was stuffed with bagel requests from Dot, Gabriella, and her husband David. Stellar bagels like these weren't available anywhere else. I didn't bother Risto, who was too busy prepping for his food tasting tomorrow. Besides, I already knew he liked onion bagels and cinnamon raisin, so I scooped up plenty of both—in separate bags, of course. Otherwise, the cinnamon raisin would absorb the onion flavor, and all would be lost. A rookie move—I shot the dude behind the counter major stink eye when he tried to drop all varieties in the same sack.

Pint containers of flavored cream cheese awaited us: scallion, lox, and vegetable. Bursting with intense flavor, they were tasty beyond anything sold in grocery stores. Not that I went looking very often. But maybe now that'd change.

I opened my fridge and gasped.

Empty.

All that greeted me were two bottles of Heineken and a Ziploc bag of lemon wedges liquefying in the fruit drawer.

I slammed the door shut as tears streamed down my face. I clung tight to the handle, my head pressing against the slick surface. A barren fridge used to be normal, a safety measure to protect me against slipping. And by slipping, I meant eating. Over the last three weeks, I'd had shocking conversations about my illness and its implications for my health. But nothing brought it home for me as much as coming face-to-face with my past.

I gripped the two door handles and flung the French doors open.

Inside, the bare glass shelves frosted over with moisture. No food spills. No crusty milk residue. Those suckers were clean enough to eat off of, especially when compared to the debris I noticed in other people's refrigerators. But why would I have that? Sticky spots meant food was present. Leaks came from having take-out containers, or the raw ingredients to cook meals. Without all those eating occasions, one was left with what I had: a pristine interior where food should be.

On the bright side, I now saw the emptiness for what it was: evidence of why I needed help and was working to change. Today was a harrowing reminder of how far I'd already come. In time, my life would be as full as my heart could bear, and I'd have a brimming fridge to match. That was all ahead of me, and I had to first crawl before sprinting.

I wiped my eyes dry with the heels of my palms and resumed my preparations. Cream cheese and fish went into the fridge to chill. Tomatoes were sliced and laid on a platter alongside an assortment of round, yeasty goodness. I knotted the top of the plastic shopping bag holding the remaining bagels to keep the steamy moisture within. With any luck, they'd still be fresh when I got back to Dot's later.

Lost in my thoughts, I almost missed the faint ping of the doorbell. I hadn't heard it in ages, since visitors typically texted from the lobby. Rebecca and Barbara must have snuck in behind another tenant.

Funny thing about West Beth. Sneaking into our building wasn't the score it might appear to be. The trick was not getting turned around amongst many floors of identically mazed white halls. Brownie points to them for finding my apartment door on their own.

I scrambled down the stairs, eager butterflies fluttering in my chest. It'd been too long. I hadn't seen my best girls in weeks and only now realized how much I'd missed them.

"Come here, you two!" I kissed their cheeks, giving each gal a tight squeeze as they entered.

Barbara wore her new uniform, dark-washed jeans and a loose T-shirt paired with holdover Christian Louboutin stilettos from her corporate days. Owning her own law practice meant she was more often barefoot in sweats than dressed up in suits, like she used to be. But then, when working from home with your fine specimen of a lawyer husband, Barbara got kudos for wearing clothes at all.

I turned to Rebecca. "Let me look at you! How exciting!"

Newly pregnant, Rebecca's baby bump was super adorable.

"All those stories about people touching women's pregnant bellies are totally true. The other day at the supermarket, my mom literally swatted a gross man's hand away with a bunch of carrots."

"For real?" I laughed.

"Wish I'd been there," Barbara said, slipping off her shoes.

"There's got to be a story in there, Les," Rebecca said. "Some bizarre reason people are so drawn to fertile bellies? I'd click on that article."

As co-owner of *Dear Diary* with Viraj, Rebecca often seeded stories from her daily life. She had a knack for it, and her instincts kept readers clicking. But my latest story would have all my attention for a while, and it was time I let them know about it.

And me.

We headed upstairs and huddled around the kitchen island to load plates from the bagel spread I'd laid out.

I felt so at ease with these ladies, friends since college who knew every intimate detail of each other's lives. Had they ever guessed my secret? If so, they never asked about it. When together, I ate my fill and had for years. What was different about being with Barbara and Rebecca that made eating okay? Maybe it was because they loved me as-is and didn't give two shits what I looked like. Well, except that time when I tried green hair. They rolled on the floor in hysterical laughter, calling me Grinch, which sent me running back to CVS for a dark brown shade to cover it up. But they'd only commented on my appearance in loving, supportive ways.

I could learn a lot from them.

"How's it going at Dot's?" Rebecca asked. "She feeling better?"

"For sure. She's coming along."

"Gabby must be home by now. Are you planning to stay out there for a while?" Barbara flicked her head toward my stack of camera equipment in the hallway.

Damn her ridiculous powers of observation.

"Let's grab food and go sit. I have some news to share."

We piled onto my sectional couch in the living room, and I filled them in about my article and how it led to my diagnosis. As I spoke, their eyes grew glassy until Rebecca hopped up to give me a hug.

"I'm so sorry for all you're going through. I've always thought you were naturally slim, since you ate as much as the rest of us when we were together. I never realized you were secretly restricting."

Barbara shifted to sit next to me, taking my hand. "I've wondered. But never knew how to ask. Your whole family is larger, except for your mom. I've heard how she talks to you, and how critical she is about what you put on your plate. I planned to bring it up but chickened out every time. I settled for ordering too much takeout and leaving the leftovers here. It's a coward's path, and I'm so sorry I never raised my concerns with you."

Overcome, I nodded, my throat constricting as salty tears trickled into the corners of my mouth. I let them fall free. I'd held them in for far too long as it was. Part sadness for the pain I'd caused myself, part regret for all the experiences I missed because they involved food. Happy moments lost forever because of fear.

"Please, don't blame yourself. There was no way you could have known. I hid it so well, I've only just put the pieces together myself. But a shift is happening already. When a mealtime comes, I eat. Sure, there's a fierce battle in my head, but I'm winning those now. That's huge for me. It's like learning to be a human all over again."

Barbara snorted. "Who says you learned right the first time? That mom of yours is a piece of work."

"Yeah, she definitely got my head screwed on backward." I took a bite of bagel and chewed. The three of us simmered in thoughts for a few beats. Mine were occupied by the odd scene of having an abundant spread in an apartment typically devoid of food. I'd wanted this countless times. Instead, I would stand over the kitchen sink, sucking ice cubes while pretending they were a succulent meal. I swallowed my mouthful and looked up to find Rebecca staring at me.

"Is that why you don't want to stay here? Too many bad memories?" Rebecca asked.

"Yeah, a little. But it's more about being near my treatment team, so they can help me through. And did I mention my aunt lives next door to Risto?"

Barbara's hand froze, the bagel hovering before her lips. "You missed that juicy tidbit. Are you together?"

"Not officially, but we still care about each other. He's made me breakfast several times this week, and I'm volunteering at his restaurant until Dot recovers."

"Sweetie, is that a smart idea? I mean, given what happened?" Rebecca's voice dripped with the same concern I had initially felt.

"I hear you, but I'm hopeful this time. I think my eating disorder had a lot to do with our problems. I'm dealing with it, and he's helping." I shrugged. "It's been... a wonderful surprise."

"Take it slow. I know you never got over him, but you need to be whole for yourself before you can show up for anyone else."

"Ain't that the truth?" Barbara arranged a tomato slice on her bagel before snuggling into her raised shoulders for a delicious bite.

For most of our friendship, the three of us were at the same stage of life. Working, dating, and leaning on each other when things didn't work out. Over the last few years, they'd leaped ahead of me on the adulting ladder. Rebecca and Kyle endured a lot, each slaying personal demons en route to a happy marriage, self-employment, and soon, their first child.

Meanwhile, Barbara plowed through a transformation of her own. She left the corporate world, started a business, and married Sebastian, the sweetest bad boy I'd ever met. I'd encountered my fair share of underworld types, and Sebastian's clean break from that life was a miracle.

Witnessing my friends' lives made it clear I was due for a fairy-tale ending of my own. One where I was healthy and had a thriving career but also had meaningful relationships. With family, friends—and Risto. Life was precious, and we deserved to be together. Instead of awkward silences, we should be making love, then waking each morning tangled in each other's arms. Was that too much to ask? To be happy with the man I loved. Our lives were inextricably woven together, and that wasn't changing anytime soon.

Did he feel the same way?

I wasn't sure.

But he'd been completely acting like it.

Now that I had food coursing through my veins, I had the energy to dream. I wanted so much more than what I'd been allowing myself, and I couldn't wait to get started.

"Tell us about the new story you mentioned." Rebecca rose with effort, baby bump forward to counterbalance her arching back.

"Becca, you're barely showing. What gives?" Barbara joked.

"Shush, you. I'm practicing!" Rebecca air-slapped at her while waddling to the kitchen.

Barbara turned to me. "Enough stalling. What are you planning for the videos? They're always behind the scenes of your work. You doing that again?"

"That's what I wanted to talk through. Since I'm such a part of this story, I was thinking of making it like a journal, chronicling my journey through recovery. I've been so afraid of gaining an ounce, but I now understand how much more I'm gaining from this process. Anyway, I'll include the background of my investigations, as always. But I'm considering being more raw and vulnerable. Just speaking from the heart and letting it fly. What do you think?" I asked.

"You just admitted all this to us. Is it wise to blast it to your followers? You don't want internet trolls to trigger a relapse so early in your recovery. Plus, you have a lot of media types following you. Anything you say will get a lot of airplay."

Barbara had a point. I got enough shit from peers as it was. Either jeers from jokers, leers from people like Kaelen Reed, or outright jealousy. In cable news, the headlining stars rarely wanted to share the spotlight. They'd use my name to draw eyeballs but didn't want the entire package. My Saturday night gig was a huge break. Would the network think I was trying to upstage my host? Or, as Viraj suspected, would they appreciate my efforts to stay relevant?

I crossed my legs on the sofa. "Making the videos would be a fresh opportunity to sidestep the narrow confines our male bosses make for us. I've been so concerned about being seen as tough, as the equal of any male reporter, that I've suppressed parts of myself. The vulnerable side. I wanted to be taken seriously as a skilled professional. But perhaps the persona I concocted only hides who I really am."

"So who are you?" Rebecca asked.

Tingles fizzed up my spine. "I don't know yet, but I'm dying to find out. And it's happening live on camera."

Chapter 24

LESLIE

By the time I pulled into Dot's driveway, I was near bursting to get in front of the camera. Alone in the car, I'd recited my video content ten times through, refining it slightly with each retelling to focus the message just right. Anyone who thought the videos they saw online were done in one take were sadly mistaken.

Looking natural and polished took practice. Knowing your stuff cold took time, and I was nowhere near the expert Dot, Tasha, or Dr. Wheaton were. But I was getting to be a knowledgeable amateur.

Dot sat in the living room as I traipsed by lugging video gear. "Don't mind me..."

"What's going on?" she asked.

"Live stream. Mind if I set up in the breakfast nook? I scheduled an episode for this afternoon. Viraj wants to be sure the team at *The Kaelen Reed Show* remembers why they hired me."

"If he's as much of a fraud as you say, why do you want to be associated with him?" Dot asked.

I heaved my camera bag onto the table while composing my thoughts. "The Saturday job keeps me on-air but away from Reed. I won't need to be on-set with him, since I'll be on every Saturday. We'll cross paths during production meetings, but I'm hoping for less alone time with him than we've had lately."

Funny how I went from swooning over Reed to avoiding the narcissistic anchor. We hadn't spoken since our last exchange after his show, and I was glad for it. I'd face him eventually, and he'd give me an earful for being away so long. He might view it as disloyal and find some way to wiggle out of my contract. While a powerful force at the network, Reed didn't have complete control over my hiring. The network ran all kinds of viewer surveys before offering me the job. I scored well enough with both men and women to secure my spot.

"Mind if I sit and watch?" Not waiting for an answer, Dot slid out a chair on the far end of the table from where I was setting up. I didn't love her sitting so close, but it was her house. I'd had scores of crew members around me at the network, so I could survive one pair of eyes. Albeit these were knowing, wise ones, and I feared she'd pipe in to correct me if I misspoke.

"Sure, but... remember I'm new to all this eating disorder and Healthy Bodies stuff. If I say something wrong, file it away and tell me after?"

Dot pulsed a brow and buried her face in her oversized tea mug. I'd seen that expression before. Usually it came right before she throttled someone. A wisecracking teenager she encountered at the supermarket, or one of Gabby's high school boyfriends, who had the nerve to say her daughter wasn't smart enough to learn Japanese within earshot of her mom.

People like them didn't stand a chance.

The ache in my bones told me I was about to be on the receiving end of something fierce, but I had no time to address it now.

I assembled my umbrella lighting and slipped on the diffusing screen before standing it on the floor next to the table. The tabletop camera tripod sat behind my laptop, then I plugged all the equipment into the wall jack nearby. Luckily, Dot's ground-floor outlets all had USB ports, and I used one for my phone. Sometimes people I knew sent helpful text messages, and it was easier to manage chat questions on a separate device. Notes handy, I settled down with a glass of water in case I had a coughing fit or my mouth went dry.

The kitchen clock ticked down until it was time for me to launch the live session. I blew out a cleansing breath and began.

"Hello, hello! Leslie Allen here. It's been a minute, but I wanted to give you an insider view of my new investigation. Thanks for all the love with my streetwalker series. Your support meant so much and helped bring attention to a group of women whose stories deserved a spotlight. They were thrilled by the exposure and the City is looking to tighten the noose on those who would take advantage of these vulnerable people. Next up is the diet industry."

I took in the space, remembering the women who had sat not 20 feet away during Aunt Dot's meeting, baring their souls. Together, they struggled against the stigmas of weight and the fervent societal dictates to live one way: thin or bust.

Their fight was now mine.

I focused my attention straight at the lens. "I'm here at my aunt's house for a while, and her work introduced me to the lies behind the diet industry. I've been interviewing experts and reading reputable research, and my mind is melting. This work helped me recognize my own disordered eating. I've seen doctors, had some medical tests, and have begun a journey to recover my health. It's a battle too many people face because of a society hell-bent on keeping us afraid of being fat. Here are a few facts you might've never heard before.

"Dieting is a waste of time because we are hardwired to fight attempts to shift our weight too far away from our set point. That's the natural weight our bodies want to be, and it's different for everyone. Dieting changes our metabolism, since our systems think we're going into starvation mode. To counteract what it views as a threat to our health, our bodies crank up powerful hunger drives. Rather than a sign of a weak mind, food cravings while dieting are actually our body's way of screaming for the food we need to survive."

This all made so much sense. Yet I'd ignored my internal messages for so long that they no longer registered. A lump formed in my throat, but I pressed on.

"When we repeatedly diet, our bodies chemically change and make us more resistant to future attempts to lose weight. After each diet, our system fights back, which only leaves us heavier at the end. But the tragedy of it all is that being heavy was never the problem. The act of dieting is what makes people less healthy."

I covered all the data about BMI and the farce behind thinner being better and healthier. The longer I spoke, the higher the attendee ticker climbed. First past 100, then 1,000, then nearly 20,000. My heart pounded to the point of distraction, but I kept going. I knew a lot of media industry professionals followed my channel and could almost hear their dismissive whispers about my content. They were like me, before I learned the truth.

Keeping my audience in mind, I covered the studies sponsored by food manufacturers and diet companies reinforcing the need to lose weight—and consume their products.

Next came the medical establishment's disgraceful suppression of large-scale studies, showing overweight and obese people lived longer than underweight and normal weight people. Then I dropped in the Minnesota study, which starved soldiers at a calorie count nearly equal to what the USDA recommended as the ideal diet. The evidence was so overwhelming, my anger boiled over.

"Shit, people! Don't you see? Dieting is all such fucking bullshit! All of it. We've been lied to for decades; some lies go back longer. It's left us feeling like crap and chasing an impossible standard most of us were never meant to attain." My chest heaved, so I leaned on the table in front of me to steady myself. I'd completely forgotten that Dot was there, and when I looked at her, she was crying. Tension knotted my throat, so I sipped water while trying to compose myself.

"Sorry, folks. It's just... I've struggled with my weight for a really long time. Since childhood, and it was all such a fucking waste. All the holidays and dinner parties I missed because I was afraid to be near food. All the nights I worked myself to the bone to avoid being overwhelmed by hunger at mealtimes. The room would spin, I was so dizzy, yet I pretended I didn't know the cause was starvation. I'm constantly cold and I haven't had a regular period, I don't think ever. This lie, this obsession we have with thinness, is putting people's lives at risk."

Tears streamed down my face, and I let them. All the pain I'd kept locked away like a shameful secret flooded out of me. The deceit, including my own, was too much to bear. How had I become someone who cried live on YouTube? Yet here I was with the viewer count ticking up past a number too big to fathom through my watery vision. Numb, I sat, a blubbering mess, wondering what to tell these people next. I couldn't be further from the polished expert I was supposed to be

.

"So what do we do now?" Dot asked.

"Huh?" I said, wiping my tears away with my wrists.

"What do we do now? Now that we know the truth?"

Only one thing popped to mind, and it filled me with such joy that I could barely contain my excitement. "We eat."

By the time I wrapped an hour and a half later, I'd answered as many of the 12,000 questions as I could and promised to answer more on *Dear Diary*—and on my next live stream. Some comments were fantastic, pointing me to new experts worth consulting. Maybe even on-air. Others were loving, supportive, and thankful. There were angry crackpots in the mix too, but love won the day.

I slumped in my chair, exhausted, as Dot broke her silence.

"That, my dear, was something special. Thank you. I never thought you would take my work seriously, given your history..." Her voice trailed off.

"Oh, you mean because I've had undiagnosed anorexia? That little thing?" I joked.

"But now you know there's a path back. You can get healthier, and I'm so grateful you never collapsed in a dangerous place."

My mind flew right to Risto. Had that caused his anxiety about my work? The prospect of me running myself so ragged I'd die? Or collapse on a foolhardy mission and end up dumped in the Hudson River, never to be heard from again?

He'd never said as much.

He'd never once asked me if I had an eating disorder.

Nobody did.

Actually, that's not right.

Everyone had, in their own way, except my mom.

They encouraged me to eat more, take care of myself, go for a checkup. Plan a vacation, rest. Refuel. Recharge. Gain my strength. Hell, Barbara admitted to over-ordering takeout just to fill my fridge. Weren't those all coded ways to suggest I needed help?

Yes. But I resisted.

I reveled in praise from people about my lean appearance. I fooled myself that those positive moments proved I was okay, using them to offset the concern from those who knew and loved me.

My answer was always the same: "I'm fine." Somehow I ate just enough to keep from collapsing, then planned regular dinners with girlfriends as sustenance hits that'd last for days.

Shit.

Almost every time I had a big undercover gig, I met the girls for dinner beforehand. Was that my way of eating without acknowledging how much I craved it in between? *God, I was sick.* But less sick than before. Step by step, I slowly moved in the right direction.

Opening up to family and friends.

Seeing the therapist.

Following my meal plan and eating multiple times a day.

The pit I'd dug for myself grew shallower and the sunshine got brighter, its warmth dancing on my skin.

Pans clinked in the kitchen as Dot set about preparing dinner. I meandered over, resting my head on her shoulder.

She kissed my cheek. "Everything will be all right."

"Promise?"

"Yes. You're on a long and difficult journey. What you did today will help a lot of people. Beginning with yourself."

Across the room, my cell lit up with an incoming call. It felt so cozy and safe here in Dot's kitchen that I forgot my show live streamed to a shit-ton of viewers. My caller was probably among them.

I jogged over to grab it before the call went to voicemail.

"Leslie! That was amazing. Scary, but amazing. Are you okay?" Rebecca asked, breathless.

"Yeah. I feel like I've been run over by a semi, but other than that, I'm ducky." I chuckled, dropping into the chair Dot had abandoned to start dinner.

"We linked to your stream from the homepage of *Dear Diary*, so it got a lot of traction. We also blasted it out on our social channels. How many people watched?"

I hadn't even looked. At some point, I'd gone from doing a live show to sitting in a confessional. I usually viewed my videos afterward to critique them, looking for ways to improve. But this was different. I would never watch that episode again.

"Hold on. Viraj is here grabbing for the phone." Rebecca passed her cell to Viraj.

"I said to go live," he said. "But you detonated a weapon."

I couldn't tell if he was mad. "I'm sorry if I—"

"No, don't be sorry! It worked. The network is calling, as are nine other outlets. They want you on. Texts are arriving every millisecond. I usually handle all the bookings for you, but we'll get one of the interns in to manage it. It's going to be a lot. That is, if you're interested."

Did I want to interrupt my treatment to become the story? No. Diet culture and the pain it caused should be the focus, not me.

"Let's keep them hungry. If I don't do press interviews, they'll come back to our channels for updates. Less is more?"

Viraj, Rebecca, and I decided to turn down all media requests. Instead, I planned a series of live streams and articles.

Dot's waving arms drew my attention. As did the places set at the kitchen counter.

"Sorry, folks. I've got to go. It's time to eat."

Chapter 25

Risto

When I pulled into my driveway and cut the engine at 11:00 p.m., Leslie waved to me from Dot's front porch. Votive candles flickered from the surrounding tables, the light shimmering off the goblet of her wineglass. Even in the dimness, I could sense a lightness about her as she swayed on the wooden swing. Until I saw her ease, I hadn't realized how tense I'd been all day.

Sharing my plans with Jose and Freddie.

Agent contracts.

Deliveries.

Recipe tweaks.

I abandoned my car in the driveway without waiting for the garage door to open.

Cricket chirps and frog peeps greeted me, their tones holding a special magic when Leslie was near. We'd spent too many hot summer nights necking in the grass while fireflies danced in the air above. We pretended to be alone on a far-off prairie. As if her aunt and my grandmother couldn't look out their windows and spot our silhouettes in the moonlight. Doing what young adults do when they're in love and no one is around to stop them.

The only people stopping ourselves these days was us.

Gravel crunched underfoot as I advanced up the walk. "You're up late."

"I was hoping to catch you." Leslie shifted in her seat so I could join her on the swing. Instinctively, my arm fell languidly, seeking her shoulders, but I fought the instinct and rested on the wooden backrest instead.

I couldn't keep on this way. I wanted her more than anything, but the idea petrified me at the same time. There were so many changes happening in my life. If I gave in, our history showed we'd likely end up where we were right now, both broken and miserable.

She set her glass down and faced me. "We need to talk."

"Okay...?" I answered.

"We've had a silly flirtation simmering since I arrived. So I'm just going to say it. I want us to be together. I've wanted it for years, but have been too afraid, or proud, or stubborn to try again. Hell, I have a bigger reason to be scared than you do. You're the one who left me. But I'm right here. And I deserve a relationship with someone who can fully commit and be present. Something happened today. Something big. It dismantled fears that kept me living life by the dropperful. I'm thirsty for love and will be happy—with you or without you. I prefer with, but I finally believe down to the marrow of my bones that I can find happiness without you. It's your decision."

I swallowed the boulder in my throat. What the fuck happened to her? There was a resolve in her voice I'd be an idiot to ignore. Had I stayed away thinking Leslie would sit around waiting for me until I was ready?

Yes. I absolutely had.

I was so convinced that she'd wait that I'd done nothing to seek her out. Leslie put so much passion into her career, it often seemed she preferred it to me. But wasn't that what I was doing to her? Choosing my culinary dreams over the woman I loved? In life, if you wanted something, you made it happen. I hopped on the opportunity to get an agent and investors but gave Leslie mixed signals. I'd treated her like the backup plan. She'd just told me in no uncertain terms that shit was o ver.

I nodded my understanding. "That's fair. But what we had before won't work for me. You in New York, doing God knows what till all hours. Me, here, pretending I wasn't gutted with worry. If you want to be together, we need to be together. Every night. As a couple. We stay honest. We talk things through, no matter if it hurts. We've got to communicate, or this thing between us will fall apart again."

"Honest?"

"Always."

"Okay. Let's start now." She downed her drink and set the empty glass down. "I just admitted to about 1.6 million people today that I have an eating disorder. It's scary as hell, and I think it's what hurt our relationship. I'm working on it, but there'll be difficulties. If you're not in, say so now and we'll—"

My lips smothered her words. I did what I'd been longing to do since she'd walked into my life weeks ago. She tasted of fruit, and love, and...

Leslie pushed gently against my chest to separate us.

"Risto. I need an answer. If you aren't committing to me, don't dive in simply because you're horny."

There's that honesty. I'd asked for it, but it sucked to be on the receiving end.

"Where will we live?" I asked.

"Here and New York for work, sometimes."

"Are you done with your adrenaline junkie stories? Not every reporter does that shit, you know."

"Yeah, but some go to war zones and crisis flare points. At least I don't do that." She teased, but I wasn't having it.

"I'm not comfortable with you using your body to ingratiate yourself with men who would do you harm if they found out you're a journalist."

She looked stunned. "No undercover work or disguises?"

"Dress up all you want. But I'm not comfortable with the faux mob moll act. Stop using yourself as bait to gain access to unsavory characters. It's too risky. I don't want you hurt or, God forbid, killed over an article."

She paused, staring at the ground while she assessed my words. Every second of delay an agony.

"Okay, deal. I can be very resourceful. I'll figure it out. What about you? How do I fit into your work world?"

"What do you mean?"

"I hear you're thinking of opening a restaurant in New York. And getting an agent. If you're going to be spread so thin, will you even have time for me? For us?" Leslie asked.

It was a good question. I wanted everything, but there was only one of me. But I deserved to "have it all." Having her by my side was exactly the right place.

"My career may take off a bit. I won't lie and say I'm not thrilled about it. But it's no different than you being on TV or streaming to millions on YouTube. Me pursuing my dreams doesn't mean you can't be a part of it. You are as much a dream of mine as growing the restaurant. I can't make any promises about my ambition, but I can always promise to love you and be an equal partner."

Leslie stood up. I thought to leave, but instead she extended her hand. "I'm in. Are you?"

I rose to face her, my hand dwarfing hers as we shook to seal the deal. "Let's do this."

She made to sit back on the swing, but I yanked her toward the porch steps.

"Where are we going?" she asked.

I stopped short, sending her colliding into me. "Home. To bed."

"Well, all right then," she said with an amused lilt in her voice.

We entered my house through my dark garage, the opener's light having long since switched off. The hinges squeaked closed behind us as I pressed my alarm code into the keypad to enter the dark kitchen.

"Welcome home," I whispered in her ear.

Leslie took hold of my head with both hands and pulled me down to her waiting mouth. I devoured her lips while she shifted to squeeze my biceps for dear life.

Holy fuck.

Desperate, we tore at each other's clothes, wishing them gone.

My fingers crept under the hem of her loose T-shirt, and I slid it off in a single, swift motion. I nibbled at her bra straps, using my teeth to slide one, then the other, off her shoulders.

"Oh my God, Risto…" Her back arched into me, pressing her small, perfect breasts toward my face. I leaned down and took one nipple into my mouth, eliciting a throaty moan.

Dizzy with want, I lost focus, the reality of finally having her hitting home. This would be the first of many times we'd make love, and I wanted it to be fucking amazing. An exclamation point on the promise that once and forever, she was mine.

I lifted my eyes to hers and near drowned in their dark intensity. Without saying a word, I knew what she craved.

Her look said, *Take me. Now. Here. And deep.*

Frantic, we stripped the other, laughing as we tangled in clothes pulled inside out, then abandoned on the kitchen floor. We slammed mouths, my hands running over her silky hips while she reached around to squeeze my ass.

"Oof! I've missed this. It's fucking delicious," she groaned.

My mouth curled into a smile as I kissed her. "Is that so? What else is delicious?"

"Wouldn't you like to know?" She exhaled, grinding herself into me like the nymph she was.

Quick as lightning, I hiked her over my shoulder and headed upstairs.

"Hey!" She giggled, kicking her legs as we ascended the stairs. At the top, I marched straight into my master suite, flicking on the light switch with my elbow.

Leslie hid her face in my back. "Sweetie? The lights?"

"Oh, sorry." I backpedaled to darken the room. Now the only light came from the glowing green clock on my nightstand.

I laid her gently on the bed, moving aside to take in the contours of her silhouette. "So many times I almost hopped in a car to come get you. I can't believe you're here. In my house. In my bed."

"Don't you mean 'our bed'?" Leslie scooted forward and wrapped her legs around me to pull me down. She then rolled us over until she sat on top, straddling me.

I caressed her curves, her skin rippling to attention as I touched her in the way I knew she craved. But I had cravings too.

I slid her onto my face so I could drink her in, together with an aromatic sweetness all her own.

"Oh, it's like that, is it?" she purred.

"Can't talk. Eating," I said, teasing pleasure out of her until she writhed against my hungry mouth.

"Holy fucking hell...!" Leslie braced herself as ecstasy ripped through her, moaning and gasping as aftershocks rippled in waves until she flopped to the mattress, boneless.

Some things never changed.

I wiped my mouth with the back of my hand, then rummaged in my night table drawer for protection, which I handed to her.

"Mind doing the honors?" I asked.

Her arm shot up, fingers wiggling in a "gimme" motion, so I obliged.

She ripped the wrapper open with her teeth, then slid the protection on, unfurling it with overhand caresses. "I love how you're a large man in every way."

She climbed onto me, both of us exhaling audible sighs.

Fuck yes.

"Jesus, you feel so good..." I moaned, more to myself than the woman driving me wild.

We savored the union, reacquainting ourselves and drawing each tactile moment of connection and release into oblivion.

Perfection.

Giving and receiving pleasure as only we two could. We completed each other and always had. I sat up with Leslie straddling me, deepening our union, and guiding her to hit me just right. Deep and hard.

Oh good God...

How was feeling this good even possible?

"God damn it, woman! You make me so crazy, I..."

"Oh!" Leslie cried as I shattered into a million blissful pieces while she succumbed to another rapture of her own. We rode the wave together until it broke against the shore and left us fizzing with afterglow.

Panting, my head swirled, barely conscious. I was hilt deep in the woman I'd dreamed about every night. Fantasies flickered through my mind of all that I'd imagined doing to her and with her, triggering another round of sensation that forced my thumping heart to synchronize with hers.

Our foreheads fell together as we gathered enough breath to devolve into giddy laughter and sloppy kisses.

"Wow," she said. "That was..."

"Yeah. Me too."

We tumbled flat on the bed, panting and smacking kisses on each other. Wrapped in my arms, Leslie snuggled into her spot. Head on my chest, curls tangled in my fingers. Right where she belonged. And where she'd always stay.

Chapter 26

LESLIE

Arguing voices pierced my slumber. Groggy, I stretched, sweeping my hand on the bed next to me, and found Risto gone. I rolled over to press my face into the mattress on his side. Both to breathe him in and to shield the day's brightness from penetrating my closed eyelids.

When I opened one eye, the sun assaulted me through the sheers masquerading as curtains. I sat up, leaning back on my hands as I squinted to adjust.

Weren't guys supposed to have blackout shades?

I guessed owning a restaurant meant you were up early and to bed late. Likely, Risto wasn't in this room much during daylight hours.

That's going to change.

The voices downstairs grew more animated.

Spanish.

Two people; no, three.

I flipped the covers off to creep over to the bedroom door and listen.

The muffled conversation was hard to make out, not that my Spanish skills were up to the task.

What was going on?

I scanned the room for my clothes before realizing they were strewn across Risto's kitchen floor downstairs.

Shit.

After exploring a few dresser drawers, neat as a pin, of course, I found the T-shirts. I slipped on a worn-out gray one from the Indiana University of Pennsylvania, the top-notch culinary school Risto attended as a scholarship student. That led to a paid externship at a glitzy bistro in Pittsburgh. He probably would have stayed out there and settled, if not for the over five-hour drive home to see his ailing grandparents. There was no way to predict at the time that his sacrifice would lead to a gig at a restaurant that would one day become his own.

I crept down the stairs, and when my legs came into view, the arguing stopped.

That was when the television audio registered. I rounded the front of the screen to see a morning news crew on a couch, a still photo of my YouTube video over their shoulder.

"... it has the internet on fire. When a respected journalist like Allen makes accusations of this significance, then disappears, it's a cause for concern. Our calls to NBC and Dear Diary *have not been returned. But the CDC has come forward, claiming it has not buried the results of the revised study."*

"Then why haven't they changed their own policies? Or mentioned it as widely as the initial false data? That organization has to answer..."

Risto clicked the television off.

Barefoot, I stood in disbelief that my YouTube confessional had gone viral in a matter of hours. I'd been too blissfully unplugged to notice. Dot and I ate a yummy dinner, took Pepper for a walk, then I sat listening to crickets until Risto arrived. Never in recent memory had I just savored being in my body. Enjoying its solidness, the strength, and later the marvelous passion, without guilt or fear.

Meanwhile, a firestorm swirled in network newsrooms.

Huh.

Even now my immediate reaction was curiosity rather than panic.

Gabby strolled over, dangling my jeans from a belt loop using one finger as she suppressed a smirk. "Need pants?"

I cracked a smile, then padded behind the kitchen island to slip them on. "Guess I poked a hornet's nest yesterday."

"My phone has been ringing off the hook all morning. When you didn't come home, I worried something bad had happened to you. The news made it sound like you were a danger to yourself, but you were fine last night..."

"News is psychological manipulation, designed to keep viewers on edge. Fear keeps eyeballs glued to screens, refreshing every minute for updates about how shitty everything is. They don't want to miss the moment things change for the better—or worse."

"You're not like that," Gabby said.

"I am and I'm not. But I think people follow my work because I give information and leave them free to arrive at their own conclusions."

"Well, their conclusion is that you're off floating in a river somewhere, having offed yourself," Gabby said. "The truth makes the panic seem really silly. But you need to go back online and let everyone know you're okay."

"Jump on the internet to say I was drinking wine on a summer evening, then had crazy sex with my boyfriend?"

"Boyfriend?!" Gabby and Dot yelled in unison, their mouths dropping open in identical Os.

"Yes. I mean, you meant it, right?" I asked Risto, half afraid his agreement the night before was a dream.

He strolled over, wrapped me in his arms, and planted a loving kiss on my lips. "I did. Every word."

Dot crossed herself. "Gracias a Dios."

"I'll second that." Gabby crossed herself too.

"Oh, come on, you two," I joked. But my wide smile betrayed my utter relief to be with Risto. This time for good.

"Okay, I've got to get to work. We have an on-site today." Gabby pried me away from my man to give me a squeeze, then linked elbows. "Walk me out?"

We left through the back sliding door, then rounded the house, out of sight.

"First, I'm so happy for you. I really hope this works out," Gabby said.

"You and me both. Risto has always been 'the one.' You get that better than anyone."

She smiled. "True. So about yesterday's video. That's a big step, telling the world about your eating disorder. Are you okay?"

Worry creased Gabby's face. I was so elated to lose the shame and reunite with Risto that I'd overlooked the bombshell I'd dropped on those around me. With the truth out in the ether, a weight had lifted. Eating disorders thrived in the shadows, and that was definitely the case for me. In some ways, bearing the secret was worse than having the disorder. Hard days lay ahead for me. But right now I chose to be optimistic, eager to take the next step on a journey that led back to me.

"Yeah, I'm good. I've been eating steady every day and getting my mind right. Plus, I'm blessed to be here, sandwiched between two of the best cooks I know."

"You could do worse!" Gabby gave me a hug, got into her car, and backed out of her mom's driveway.

When I got back inside, Risto was cooking, and Dot sat sipping her coffee.

"So," she said. "Am I losing a roommate?"

"Not until you're fully well," I said and meant it. Three weeks post-surgery, and she was already resuming some normal routines. We'd gone for walks daily, but I still did all the lifting for groceries and laundry baskets and had been handling the cleaning.

"The doctor said if I'm good after next week's visit, I can resume yoga."

"That's great. Maybe I'll give it a try."

Dot almost spit out her coffee but recovered, dabbing her chin with a napkin from the dispenser on the counter. "I'd like to see that."

Risto divided eggs, chorizo, fruit, and toast onto two plates and slid them before me and Dot. "It's been lovely, ladies, but I need to get going. Big day today. The investors are coming."

I'd been so consumed with my situation I'd lost track that Risto had a busy life too. And a huge opportunity waiting for him.

"Nervous? Excited? About to puke?" I asked.

He laughed. "All of that, and more." He paused. "I hope it goes well, but I'm scared shitless about what it means for it to go well. Basically, I'm a wreck."

He'd been preparing for this moment his whole life. He deserved to enjoy it.

I rounded the counter to give him a hug. "You'll be magnificent. No matter what happens, you're already a success. If this is what you want, you'll find an investor. Today, or another day."

He kissed my waiting lips. "Thanks."

Risto opened a kitchen drawer and pressed a set of keys into my hands. Without another word, he left.

I opened my hand to see the key chain and startled. The loop held three keys and a mini picture of the two of us on the amusement park ride. I looked up to see him through the front picture window, backing the car out of the driveway. The man I loved had been prepared for us to reunite. A knot tightened in my chest, forcing tears out of my eyes. I looked up to find Dot watching me.

"Come here, muñequita." She opened her arms. I sank into her embrace, her soft hands stroking my head. "There's a lot of love there. You two will make it. I've always known. But we also need to be sure you're well on your own. You'll be no good to anyone if you're not whole for yourself."

I knew she was right. Talking big on YouTube was one thing. Making it work in my everyday life was something else. I hadn't considered all the implications and unintended consequences of feeding myself. I'd read so much about set points, I was curious to find out where my body wanted me to be. What it would mean for me to live in a larger body, especially one like my aunt's and Risto's. How would the world treat me? How would Mom react?

I stiffened.

Fuck.

My mom.

She had to be one of the many calls I'd missed while I was with Risto. I scrambled around the living room, looking for my phone, finding it on the entryway table. Of the scores of missed messages I'd received from Viraj, Rebecca, Barbara, Dad, editors, and producers I worked with, including from *The Kaelen Reed Show*, many were from my mom. Her last one left my blood cold.

"Call me, or I'm coming."

Oh no.

Those words fried my nerve endings, sending my fingers fumbling with the phone until I dropped it on the floor. *Shit.* I picked it up and jogged up the stairs.

"I'll be right back," I hollered to my aunt, who had probably never seen me move that fast.

Once in Risto's bedroom, I shut the door and braced it with my back. This was not a conversation I wanted to have with my mother. Perhaps ever, but certainly not right now. Not when I was just getting my footing and could easily slip back into an abyss.

But I'd changed.

I could no longer be manipulated into thinking the way I'd been living was good for me. Plus, I was an adult with a loving family around me that would support me as I got well.

My panic eased, replaced by rebellion. I wasn't six years old and no longer had to observe her food fetishes. That was what they were. Hers. She'd successfully indoctrinated me, with zero regard for my health or safety. I was sure that wasn't her intent, but the result was the same. The woman who gave birth to me and raised me was also the one who set me on the path to being sick.

A jumble of emotions warred for supremacy. Anger. Frustration. Fear. Righteousness for my new way of thinking. Sadness for all the years I wasted blindly following a woman I now knew to be ill herself. I couldn't let anyone, not even my mother, inject doubts into my orbit that'd only tangle me up. I wasn't going back to the cage. It only kept me alone and spiraling. The new me had grown beyond its boundaries.

Inhaling deeply, my burning lungs were rewarded with Risto's scent. The rumpled bedding of where we'd slept lay before me. We'd live here and build a life together. I strolled to his side of the bed, sitting next to his pillow and hugging it to my chest for protection. His personal essence reminding me I was no longer alone. A mix of shampoo, laundry detergent, and musk—mashed up into a botanical signature all his own. With Risto at work, his fragrance would have to suffice.

I tapped my mom's number while reclining on my side, cupping the pillow like a swollen, pregnant belly. It was the first time the idea of living in a large body struck me as wonderful. Life-giving. Maybe I'd birth a new and better version of myself. One who wasn't so hungry and pissed off all the time.

Mom answered midway through the first ring.

"What the hell is going on?! I wake up to find my daughter headlining every news channel? I knew going to see those people was a mistake. Now what you need to do is—"

"Stop. Just stop. Did you even bother to watch my video, or did you blow up after hearing distorted summaries?"

I could imagine her shocked blinking across the miles.

"Yeah, I thought so." I moved Risto's pillow away so I could stand. "You have a distorted relationship with food and passed that along to me. I've been miserable and sick, stuck in a weird limbo ever since. I've felt like crap for years without fully understanding why. But that's over. I've been so afraid of gaining an ounce that I've stayed away from the people I love. It's wrong. You've been wrong all along."

"Now wait just a minute—"

"It's a sickness. You can stay this way if you want, but I'm getting help. And for the time being, I think it's best if we didn't talk to each other."

"What have they done to you? Your head is filled with a bunch of lies, and suddenly I'm to blame? So what? You're going to eat yourself fat and die?" Her voice dripped with the disgust I heard from the rest of society. The ones who hadn't yet realized they were trapped in a hamster wheel, running for the amusement of the industries growing rich with profits. Well, fuck that. I was stepping off.

"I'm following the treatment plan the doctors have given me. If my body is meant to be fat, then that's where I'll end up. Are you saying I'm only worthy of your love if I starve myself? If I struggle in a depleted body incapable of giving you a grandchild?"

"What?"

"Need a period to have a baby, Mom."

"You don't get periods?" she asked, genuinely shocked.

"No. I never have gotten them regularly. Only right after my summer visits here. They'd return for a short while but stop once I got home. Now I know it's because I ate properly for long enough to kick-start my system. Mind you, I'm not dying for my monthlies. But I'd love a sign that my body has what it needs to give life."

I rotated to face Risto's room. Our room now. I'd never thought about having a baby. But the idea had fluttered across my brain twice in the span of a few minutes. Maybe it hadn't before because I lacked a partner and presumed my plumbing wasn't up for the job. The concept of being responsible for another person made me want to get well all the more.

Mom's crying drew me back.

"I just wanted you to be healthy. To have a long life and be happy. You're going to undo everything we've worked for."

I pictured myself walking through open cage doors and filling my lungs with the air of freedom.

"You're right. And I've already started."

Chapter 27

LESLIE

I returned downstairs, where Dot sat fidgeting on the sofa. She stood as I entered.

"Was that your mom? What'd she say?" She vibrated with the love and concern I craved from my mother. Emotions Mom was incapable of expressing. I was fortunate to have other sources.

"She's not happy, but I need to do what's right for me. It's the only way for me to get well."

I fell into Dot's arms while sobs wracked my body. I hated myself for wanting Mom's approval. Too often I twisted myself into a pretzel to earn praise she doled out by the meager teaspoon. Too little to satisfy but just enough to make me think more was possible. That, of course, was a fantasy. Mom would more likely raise a pitchfork against me than shower me with love. I could hear her sharpening the tines as retribution for losing her most reliable disciple. Her robot assistant. But I refused to parrot her dogma anymore, and scant else bound us together. Estrangement had long since become our norm, and right now that was fine by me.

I lifted my head off Dot's soaked shoulder, wiping my face dry with the hem of Risto's shirt. "Sorry for that."

"We all need a good cry sometimes."

That must be true, because as my sadness dissipated, a lightness took over. Free of the guilt and shame, I centered on a sensation that was growing more familiar by the day. Hunger. It wasn't a nagging hollowness, doomed to be ignored. It was a tap on the shoulder, a reminder to take action.

"After I finish eating the breakfast Risto made, I'd love for us to go to the grocery store," I said. "I'll head over to your house shortly to get ready."

Dot left and I sat before the plate my sexy hunk of a boyfriend fixed for me.

Devoid of the morning's excitement, the only sounds came from the undercurrent of Risto's house. The barely audible hum from the refrigerator. Water droplets settling down the kitchen drain. Muffled tweets from the area's songbirds outside. Alone, I savored my breakfast like I belonged here. Risto welcomed me home last night. Today, the house sighed its own greeting. I hoped it could tell how much I treasured the welcome.

A calm awareness settled over me that I rarely permitted. My belly was full but comfortable. I'd left half a piece of toast and some egg untouched on my plate, knowing this was only my first meal of the day. There'd be more. Today. Tomorrow. The next day. I'd have to keep reminding myself.

I slotted my dirty dishes into the dishwasher and made ready for another milestone.

Dot glanced over from the driver's seat on our way to the grocery store.

"When you're at the beginning of your recovery, food shopping can be scary. For some, it's akin to being let loose in a candy shop. But the point is to build a new relationship with food, one where you take back the control and make decisions for yourself without guilt or fear."

"Sounds like heaven," I joked.

"It is. But after the joy comes the anger. All the years you wasted restricting, implementing strict rules, and punishing yourself when you couldn't measure up. You're about to learn a better, healthier, more empowered way to live. I'm excited for you to learn and then share it with the world." Dot beamed with pride.

No pressure.

Unlike other people suffering from disordered eating, there was a public service aspect to my journey that was impossible to ignore. Chronicling my progress, and reporting back, would be an essential part of bringing authenticity to this important topic. I would be a counterbalance to all the celebrity false prophets hawking diet plans that failed so spectacularly they ran straight to diet pills after they regained their weight. Those would also fail because we were human. The sooner the masses got this message, the better off we'd all be.

But it started with me.

Dot parked at the far end of the parking lot and turned off the ignition. "Every step counts."

I loved how determined she was to get back to her usual routine. Already, I found it hard to keep pace with her when we were out walking Pepper. Dot planned to return to yoga next week and insisted I go with her. An exercise class was something I never would have been able to attempt before, since I got lightheaded and clumsy at the slightest exertion. Now fed, the competitor in me looked forward to seeing Dot in action at the studio, even if she wasn't yet teaching the class herself.

The world certainly underestimated the fitness abilities of large-bodied people. Dot recommended I follow a bunch of body-liberation creators on Instagram. Each posted video after video showing fitness moves impossible for me to contemplate doing myself.

Lifting heavy weights.

Bending and stretching with fluid, controlled movements.

Hiking in forests and across mountains.

Multi-day kayak trips with overland portages.

Biking and swimming.

These influencers honored their large bodies in tight spandex that hugged every curve, roll, and cellulite dimple. They proudly reclaimed fitness wear formerly reserved for the lithe and trim. It was a positive reminder that movement was for everyone. It led to stronger bodies and freer minds, and I'd have to make moving a priority.

But first I needed to buy the fuel.

At the market entrance, I yanked an enormous shopping cart from the corral of nested carriages and followed Dot through the automated doors.

"We'll go up and down every aisle and see how it goes," she said. "This entire store is yours and you can buy—and eat—anything in it. Some foods are more nutrient dense, have more whole grains, and will keep you feeling fuller longer. They also have more vitamins and minerals, but you aren't a better person for choosing a melon over a bag of chips. It's just food. Right?"

I nodded but knew that was my first lie. I'd absorbed too many negative body messages down to the cellular level. Anxiety crept up my legs, so I clutched the cart handle tight to center on its solidness.

I was screwed. We were only standing in the produce section. What would happen when we got to the cookie aisle?

Dot paused by pyramids of apples and oranges. Across the aisle, clear plastic cartons of berries called to me. I crossed to stand before the strawberries, lifting the container to inhale their fruity perfume.

I imagined red, juicy berries, cut in half and topped with plump blueberries.

I picked up a box of each, holding them against my chest, waiting for a store alarm to sound. Like I'd snatched a jewel out of a display case guarded by a laser-triggered security system.

Dot suppressed her amusement. "It's okay for you to touch things here. No one is going to tackle you in the aisle for buying food."

I let out a breath and placed the berries in the cart seat, flipping the plastic guard up so they wouldn't slide through the gaps. Next, I got some apples, baby spinach, walnuts, cranberries, and a creamy salad dressing that would've made my mom shudder with anger at the mere suggestion. It looked like garlicky, creamy heaven in those refrigerated glass jars. I pictured myself ripping the top off and chugging it, white cream dripping down my chin.

Yeah, not a good look.

We rounded the produce section to the refrigerated meat cases, and I selected a package of boneless chicken breast. Dot said she'd show me what to do with it. Visions of grilled chicken fluttered in my head as we hit the cereal aisle. Colorful boxes flashed across my field of vision, fueling my desire for Peanut Butter Cap'n Crunch. Mom barely let me eat cereal and certainly not anything sugared. Once after a sleepover at a friend's house, we woke and ate the crunchy, sweet balls. They bobbed in my milk as I dipped my spoon in, leaving me with a delicious milk treat that I drank from the bowl after my friend slurped hers. Delighted, I begged Mom to buy some. She not only didn't buy it, Mom never let me have a sleepover at that girl's house ever again. Hurt, the girl drifted away, leaving me friendless. I lost my best friend over fucking breakfast cereal.

I snatched a box off the shelf, grasping the Peanut Butter cereal so hard, the cardboard sides puffed out. Then I tossed the Crunch Berries flavor in the cart too, alongside the Original variety. I was staging a three-box breakfast cereal rebellion.

I grinned up at Dot, who barely pulsed an eyebrow.

"Where to next?" I asked.

She stepped aside. "Why don't you lead the way?"

We took care to walk up and down every aisle. Instead of the usual overwhelm that typically left me fleeing the store empty handed, cartoon-style through the wall, I calmly browsed. I read labels, and Dot and I discussed the importance of eating a variety of foods. While I was now following a specific meal plan to restart my system, eventually my hunger signals would return. Once that happened, I'd be able to follow my cravings like the women talked about at Dot's meeting. So odd to think of trusting my body after fighting it for so long.

We entered the refrigerated dairy aisle, and a tub of rice pudding called to me. I reached for it but stopped myself.

"I always wanted to buy this. Once I had it at someone's house and thought I'd died and gone to heaven."

"What's stopping you?" Dot asked.

I scanned my overflowing cart. While my usual shopping trips barely filled a handbasket, this sucker was full. I'd always envied shoppers when in the checkout line. As I starved to the point of near fainting, I watched their delectables travel down the black conveyor belt where the cashier would bag them out of sight. I dreamed of launching myself onto the slick surface to sneak home with them. Instead, I'd haul my meager provisions to my apartment and stand in front of my empty fridge to draw nourishment from the chilly air.

I shivered, thinking of it. Of who I used to be.

Today was my first day going to the store and buying whatever I wanted. Would I be able to eat this stuff? Actually, get it past my lips? I trusted Dot, but it still seemed unlikely that once I started eating I'd be able to stop. In my head, I'd keep eating and eating and eating, ballooning out until my body exploded undigested food all over the walls. Looking at the pudding carton near my hand, a wave of nausea rolled through me.

"I changed my mind." Body erect, I turned to leave.

But Dot blocked the cart with her body. "Hold on now. Tell me what just happened?"

My shoulders sagged. "Do I have to?"

"Muñeca, you're stuck in a polarized way of thinking. You're either starving yourself or you're an enormous human ball rolling down the street. Am I right?"

She had me. "Kinda. Yeah."

"Have you ever imagined yourself in the middle? Where you enjoy eating food that tastes good, have what you want, then stop?"

"Is that even possible?"

"Yes, but you need to learn to trust yourself." She lifted the carton of rice pudding. "Rice pudding is fine to eat. It's no better or worse than anything else in the store. Tell me the truth. If we leave this pudding behind, what happens?"

"I get home and wish I had it."

"Then what?"

"I'd obsess about it and make myself miserable."

She laughed. "I'm the same. Only difference for me was that I'd launch into a binge. I'd keep eating things, wishing they were the item I craved. By the end, I would have consumed way more than I intended or wanted. When I dieted, bad days became 'free days.' I killed my diet for the week already, so what was the point of trying? But I was searching for something I couldn't put in my mouth."

"What was it?"

"So many things. Happiness. Love. Companionship, when I was missing your uncle Arty. Peace when I wanted to calm down about a frustrating situation. If I finished a book and was sad it was over. It could be anything. But what was the one thing I never hoped to fix?"

I shook my head, not knowing.

"Not once was I ever hungry. I was overcome with another emotion and used food to fill the gap. What were you feeling when you reached for the pudding?"

Visions of me in a pink lollipop wonderland flashed to mind. I was smiling and sitting in front of a table with a clear glass sundae cup full of rice pudding. The goofy vision made me smile. "Happy. I felt happy."

"And when you pulled away?"

Fear.

After eating too much, I'd stroll into the street and be surrounded by jeering people. They'd stop, point, and laugh at me and my fatness. I'd end up lonely and unloved because I was too weak to resist a fucking bowl of pudding.

Shoppers rolled carts past where we stood in the center of the wide dairy aisle. Not a single one giving either of us any notice. They didn't care. Why was I so scared of offending strangers? They'd pass by into their own lives, and I'd never see them again. They'd have no memories of the gal they saw at the supermarket, petrified by a tub of rice pudding.

Dot still held it. A glossy white container with an image of a purple tablecloth under a mounded dish of rice pudding sprinkled with cinnamon. This time, the tub didn't make me happy or afraid. I felt nothing. But I might like to have some later, so I lifted it off her flat palm and placed it in the shopping cart.

She gave me a kiss. "I'm proud of you."

"For choosing pudding?"

"For taking control of your life." She bumped me with her hip as she took over the cart and headed toward the checkout.

A glow warmed me from within as I strutted behind her.

I'm proud of me too.

Chapter 28

RISTO

Instead of dirtying my home's kitchen, I stood, arms locked on the counter, visualizing the meal. In my mind's eye, ingredients scattered everywhere, service swirled around me while I plated stunning dishes with tweezers that were swept away for waiting diners. Manicured meals were a far cry from the homier fare I typically served. But wasn't that the whole point of stretching myself? To make dinner an event worth remembering?

"Penny for your thoughts?" Leslie's hand caressed my back before I sensed her presence. Having her in my house was still a thrill, and I planned to take full advantage.

I turned, wrapping my arms around until they cupped her ass. With one solid squeeze, I held proof her new meal plan was working. Which made me wonder.

"Can I ask you something?" I kissed her forehead.

"Sure," she said.

"Why didn't you ever tell me about your struggles with food?"

"Oh, that little thing?"

She nestled into my chest. "I... I don't think I had the words to express it. I just thought it's how I was and that it wouldn't change.

That sounds silly now. But I can't explain it any other way. Learning that I have an eating disorder threw me for a loop. It was a surprise, a relief, and a hard, scary truth mashed into one. All those times I felt like crying because I was so hungry, fear kept my lips closed. From food, and from you."

Leslie tilted her head, her brown eyes liquid with longing. *She loves me.* And she wanted a kiss, which I gladly delivered.

"I wish I'd been able to handle things differently," she said.

"Well, we can now. I've learned so much from you and Dot. Sometimes giving our feelings a name helps make sense of them. It lights a path forward that was too dark to see before."

"Thank you. That's a beautiful way to put it." Leslie pulled away and glided around the counter to the opposite side. She ran her fingers over everything, the milled-maple cabinets, the smooth quartz, the rough baskets holding my aromatics—onions, garlic, and shallots. I swore, I'd never seen anything hotter than watching Leslie touch the tools of my trade. Making peace with a world she denied herself for so long.

At last, she met my eye.

"Since we're coming clean, tell me more about this whole restaurant thing. How much do you want it and how much are you trying to please a bunch of fancy people from Manhattan?"

"There's only one fancy person from Manhattan I care about."

"Be serious," she pleaded.

I sighed. It was a good question.

While I pondered my answer, I grabbed a bottle of wine and two glasses from the bar area. I handed them to her while I opened a drawer for a picnic blanket.

"Let's discuss this under the stars," I said.

We exited my home's rear sliding doors and strolled across my backyard to a clear spot under the night sky. Inky black surrounded stars twinkling brightly within the infinite cosmos. Crickets chirped, sparring with the frogs from the nearby stream. During heavy rain, the water roared, rough and furious. Tonight its shimmering surface quietly flowed without end.

Leslie breathed deeply, stretching toward the heavens. "Anything seems possible out here."

As teens, we'd spent countless nights giggling in the grass while our guardians slept inside. Desperate kisses escalated to hushed confessions of love and dreams for the future. Some came true. Others smashed against stormy shores. But here we were, shining as brightly as the stars above us.

After spreading the wool blanket, we both sat. Glasses in hand, words failed me. But I owed her my truth. I sipped my wine and gazed into Leslie's moonlit face, its contours never more alluring.

"I want to be famous. I want the world to eat my food, love it, and crave more. But most of all, I want them to remember it was me who prepared it. It sounds shallow, I know."

"No. It's honest and real. You're amazing. Why wouldn't you want everyone to know? We're so often taught not to dream. Not to aim impossibly high, that it's too risky. Even that ambition is selfish. But where would we be without people driven enough to think they can make a difference?"

"For me, it comes from a place of giving. The dishes I create—especially this new menu I've been working on—they're both tasty and transformative. I want everyone in the world to experience that joy. It's what drives me to create."

"Sign me up." Leslie leaned over for a fruity kiss, the tang of pinot grigio fresh on her lips. I pictured her naked in a sauté pan, slathered in caramelized onions and a savory reduction. Mixing metaphors, for sure, but this woman was good enough to eat.

We downed our wine and lay amongst the crickets, talking for hours. About our hopes and our fears. About what we wanted in life. Under these stars, we bared our souls in a way we never had before. Raw honesty scraped off the artifice, then bright moonlight rinsed us clean.

Leslie was mine, and I was hers.

Whatever came next, we'd conquer it together.

Chapter 29

RISTO

Energy flowed through me, like the saffron dough I cranked through the pasta roller for the special arroz con pollo dumplings. I would serve them with a garlicky pimento broth. The idea came to me in the middle of the night a few weeks back after seeing a ravioli commercial on TV. Once I balanced the flavors, the dumplings tasted identical to the original dish. It'd be a sensation as part of today's tasting menu for the investors.

Jose dropped the lid on my simmering broth with an aggressive clank. "I thought you were going to stick to our current menu? Hmm? Why are you making all this deconstructed bullshit that has no soul."

He paced closer to where I was forming little mounds of filling on my fresh pasta sheet. I had to keep working to ensure it all was perfect. There was no time for tirades. But Jose wasn't finished.

"You think people are dragging themselves here from Brooklyn to eat this?" He gestured to my work. "No. They're coming for pasteles like their grandmother made. Succulent pernil without the work. A sip of coquito at the holidays because it brings them joy."

It was impossible to explain to him how or why the act of creation was vital to my well-being. It defined me as a man and as a chef. Yes,

I loved those flavors. They made me sing and inspired me to elevate them still further. A New York City restaurant would be that chance. To take the dishes swirling in my head and give them a home. They felt out of place on the Boricua menu. Jose was right. But what if I crafted an entirely new dining experience? Transformed familiar dishes into something completely new? THAT would show the culinary world I'd arrived. Even better, it would prove that Puerto Rican food was worthy of notice.

New York was THE destination for restaurateurs. This opportunity would catapult my career. At 37, I had the skills, business savvy, and experience to get called up to the big leagues. My normal Boricua menu wouldn't cut it. Not for Manhattan. And not if I wanted to be taken seriously as a chef on the rise worthy of an agent like Brock.

I flowed a top sheet of pasta across my fillings, then pressed the sheets together with a fluted cutter. "I have a vision for this meal. You need to trust me."

Jose grabbed my arm to still me. "Why are you doing this? It's our big shot, and you're blowing it with distractions. With ravioli and sea urchins. What the fuck?"

"Please. You know we're serving each dish alongside the reimagining. They WILL eat our food, so stop worrying." I nudged him with my elbow, smiling as I looked up at Freddie. His head bowed back to his work like he wasn't just watching me and Jose battle.

"What? You too?"

Freddie sighed. "Why are we doing all this extra work when we have a solid menu people cherish? It's like you're ashamed of us and trying to be something you're not."

Anger shot me upright from my hunch over the counter. "And what's that? A chef? A creator able to take the foods we love and innovate them? Anyone can cut up pork in different shapes. These flavors deserve a wider platform. I want to push it and see where they'll go "

"But why today, mijo? Win them over, then introduce the new dishes slowly." Jose pleaded with me to listen, but all I heard was my mother's voice urging me to dream big.

Silas saying more people deserved my food.

Brock declaring I was a man of consequence.

All those people were depending on me to be unforgettable today, and I damn well was going to.

I wiped my damp forehead with my forearm. "Let's get back to work. They'll be here soon."

Afternoon sun splashed across the tables in the dining room, sparkling on the tableware I'd set in the center of the space for the occasion. Instead of coming during a meal service, the investors wanted a leisurely opportunity to dine, then stick around by the bar to watch dinner afterward.

First to arrive were Ruben Santiago and his wife, Anita. A native New Yorker of Puerto Rican descent, Ruben led a restaurant group with holdings in the US and the Caribbean. With copper skin and a neatly trimmed beard, he wore a crisp white shirt and jeans. Anita's flouncy blue dress with ruffled short sleeves mingled with her long, dark curls. Seeing them together reminded me I was about to have a future with Leslie. One dream come true. Was I due for another?

"Hello! Welcome to Boricua!" I said, extending my hand to each of them. "I'm Chef Evaristo Zaldo, but everyone calls me Risto."

"Thank you for having us. The others will be along shortly."

"Is that Brock?" Anita turned toward the hostess stand where my soon-to-be agent was removing his sunglasses.

"It is! You're lovely as ever, Anita."

Brock strolled in and embraced Ruben's wife.

While they hugged, Ruben leaned in to whisper to me. "Be careful with that one. He's slippery."

"Brock?" I mouthed, and he nodded before plastering on a smile to greet him.

I wasn't sure how to take the comment. If all went well, I'd be negotiating with Ruben's company, and his interests didn't necessarily align with mine. Could be he was trying to weaken my position. Or, given Brock's attempt to elbow in on my future franchise revenue, I should heed his warning and keep a sharp eye on them both.

The other two partners arrived, so I signaled to my staff. A server entered to fill the water glasses while my bartender greeted my VIP guests and took drink orders. Once everyone found their seats, I stood beside Ruben at their round table.

Here we go.

"Welcome to Boricua and thank you for making the trip out. I'm a proud Puerto Rican American and have long been fascinated by the flavors of my culture. Today, I've prepared a special menu, which pairs some of our most popular dishes with innovative interpretations. My goal is to take you on a culinary journey. Then we can unleash the potential of any business partnership we pursue together. Please ask as many questions as you want. And after we're done, I'll return to have dessert."

I bowed my head and left the dining room, pushing my way through the swinging doors to the kitchen.

"We ready?" I asked.

"Yes, Chef!" the staff cried out at once.

"Fire six app platters."

"Six app platters, heard," Jose called out, mobilizing the rest of the staff. We typically had assorted standard appetizers on our menu, plus a few specials. Today, we'd made them all, alongside two new ones. A sea urchin halved and splashed with some wine and shallot foam, and chorizo grilled alongside squid, sprinkled with cedar smoked sea salt.

Once composed, the plates looked magnificent. All my servers were present to simultaneously table each diner's plate, then exit.

"My!" Anita clasped her hands together. "This looks wonderful!"

Steve Taylor, the oldest and richest of Ruben's partners, sported white mussed hair and a ruddy complexion. He perked up in his chair and cupped a hand to flow steam toward his face. "I believe we're in for a treat today."

I described each dish, sharing where we sourced ingredients and explaining the special techniques we used to bring them to life. They asked questions, examining their plates at eye level before taking bites. Deadrick Jones, the last of Ruben's partners, was a force in the restaurant world. A smooth-headed Black man with a trim white goatee, he mumbled voice memos into his phone so artfully I couldn't catch a word. It was likely a skill held over from his days as a food critic a t *The New York Times*.

My nerves buzzed with anticipation as these culinary titans decided my fate. Would they understand my concepts? Enjoy the flavors? Want to invest? I gripped my wrist behind my back, digging the nails in to settle myself. I had to remind myself that even if they passed on the investment opportunity, all wouldn't be lost. There would be others enthusiastic about my food.

But I had a good feeling about my chances.

Our carefully crafted flavors exploded in their mouths, sending eyebrows arching and eyes rolling in pools of pleasure. Imperceptible nods came next as they savored mouthfuls, wanting them to endure. "Mmm" and "not bad" murmurs of surprise rounded the table. As much as they tried to play it cool, these folks were impressed.

Servers swept away their spotless plates to begin dinner service. Each entrée featured a Boricua favorite paired with a reinterpretation. Authentic flavors shared two ways. It was time to see if my whimsy would fall flat or pay off.

First up was my ravioli, which left my guests staring at their meals in confusion.

Ruben lifted his arroz con pollo ravioli to eye level, inspecting the dish up close while savoring the pimento steam from the pasta side. "I've never seen anything like this."

One of my grandma's favorite dishes arrived next.

Deadrick shook his head, motioning to his plate with his fork. "Chef Zaldo, is this recipe from Ponce?"

Not waiting for my answer, he dove in for another bite, unable to contain his delight. The man's enthusiasm brought a smile to my face.

"Yes. My family was from Ponce. It's my twist on a family recipe."

That Deadrick recognized the distinct spicy/earthy flavors of cocido ponceño elevated him 50 points in my book. It was a traditional dish of stewed pigs' feet, bathed in a rich sauce of coriander, sofrito, and chorizo sausage, then thickened with potatoes and chickpeas. My twist offered pork belly crusted in chickpea flour surrounded by the strained stew sauce, so smooth it shimmered in the afternoon light like a fiery sunset.

I knew the meal turned in my favor when they abandoned all pretense of hiding their delight. Gone were the stoic notes and voice memos, replaced by lively conversation, clinking flatware, and laughter.

As they devoured their last dessert, I joined them in the dining room, and they greeted me with a standing ovation. Brock blasted a sharp whistle with his pinkies, sending Steve's hands cupping over his ears. Hearing the commotion, my team stepped through the swinging kitchen door to bask in genuine adulation. Too enthusiastic to stop, I finally hushed them with my arms and motioned for us all to sit. I pulled up a chair tableside to join them.

"That was magnificent. Truly outstanding," Ruben said. "Gentlemen, and lady, we have a standout here, and it's incredible that we get to introduce his talents to the world."

He lifted his wine glass. "To our mutual success."

I bowed my head as they toasted.

"Now I understand the chatroom furor. You, my friend, are a talent." Deadrick reached across the table to shake my hand.

"We'll regroup and begin working on the offer. And don't worry, it will be generous. Upscale Puerto Rican would be entirely unique in the City. No one has done it yet," Steve said.

"It will be the most exclusive dining experience this cuisine has ever seen," Deadrick added.

Ruben furrowed his brow. "There is a lot to discuss. Puerto Rico is a humble place with bold flavors. We could make a killing with a more accessible price point."

"We can make a bigger killing at a higher one," Steve said with a laugh.

Ruben seemed to hold his next thought, choosing to swallow a sip of water instead. The power dynamic among these three men was clear. He with the largest bank account won. And from his Forbes ranking, that was Steve.

But I'd worked too hard not to have a voice in my future.

"My thinking was that our New York location would deliver the elevated version of the menu I presented today. I'm excited about the opportunity."

"Then you made a grave mistake, chef." Ruben turned to me. "You wowed us with sophisticated food, yes. But you also captured the soul of a nation on the other side. You can't yank that away. It's the culinary story of your heritage. Of your chef's journey. And that story needs telling."

Ruben drove his finger into the table to emphasize the point.

But Steve was not to be deterred.

"Chef Risto took humble flavors and made magic. That's a skill people will pay for. Pork belly and sea urchins, hours of crafting and creativity has a price tag. Be honest, Ruben. You got nostalgia for the arroz con pollo, but you wept over that saffron broth. Don't lie. I was right here watching you."

Steve wiggled his empty wineglass, and Brock refilled it. While he poured, my would-be agent pulsed the briefest of head shakes.

Brock's message was clear.

Keep quiet. Don't blow it.

I caught Ruben's eye, and he arched an eyebrow. *We'll figure it out, so we're all happy.* Their good-cop/bad-cop routine had my defenses melting. And Ruben knew it. He borrowed an empty wine glass from the next table and placed it in front of me. Brock poured, and the ruby liquid settled into place. Finding equilibrium.

That's what I had here at my restaurant. A world of my making where I ruled supreme. Taking an investment would upend it all. As I saw it, the situation would likely end in one of two ways: I'd achieve wild success or be left in tattered ruins.

Only time would tell, and these people wanted answers.

Now.

I tipped my nose into the wineglass, its fruity tang electrifying my senses. Swirling the legs, I thought about what it meant to toast with these people. How my world would change. How proud my parents would be if I could make it in New York City. Success at this scale would mean a financially secure future for me and Leslie. Done right, we could be set for life.

I raised my glass. "To us. Que siempre soñemos en grande."

I'm dreaming big, Mom.

Chapter 30

Risto

A month after hosting the tasting menu, I was still flying high in my morning shower. We'd begun conceptualizing the new restaurant, and after many conversations, the investors had won Ruben over to the upscale Puerto Rican positioning. My mind swirled with concepts and flavors, and Jose and Freddie were warming to the idea of getting me out of their hair.

As for my hair, I had cropped it close in anticipation of the two days of photoshoots Brock scheduled. He wanted to beef up my social presence and book media interviews. All that took planning—and pictures. Yesterday, they focused on candid shots of me cooking in the kitchen, then sprinkled in staged scenes, both inside and outside the restaurant.

The lighting crew, photographers, and makeup artist encouraged me along as I posed. The attention made me glow like a bride, and visions of my Leslie in a wedding gown had me sparkling all day. They all said the images were amazing.

I was toweling off in the bathroom when Leslie walked my cell phone into me. "Brock. He called eight times in five minutes, so I answered. Thought it might be important."

"Thanks." I took the phone, and she closed the door as she exited.

"Is everything okay?" I asked.

"Um. I have something to discuss with you. Mind if I stop by?" Brock asked.

"Sure, but can't we talk at the shoot in an hour?"

"There may not be one today. That's what we need to talk about. Mind coming down to let me in?"

He was here?

"I'll be right down." I hung up, dazed.

Why would Brock show up at my house unannounced, threatening to cancel? Had the pictures come out worse than they said?

Mild panic took hold as I envisioned him triggering our 30-day "out" clause. The restaurant group would follow, causing my dream to vanish like the hot shower mist swirling around my damp head.

I finished drying myself, then tossed on a pair of sweats and a T-shirt to dash downstairs. Leslie had already let him in and was pouring him a mug of tea, the little paper tag fluttering helplessly from the string.

I could relate.

"Ah, here's our man," Brock said, walking over to shake hands like the pro he was.

Ruben's words flashed to mind.

Be careful. He's slippery.

He hadn't been yet, but this unannounced visit had my sirens blaring.

"Is there somewhere we can speak? Privately?"

Leslie jingled her keys. "You two stay. I'm heading out for my walk with Dot and Pepper."

She pecked me on the lips and left through the back sliding door.

I still hadn't spoken. Scared anything I'd say would burst my fantasy. Like an eager home buyer, I'd mentally moved into my Manhattan restaurant, picked furniture, hung drapes, and unpacked my clothes. That's how real it felt. But something told me Brock was about to make my dream evaporate. I wanted to cling to it for dear life, but curiosity got the best of me.

"What couldn't wait an hour?"

Brock set his laptop on the kitchen counter and flipped it open. "The photographer sent me yesterday's proofs, and there was something not sitting right with me about how you appeared in the shots."

"Don't tell me. I had food stains." My chest lightened.

It's about the photos. Whatever it was, it could be fixed.

He tapped through screens and loaded one filled with pictures. "Tell me what you see."

The lighting was fantastic, and I looked both focused and determined. I'd never seen myself cook but recognized the expression Jose teased me about. Steely intensity, like nothing was more important than getting the dish right. Any of these would make perfect promotional materials.

"These are great. But it sounds like you disagree?"

He sighed his frustration, tapped on one picture, enlarging it until only my torso showed and the remainder cropped off the screen. "I know that you removed the clause about weight, but fuck, Risto. My eye goes right to those rolls. What do you think the rest of the world will see? Their eyes will zoom right there, and we'll be finished."

Brock pressed the digital image so hard his fingertip turned white. Beneath it, two rolls of fat that I'd never noticed protruded from my waist, perfectly highlighted where my black chef's coat contoured around my body.

Brock decapitated my picture, reducing me to faceless parts. All of them big. All of them fat, but none had ever defined me. I'd always been proud of who I was and felt at home in my skin. My parents and grandparents had encouraged me to live life to the fullest. What's more, I was well respected in our community, had built a successful business, and now had investors throwing themselves at me. My cooking was what mattered. Who cared what I looked like?

My vision blurred with the headless man on screen.

"Chef, the cold truth is that diners want to enjoy their food without an in-your-face reminder that eating makes them fat. It's a killjoy." Brock shifted his hand to gently squeeze my shoulder. "Having you slim will liberate people to dine freely. Don't you want your guests to have the best dining experience possible? This is going to help. Trust me."

His expression was so earnest.

Could he be right?

Did people view me as a repulsive fat man?

I'd never cared what others thought of me, but I'd hired Brock to make the masses love me and flock to my restaurants and appearances. We'd already started talking about a cookbook. But that all depended on fans being drawn to me. Up until now, my joyful spirit, delicious food, and giving nature won praise all around. My appearance never factored into the equation. But according to Brock, I was just shy of repulsive.

"I've never been thin. No one in my family is thin. I'm a chef because I love food and love sharing that enjoyment with others. It's central to who I am."

"You're about to become a famous chef, opening a new restaurant in Manhattan. Your photos will be everywhere. Is this how you want to appear to the world?"

My offense boiled over. "I don't get where this is coming from. You're the one who pursued me. You knew who you were getting."

Brock sighed as if I was an idiot. Shooting me a sideways glance, he slid his computer in front of him and opened a file of "Before and After" pictures of his chef clients. "Chef Chow lost 80 pounds. He went from a guest panelist to having his own show. Chef Morgan transformed from a plump girl next door to a fiery vixen on magazine covers. She has cookware and is about to get a talk show. Chef Tanzanini is the top-rated host on the Culinary Network. He's every damn place you look, but not till after he lost those 45 pounds."

I'd always pitied Chef Tanzanini. Skeletal since he dropped the weight, his perpetually pissed off expression was downright creepy. Yes, he was uber famous. But the dude looked miserable at being forced to be around food. A joyless wisp of his former self, he seemed better off in his "Before" picture.

"I'm not a twiggy, bony guy. Yet you signed on anyway." I hated the pleading tone of my voice. Like I was already giving in.

"Chef Risto, we have an opportunity here. I want to help you become the biggest thing going, but that requires you being smaller.

Lose 30 to 40 pounds and commit to some back and ab exercises. Trust me. You'll be amazed by how much better and leaner you'll look in these photos. Until then, we'll use what we have. They can be cropped and airbrushed to perfection. But that won't work during live appearances. Or on television. Do this for me, and I promise the results will speak for themselves."

He slid a paper in front of me. "This is the diet Chef Chow used and the exercise regimen used by Chef Tanzanini. Try it for a month and see how it goes."

He rose to leave.

"What about today's shoot?" I asked, already emotionally flattened.

He shouldered his backpack and strolled to the front door. "I canceled it. Yesterday."

Brock dipped his head in faux reverence and was gone.

Stunned, I stared after Brock as though he was going to pop back in and yell, *April Fools!* But I was the only fool in sight. He never intended to have today's shoot. He saw me on camera yesterday and was repulsed.

I let that sink in.

I returned to the bathroom and stood before the mirror. Honestly, I never thought much about my appearance before. People liked me. I liked me. Leslie said my ass was perfect. What was the point of fretting over my weight?

Instead of taking in my entire reflection as usual, I focused on the parts troubling Brock. I had wide shoulders and powerful arms, not chiseled and defined, but capable of lifting hundred-pound cases of meat, canned goods, and fruit like they were child's play. I spun around, glancing over my shoulder. My shirt pinched where the rolls met, sloping down to a flatter bottom and thick legs. The ones that never failed me despite working 18-hour days, most of those spent standing.

My stomach rumbled, so I made my way back to the kitchen. And Brock's new sheet. His breakfast dictated one egg, boiled or poached, one slice of whole-grain toast, black coffee, and three glasses of water. There'd be an apple for snack at 10:45 a.m. Then a lunch of fish over a bed of greens, drizzled with lemon and a splash of olive oil, salt, and pepper. Dinner comprised a few ounces of lean protein and some vegetables, followed by a nightcap of tea.

That was it.

No daily variety.

The same meal every day.

No wonder Chef Tanzanini lived in agony.

This was how Leslie starved herself.

Now Brock insisted I do the same? I knew this was trash from the get-go. Yet I asked to ride on the celebrity train. That decision had consequences.

I held the sheet detailing my bleak future.

How could I eat this way after supporting Leslie in her recovery? What kind of message would that send her?

A bad one.

If I did this, she mustn't know. She was making amazing progress. In two months, her body had transformed, filling in and rounding out after following the doctor's eating plan. Her care team didn't focus on weight, but they were pleased by the steady weekly gains. Her skin glowed. She had more energy, and she was happier than I'd ever seen her. And not for nothing, her breasts had never been more spectacular.

It smacked of disloyalty and ignorance to follow Brock's demands, given all Leslie had been through.

Then my agent's words came rushing back.

I can't see anything else but your rolls of flab. What do you think the rest of the world will see?

Fuck me.

Could I really do this? Avoid the foods that made life worth living?

You wanted to be famous.

Yeah, but at what cost?

It's only a month. Suck it up.

I sighed in defeat.

It might not be hard to keep it a secret. Leslie and I rarely ate together as it was. I fixed her breakfast, then headed out, eating most of my meals at the restaurant. I'd just convince people I ate at the other location and sneak my meager meal when no one was looking. Aside from hating myself, and disappointing my grandparents, a diet was workable.

Yes. I'd humor Brock for the sake of the damn pictures, so he'd leave me alone. Starve for a while, then be done with it.

I rounded the kitchen island to the refrigerator, and for the first time in memory, I dreaded cooking. Without taking a bite, I knew my new breakfast was barely better than not eating at all.

Chapter 31

LESLIE

I'd been practicing yoga moves at home with Dot for six weeks to get ready for her first class back as an instructor. I had only a fraction of the flexibility and strength she'd honed over years. But I improved day by day, especially in my arms. And that was only possible because of the beginner modifications she demonstrated.

As we walked into the studio, her students clapped and swarmed around, giving her hugs and saying how glad they were to have her back. I lingered in the rear, my usual route to unobtrusive observation. That was how I noticed the crew of three women whispering to themselves and shooting nasty glances toward Dot's admirers.

I ambled over to listen.

"This is bullshit. How can they just switch instructors like this? I mean, look at her. She's as big as a house."

"If you have that much cellulite, you shouldn't be wearing spandex."

"They shouldn't MAKE spandex in that size. Christ, it's an abomination."

"Should we complain? Or stay for the laughs?"

"Ugh. You two can stay. I'm leaving."

A rail-thin blond passed me, her ponytail swaying like a windshield wiper against the yoga mat slung over her tense shoulder. Her companions looked torn. They'd obviously come to move their bodies. What difference did the shape of the instructor make?

They shrugged and sheepishly made their way out, but not before giving me a hard look up and down with a disgusted expression.

Good riddance.

I rolled out my borrowed mat and watched the room's hubbub reflected in the mirrored wall at the front of the room. Women moved around the studio in all manner of yoga outfits, including someone wearing an identical set to mine.

Hold up.

That's me.

My 5'4" frame had filled in, leaving me stronger and thicker as I stood with my legs hip distance apart. Speaking of hips, I had some. Along with an amazing rack.

No wonder Risto had been luxuriating in my boobs. I wanted to myself, despite being in public.

I migrated to the side of the room, where the mirrored walls joined in a corner. On closer inspection, all was not awesome. The spandex clung to my new curves and foreign physique. I'd always had a pear shape, and flesh gently bulged over where my elastic waistband rested at my waist. I'd been floating in such positivity that I expected the body housing my newfound confidence and vigor to be... smaller.

I ran a hand over my stomach. Mom raised me to believe that strength, beauty, and success required living in a lean frame. How was it possible for me to feel this good, yet look so lumpy?

Icy tingles shot down my back at a shocking realization.

The hostile glance I got from those bitchy yoga gals wasn't for Dot.

It was for me.

Anyone familiar with journalist Leslie Allen could certainly see the pounds I'd gained, courtesy of my closely monitored eating regimen over the last three months. The rest of it was muscle from my regular exercise, which included long walks twice daily with Pepper, plus home yoga. Old me would have been visualizing a smaller me, carving off fat like I was made of gray clay. Toxic thinking, for sure. New me was strong, slept well, and had enough energy for stupendous sex with my hunky man. I chit-chatted with strangers in the park, free of judgment about my body, or theirs, for that matter. That was another surprising development. I hadn't realized how much I had judged other people's weight in comparison to my own. Without all those warped expectations, I could respectfully engage, human to human.

The benefits of eating never failed to surprise. I wasn't cold all the time. My mind cleared and sharpened. I had more energy and sex drive. My skin and hair were glossier, and my nails no longer splintered. (How was that even possible?) My cravings for isolation and darkness lessened, and I enjoyed the warm glow of light in the evenings. (Well, except in bed with Risto). As my mood and body improved, I stopped my mouthwatering stares into trash bins. I had never eaten out of them, even at my worst. But damn it if I hadn't considered it on multiple occasions. These days, I devoured as much food as I wanted right off my plate.

Yes, in healing, I finally understood my worth, regardless of size. I deserved love and goodness, and that gift was priceless.

Food was medicine, joy, pleasure, and life all rolled into one, as Tasha said so often in our sessions. This version of me proved it.

I explored my body, fingering the softness beneath my skin.

This is how I should have been all along.

I was learning to love her.

I'd been in a supportive bubble the last few months. A cruel world lurked outside my door, waiting to pounce like a mob of rabid yoga gals. My articles and YouTube videos had been going well. The more I shared about my struggles, the more love I got from fans in return. Those voices countered Little Diana whenever she reared up to whisper negative thoughts in my ears. Risto and Dot stood right by my side, so much so that I'd stopped looking at my mom's threatening texts.

I knew better. But internalizing change down to the marrow of my bones would take time. I'd have to allow myself grace a little longer.

"Okay, class, let's get going," Dot shouted over the din of voices.

Those not already on their mats jogged back and sat.

Through the glass studio door, one of the nasty girls noiselessly ranted at the receptionist. The woman's accusing finger pointing toward our class. Without hearing her venomous words, her true self lay exposed. A venomous, ignorant person who probably resented me for not being hungry.

Huh.

Was part of her anger actually jealousy?

I could almost hear her Little Diana's voice ranting. *If I have to be this way, starve myself and take yoga classes when I'd rather be sleeping, why doesn't everyone? These fatties shouldn't be allowed to be happy and exist where I can see them? They're living reminders of my choices.*

A smile crept over my face.

I endured as a living reminder of my choices, emphasis on the living. Too many people with anorexia nervosa didn't make it.

But I would.

I strolled over to my purple mat and sat, feet together, knees flopped to the sides as far down as my muscles allowed. It wasn't about being perfect anymore. It was about showing up and trying. That I could do. This class was another first in a litany of firsts, and I yearned for more. To feel, to move, and finally to love the body I was in.

Chapter 32

LESLIE

After class, Dot stayed behind to hang out until her next one. No clue how she could manage another class, as my muscles could barely make the 3/4-mile walk back to her house. My damp yoga mat slung over my shoulder, feeling like a hundred pounds. But I'd finished the class, and that was another huge accomplishment.

As I walked, I registered a gray sedan creeping alongside me.

I turned as the driver lowered the passenger window.

"Mom? What the—"

"Get in."

"Wait, what? No, what are you..."

"I'm not asking again."

Two lithe women hopped out of her car and grabbed me by the shoulders.

"Have you gone mad?!"

"Stop struggling."

"No! Where are you taking me?" I tried to shove them away, but they clung fast, their bony fingers digging into my arms. Tired as I was, my attempts to resist were met by a firm shove into the back seat.

My mom floored the gas pedal before the car door was even closed, making me wonder if she'd done this maneuver before. Perhaps one of her sidekicks had been a prior victim.

I wiggled free from my captors, hugging myself. "Mom. Stop the car and let me out."

"Not until I get you somewhere safe. They'll deprogram all the bunk you've gotten into." She stopped at a red light and twisted to glare at me over her shoulder. "Look what they've done to you. You've gained, what, 40 pounds?"

I turned to the strawberry blond woman next to me. Her pale skin was slightly ashy and covered in the same fine hairs I recognized as a symptom of anorexia.

"Who are you and why did you let my mother trick you into kidnapping me?"

She pursed her lips. "I'm Janet, if you must know. Your poor mother has been broken up since you started ballooning on YouTube. She's right to want to get you well."

While under treatment, my weight was a closely guarded secret. From the new clothes I bought, it was impossible to hide that my size had increased to a number that would have had me cowering in the past.

The nasty glances in yoga class flashed to mind.

Living my life without a scale had been a blissful relief. Would everyone outside my family react as my mother had? I tightened my arms around my middle to conceal where my body pinched from sitting.

Not five minutes into our drive and a blanket of shame had already draped over me, its burden impossibly heavy. I carried it for years without noticing, but the oppressive darkness was impossible to ignore. This wasn't a life I wanted anymore. And yet the pull was so strong. So familiar.

Was she right? Were the last months a warped fantasy?

"This is for your own good," Mom snapped.

"C'mon, please. Pull over and let me out."

Rather than slow, she floored the gas pedal, slamming me and her co-conspirators against the back seat.

"This is so upsetting. You were perfectly fine before you got here!" Mom screamed at me via the rearview mirror.

"I was sick. And so are you. What the hell are you thinking? Grabbing me off the street?"

"You don't want to be this way. You'll be miserable and alone and die."

You mean like I was before?

"It's not too late to get you well."

This I'd like to see. Her? Get me well? She was the reason I'd lived my entire life with an undiagnosed eating disorder. Why my organs had nearly shut down. Her mania was why I stopped responding to her texts weeks ago.

But her rant got me wondering about one thing. My care team never mentioned the end goal for me. Where would my refeeding lead, and how would I know if we'd gone too far? I'd never admit these doubts to my mom. For that I needed Tasha and the doctors. I had to get away.

Without thinking, I lunged for the door handle, stretching across sidekick number two. I wrestled with the gray-haired woman, whose locks were so long I nearly got tangled in them while struggling for supremacy. Janet grabbed me around the neck from behind, cutting off my air and forcing me to let go of the door to fight for breath.

"Janet, good God! Don't choke her!" Mom screamed, watching us instead of the road. A horn blared, and Mom swerved right to avoid an oncoming car. The move slammed Janet into the side window and off me.

I coughed, gasping for air, while my gray-haired nemesis pushed me off her.

"I didn't sign up to die!" Janet spat at my mother. "Watch the damn road!"

"Fool. You could have killed her," Mom yelled back. "We're here to save her, not end her life."

Throat tender to the touch from being choked, I sat mute, recovering from our battle and wondering where they were taking me. Of all the risky situations I'd been in, not once had I ever been attacked as violently as by my mother's gang.

After another 20 minutes, the car slowed and turned into the driveway of a two-story colonial home. The lights were on inside, and the moment we cut the engine, a woman holding a clipboard stepped out through the screen door. She wore office attire—black slacks, a blouse, and a blue blazer.

I don't like the look of this.

My captors exited the car, leaving the doors ajar for me to follow. I had half a mind to lock myself in and lean on the horn until a neighbor rescued me.

My phone!

I slipped it out of my back pocket, snapped a quick picture of the home, which had the street address and house number affixed to the porch post in black script letters. I texted it to my chat thread with Dot and Gabby:

Me: My mom grabbed me off the street. Help!

Just as I pressed Send, Mom snatched my phone away and smashed it on the paved driveway.

"God damn it," she whispered. "Why do you always have to do things the hard way? Quit fighting and get inside."

I slid out of the back seat, tugging my torn shirt into place as I ascended the steps.

"Hello, Ms. Allen. My name is Phoebe Lansen, Director of the Wellness and Rejuvenation Center. Your mother hired me to work with you. She's concerned about your welfare. And after watching your videos, I understand why."

"I was dragged here. Against my will," I said through gritted teeth.

"That may well be. But let's go inside. What we have to say might change your mind."

My mom flicked her head for me to listen. But all I could think of was an imaginary SWAT team descending, guns drawn to whisk me to safety.

I crossed my arms, looking away.

Phoebe chuckled. "Oh, come now. There's nothing to fear. We're all friends here. We've gathered to help you through your current crisis so you can reach the other side. Many clients are referred by family." She entered and bade me follow.

This time I did.

The Victorian house was unassuming. Lace curtains, upholstered furniture with carved mahogany legs in the entryway, and the living room beyond. You'd never know it wasn't a private home, except for the stern-looking people sitting on folding chairs in a circle. An empty chair sat awaiting a body, and I didn't have to guess whose name was on it.

"Before we join the others, let's get you checked in." Phoebe ushered me into a small room and closed the door. There, she took my height, blood pressure (high—shocker), pulse (also high), and stepped me onto a medical scale. Instinctively, I turned backward, and Phoebe laughed.

"Oh, is that how they hide the truth from you? Turn around. We want all our patients to be active participants in their care."

She adjusted the counterweights, and I squeezed my eyes shut to avoid looking. She clicked the block so many notches to the right, my resolve evaporated. I peeked, stunned by the scale's verdict. I swallowed hard. She saw my throat bob and pounced.

"See? Knowing your weight is the first step to addressing your problem."

"I have an eating disorder. My problem is already being treated, under close medical supervision," I said, shocked that my voice lacked a whiff of conviction.

Phoebe pressed her lips together, saying nothing, before sighing

"Leslie. You're a beautiful, talented woman who's gone off the rails. Your mother only wants what's best for you. And your career."

That got my attention.

She took a few pictures of me, then opened the door. I followed her to join the others. Phoebe ushered me to the vacant seat and stood to address everyone.

"Thanks for gathering today to welcome Leslie. Dear, your mother is concerned that you are spiraling and need a steady hand to right the ship. That's where we come in. Our center helps people overcome poor habits with food. By following our proven system with sensible meals, nutritious shakes, and dietary supplements, clients lose tens of pounds in a matter of weeks."

One by one, each participant lifted their intake photo and proudly proclaimed their weight loss. Applause rounded the room, again and again.

15 pounds.

47 pounds.

150 pounds.

Speakers were barely recognizable from the images they held beneath their beaming faces. The photos displayed dejected, slumping people living in larger bodies than they had now. Meanwhile, my journey over the last few months had transformed me from the After photo to the Before. Yet my care team cheered me every step of the way. So much so, my mother felt compelled to grab me off the street to reverse the damage.

These two realities couldn't coexist.

Was I a walking tragedy then or now?

The second researcher I spoke to popped to mind. The one who took each point Professor Hawley had said and tossed it in a trash heap. He'd lost a ton of weight and committed his life to staying slim. Exactly what Mom and Phoebe thought best. Their view contradicted the sober warnings from my care team, who declared me on a dangerous path to an early grave. And they had the test results to prove it.

Sixty eyes stared at me. For once, I had nothing to say.

Tears of confusion streaked down my face. My chest heaved as my pulse thumped wildly in my ears. It was all so fucked up.

"I... I... I can't do this..."

I ran out of the room and down the hall. My head whipped side to side, searching for a bathroom. Passing through the last door on the right, I slammed it closed, locked it, and sat on the toilet lid, rocking.

Who to believe?

Two pathways stretched before me.

One led to Risto, Dot, and the happiness I'd experienced over the prior three months.

But that ignored the cold reality Little Diana had warned me about. The one I wanted to pretend didn't exist. It finally arrived in spectacular fashion, tossed me in a car, and choked me for good measure. People like my mother viewed fat as wrong and repulsive. Those who made peace with their bodies were lazy, undisciplined, weak, and looking for any excuse to avoid the rigor of dieting.

Which was right?

"Leslie, please. Come out of the bathroom this instant. Phoebe and her staff only want to help," Mom said.

"You shoved me in the back of a car. Forgive me if I don't trust you," I yelled through the closed door.

"You've got to know I only want what's best for you. This program shows marvelous results. You can lose the weight and be right as rain before your new job starts next month. There's time to turn back the clock on all the damage you've done to yourself."

She slid a photo under the door. What she hoped was my "Before" picture. Dead eyes stared blankly, already resigned. Hair mussed, clothes torn, with faint bruising visible around my neck.

It was as if the hurt from all my years of disordered eating was finally noticeable on the outside. The pain of hiding. The sorrow of lost relationships. The relentless fear. Despite Mom's accusations and fears, I'd never felt more free or more... happy.

Yes, I'd been happy lately.

The conversation with Dot on my first day in town came flooding back.

"Are you happy? Do you ever pause long enough to find out?" Dot had asked.

"No, I can't say I am. But maybe not everyone is meant to be happy. Maybe people like me have to settle for being okay."

The picture loomed on the floor, projecting the misery of my former self. The emotional truth of another time. Another me. A woman I never wanted to be again. Realization hit me like a truck. This whole stunt wasn't about me at all. Healing myself threatened Mom's entire worldview. It meant I was sick. And if that was the case, what did that mean for her? It was far easier for her to stuff me back into the hamster wheel than face her own demons.

Well, fuck that.

I flung the bathroom door open. "You and me, Mom, we're sick. We have eating disorders. I've chosen to get help. You're a grown woman and can make your own decisions. Enjoy your juice cleanses, rabid exercise routines, and nine gallons of water a day to chase away the hunger. But that's not how I want to live."

"Les—"

"I'm not finished. I've been getting treatment from a nutritionist, a doctor, and a psychiatrist." I ticked off the roles on my fingers. "My focus is on healing the damage I've done to my body, unlearning all the lies you've fed me instead of food. I was so close to organ failure, they almost admitted me to the hospital. Now that I'm beginning to find my way, you want me to book a stay in the paradise of an early grave? No. No more."

I stepped around her and her gaping mouth and headed for the front door.

"Leslie. Stop. You're making a huge mistake."

"No. My mistake was not getting help sooner." I paused in the doorway, where the group session was in full swing. I considered saying something to them. To help them break free of their own bonds, but they'd need to find their own path. Hopefully, me publicly stepping forward as I had would start some overdue conversations.

The screeching of car brakes from outside grabbed my attention. I strode to the screen door to see Dot's car parked crookedly at the curb. Gabby jumped out.

My SWAT team had finally arrived.

The two women hurried to the porch steps as I stepped out.

"Are you alright?" Gabby wrapped me in my arms, her silky blouse caressing me through the gaping tears in my shirt. Goodness knows what other wounds I'd have from this ordeal.

Dot stormed up to my mom, who had joined us. "You are a twisted, evil woman. Look what you've done to your daughter! Thanks to you, she almost died. Did you realize that? You and your—!"

I rested a hand on Dot's shoulder. "Let's just go."

Dot turned to cradle my head in her hands. "Are you hurt? Two women from class saw you get shoved into a car and came running back. The moment they mentioned a New Mexico license plate, I guessed what happened. Then your text arrived."

She flashed a death stare at my mom.

"You come near this girl again, and I'll call the police myself. In fact..." Dot turned to me. "Do you want to press charges against these people for what they've done?"

I looked over at the trio. My mother, waif thin and swaying. Likely from over-exertion. The other two sat on a wicker bench, fretting with their hands. A pathetic lot, by any measure. Ms. Wellness was nowhere in sight, proving she was the only bright one in the bunch.

"Nah. But, Mom," I called over. "I'll expect you to send money to replace my broken phone and torn clothes. And pay for a shit-ton of groceries."

Linking arms with my aunt and cousin, I walked to the car. My mother stood alone, clinging to her toxic beliefs as if they had the power to save her.

Chapter 33

RISTO

Two weeks into Brock's diet was the worst time for me to prepare my new menu for Silas. Giddy, he'd ambushed Ruben at a cocktail party and insisted on an "off the record" sampling of what would become the centerpiece of Boricua New York.

When I last cooked these dishes, I fizzed with the joy and creativity of a child on Christmas morning. Today, I felt flat and angry. I'd snapped at Jose and Freddie without mercy, sending them fleeing out the door for their midday break. Intoxicating scents filled the kitchen in their place, forcing me to put on music so my guest wouldn't hear the roar of my empty stomach.

Maybe the smooth jazz would take the edge off my mood before Silas arrived.

Lifting the lid off the saffron broth, I stirred, steamy visions emerging in my mind. First, I slurped the pot dry, then devoured the pasta bobbing merrily in the boiling water nearby. I returned to preparing a light salad. I had eaten a version of it earlier, with some pan-seared fish, the memories of it having to suffice, given that I'd already gone off-menu by skipping the lemon and having the vinaigrette dressing I'd made for Silas. I had to taste the dish. Even dishes I had prepared a thousand times had to be sampled, so the balance and seasoning landed just right. New menu items, all the more. My instincts and muscle memory for pouring and spicing had yet to take over. Jose did the honors during today's lunch service, but it'd be hard for me to avoid these "unscheduled snacks" while working as an active chef.

Of course!

Now that I thought of it, Chase Patel, my culinary school classmate, had looked way leaner when I'd watched him on television. There might be a darker, hungrier reason behind his absence from the kitchen.

"Chef Zaldo?!" Silas called from the dining room.

"In here!" I answered.

A moment later, a cheery Silas entered, sporting a fresh tan. "Ahh! This kitchen smells like a dream!"

I swelled with pride.

Everything would be okay. As long as the food hit the spot, nobody cared if the chef was tired, or hungry, or pissed off, or stressed beyond measure. All that mattered was what was on the plate, or in the case of Silas' first menu item, a small appetizer medley.

He sat at the side table I'd prepared for him, his eager palms scratching their approval as they rubbed together.

I plated his first course, an appetizer of three items, including the sea urchin dish with smoked salt. I proudly set it before him.

His brows furrowed, but he recovered and pressed a closemouthed smile before digging in.

Silas sampled from the dishes, finishing none, then reclined in his seat.

"I'm ready for the next course," he said without making eye contact.

A dagger pierced my heart.

No moans of pleasure.

No acclaim.

Just "next course."

I hurried back with my arroz con pollo raviolis in a saffron broth. This garnered a confused look before he dipped his spoon in.

His eyes closed behind his fogged lenses. Silas nodded as he went for another bite, then another.

I had him.

As with the appetizer, he sat back before finishing and gestured for me to clear.

What the hell was happening?

Dish after dish continued the same way until I served my last dessert and took a seat across from him.

"Thank you for sharing your new menu." His voice was stiff and devoid of any enthusiasm. "Can I speak frankly?"

"Please. Yes," I said.

"The food was tasty, without question. But I could have it at any restaurant in New York. It's not special. It's not unique. And, I fear, won't lead to the success I've encouraged you to expect."

I covered my mouth in shock. How could he reject a menu that had my investors leaping to their feet in a standing ovation? Steve called it a revelation and demanded we go with it, over Ruben's protests.

Ruben. He'd been the one person at the table not wowed by the modern dishes. I'd overlooked his response, given how mesmerized he was by the overall experience. Given Silas' reaction, my menu was obviously not the slam dunk win I'd expected.

I met his dejected stare. "What's missing?"

He sat pensively, though he didn't seem to be collecting his thoughts. It was more him deciding whether to reveal his true opinion.

Finally, he spoke. "Soul. It's missing soul."

I huffed a laugh. "You think this meal is soulless? Fantastic."

"There's skill, yes, but no joy. No identifiable culture. Nothing to trigger memories and love and experiences that we each bring to the dining experience. The flavors were delightful, and the technique, extraordinary. But I tasted the work when I wanted to enjoy the emotional essence of your usual menu."

I hated that word. "Usual." Foodies wouldn't pack my tables for ordinary meals.

"My menu is good enough for small-town Pennsylvania. New York demands more. I don't want to get lost in the shuffle. I didn't need to go to culinary school to make my grandma's food. She taught me that when I was ten."

"Are you planning a gallery installation or a restaurant? Some of the best meals I've eaten around the world were modest ones prepared by self-taught cooks," Silas said.

Cooks. There, he said it. I wasn't a cook, I was a chef, and there was a huge difference. To me, and for the career I hoped to build. No one asked a cook to sit on a television panel or at a food festival. If I showed up in New York—the humble brown boy I'd been up to now—I'd get eaten alive. I wouldn't open a new restaurant only to have my food called pedestrian. Not happening.

The menu might need work, but I wasn't giving up yet. Not by a long shot.

"Thanks for stopping by today. I appreciate the feedback." I rose, expecting Silas to stand. But he remained sitting, staring at me with an expression I couldn't place.

It reminded me of my elementary school science teacher, Mr. McKinsey. I was a quiet kid, struggling with my lessons after my parents passed. He knew my dad worked in a restaurant, so my teacher taught me the chemistry behind cooking. How temperature impacted proteins and liquids. How it caramelized sugars and shrank some muscles tight and loosened others. I'd completely forgotten how much that man rekindled my fascination with food after my father died. I got the sense Silas was about to do the same.

"No one ever tells you no, do they?" he asked. "Says try again, go do better?"

I crossed my arms. *Where was he going with this?*

"Like most successful men, you have a chip on your shoulder. Probably afraid you don't measure up as you are. That you need to prove something. But I didn't fight for you to get on that *Philadelphia Metro* cover because I thought you lacked talent. This meal was very good for most chefs. It just wasn't good enough for you because you were nowhere on the plate."

"That whole menu was me!" I yelled. "Everything on it, I dreamed up in my head. Isn't that what diners want?"

Silas stood. "No, my dear Chef Zaldo. They don't want what's in your head. They want what's in theirs."

He dropped his napkin on the table, bowed, and left.

An hour later, I sat slack-jawed next to the remnants of Silas' half-eaten meal. What the hell did he mean by diners wanting what was in their own heads? How was I supposed to know what was in their heads when I couldn't decipher what was in my own? It was ludicrous.

The backdoor hinges squeaked, and Jose walked into my disaster of a kitchen.

"Shit, mijo. What happened?"

"He hated it. Said it was food he could eat anywhere."

Jose grabbed my abandoned knives and cooking utensils, dropped them into the wash basin, and began filling it with soapy water. "Not for nothing, but I told you that food was bullshit."

My head jerked up. He had. But I didn't listen.

"What would you change?"

"I'd drop all the gastronomy crap, be us. Be Boricua. People drive hours to get here and wait weeks for reservations. Yet you seem to think we're not good enough as we are."

That was where he was wrong. My restaurant rocked. I was simply tired of cooking other people's food. Tasty dishes, yes. But anyone could find similar recipes on a Goya beans label. I wanted more, and I thought diners did too.

Speaking of more, my wristwatch vibrated, signaling it was snack time.

I strode into the walk-in fridge and grabbed a tangy Braeburn apple from a produce bin.

Tossing it in the air, I walked to the sink to rinse it next to where Jose washed my dirty dishes. He eyed the fruit, then me, with suspicion.

"What gives? You never eat in the afternoons?"

"Nothing. I'm just having a snack."

"You're acting weird today. Sulky one moment and a total asshole the next." Jose transferred dishes between the wash, rinse, and sanitize sinks before resting items in the drying rack.

"Yeah. I'm fine." I bit the apple, then aggressively tore away a bite that snapped the fruit in two.

He raised his eyebrows but let me be to join in the cleaning.

A short while later, my phone rang from my breast pocket.

Dot sounded frantic.

"It's Leslie. Come home. Fast."

Chapter 34

LESLIE

The second Dot drove away from my mom, I crumbled in Gabby's arms in the backseat. As intense as my mother had been over the years, never could I imagine she'd do something like this. Force me into the back of a car with strange women assaulting me?

"Let me see your neck," Gabby said, gently lifting my chin for a better look. She tapped Dot's shoulder. "Should we take her to the hospital to be checked out? She's all bruised."

Dot kept her eyes on the road. "Let's get her home and washed up and then Leslie can decide what she wants. Are you hurt anywhere else besides your neck?"

It was hard to tell what hurt from my backseat wrestling match and what Dot inflicted during her yoga class. "I don't think so. Maybe some random bruises here and there from them mauling me. I mean, where did she find two women who would do such a thing? Jump a friend's daughter and strangle her?"

"For all we know, she hired them. Your mom never had many friends, let alone ones willing to drive up from New Mexico for a stunt like this."

That was far worse, but it was true that my mom rarely mentioned whom she spent time with the few times we were on the phone and not talking about my diet regimen. Which wasn't too often. She once mentioned a boyfriend, but for all I knew, he was out of the picture.

I leaned into Gabby's shoulder and closed my eyes. Suddenly my body felt leaden. All I wanted was a hot soak in Risto's bathtub.

Dot pulled into her driveway, and the two of them accompanied me next door to Risto's house.

"Did anyone call him?" I asked.

"I'll do that right now," Dot said. "Gabby, why don't you help her get a bath going?"

I followed my cousin up to Risto's bedroom. She deposited me to undress and went to the bathroom. The tub faucet splashed to life, then quieted as the water filled. Cabinet doors opened and closed.

"Aha! I knew it." She stepped into the doorway to wiggle a bottle of lavender luxury. "Guess you're in luck. Risto once mentioned taking a bubble bath, turned beet red, and never spoke of it again."

That man is full of surprises.

I stretched to lift my yoga shirt over my head, tangling myself in the gaping tears. Guess those women did more damage than I thought.

"Gabs, can you help me get this off?"

My cousin pulled the bathroom door closed to detangle me from my top.

She lifted it off and gasped. "¡Dios mio! I'm sorry, but you've got to press charges."

"That bad?" I asked, not wanting to look.

But she spun me around to face the wall mirror over Risto's dresser.

My neck was one deep red blotch, and my shoulders and upper arms bore finger imprints from where the women had grabbed me. There were random other bruises on my torso. Alongside those were the fuller belly, rounded hips, and curvy Molina ass my mother hated.

A chilling thought emerged. The world may not like the new me any more than my mom did. But I had to be okay with that. People embraced me before and I was still miserable. It wasn't until I loved myself that I began to live.

"Do you mind?" Gabby held up her cell phone. "We should probably document your injuries. Just in case."

I nodded, and she moved me near the window for better light. I twirled to help her capture every angle.

"I'm so sorry it came to this," she said, giving me a hug. Her warm tears fell onto my bare shoulders.

"Gabs?"

"Hmm?"

"You might want to check the bath before it overflows…"

"Oh, shoot!" She dashed into the bathroom, where a mountain of suds crested over the tub edge. "Guess I put too much in!"

I followed. We stared at the tower of bubbles, then each other, and burst out laughing.

Ten minutes later, all the stress had melted away, the hot water caressing the day's tense events out of my muscles. Gabby sat on the closed toilet seat, the two of us chatting about all the absurd things my mom had done over the years. Dot joined in, and bath time became a cathartic purging of Diana Allen from my mind, my psyche, and my heart.

Little Diana drowned today too. She gurgled for mercy before I sloshed her down the overflow drain, then blocked her escape with a pruned toe. A foreign lightness came over me, from being in my body alone. The thoughts were mine, and the hopes were too. I luxuriated over my skin, sliding my hands over its curves and newfound muscles. The bruises would heal. Just like the rest of me.

"Leslie? Leslie!" Risto's panicked voice boomed from downstairs.

"Up here! In the bathroom!" Dot yelled.

Risto thundered up the stairs, arriving breathless as he braced himself in the doorway. "What happened?"

In our giddiness, we burst out laughing.

"Diana happened, that's what," Gabby said, barely able to contain herself.

By the time Risto got the full story, my water grew tepid. Gabby and Dot excused themselves. Gabby to head home, while Dot figured we'd want some privacy for the big reveal. I'd been hiding my wounds under collapsing bubbles.

The second I stood in the tub, Risto fell apart.

"Jesus, Leslie! It's... you're..."

"I'm okay now. It looks worse than it feels."

"How could she do this!?"

My body glistened with wetness, which soaked his clothes the moment he wrapped me in his arms. I clung to him as he guided me out of the tub, then blotted me dry with a fluffy towel. Not since childhood had I been so carefully tended. Risto's face lined with worry and concentration as he worked, lifting my elbows to blot every patch of moisture off my skin. His tenderness was exactly what my broken soul needed.

When finished, he planted a whisper-light kiss on my lips. "Why don't you get dressed, and I'll make you some dinner."

"You're not staying?"

"Huh?" he asked.

"You said, make me some dinner. Are you not eating?"

Risto flustered. "I'm, I didn't mean...."

"Jose and Freddie can cover for you tonight, don't you think? That's what you meant? Going back to the restaurant?"

He exhaled, hugging me again. "Of course, yes. Make *us* dinner."

We exited the bathroom, the bedroom's air conditioning rippling goosebumps across my skin. Risto headed downstairs, where the comforting sounds of kitchen activity filtered up the stairs. A short while later, I joined him and set the table for two, lighting the candle tapers that stood at attention in their wrought iron holders.

The wicks crackled in objection, dancing shadows around the space. I sat to enjoy the view of Risto making magic with his hands.

"What are we having?" I called over.

"Pan-seared fish and some greens. I have leftover rice and beans too, if you want."

I was about to say, *I'd never turn down rice and beans,* but that wasn't true. For years, I declined, regretting it every time. Watching others eat, I wished to be like them, yet feared the consequences more. Ease settled over me, now free from Little Diana's pre-meal poison. The only voice that came was mine. "I'd love some rice and beans. Thanks."

Moments later, he pinched greens out of the pan with tongs and swirled them into hubs on two plates. A filet of salmon leaned against each, its edges golden and crispy. Risto returned to snatch a bowl of rice and beans, which he placed in front of me on the table.

"Aren't we sharing?" I slid it between us.

"Not in the mood tonight." He shifted it away, into my plate's orbit.

"Suit yourself!" I chirped, digging my fork into the source of the briny aromas. Peppery with a hint of garlic, the salmon was just what the doctor ordered.

"This is heaven. Thank you."

I leaned in and we shared a luxurious kiss. Warm and wet, the zing awakened my longing. But I'd need energy for what I had planned for that man. We refocused on our plates and ate in silence, the soft music Risto had playing finally registering.

I sighed, my eyes dipping closed to take it all in. Bruised as I was, I'd never felt so at peace or so totally nourished. Heart, mind, and soul.

Chapter 35

Leslie

A week later my bruises had faded, but there was no doubt my mom's insults left a mark. I began sneaking peeks in mirrors, skipping meals, and increasing the length of my dog walks with Pepper. After two weeks, I could tell the pace of my weight gain had slowed, and it was impossible to suppress the thrill that had fueled me for decades. Unable to help myself, I wandered into a local gym, past the receptionist, and straight to the locker room scale. Old me would have barfed in my mouth at the number, but I hadn't gained nearly as much as expected from when the woman weighed me at the "wellness center."

That precious secret I held close. No one in my life would understand how hard it was to know something was logically right, yet still reject it.

The moment I stepped on the scale at my next hospital check-in, the jig was up.

Tasha peered over my shoulder, then shot me a questioning glance. "How have you been since the ordeal with your mother?"

"Okay. Good." I stared straight ahead, avoiding her face.

She wasn't buying it.

"That's got to be the shortest answer you've ever given." Tasha stepped toward the doorway, and I knew to follow her into her office. She closed the door gently behind us and gestured to a seat.

Opening a drawer, she slipped out a blank sheet and a pen. "I noticed you stopped using the meal planner app, so why don't you write down everything you ate yesterday and so far today?"

Shit. I totally forgot about the damn app. If I had my head right, I'd have logged fake meals. Without that buffer, my nonexistent weight gain was suspicious as hell. Especially since I'd gained at a steady clip until today. My hands fumbled in my lap.

"Go ahead," she prodded.

I lifted the pen and wrote "coffee with cream and sugar" for yesterday's breakfast. Risto dashed out in the morning without eating, saying he'd grab a bite at the restaurant. Full after the coffee, I didn't eat anything until a small afternoon snack with Dot. I added "banana" and left the rest of the page blank. I'd planned to eat during my shift at Boricua, but Dot decided to go in instead, leaving me solo at what should have been a mealtime. Today, I'd had a miniature bowl of wheat flakes and a few blueberries, no milk. I slapped the pen down and crossed my arms.

"What has made you want to restrict again?" Tasha asked.

"Oh, I don't know. The reality of the outside world? When I'm here with you and my aunt, everything is fine. Once I step back into my life, they'll take a look at me and wonder what the hell happened. It's already started."

A nasty string of texts from Kaelen Reed flashed into my mind.

"And?" Tasha asked.

"Colleagues will sneer at me or laugh. It's just... I saw my weight and panicked."

How stupid of me to get triggered over a bathroom scale! A square of metal and springs had complete power over me, like a holy oracle.

"Since you've gone back to restricting, how do you feel?" she asked.

"Emotionally better, physically worse. Actually, that's not true. I'm less afraid of outside criticism, but also more afraid of what would happen if my family found out. I'm not sleeping as well and I drag when trying to do any physical activity. It sounds awful when I say it out loud, but I haven't had control over much lately and it thrilled me to own something."

"So you own your disordered eating?"

"No. Yes. Well, no, I hadn't quite thought of it that way," I admitted.

Tasha and I talked things through, and I agreed to go back to using the meal planner app and promised to stay away from scales. Risto and I were heading out for a two-day trip to Manhattan for Risto's restaurant expansion, and I was thrilled about the change of scenery. We'd scout a few restaurants and check out executive chefs he might want to poach. He'd also look at a few locations under consideration for his new venture.

Tasha loved the idea, and her positivity was the reset I needed to get my mind right. I committed to enjoying myself and embracing opportunities to savor the amazing food I'd be eating. Since we planned to stay at my apartment, I'd bring some groceries to stock the fridge and avoid weighing myself. To be safe, I texted Rebecca and asked her to sneak over to my place and remove the scale.

I hated myself for regressing. But Tasha said after my ordeal, she'd have been more surprised if I hadn't slipped. As I headed home to pack, a lightness settled over me that I'd missed since that day after yoga.

Suitcase open on our bed, I was midway through folding one of the flouncy dresses I'd been wearing lately when my cell chimed. Viraj's face filled the screen as I answered.

"How are you?" I said.

"We may have a problem with the network. They want a meeting. I hope you don't mind. I mentioned you'd be in town. They've scheduled a face-to-face for tomorrow afternoon."

My stomach dropped. While chronicling my journey on YouTube, the support had been overwhelming. But there was a growing percentage of nasty comments posted under my videos, accusing me of "letting myself go" and being "disgusting." Kaelen Reed's texts were especially cruel.

Until my recent setback, I had observed my body with amazement as it transformed. Gone were my gaunt cheeks and gray pallor, replaced by sparkling eyes and luxurious hair with an impossibly silky texture.

But my critics saw none of that in my videos, nor the energy I displayed, which enabled me to answer viewer comments live for over two hours without wilting.

Their sole focus was commenting on my weight, perpetuating the darkness that shadowed me for far so long.

I sighed. "Need I ask why they want to meet?"

"Les, I think they're spooked with the fervor you've brought to this story. And how it's changed your appearance."

"They should be worried. This whole food-diet-industry thing is the most corrupt machine I've ever investigated. They wield massive power over our culture and lives at a scale that's hard to comprehend. I have all the data at my fingertips and still marvel at the absurdity of it all. People must hear about it so they can make informed choices."

Viraj pinched his brow with his free hand. "I get you. But look at it from their side. They think you're mentally unwell—"

"I was. Before. They never cared when I was starving myself. Now that life is coursing through my veins and I'm recovering, they've decided to care about my health? This is bullshit."

I paced to my underwear drawer, grabbed a handful, and stuffed the wad into my suitcase. I then slammed the hard-sided lid almost closed. Cradling the phone between my neck and shoulder, I wrestled with the zipper, straining to get the teeth to match up.

Then a horrible idea struck.

"Shit!"

"What?" Viraj looked worried.

"I have nothing to wear to meet them. My old clothes will be too small."

"Buy something new. It's New York."

"Yeah. Right. I forgot." I huffed relief. "Not much shopping out here."

I took the meeting information down. The timing forced me to miss Risto's restaurant site tour, but it couldn't be helped. He wanted me there for moral support and to share his exciting moment. Meanwhile, I wished he could come with me. Walking into the network would be no picnic. While I was hiding out here healing, the rest of the world saw a woman in crisis. They looked at me and projected the same negative stereotypes that my mom spouted for decades.

Fat.

Lazy.

Undisciplined.

Soft.

Mentally weak.

Unprofessional.

What a fucking insult. The truth was 180 degrees opposite. I was smarter, stronger, and happier than I'd ever been. But they wanted the old me. Well, too fucking bad. She was gone, and I was fighting hard to ensure she never came back. And they'd better watch out because the new me was an even bigger force to be reckoned with.

After an amazing dinner at a restaurant in the Meatpacking District, Risto and I strolled the short walk to my apartment. Hand in hand, our footfalls echoed on the dark sidewalks and cobblestone streets.

I'd missed this.

The city sounds humming around us as we wordlessly melded with our surroundings.

Then Risto stopped short, tugging me into his arms. "I love you, you know."

"I love you too." I lifted onto my tiptoes to reach his mouth, the tang of after-dinner port dancing on his lips. "It's great to see you so relaxed. There's a lot riding on your shoulders."

"And yours too." His mood darkened, and we resumed walking.

"What did you think of the chef?" I asked. "You looked excited when the food arrived, but you didn't eat much. Was he not as good as you thought?"

Risto startled. The glossy whites of his wide eyes shined like two beacons in the shadows.

"Um. No. Not at all. He was better than I'd hoped. I guess… my mind was wandering to restaurant planning, and I forgot to eat."

Forgot to eat?

What the hell?

Warning bells blared in my head. Of all the lies I'd told to avoid meals, "I forgot to eat" was chief among them.

His profile silhouetted against the streetlight overhead. In recent weeks, it'd become more angular, and I noticed he'd taken to wearing a belt on his loosening pants. I didn't want to start an argument, or manufacture food disorders everywhere, simply because I had one. But if he was doing this on purpose, we needed to talk about it.

"Sweetie, you seem to forget meals a lot lately. You stopped cooking breakfast before work, then skip eating at the restaurant. Jose keeps dropping off your uneaten dinner at the house. Take it from a pro: It's not a good habit. Jose is worried. Is there something you're not telling me?"

He pulled my hand to his smiling lips. "Of course not. I'm fine. Really. I've just got a lot on my mind."

"Promise?"

"Yeah."

He held me close and devoured me with his mouth, spiking my desire sky high and evaporating any concern I had for him. We rushed the last few blocks home and were barely past the closed door when we each tore at the other's clothes in search of skin.

Risto hiked me up, and I circled him with my legs as he bit at my bra strap with his teeth. We turned toward the staircase, and he set me down on the second step. I swallowed my surprise at not being tossed over his shoulder and carried upstairs, as he so often did at home. Now that I think of it, he hadn't hauled me up in weeks. I forced a closemouthed smile and climbed up. Instead of the bedroom, I led him to my living room so we could make love beneath the darkened Manhattan skyline. A thousand twinkling buildings were our only sources of light.

Risto dropped to his knees on the carpet, tenderly kissing my tummy with his pillowy lips as I lay on the floor. I'd grown to appreciate my newfound curves, but he relished them, caressing my contours like I was a Grecian goddess. Squeezing my ass and using it to pull us closer together as his breath tickled the skin around my navel.

He inhaled deeply, hissing a reluctant release. "I dreamed of this scent for years. Now I have it every day. How did I get so lucky?"

I giggled, tangling my hands in his wavy brown hair, his broad shoulders highlighted by the ambient light. I never felt more safe and loved than when I was with Risto. He was like a cozy warm blanket after a night of sleep that I wanted to wrap around me.

And never let go.

Was that what love was? A hug that stayed with you long after the embrace ended? A safe place to nestle when the world got to be too much? Where it could be just the two of you because your lover understood you better than you understood yourself? When we were together making love, our connection exploded into something more. Our barest selves fused into a pulsing orb of light that was pure peace and love and sensation.

I needed that.

Now.

I shifted to sit on the coffee table and cupped his chin in my hands so I could devour his mouth. My legs wrapped around his torso and the rock hardness straining against his pants. He hit my sweet spot through my panties, making me arch into him.

"Oh, you like that, do you?"

"Mmmm," was all I could manage.

He ground into me like the devil he was, sending me gasping into his arms. He laid me on the coffee table so he could peel off my panties. Between my legs, his warm, wet tongue went to work, sucking pleasure out of me as if he had a straw. My pulse quickened, tension cresting until my breath froze in eager anticipation.

I tangled my hands in my hair, seeking relief from his pleasure torment. "Risto, I can't take... Please..."

A kiss to my inner thigh was his only response, before intensifying his pleasuring, driving me wild, until...

"Oh my—!" Tingles rippled across my skin in a soundless song. Every pore was alive and fizzing with life. Transported, I floated on a blissful river of satisfaction, bobbing on waves without end. And just when I thought he was done, he filled me with a deep thrust.

"Holy fuck!" Ecstasy jolted through me, so intense I nearly passed out.

Risto pulled me upright into his hungry kiss.

"I feel pretty godly right now," he moaned, holding me up while ramming into me with a ferocity I'd never experienced but would crave forevermore.

My arms draped around his shoulders as we fucked. That's what this was. Raw and nasty, and I never wanted it to end.

Pleasure liquefied my bones, yet Risto held fast, driving into me with determination. His breaths grew shallow as his muscles stiffened until...

"Arghhhhh!" he yelled, throbbing the release I could no longer muster.

Meanwhile, I was a pile of mush in his arms.

His muscles flexed under my fingers, stiff, then softened as he recovered. Then Risto shifted us onto the carpet.

We lay there panting, a tangle of limbs, the dark room a blur through my droopy lids.

He planted a kiss on my forehead and drew me in.

"That should be illegal," I exhaled in a breathy whisper.

"It probably is, somewhere."

Immobile, our breathing gradually synchronized as sleep took hold. Dreamland approached, then receded as Risto jostled to standing. He offered me a hand.

"Let's get to bed. We both have big days tomorrow."

I rose, slapping my feet in protest as he steered me across the wooden floor to my bedroom. I wanted no part of tomorrow. Tomorrow meant going to the network. Tomorrow Risto would tour real estate. Tomorrow, everything would change.

We crawled between the sheets and assumed our snuggle position at the center. Despite our passion, his skin seemed oddly chilly. I tossed a blanket over us both and drifted back to dreamland, hoping tomorrow would never come.

Chapter 36

LESLIE

"**N**othing fits!" I screamed at Risto from my spot in front of the closet. My trusty white blouses, blazers, and slacks hung limp and useless on their hangers. In frustration, I grabbed the camel jacket Kaelen Reed hated and held it up to myself in the mirror.

Had I really worn this three months ago?

I stretched out my arm, gripping the fabric with my palm. Its width was about the same as the empty sleeve.

Yeah, not happening.

I mourned for my clothes. They gave me a professional style, in front of and behind the camera. They kept me warm despite the frigid television studio temperatures. I slid hangers aside, spotting one of my *other* work uniforms.

All straps and mesh, I paraded around in this hooker outfit as if it were a job requirement. Like being a journalist meant I had to prostitute myself. Literally. Could I succeed without using my body as bait? Let my words speak for themselves?

Yes. I could and I must.

Plus, that's what I'd done all summer with my YouTube show.

Viraj was right to suggest I stay in the public eye. My videos had millions of views, and the comments I received showed my message was changing lives. Most of all, mine.

I accomplished all this without prancing the streets in a hooker outfit. Not once did I pretend to be in love with a mobster or lurk in a dive bar waiting for an informant. That was my normal MO, but I was playing a character. The crackerjack journalist I thought everyone wanted me to be. No, that wasn't quite right. I dressed up because I enjoyed being someone else more than living my pathetic life. Compared to my alter egos, the real me had always been a lousy alternative.

But I'd changed.

The clothes morphed before my eyes. Instead of thrilling adventures, I saw them for what they were: straps of restraint. Prison garb, no longer representing who I was and who I wanted to be. Tears trickled down my tightened throat in sorrow for the woman who wore them. I hoped to never be her again.

I shut the closet door and slipped on a dress I packed. It was 11:00 a.m. I had plenty of time to get a new outfit, then hop over to the network for our 2:00 p.m. meeting. Finding clothes had always come easily to me. I wasn't fussy, favoring classic cuts and solid fabrics. Hopefully, I'd find suitable garb quickly and squeeze in... lunch?

Wow. I had definitely changed.

Risto entered the room and drew me into a hug. "Go buy something new. My treat."

"You're bankrolling my shopping spree?"

"Yes. You work hard and deserve it."

I kissed him. "Thank you. You're the best."

"Yeah, I am." He squeezed my ass and headed out for his day.

I faced the storefront of my favorite store and immediately knew I was in trouble. The display sizes mirrored the ones in my closet, and I wondered if the shop carried anything that'd fit me.

I pulled the glass pole of a door handle and entered the retail space. Women's clothes were to the right. Fall items were up front, so I went to the back of the store where summer hadn't yet left the building. Garments hung limp on every rack, with more folded in incredibly precise piles on white display tables, likely arranged using a ruler.

A salesperson approached. Young and blond, her pale skin was identical to the translucent pink top she wore over black leggings and sensible flats.

"Looking for a gift?" she said in a cheery voice.

My brow furrowed in confusion. "No. I'm shopping for myself."

Her smile fled as she looked me over. "Um."

"Is that a problem?" I asked.

"It's just... We may not have anything for someone of your... shape."

"What shape am I supposed to have to shop in your store?"

"It's..." The girl dropped all pretense of civility. "Look, I don't make the clothes. Are you going to make me say it?"

I lifted my chin in defiance.

"Our shoppers wear skinny cuts. Your proportions... I mean ... well... curvy people are better off somewhere else." She shrugged, looking over her shoulder, hoping another customer would rescue her with an interruption. But we were alone.

I pivoted to face her, crossing my arms across my chest. "So you discriminate against anyone who's not a size zero?"

"No, not at all. I mean, you're not huge, but you're..." She pantomimed the arc of my new hips and round butt. The one that drove Risto wild and made me feel sexy as hell in bed. Seeing my stormy expression, the salesperson gave up.

"I think it's best if you leave," she said flatly, crossing her arms.

"I'm way ahead of you, sister." I hiked my shoulder strap and headed for the door.

Would this be the treatment I'd get everywhere?

Curvy people are better off somewhere else.

Like having curves was a bad thing. Suddenly, my shopping trip became a mission. How many shops would toss me out? I made a quick voice memo on my phone, noting the store and the first name of the sales associate.

I hopped straight next door, not even looking at the style of clothes displayed in the window. Yet I had identical results. Store number three went the same way. Then I tried a department store. The departments I frequented before had the latest in cute styles. But to find something that fit my hips and butt without pinching, I had to journey to the "women's" section. Oddly positioned beside "petites," a stark reminder that I was now an "other." Shapeless sacks of cloth hung from hangers. Depression personified. Did no one in the fashion industry think that "curvy" people wanted to be stylish?

I huffed out of the store and paused against the storefront window to open a browser tab on my phone. I could forget about lunch. At this rate, I'd show up at the meeting looking like an upholstered sofa. Not the powerful impression I was going for. I had to find something that screamed, *You made the right decision in hiring me.*

All the places that populated my web searches were exclusively online shopping. While the fashions were cute—and I'd definitely return to them later—that did me no good today. I needed clothes. *Now.*

Frustrated, I dialed my cousin Gabby.

"What's the matter?" she asked.

I swallowed a sob, plugging my ear from the traffic blaring around me. "I've been to four stores and can't find a decent fucking thing to wear. Everything looks like a tent."

Gabby sighed. "Welcome to my world."

"Shit, this is awful. I'm definitely doing a story on this next. Total bullshit."

"Where are you?" she asked.

I wasn't even sure. I started by Herald Square and meandered uptown. The green-and-white sign anchored me at 40th Street and Fifth Avenue. The likely reason my comfortable shoes weren't. I sank onto the front steps of the New York Public Library, the stone lion giving me as much love as the crabby salespeople. The NewsOne building was a quick walk away, but time was running out.

"I'm by the main branch of the library. Near 42nd Street."

"Perfect. Go to B'Cause. It's nearby and you'll have a gorgeous outfit in a flash. They're not cheap, though."

"Risto's treating me. He might regret it!"

Gabby whistled. "Jackpot. Get going and let me know how it turns out."

I hiked the eight blocks up Fifth Avenue to the store and breathed easy when a full-figured beauty stood behind the checkout station. Dressed to the nines with sparkling accessories, her green eyeshadow and plum lips complemented the deep tan tones in her complexion.

"Wait! No! Shut the front door! You're Leslie Allen!" Her glossy dark curls bounced as she clutched her hands, squealing.

"Um, yes." People recognized me sometimes. But never with so much enthusiasm.

"I've been watching your YouTube series. We all have." She turned and yelled to her colleague across the store floor. "Grace! Grace, come quick."

The second clerk looked up from her work refolding shirts. She used a folding board to get each shirt the same width, bending round at the front. "Is that who I think it is!?"

"Yes, can you believe it?"

As overjoyed as I was to be gushed over, the clock was ticking.

"I'm kinda in a rush. I have a big meeting in an hour and have to look the part."

"Do you have an outfit in mind? Dress, pants?" Grace asked.

"Something that says 'don't eff with me' but also shows I'm a woman. Got anything like that?"

"Definitely." The pair scattered across the store, grabbing hangers, belts, and shoes before shooing me into the dressing room.

A few changes later, I looked like a million bucks. Black slacks with an ivory sleeveless cowl-necked blouse, topped by a black jacket that cinched at the waist with a sparkly marcasite belt. They even let me use the staff bathroom to freshen up and reapply my makeup.

I stepped out to meet Grace, who was holding up onyx hoop earrings with sparkly edging that glinted in the overhead spotlights. "You need these."

I slipped them on and my outfit was complete. "Perfect. Thank you. Time check?"

"One thirty-six," Salesperson #1 said, now recovered from her initial shock and thoroughly invested in my meeting.

The pair rang up my purchases, and I tried to ignore all the decimal places. No way Risto was paying for this. He'd have to spoil me another day.

"You ladies were lifesavers!" I stuffed my sweaty dress into my handbag and dashed out. Five minutes later, I flashed my badge at the lobby security guy, who did a double take and smiled. That slight pause of approval made me feel beautiful, confident, and ready to meet the network team.

I rode to the 41st floor and knocked on the producer's closed door.

"Come in!" I heard her yell.

I entered to find Maureen sitting at her desk, opposite her star anchorperson, Kaelen, and Jay Key from the legal department. My internal warning system blared.

Why was a lawyer here?

This meeting smelled of dismissal. And while I was nervous, never had I entertained a scenario that ended with me losing my Saturday host spot.

"Come sit down." Maureen gestured to the empty chair between Jay and a smirking Kaelen.

I stashed my purse under my seat. "What did you want to discuss?"

"As if you don't know." Reed eyed me up and down with disgust before looking away.

Maureen side-eyed Reed before centering on me. "Leslie, when we signed you on, we were so happy for you to be our Saturday host."

"Were? Has something changed?" I didn't like where this was going.

"Well, yes. You have. Quite a bit, if I'm to be frank. You're noticeably larger and, I believe, are in violation of your contract's weight clause. It mandates that you stay within the designated percentage gain from when you signed the deal. While we appreciate that you're accustomed to being a freelancer and doing as you please, as on-air talent your choices now have consequences."

Jay handed out copies of what I presumed to be my contract. Thirty pages deep, I found a paragraph highlighted yellow. Sure enough, I committed to a weight clause. I had a vague memory of it when reviewing the original contract language. But having never strayed from my starvation diet, I'd only given the passage a cursory glance when Barbara pointed it out during her legal review. Now I wish I had taken it more seriously.

I looked up from my paper to meet three sets of unyielding eyes.

"Here are your choices." Maureen leaned forward on her crossed forearms. "If you commit to dropping back to your original weight and staying there, we're all good. If not, then I'm afraid this triggers the termination clause."

"You're not serious? Do you know how sick I've been?"

"Leslie, we—"

"Just listen. I was nearly hospitalized. My weight was so low that my organs were failing. You want me to go back to that?"

"Shit, Allen. No one cares about your fucking sob story. They just don't want to turn on their television and see a blob." Kaelen's expression dripped with disgust.

Jay shot Reed a silencing stare. "What Mr. Reed meant to say is that we have these clauses for a reason. You were hired because of the package of attributes you brought to the network, including your appearance. Given your weight gain, we are no longer getting what we signed on for."

My mind flooded with memories of sex workers standing on street corners. How they strolled in the dark, selling their bodies for cash. Sure, I was sitting in a skyscraper. But how would I be any different if I agreed to these terms? That would surrender control of my body to a corporation while reinforcing the impossible standard I railed against to millions of people on YouTube. The diet industry would win, yet again.

Then it hit me.

"A sponsor complained." I didn't ask.

Maureen squirmed in her seat.

Jay stared at his wristwatch.

Kaelen skewered me with an icy stare.

"Someone has to pay the bills, Allen."

Of course.

When we watched Kaelen's show over the summer, Dot would change channels, complaining about all the ads for diet plans, weight loss drugs, and empty-calorie diet foods. With Kaelen's maniacal diet regimen, it figured he'd court diet-industry advertisers, none of whom were likely happy to have an anti-diet crusader on the staff. As a recovering anorexic, I'd become a living example of the dangers of their lies.

Maureen cleared her throat. "Regardless of any complaints we might or might not have received, the fact remains that you've violated your contract. It's right here." She waved the papers for emphasis.

"Yeah, well, it's bullshit. Rodney Cox, Morgan Finch, Steve Gruber." I ticked the names off on my fingers. "All three anchors are large-bodied and on-air. Why am I held to a different standard? Because I'm a woman?"

Kaelen snorted. "Don't be thick. They were always fat. You're the one who did a swan dive into an all-you-can-eat buffet."

"That's enough," Maureen snapped at her superstar turd.

"I'm sorry, Ms. Allen." Jay handed me a letter. "This is your official warning. You have 48 hours to reply, in writing, about your intentions."

Jay and Kaelen rose and left, leaving the door open behind them. But I wasn't done.

I grabbed my bag and followed them out. Jay turned a corner and disappeared, but Kaelen strode ahead.

"Kaelen! Kaelen, wait." I hurried after him. "Don't do this. Please."

He stopped and turned to face me, fuming. "This was your big break. Network brass had plans for you. Now you're a fucking mess. I mean, look at you!"

"Because I stopped starving myself? This is bullshit and you know it. My YouTube videos get more viewers than two cable news networks combined—as I am. Why leave ratings on the table by cutting me loose?"

"I don't make the rules here," he said.

"Do you seriously think viewers care what I weigh?" I asked.

"I do. The lookers across the dial attract viewers for a reason." He flicked his head, and I followed him into an empty conference room. He slipped out his smartphone, tapped it a few times, and handed me the device.

Survey results.

In your opinion, does Leslie Allen look better in picture A or picture B?

The question was above two pictures. One of me on the red carpet at a news industry gala, slim and smiling. The other, a grainy picture from YouTube, my face blotchy from crying, chin retracted to make it look like my neck had eleven rolls.

For fuck's sake.

This was a bullshit setup to get me off-air and silence my voice. If he watched my videos, then Kaelen damn well knew how sick I'd been. The network expected me to reject their terms. They wanted no part in exposing the incestuous connections between the diet industry, government researchers, pharmaceutical companies, and the medical establishment. All the sectors profiting from keeping people chasing an illusion.

Kaelen sighed. "For what it's worth, I'm sorry it ended this way."

"Then why not stand up for me? This is your show. You have power."

"Allen... Give it up. No good will come from making a fuss." He strolled across the room, staring vacantly out the window. The hazy view a perfect metaphor for the network's foggy reasoning for firing me.

"There's a story here. I'm living proof." I handed back his phone. "Isn't the journalist in you the least bit curious? Don't you want to know whether that health regimen of yours is motivated by faulty science?"

Kaelen stiffened in anger. "Getting healthy changed my life for the better, and it's doing the same for every kid I work with."

I sighed in frustration. "Then you're just as brainwashed as the rest of them."

"Not brainwashed. Smart enough not to bite the hand that feeds me."

I shouldered my bag and stormed out of the network offices, mind raging with anger, confusion, and despair for a career suddenly off the rails.

But if they thought I'd go away quietly, they were sadly mistaken.

Chapter 37

RISTO

I checked my watch, wondering how Leslie's meeting was going. The network was probably fuming about her recent commentary on the diet industry. Shutting it down was likely first on their list of priorities, which would go over about as well as my day had.

Listless, I found it hard to focus during the location tours with Ruben. After visiting three vacant restaurants, they blended together in a mash-up of silver air ducts and exposed wiring lit by bare light bulbs.

At our fourth site, he pulled me aside.

"So, any preference between the places we've seen?"

The last thing I was sure he wanted to hear was that I couldn't tell them apart and was too tired to try. I did my best impression of excitement.

"They're all good. What do you think?"

"Chef, imagine it filled with guests, savoring your arroz con pollo pockets, their eyes arching in surprise. You peek out the kitchen door here." He stopped for emphasis. "Walk past an amber backlit bar... and take in your dream. Can you see it?" He grinned, facing the space.

I wanted to, more than anything. The luxurious interior. The success. But my vision was clouded, leaving me swaying in confusion while Steve chatted by the front door with the real estate agent.

"Chef Zaldo?" Ruben asked.

"Hmmm?" I answered, noting his confused stare.

He stole a glance at Steve, then took me firmly by the arm and tugged me over to a shady corner.

"Are you planning to back out of this deal? If so, do me the courtesy of telling me now, because you look bored. And it's way too soon for that."

"What? No. What makes you think that?"

"Oh, I don't know. Maybe because I've seen zero enthusiasm coming from you since we signed the letter of intent. The fire's gone from your eyes. You barely say anything unless we drag opinions out of you. Plus, after visiting six restaurants to evaluate chefs, you can't describe a single dish. What's going on?"

Shit. I hadn't realized my struggles were so obvious. Mired in hunger, if I wasn't distracted or sleepy, I was consumed with the desire to eat. And not just my two-egg ration. There was a difference between thinking about composing a meal and fantasizing about eating the ingredients raw. Before Brock's diet, I ate when hungry and was done with it. Now thoughts of eating consumed every waking moment, except at mealtime. By then, I was so petrified I'd overeat that skipping meals became preferable. Small portions brought me no joy. Succulent flavors, aromas, and textures were replaced by twisted visions of what the food would do to my body. Fat globules attaching to me like an encrusted pan, impossible to scrub clean.

I knew Ruben wanted to taste the updated menus too. But creating dishes meant tasting, over and over again. That didn't jibe with Brock's constant weight commandments. He had me weigh myself every morning and text him the plummeting figure. I refused at first, repulsed by his obsession. But he'd worn me down. I approached the scale with excited anticipation. A lower number than the day before validated that my diet was working.

It was my only joy lately. I pledged to stop after a month, but Brock kept moving the goal posts.

Last night was the first time in two weeks that Leslie and I had sex. I'd drop into bed each evening, exhausted, and rise weary in the morning as if I hadn't slept. What's more, I hated the temptation of being around food. The colors and spices that used to transform any kitchen into home now provoked icy terror.

I'd become too hungry to cook.

How was I supposed to be the next super-chef if food made me miserable?

I scratched my chin, my sharpened jawline unrecognizable. "I'm so sorry, Ruben. I'm wrung out, but I'll do better."

His eyes brightened. "Ahh, I see. You've been 'Brocked.'"

"What?"

"I told you Brock was slippery. He's good at what he does, but every chef he works with ends up an emaciated mess."

"But famous." I cracked a smile.

"Yes, that's true. But there's more to life, Chef. Food is love. Food is life. Food is family. Why deny yourself those things to fit into a pair of skinny jeans no one but Brock wants you to wear? The man I chose to run this restaurant is the burst of life I met at Boricua. That's the genius who impressed us and will thrill every New York foodie who has the privilege of dining at your table. But is that who you still want to be? Because the guy I'm looking at…" Ruben looked me up and down. "He'll get eaten alive, and you're trending toward an amuse-bouche."

I swallowed hard, watching every tic of Ruben's jaw.

"I need a chef who has their shit together. That's not you. At least, not anymore."

Ice flushed my veins as the truth of his words hit home. In trying to become what Brock wanted, I'd morphed into a person I didn't recognize. Besides losing pounds, I'd lost my drive, energy, and love for the one thing that defined who I was as a human: food.

Leslie had been worried.

Jose delivered meals to my house if I didn't eat at work.

Now Ruben was about to pull the plug on our deal.

I stood dumbstruck as he squeezed my shoulder. "Chef, you have to do what makes you happy. I don't care what you weigh or how you look. And neither will your guests. We all want the same thing: magic on our plates. Can you do that?"

I choked down the lump in my throat. "Yes. I can do that."

"Good. Then which restaurant location do you like best?" he asked.

I cranked my neck around. Light flooded the space through the dusty, second-story windows. The spot had once been a bank. Stone columns reached up to a vaulted ceiling. We could transform the cavernous room into an indoor veranda. Special lighting could make it appear sunny during the day and like a starlit evening at night. We could even add some swaying palms.

I stepped into the area that would be the kitchen, imagining gleaming stainless appliances and work surfaces. A walk-in fridge and freezer that kept my market treasures fresh and full of flavor. This was the space I wanted.

But more importantly, this would always be the place where I remembered who I was. Evaristo Zaldo, a chef from Pennsylvania who dreamed big and lived bigger. I'd build my second thriving restaurant—and my name as a rising star of consequence.

I turned to face Ruben, who had trailed me at a respectful distance. "Right here. This is where we'll make food magic."

On the way back to Leslie's apartment, I stopped at four markets to gather ingredients. The first for meat. The next for vegetables, then spices, and finally, seafood. A feast was in order. Creativity coursed through me like a raging river bursting through a dam. The shame of keeping my secret slipped away. Leslie had been honest and vulnerable with me about her food struggles and deserved the same in return. She probably suspected something was wrong with me. But if we were going to survive as a loving couple, I had to do better about letting her in.

I dropped the spare key she'd given me on the table next to the door and jogged up the stairs with my groceries.

"You home?" I deposited my bags on the counter and started unpacking. "I'm making us dinner. There's so much to tell you."

I put the dairy and produce in the fridge and turned back to see the top of Leslie's head peeping over the half wall separating the staircase from the living room beyond. "Hey, what are you doing over there?"

Leslie didn't move or speak.

Something was terribly wrong.

I abandoned my ingredients and found her sitting on the sofa, hugging her knees. Tears and black mascara streaking down her face. She let them fall freely, staining her cream-colored blouse, the one she must have purchased today for her big network meeting.

"What happened?" I asked.

"They fired me."

"You have a contract. How is that possible?"

She tossed a stapled stack of papers at me. It hit my chest and splayed out, pages bent every which way. I gathered it together to see. The title page with Leslie's name and the network's.

"According to this worthless agreement, I'm too fat to be on-air. I ran it past Barbara, and it appears they're on solid ground. I'd been the same weight for years and laughed at her when she originally pointed it out. *I laughed.* Ironic, huh? That fucking clause ruined my career. Kaelen was so disgusted he could barely look at me. He called me a blob." Leslie shuddered. "All because I stopped starving myself. I've never felt better, but all they see is bulk. This is... it's so...."

Her head dropped to her knees as heavy sobs wracked her heaving shoulders.

I sat beside her to draw her in, trying to press my love and support into her. Seeing Leslie this way cracked my soul wide open. She'd always been so strong, definitely the rock between us. Yet she shed her hardened exterior to be vulnerable and selflessly invited the world in to benefit from her journey. She gave and gave, and now there was nothing left. Not even her job.

I couldn't help feeling partially to blame.

With Brock's urging, I was perpetuating the same anti-fat stereotypes that cost Leslie her job. Only slim people were worthy of being seen. Large people were expected to hide away in shame until we were deemed small enough to be presentable. How stupid I'd been to listen to Brock. He'd made it seem like his was the only way. But everything was fine before his meddling. I became the success he now wanted to diminish. I had allowed him to reduce me in every way, but no more. The scale I kept hidden from Leslie would be trash as soon as we got back to Pennsylvania.

Brock worked for me, and I had a choice. She deserved that same opportunity.

"There's nothing we can do?" I asked.

"Don't laugh, but my one out is going back to starving myself. Forever. After I've fought so hard to get well, this job depends on me being sick? Can you imagine?"

I could. Popular thinking said thin equaled success. Opportunities opened for the lean, while the heavy got doors shut in their faces. Employers hid their bigotry in coded language and fine print because they knew how discriminatory it would sound to voice it aloud. The Brocks of the world wanted to be bigots without consequences. Scribed in black-and-white and sanctioned by their legal team somehow made their bigotry acceptable when it was anything but.

I sat beside her, planting a kiss on top of her head and squeezing her tight until her heaving subsided. Dusk settled around us, leaving the room in semi-darkness. After a while, vibrations of my stomach's grumbling jerked us apart.

Her lips rounded into a smile.

"Seriously?" she joked.

"Well, it is almost dinner time."

"Are we eating?" she challenged.

"We are. I am."

"Are you going to come clean?" Leslie swiveled to face me on the sofa, crossing her legs.

"Brock pressured me to lose weight."

She clapped her hands in triumph. "I knew it! I knew you haven't been right, but I wasn't sure if you were doing it on purpose."

"I was. And honestly, I hated every minute. Was it that way for you?"

"Definitely, but I was more petrified of the alternative. What happened today makes my fear feel justified."

"But their actions are not justified, you understand that. What they did to you was gross. If people only knew—"

Leslie leapt to her feet. "You're a fucking genius!"

She grabbed my face with both hands to plant a sloppy kiss.

"What'd I say?"

"If people only knew. This nastiness festers because it's kept secret. Shady dealings negotiated behind closed doors and buried in contracts. We watch shows, thinking everyone is naturally thin and that there must be something wrong with us if we're not. Occasionally, they let one or two fat people slip through as sad examples of what not to be. This behavior will never stop until someone exposes the powers that be for the shallow bigots they are."

Leslie fisted her hands, pacing. "They sat there, insulting me to my face like it's a perfectly normal activity. Because it is. People in larger bodies get insulted in broad daylight. We're called diseased and told we'll die if we don't change our ways. Well, fuck that. This has to stop."

While her chest heaved in indignation, I thought of all the forces aligned to keep us repulsed by largeness. While the studies Leslie shared over the last many weeks lit a bright path in the right direction, doctors, food execs, big pharma, and government agencies were totally invested in their crusade against fatness. If they kept walking us off a cliff, there'd be nobody left to warn the rest of the line to turn around. I'd be forever grateful to Ruben for his warning cry. But Leslie and I were just two people against a gigantic machine that'd been chugging along, full steam, for hundreds of years.

"I've got an idea," she said, interrupting my thoughts. "Reed has his regular guest spot on *Sunrise New York,* the day after tomorrow. He'll be on that couch with a huge glass window behind them."

"And?"

"I think he needs some fans to show him and the network some appreciation. Don't you?"

Chapter 38

LESLIE

The whisper campaign began with me emailing the 17,000 people on my mostly defunct newsletter list with a call to arms. I explained what happened and invited people to show up at 4:45 a.m. on Friday to get choice spots by the *Sunrise New York* studio window.

I then called Dot and Tasha and asked them to spread the word in their networks to mobilize more people. They said they wouldn't miss it and would do what they could to help. Tasha said she'd reach out to a bunch of body-positive influencers she knew on Instagram and TikTok, so they had time to quietly amplify the message. Gabby, her sorority's rep on an intercollegiate Greek council, blasted an email to her co-chairs. That had the potential to engage college students as well. My favorite cousin would arrive later today to help prep and join us in person.

I looped in Rebecca and Viraj, who used the *Dear Diary* magazine private message forum to post what had happened to me and ask anyone local to show up in force to support the cause. Meanwhile, I hopped on my computer to design some flyers and signs that I had printed at Staples. I also bought supplies to make poster-sized boards to hold up by the window.

It all came together remarkably fast.

We planned to rendezvous by the nearby park, then march over in force. Asking random people to show up in the middle of the night on short notice might be a fool's errand. But I'd worked too hard for an opportunity like this. I was finally recovering from an eating disorder and hoped to stay on track. Inner strength surged to keep me well, fueled by the food and grace I'd denied myself for so long. Now the network forced me to choose between my health and my career? All to meet a ridiculous clause that should be illegal? How did that compute?

My laptop beckoned, so I poured my soul into an article that would run tomorrow in *Dear Diary*. A blog this important usually took days to write. I would polish and reorganize the information until the ideas flowed like silk and the impact sliced like a razor. Today I had barely two hours. If not eloquent, at least my words were raw and vulnerable. Opening myself up this way was becoming much easier, and I scored that as a win.

After sharing the piece with Viraj, I dialed up my favorite reporter.

"I'm trying to keep it quiet, but if you're open to covering the story, I'll give you an exclusive."

"Oh, I'm in." The twinkle in Victoria's voice was unmistakable. "This is so overdue and couldn't happen to a better guy."

After Kaelen shamed her on-set with the goiter comment, Victoria never returned. Instead, she got a recurring spot across the dial on a rival show. I heard Reed was furious, but he only had himself to blame. You couldn't treat people like trash and expect them to return for more.

"Do you want to join us with a camera crew? We're going to make some waves," I said.

"I'll talk to my producer on the down-low. Okay if I tell a few trusted people? It might get you wider coverage."

"I'd love that. Thanks. I'm hoping this rally makes a gigantic statement. If it fizzles, I've failed."

By late afternoon, I heard about organizations renting buses to come. Thousands of emails and comments flooded in from eager people clamoring to be part of a movement that they named "Operation Fat Justice."

Then pictures showed up on social media.

"Holy shit, guys!"

"What is it?" Barbara asked from her spot at the kitchen counter, painting signs alongside her husband, Sebastian. Behind them, Risto took a protest break to whip up some dinner.

I handed around my phone to show Instagram posts of women, all sizes, colors, and ages with "#OFJ" written on their faces in lipstick, holding up pieces of paper that said *Tomorrow*.

"This is huge," Sebastian said. "OFJ. It's got a nice ring to it. By the way, I told my mom, and everyone in our neighborhood who can is coming. She's a regular town crier."

"That she is," Barbara said with a knowing smile. I loved that Barbara again had a doting mother figure in her life, Sebastian's mom. Barbara's mother had lost her battle with cancer years ago, but between Barbara's family and Sebastian's, my bestie was surrounded by the strong support system she deserved. Taking in the scene before me, I felt the same way.

"OFJ? We should add it to the signs. Don't you think?" I asked.

"Definitely." Barbara dabbed her brush in black paint and added #OFJ to the corner of her sign. "I'll repeat it on the others."

"First, I was worried no one would come. Now I wonder if I should have gotten a permit." I bit my lip, envisioning myself getting hauled off by the cops. I'd always managed to stay on the right side of the law, despite my underworld dabblings for stories. "I'll call an NYPD source to give them a heads-up. We only need to be there long enough to get on air while Reed is on the couch. Might be good to have some police presence in case network security gets rough with us."

I walked off to speak in private, not wanting anyone to overhear the name of the person I was asking for. The people in the room were family to me, and I preferred not to involve them more than necessary.

"They screwed with the wrong gal," Barbara called after me.

Phone pressed to my ear, I turned to face her. "Yeah. They did."

Laughter rounded the dinner table when my doorbell rang.

I set my wineglass down. "That'll be Gabby."

A pleasant fullness registered as I stood to greet her, but when I opened the door, I got a happy surprise.

"Dad!" I wrapped my arms around his neck, squeezing tight, just as I did as a child. The moment he walked through this door each night, it was like the cavalry had arrived. His joy and laughter offset the worry and tension swarming Mom, and me, by extension.

"Ready to start a ruckus?" He slipped off his Yankees cap and matching jacket.

"Do you blame me?" I had filled Dad in the day before, not expecting to see him. It'd been too long, though. I'd have to do better about staying connected.

"Come up, we're just finishing dinner, but there's plenty." I started up the stairs, but he grabbed my hand.

"Let's step into the study first. To talk in private."

By study he meant his old writing space that now doubled as a storage closet for random belongings from my divorced parents. They refused to take them, or pay for storage, so I stuffed them in Dad's former office and rarely entered.

We pulled up two chairs and sat. Dad spoke first.

"I wanted to apologize. It's long overdue, and I've been a coward for not coming to you sooner."

That was quite the intro, but I had no clue what he was talking about.

"This business with your mother. It's all my faul—"

"Dad, no!"

"Let me finish. Your mom's always been rigid as a tree. She gets an idea in her head, and there's no changing it. I used to find her stubbornness charming, if you can believe it."

Dad huffed a laugh, but I didn't respond, not wanting to break his train of thought.

"I'm a big guy, as you know, and Diana has always been slender. But food wasn't an issue for her when we met. She was regular, ate the same as me. However, that all changed after we had you. Di was obsessed with reclaiming her pre-baby body. That's when the strict dieting started. But even after she took the weight off, she kept going. It became a lifestyle. She got thinner and thinner and nagged me to do the same. I put a stop to that pretty quick, but I hadn't planned on losing my wife to a fanatic obsession with weight."

Why had I never heard this before? That the woman who ran my life like a drill sergeant had an origin story of her own?

"Did you ever talk to her about it?" I asked.

"Of course. I even got her to go to a doctor, but that was the worst decision I could have made. They said her weight was healthy, completely ignoring her compulsive behaviors. Instead of taking her situation seriously, they turned on me, insisting I was the one with an eating problem."

I'd been learning about the medical industry and their twisted habit of praising patients exhibiting disordered symptoms because the clinicians relied on BMI charts. Thin was good, fat was bad. Within that framework, no wonder Mom never got the help she needed.

He reached out tenderly, lifting my chin to inspect the faint bruise on my neck, barely noticeable at this point. "Your mom has been unwell for a long time, and I let her drag you down the same path. I should have done something sooner to save you. Do for you what I was unable to do for Diana. I'm so sorry to have failed you."

Dad stood, drawing me into his arms, while blood thumped in my ears. I loved my father, but he knew what was happening and did nothing.

"You took Mom to the doctor. Why not me, especially when you saw how she was raising me?"

I hated piling on after he'd already apologized, but I deserved answers.

"The doctors said Mom was fine. I figured even without Diana knowing, the result would have been the same. Your overweight dad would have been to blame. I didn't see a way out."

Hard as Dad's inaction was to accept, I understood. To the medical establishment and society, thinness was the ideal. Who knew? They might have viewed him as a poor parent for trying to fatten up his daughter to be like him.

Then an idea clicked.

"You sent me to Dot's each summer on purpose?"

Dad pulsed an eyebrow. "It was all I could think of."

At the beginning of each visit, it was hard for me not to feel abandoned. Sure, I had fun adventures and loved my aunt and cousin. But the distance made me wonder if they'd be happier without me; two artists having wild times. But I couldn't have been more wrong. The trips were my dad's loving way to nourish his daughter in a world unable to see disordered eating as the danger it was.

"Seems like you were in a tough situation and did the best you could. It sucks, but I understand."

Given Mom's mantra about thinness equaling health and my sketchy medical insurance coverage as a freelancer, visiting the doctor regularly had never been a priority. I had no obvious health issues. But I didn't know what I didn't know, and that was when a boatload of trouble happened.

Like the protest I was planning for tomorrow.

"C'mon," I said, standing. "Let's go join the others. You might not have been able to fix the situation then, but you can paint some signs and help now."

He pinched my chin. "I'd love nothing better."

Chapter 39

The dark streets glistened from the overnight rain as we approached the rendezvous point. Besides me, Risto, and Gabby, we had Barbara and Sebastian. Kyle and Rebecca would come later, as we didn't want our mother-to-be standing for that many hours. Disappointed, she battled back with a fury but relented when we mentioned the possibility of her getting crushed by what would hopefully be a sizable crowd.

I rocked a new outfit: black jeans with an electric-pink top and a yellow blazer. This time I let Risto pay the stunned clerks at B'Cause. Outraged after hearing why I needed more clothes, they tracked down the company founder, who planned to attend the rally herself.

"Do you hear that?" Risto asked.

I did.

Over the swiping noises of our poster-board signs as we walked, there was an unmistakable murmur of a crowd. People energized at 4:00 a.m. We turned the corner and entered the park, when someone yelled, "There she is!"

My yellow jacket is apparently doing its job.

The attendees cheered as I approached and cleared a path for me to pass through to the front. I ascended the steps of the vacant amphitheater where a revival of *STOMP!* would perform for a lucky audience hours later.

I shifted my picket signs to Risto's arms. "I should have prepared a speech or something. It was all so last minute..."

"Just speak from the heart." Risto stood back so I could take center stage before the quieting group of faces.

"Wow," I laughed, dismayed and overwhelmed by the sea of shining people before me. "Thank you. Thank you for coming out on a damp night to support my outrageous idea—that we should be loved and appreciated and respected for who we are. No matter the size we come i n."

People clapped and cheered. A shout of "You go girl!" cut through, making us all laugh.

"I'm trying. I swear," I said. "By now you all know that I was hired for a job as a permanent Saturday host for *The Kaelen Reed Show*. It was my dream opportunity to be on television. But all that vanished two days ago when my contract was terminated. The producers told me I was too fat."

"Booo!" the group roared.

"Right? I thought so too. I was still the same person they hired, only more in every way. That's because I was no longer starving myself. I never realized I was sick. I had anorexia nervosa and was terrified of food. Healing myself was the hardest thing I'd ever done. To feel happy, creative, and energetic. I got my fucking period back, people!"

They laughed again.

"I mean, it sucks, but that's a huge win for me. When we're hungry and endlessly dieting, beating ourselves down for not fulfilling some impossible ideal, it's about so much more than food. Because in denying ourselves, what we give away is power. What we give away is agency. What we give away is the freedom to live life on our own terms. These values are too precious to let slip through our fingers. We must hold them close. But society wants something different. They want us afraid and hollowed out at a physical and spiritual level. Cowering in shame. Covered up and living small. Are we ready to say, 'No more!'?"

The crowd cheered, "Yes!"

"Are we ready to own the room?"

"Yes!" they yelled.

"Feel right in our own skin?"

"Yes!"

"Tell the suits to go fuck themselves for having 'weight' clauses in employment contracts?"

"Yes!"

"All right then. Let's march! And remember, keep your signs hidden until I give you the signal. I don't want them to know why we're here until Reed is on set." I stepped back, and Risto pecked me on the lips, so gently, he avoided marring my makeup. A total pro.

"That was pretty awesome," he said. "Ready to battle another corporate giant?"

"Can't wait."

As I bent to pick up a cardboard sign, a familiar pair of legs in fishnets approached. Mo'nique, one of the subjects of my sex trafficking story, spread her arms wide.

"Give me some sugar," she cooed.

"What are you doing here?!" I squeezed her tight, her faux fur collar tickling my cheek.

"Had to come support my girl." She stepped back to take me in. "Glad to see you put some meat on those bones."

I sighed, recalling all the times I declined one of her Larabars. I figured she needed them more than me. Yet another thing I got wrong.

"Apparently too much for the network. We'll see if today makes any difference." The crowd was getting restless to march over to the network's viewing plaza. A lump clogged my throat. Hundreds of people showed up in the middle of the night to support this cause.

"Us curvy gals gotta stick together. Shall we?" She hoisted a picket sign onto her shoulder. It said #OFJ in big block letters.

I shouldered mine and led the group to the NewsOne studio window, taking our place against the glass. Inside, the 5:00 a.m. show was in full swing, the studio window lit up like a beacon. Unlike other networks, they didn't have a huge fan base watching the show each day. It was more a random series of people waving behind the anchors or holding up Happy Anniversary signs. An immense crowd arriving all at once earned worried looks from the early morning crew on-air before the weekday A-team arrived.

We smiled and waved, and they grimaced tentatively, whispering during the commercial breaks while shooting glances over their shoulders. It was still dark, but they might have spotted me in dawn's first light outside. *Yellow jacket strikes again.* Either that, or the trending social media posts caught more press attention than I'd hoped. I pulled my phone out of my pocket to check on the

#OFJ hashtag. There were thousands of posts, including pictures from people in our morning crowd. At this very moment, two influencers were streaming live interviews from behind where I stood.

Shit.

I wanted the crowd energized, but I needed to save the surprise until Reed hit the couch. If he found out in advance, he might bail. Cowardly, yes. But he wasn't stupid.

Over the next few hours, sunlight flooded the plaza, as did more people. One group included my visibly pregnant best friend. Rebecca nearly dragged Kyle through the crowd, leading with her belly.

"Excuse me! Pregnant lady coming through!" She smiled but meant business, arriving out of breath. "I can't believe this turnout! It's amazing!"

I hugged her. "Yeah, but it's making me worried we'll tip off the enemy before we confront him."

"With good reason," Rebecca said. "Viraj called me this morning. Reed got wind of it all last night and tried to cancel his appearance. The network is forcing him to come, but he might not. Anyway, here's the megaphone you wanted to borrow."

Rebecca passed it over from Kyle. It was the same white-and-blue, battery-powered bullhorn we had used in college at football games to taunt the opposing team. Rebecca's mom got it after a failed political campaign disbanded. Flat broke, the former candidate sold off everything that wasn't nailed down. If I had my druthers, I'd strip this building the same way.

The network treated on-air talent like trash. The nasty conversation from the other day streamed incessantly through my brain, an on-screen news chyron I couldn't shake. I imagined the messages scrolling by.

Breaking news: Leslie Allen got too fat to host our show.

Breaking news: Victoria Cooper Rawley has a neck like a goiter.

Fuck that. No way was I letting Reed and the network brass slither out of this one.

"Reed wants to bail? Then let's make it impossible for him to ignore us."

I scrambled onto a concrete planter and switched on the bullhorn. "Hello, hello, hello!" My voice boomed through the megaphone. "Are we ready to be heard?"

Cheers and hoots erupted.

"Kaelen Reed is trying to avoid coming to the show this morning!"

"Boo!"

"Do we want him to come see us?"

"Yes!"

"Does he need to answer for his bias against larger people?"

"Yes!"

"Should the network let me on-air, as I am, every fabulous inch of me?"

"Yes!"

I winked at Risto at that one, launching him into a wide grin as he cheered, "Yes!" alongside the growing crowd.

From my perch on the planter, I could see a group of cops gathered at our periphery. Shoulders relaxed, fingers hanging from their waistbands, they ignored a woman in a gray skirt suit screaming at them and pointing in our direction. The gal stormed our way, but a uniformed police officer put herself between the network patsy and the edge of the crowd. From the looks of it, urging calm.

My heads-up call to police HQ seemed to be working.

While I eyed the police happenings, a crowd chant started.

"Too fat to watch news. Too fat to watch news. Too fat to watch news..."

My cell vibrated in my pocket, Dot's face filling up the screen.

"Hey, how's it look on TV?" I asked.

"It's on all the channels. They just showed you with a megaphone. What's that?" Dot muffled the phone with her hand. "I've got my ladies' group here as a command center. There's footage of five people protesting at the network headquarters in Los Angeles and another ten in Chicago. I'll keep you posted."

"Wow, thank you!"

I hung up, unable to make out much of what Dot said over the growing din on the plaza. A small group started marching in a big oval, chanting, "Shame on Reed! Shame on Reed!" over and over.

I hopped down and grabbed Risto's hand. We joined the chants, walking and shouting. I added my megaphoned voice to the mix.

Energy channeled through me, every cell of my body alive and pulsing. Our cause was just. This was far bigger than me. This was a movement calling for all people to be treated fairly, no matter our size. After a half hour, someone tugged on my arm.

Victoria had arrived with her camera crew. "Got a sec for an interview?"

We maneuvered back to a space next to the studio window, where Gabby stepped aside to make room.

"I never thought you'd be the one starting a ruckus over weight!" Victoria joked, talking close to my ear given the crowd noise. "I can't tell you how many conversations I've had about my own contract over the years. Took an Emmy nomination and seven journalism awards to get my weight clause removed."

"Sounds like I should be interviewing you!" I said.

"Oh no. You're the headline here, girlfriend. Let's get you miked up."

As they clipped a lapel mic to my jacket, I glanced over my shoulder to where the news crew inside looked to be in panic mode. The last thing they wanted was to be making headline news on another channel or being the top story on their own show.

Victoria's cameraman lit us, and we began our interview. She asked me why I was there today and followed up with a few solid questions, asking me to justify my claims about fatness not being a death sentence. Facts poured out, the ones I learned from Tasha and my care team and then backed up on my own. The details I gained from Professor Hawley and how they contradicted the opposing research I'd found. Then the key question arrived.

"What do you want to say to Kaelen Reed?"

"I challenge him to an on-air debate. On his show. He needs to publicly account for his behavior. I also want the network to repeal my dismissal. I love working for NewsOne and look forward to doing an amazing Saturday anchor job for them when and if they lift their use of weight clauses in contracts. If fat people and our allies turn off TV news, perhaps the network will finally take notice."

Victoria finished up, gave me a hug, and wiggled her way out of the crowd, but not before getting mobbed with people wanting selfies with her. She posed for a few, then waved her goodbyes and inched toward the news van parked near the police.

I checked the time on my phone, then noticed a missed text from Viraj.

> Viraj: Network let Reed bail. Not happy with you going public about the weight clause.

> Leslie: Yeah? Well, I'm not happy with them treating me like garbage.

I could almost hear Viraj shrug across my text screen. He had worked in media for over a decade and knew the deal as well as me. The producers wouldn't budge until forced. But wasn't that what I was doing here? Hundreds of women of all sizes showed up to demand better. In the middle of the night, no less. Despair grabbed me by the ankles and tugged, but another Viraj text pinged through.

> Viraj: On a bright note, we've gotten major coverage. All the other morning shows are covering it and we're trending on social. They'll not be able to ignore you for long. Interview requests are pouring in, and we can use that leverage to get you face-to-face with Reed. At least, if they're smart. You in?

> Leslie: Set up as many as you can. Rival networks included. If NewsOne doesn't want me, let's show them the long line of people who do.

Not waiting for an answer, I pocketed my phone and swapped it for the bullhorn. Starting a fresh round of chants, we celebrated being here, loud, and together. Women laughed and danced. Men hugged their curvy ladies—and curvy men. I'd felt so alone with my food struggles. Starving and binging, restless and hollow. Wrong as it was, it was the only way I knew how to live. But I'd changed, and a healthier, fuller future awaited me. And Risto.

I searched for his face and found him leaning against the stone building, chatting with Kyle, Rebecca, and Gabby, while Barbara and Sebastian danced to the music of a kettle drum someone set up. Life had certainly taken a wild turn for Risto and me lately, and it would remain unsettled for a while longer.

But after today, I had no doubt we'd land on top.

Chapter 40

RISTO

Leslie and I collapsed into bed the moment we dragged our weary bodies back to her apartment. When I woke the next morning, Leslie's limbs splayed across the mattress like a starfish. Mouth open, she was zonked. She didn't as much as twitch when I slipped out and closed the bedroom door.

As I splashed water on my face, my mind's eye teemed with the animated crowds from the day before. How phenomenal to see so many people enthusiastically supporting the woman I loved! Having her vibrant and healthier made our future together seem limitless. Despite her public battle with the network, I expected her to get offers from other organizations who would smartly pounce on Leslie, given her high profile and stellar reputation for integrity.

Reed was getting pilloried on every social platform. Loud calls for his firing crammed my social feed, as did posts about boycotting his program. The boycott cries then expanded to other shows that used discriminatory weight clauses in their contracts.

Legal experts spouted from every TV news panel. Few could justify the contract language without also admitting the bias inherent in so narrowly limiting staff to slim reporters.

Then more evidence poured in. Redacted screenshots of contracts and rude emails from industry execs, casting directors, and producers ranting about a talent's fatness or berating thin ones for gaining two ounces. Leslie's protest ripped open a festering wound, and people were clamoring for disinfecting change.

I braced my arms on the sink, face dripping as I inspected my reflection. The roundness I'd seen my whole adult life had angled. My skin was ashy gray, like a piece of chicken cooked in a microwave. Dark circles took up residence under my eyes, displaying the relentless weariness that had settled in my bones.

I looked hellish and felt worse. But worst of all, I no longer recognized myself.

Being around proudly fat people yesterday had reinforced Ruben's concern about my health and well-being. And his warning about Brock's influence. My thirst to be a star blinded me to the idea that anyone would want me as I was. A chef of food so amazing that Manhattan diners drove three hours to taste it. Eager fans lit up chat forums and made Silas Greene barge into my kitchen, demanding to be served. Food that earned me a magazine cover and enthusiastic investors.

Why was I risking it all to starve myself? Like Brock's other clients, I'd only grown more miserable by the day, until being around food had become torture. Yesterday's lessons confirmed for me that my days of dieting were over. I'd already texted Brock with the news and had yet to hear back. His silence was deafening, but I had bigger concerns. I owed the investors the new restaurant's menu.

Was my reinterpretation of humble Puerto Rican dishes another attempt to twist myself into someone I wasn't? The flavors of our cuisine needed no altering to be worthy of a NYC address. Creating complex recipes that tasted like the original justified the higher price tag, but left Silas unimpressed. Somewhere along the way, the food lost its soul. Jose and Freddie rolled their eyes at the hours I spent manipulating pricey ingredients onto spare plates. Was it because I thought my regular food wasn't good enough? Or because I felt inferior to the famous chefs on TV?

A thunderclap of truth knocked me near-senseless.

Silas was right. I'd gotten the entire NYC menu horribly wrong.

Yes, I loved my delicious intellectual puzzles. But was that what I wanted to be known for? Elite, unrecognizable Puerto Rican food? Or did I belong preparing the authentic article with love using time-tested, if slightly modified, recipes that tasted like home?

The chemist in me wanted to experiment and innovate. That's what the investors signed up for. I'd only presented them foods two ways to show them the difference if they were unfamiliar with the original flavors. They'd fallen in love with elevated dishes while savoring traditional ones. They had the benefit of both. Shouldn't all diners? Both sides were part of me. I was sophisticated and humble. Innovative, yet yearned for tradition, family, and friends.

I didn't have to choose.

I had always been my own man, creating meals that sparked happiness. But all the nonsense with Brock twisted me into someone who hated food. The menu for the new restaurant would be me. All of me. The fancy culinary school me and the sweats and T-shirt me.

The guy who lovingly tended pernil until the pork was marinated to maximize flavor and roasted until golden and succulent.

All of me would go into this restaurant.

And people would make reservations months in advance to get a taste.

I dried my face, grabbed my keys, and was out jogging to the market before the recipes fled out my ears, never to return. I craved the stove like air. These dishes would breathe life into my new vision. Two me's. Two ways to enjoy the flavors of Puerto Rico. I'd call it Boricua 2.

Hours later, every pot Leslie owned bubbled on the range and meat sizzled in disposable roasting pans jammed into the oven, surrendering to their roasted selves. The oven heat first dried the cuts, then hardened, then tenderized. Taken out at the wrong time, the meal would be a disappointing disaster.

As I almost was.

But I eventually made it through, coming to understand and trust my true self. I'd been a happy, satisfied chef before, confident beyond my years or life experience. When the idea for the new restaurant surfaced, my instinct said to walk away. Instead, I'd agreed, half-assing my way toward a future I thought I should want but didn't. Not if I were honest with myself.

With the cloud lifted and my goals clear, New York cemented itself as an inevitable part of my destiny. I craved it and the creative potential it represented. The yearning throbbed in my veins with a passion typically reserved for Leslie.

"That smells delicious." Leslie crept close, caressing my back.

My head bobbed in time with my knife chops. "You have no idea. It's extraordinary. Taste."

I snatched a shrimp from the sauté pan and dropped it from my fingers into her waiting mouth.

Her eyes shut as she savored the flavor. "Mmm. That is fantastic."

She reached for another, but I swatted her hand away. "Not yet. Everyone will be here soon."

"You're seriously denying me food?"

I pulsed an eyebrow. "Good point. Go ahead."

She took a second shrimp from the pan with her bare fingers, licking them slowly and seductively while batting her long lashes.

"Oh, it's like that, is it?"

She shrugged. "We have time."

I glanced at the stove and saw my concoctions bubbling happily or turned off and resting.

We did have time.

Torn, all my resolve melted when Leslie slipped her black dress over her head and dropped it on the kitchen floor. Braless, her firm breasts taunted me as she backpedaled toward the bedroom wearing only a black pair of panties and a curled finger.

"Now that's not playing fair," I said.

"I never play fair, Chef." She posed, arching her back against the wall while tangling her hands in her luscious curls.

That was my job. And she knew it.

"I love you, but I'm not burning dinner…"

She sashayed down the hallway, then straddled the bedroom doorway like it was me.

"Fuck it."

I was on her in an instant, flipping her over my shoulder and taking a more than playful bite out of her ass.

"Hey!" She giggled. "Who's not playing fair now?"

I bounced her onto the bed, tossing my apron at her and slipping off my clothes. By the time I looked up, she'd tied the black apron on but wore nothing else. Mouth deliciously pouted, her breasts exploded from behind the narrow bib slung around her neck.

My body ached to have her. I imagined slipping into her like a glove. Tight. Warm. Wanting.

I crawled to meet her on the bed, yanking her up to her knees and devouring her mouth until the call of her throat overwhelmed me. Her herbaceous scent was a meal far better than any I could manufacture.

Leslie released a deep, throaty moan. "I should wear an apron more often!"

"You should, but only in bed."

I reached for the night table drawer, but she pushed my hand away.

How could I have forgotten?

Both clean and with birth control pills active, there was nothing to keep us apart. Our bond was unbreakable. She'd be mine forevermore. I flipped her around and entered her, deep and hard, surrendering to a torment of colliding senses. I moaned as the silky texture of her skin set me on fire. I bent flush with her back and sank my face into her curls, delighting in the sensation of being skin to skin.

"Oh, baby. You feel too good."

I gripped her waist, Leslie's breasts grazing my hands as we joined and released. Teasing me. Tempting me to flip her over to suckle like the drowning man I was. But I was too lost in the fiery pleasure lapping at my edges, like a siren call. I bit my lip, but the pain only inflamed me further.

Leslie withdrew, flipped over, and tossed her legs over my shoulders. I knew what she wanted, but I had other plans.

I devoured her wetness, working her most sensitive spot the way I knew she wanted.

"Oh, oooooh! Right there, right there..." she cried, grabbing my head, holding as she arched. Leslie drifted in her private cosmos before falling limp on the bed.

Sick with lust, I thrusted, our union sparking her back to life. We joined and released in a rhythm perfected over years. From loving someone more than you loved yourself. From igniting their pleasure, then fanning the flames into a white-hot inferno. From wandering together in dark places. From sunning in bright ones. From knowing what they needed to soar. Soulmates in every sense of the word.

Pleasure crested until the call was too strong to resist. I let go and broke into a billion pieces. My cry echoed off the walls, blending into hers until we were one, collapsing into a heaping mass on the mattress.

We lay panting and immobile, floating through the mists of sleep, when the stove timer sounded.

Fantastic.

Visions of ruined dishes had me alert in no time. I jumped up and quickly washed and dressed before returning to the kitchen.

The roasted meat glistened as I removed it from the oven and set it aside to rest.

The tomato sauce had reduced into what would become the thick base of my pink beans. I put the new pot on the stove, dribbled olive oil into it, and added a spoonful of sofrito. The rich mix of peppers, onions, garlic, and herbs sizzled in the pan. I stirred beans in, then ladled in tomato sauce, salt, and pepper and set it to simmer while I got the rice cooking.

Lost in my preparations, Leslie's presence went unnoticed until her soft lips connected with my back. She'd slipped the abandoned dress back over her curves like nothing had happened. Like she hadn't just destroyed me in bed.

"We're both lucky I set that kitchen timer. I would've lost it all." I drew her in with one arm. She tilted her head back, her wordless request for a kiss, which I granted.

Leslie moved to the cupboard and removed a stack of white clay plates with lipped edges. Arms straightening under the weight, she made her way to the dining table to set it for eight. It was a homey scene. One I'd wished for far too many times to admit to anyone out loud. Not even Leslie. But we were here. We'd made it. I'd fight like hell to keep anyone from harming the woman I loved.

But the world outside this apartment might have very different plans.

Chapter 41

Leslie

Candles flickered on the table as the eight of us broke off into side conversations. Most centered on two topics: Ruben's restaurant empire—and his latest prodigy in Chef Risto (as Ruben insisted on calling him)—or the networks scrambling to save face.

Every media conglomerate had released press statements, both for and against weight clauses for on-air talent. Some claimed the practice simply responded to studies showing viewers preferred trim personalities. It was a public service to provide healthy role models whose weight complied with government guidelines. Others admitted the practice might be antiquated and committed to investigating how to eliminate or ease the requirements. No comment issued from NewsOne, about me specifically or their talent policies.

Kaelen Reed had gone radio silent after texting me, *nice try*. But he couldn't continue to ignore the fervor demanding that he address what happened. His show sat at the epicenter of what some called Earthquake Leslie. Unflattering cartoons had surfaced. Most featured some version of a porked-out me with a pig snout, jumping up and down to ripple the earth's surface while network logos bounced in the air like rubber balls. My favorite headline: "Allen feasts on networks."

Old me would have turtled in shame, as my mother must be doing. She'd left me no less than sixteen messages, and I didn't need to listen to a single one to sense her palpable horror. My dad simply texted: *That's my girl,* with a heart eyes emoji.

How did those two ever marry? They were so different. I guessed it was lucky for me, though. Mom's tenacity with Dad's humanity produced the perfect combination for the career I loved.

"Leslie?" Rebecca asked.

"Hmm?" All eyes at the table were on me. "What'd I miss?"

"We're just wondering if you're going to accept any of the network interview requests."

I slumped back in my chair. "I was holding out for NewsOne. Figured I should give them a shot before my job there is officially gone."

Risto scratched his beard. "Hon, you never answered their warning in writing. Doesn't that end things?"

He wasn't wrong, unless my protest sign outside their studio window counted.

"The way I see it, they can forever appear like the bigoted cowards they are or make peace with me and save face. It's their choice."

"Have you sent that request to them?" Barbara asked.

"No, I just thought of it right now. It's a great idea, don't you think? A one-on-one interview with me and Kaelen Reed. We'd hash it out in a TV special. If it went well, I might even get rehired."

Barbara winced. "You don't honestly want to work there, do you?"

"Yeah, I kinda do." I smiled.

Rebecca and Barbara exchanged glances, but it was Ruben's wife, Anita, who spoke next.

"You deserve your own show."

I laughed, reaching for my wine. "Sure, I can have a nightly interview program. I'll grill notable people, and we'll call it *The Hot Seat*. Reed will be my first victim."

"I'd watch that," Sebastian said.

"Me too." Ruben raised his glass.

"Let's pitch it!" Rebecca clapped merrily, her eyes aglow. I knew that look. It always happened before trouble.

Barbara shrugged in approval. A "why the hell not?" mutiny.

"To *The Hot Seat*!" Anita toasted.

Glasses clinked, and suddenly I felt like I was in a frying pan myself.

I caught Risto's eye from the far head of the table opposite me.

He raised his glass. "¡Sueña en grande!"

Dream big.

It didn't take long for the "hot seat" idea to sprout roots and embed itself into my psyche. Maybe I was thinking too small. If I went crawling back to NewsOne, I'd forever be battling with Reed. A petty, vindictive man with way more clout than I had.

Pitching the idea to rival networks would give me a fresh start at a new home. One far away from a huge asswipe who likely had no use for me now that he no longer wanted in my pants. I crafted a proposal that included two pages of potential topics with three guests each. It would cover a year of weekly shows, not counting the ripped-from-the-headlines themes that might arise and demand attention. Ideally, my show would air opposite Kaelen's Saturday episode but tape during the week so I'd have weekends free. The more I refined the pitch, the more I imagined myself as a host, grilling big names and taking no prisoners.

But first, I had to find a network home.

Viraj worked his magic and got me interviews at three cable networks and one major broadcaster that hoped to replenish a recent talent drain in its news division. After several rounds of meetings, two offered contracts.

Then my phone rang, the caller speaking before I could.

"It's Maureen from NewsOne. Do you have a moment? I'm here with Jay and Kaelen."

The producer, the lawyer, and the pig-headed blowhard.

They must have gotten wind of my meetings.

While my instinct was to hang up, curiosity got the better of me.

"Never thought I'd hear from you again," I said.

"Yeah, well, we never expected you to amass an army of protesters and fuck over the people who gave you a chance," Kaelen snapped.

"Kaelen, please," Maureen said.

"If you recall, you were the ones who rejected me. You have it backwa—"

"Actually," Jay interrupted. "If you look at the contract language, we 'may' dismiss you for cause. We never officially did. That means you are still bound by the terms of the deal you signed."

Could that be right? No. Not at all. My heart pounded so forcefully I got light-headed. Barbara and I checked the agreement. Carefully. No, they were trying to pull a fast one now that the competition was sniffing around. I held my cell phone against my chest while I composed myself.

"Allen? Still there?" Jay asked.

"For the moment, but you're really wasting everyone's time. You've conveniently forgotten the dismissal letter. The one you gave me ordering me to lose weight? Remember that?"

"Jay, what's she talking about?" Maureen asked.

"According to that, our relationship ended 48 hours after our meeting," I said.

"Only if you replied in writing, which you never did," Jay replied, though he sounded unsure. The sounds of paper shuffling replaced the conversation as they frantically searched the pages of my contract, looking for answers. Then muffled voices escalated before a shout and a door slam.

Radio theater at its finest.

"Hello?" I said.

"Kaelen left," Maureen said. "Listen, Allen. We admit we didn't do right by you. This whole thing got blown up way bigger than it had to. But now there's this new show you've been shopping around. We'd love for you to come in for a conversation. If it's as good as the rumors suggest, we'd like you to consider NewsOne."

They had to be kidding. They expected me to trust them after everything that happened? After they just tried to trick me into thinking I was still under contract? Did they forget what a major dick

Kaelen had been to me since then? He posted nasty comments about me on social media, both on his own feed and others. Plus, Kaelen's show aired Saturday nights. They didn't even have a spot in the lineup.

Holy shit.

That's why Kaelen left.

They were planning to offer me his Saturday time slot.

Given what happened and how they treated me, I had no intention of going back. But I could give them an incredible program differently.

"Before I entertain your ask, I want a one-on-one interview with Reed. Live. He has to face this head-on. It'll be good for both of us and go a long way to repairing his reputation—"

"Done."

"What?" flew out of my mouth before I could stop it. "You're serious?"

"Yes. I was authorized to offer this should it come up."

"Then I look forward to clearing the air. In prime time."

It took a few weeks to arrange my TV special with Kaelen. I demanded a clean set, two chairs facing each other equally. We were long past the host/guest bullshit. I was his peer and equal, so the optics should reflect that. He'd kicked and screamed, but the network caved. Especially since the show was being billed as a Kaelen Reed special event.

My goal for the episode ran deeper than getting him to apologize. I wanted to understand what made him tick. Something from his background had triggered his deep loathing for fatness. I dressed in jeans and a cute top, grabbed my bag, and headed out to the neighborhood where he grew up: Bensonhurst, Brooklyn. It was an immigrant mecca now, known as Brooklyn's Little Italy. With large Italian and Jewish populations when Reed was a kid.

I'd scheduled a meeting with the principal at his elementary school. Hopefully, talking to staff there would give me some clues about who Reed had been as a child.

I hopped on the D train and took the subway to the 20th Avenue station in Brooklyn. I then walked the remaining five blocks to Public School 348. The secretary signed me in and handed me a visitor lanyard before ushering me to meet Principal Athena Woods. She'd worked in the district for 32 years, rising from a teacher to hold her current post for 12 years.

I sat in a wooden captain's chair after shaking her hand. "Thanks for seeing me today."

She chuckled. "It's not every day a face from television knocks on your door. I presume you're here about Kaelen?"

"Yes. I'm trying to learn more about him as a child."

"He's a favorite son around here. A smart child who became a great man. Mr. Reed is here regularly, talking to the kids and encouraging them to be kind to each other—and follow their dreams." Principal Woods leaned forward in her chair, and I got the overwhelming sense that Reed had a powerful ally in her.

Not at all what I expected.

Kaelen's visits must be unannounced, surprising given what a media hound he was. Why wouldn't he plaster the newsroom with pictures of him posing with neighborhood children? Sure, they came by the studio. But I'd seen no photo-ops, articles, or learned any reasons for their visits.

"The school obviously meant a lot to him."

"He was such a sensitive child. We do our best to stop the bullies, but kids always find a way."

Sounded like Kaelen's bullying must have started early.

"Do you remember what the issue was? What made Kaelen bully the other kids?"

Principal Woods leveled me with her deep brown eyes. "Kaelen would never and has never been a bully. He was the target. The victim."

"My apologies. Given my adult interactions with him, I just assumed..."

She sighed, lowering her voice. "Kaelen was a chubby child. The kids picked on him for being different, especially because the Reeds were only one of two Black families here at the time."

A pang of sorrow seeped into my bones, thinking of little Kaelen. Wanting so badly to be like everyone else while the other children only saw the color of his skin. My elementary school had a lot of biracial children, as well as Hispanic and Chinese children. Sounded like Kaelen could have benefited from a more diverse learning environment than the one he had here.

"If his past was so painful here, why does he come back?"

"Oh, that's easy—Mr. Marinelli."

Principal Woods explained how a gym teacher took young Kaelen under his wing. The man spent hours with Kaelen every day after school, getting the child into better physical shape. Running laps around the gym. Shooting baskets in the yard, doing sit-ups and push-ups. By the end of his elementary school career, Kaelen was so strong, he tried out—and made—the basketball teams in junior high and high school.

"He comes every year for the physical fitness tests we hold. He cheers the kids on and has even helped a few kids in his private time, like Mr. Marinelli did for him. When his star rose and his schedule made it difficult to make time, Kaelen began sponsoring scholarships to a local gym to help overweight and obese children get more physically fit."

It jarred me to hear those "o" words spoken so freely. There were so many lies behind the concepts of "overweight" and "obesity," but kids had zero chance to avoid them.

The principal beamed with pride, while I had traumatic flashbacks to my elementary school physical fitness tests. They created a pecking order, with me always at the bottom. Too tired and weak to participate fully, my scores were habitually low. Now I knew why. My lack of calories denied me the energy needed to run, play, and adopt a healthy love of movement. With Dot's help, that was one more change I'd made for the better.

When I moved now, it was because I enjoyed it, and it made me feel good. I relished the strength and endurance of my muscles, marveling at how far I could walk and how much better I slept. Ironically, I was more active in my current body than I ever was at lower weights. Encouraging movement was admirable. But forcing kids to move as a proxy for losing weight fueled resentment for exercise by forever associating it with not being good enough as they were. Movement for the sake of health was best, regardless of the impact on the scale. I doubt that was the approach they took with the children.

It was great that Kaelen was encouraging kids to be active, but I didn't have to wonder at the underlying message. In his world, the purpose of moving was to lose weight, avoid shame, and become like everyone else. Programs like this reinforced the notion that there was only one way to be, and that was as thin as possible. What started out as a well-intentioned gesture had likely developed into an unhealthy obsession with thinness that transformed Kaelen into a bully himself.

To me.

To Victoria, and to everyone who didn't fit into his narrow ideal.

I thanked the principal for her time and headed home, ideas zinging around my brain.

When the time came for my battle with Mr. Reed, I'd be ready.

Chapter 42

RISTO

Ear-splitting construction noise jarred me as I navigated the hive of workers putting finishing touches on Boricua 2. We were less than two weeks away, and I longed for this next phase to begin.

Electricians on ladders installed wall sconces while contractors on scaffolding affixed sound proofing tiles to the ceiling. I wanted our cavernous space to welcome intimate conversation once filled with diners.

I rounded a bar area where glass shelving was being carefully fixed in place. The foreperson nodded to me as I passed through the archway to the work of art that was the kitchen. Having just remodeled at my home location in Easton, I supersized the same models here. I also ordered the additional equipment we needed to simultaneously cook the "paired" dishes I'd centered the menu around.

Then my eyes landed on Brock.

Once he returned my call and agreed to behave, we'd started a new chapter. I explained how his urging almost tanked the whole deal, and he blanched in shock. I could tell his apologies were insincere, so encouraged him to dig into the information I shared from Leslie. He admitted his rail-thin mandate might be overkill and eased up on me and a few of his other clients. Since then, I'd received six emails of hearty thanks from other chefs, alongside offers for unlimited free dining at their restaurants. I laughed it off at first, but Leslie insisted we collect.

With the restaurant opening and my favorite journalist planning her battle royale with Kaelen Reed, our leisurely dinners would have to wait. NewsOne launched a huge campaign, featuring Leslie and Kaelen sneering at each other. A bus rolled by me this morning on my walk to the Boricua 2 site, so I snapped a picture to text Leslie.

Looking good, I'd written.

Back atcha, she'd answered.

Eating normally had me feeling myself, and Jose gave me his thumbs-up when I returned home for a week to check in. Not once did I skip lunch or dinner. Though the few dishes he'd introduced from his family recipes made that impossible. Boricua was in excellent hands with Jose and Freddie, but I missed them terribly. All the recent staff hires in Manhattan reminded me about my second job: forging close working relationships with my new team. If I was lucky, they'd eventually turn into friends as Freddie and Jose had.

Brock's shoes clacked on the concrete floor as he approached.

"They just posted a billboard of your wife smack opposite my apartment window. Is that your doing?" he joked. Though he knew Leslie and I weren't married, I'd stopped correcting him.

I loved the sound of it.

My wife.

I'd dreamed about it for years. But with everything going on, adding wedding chaos to the mix was out of the question right now. Leslie and I had begun talking about our unified future as if it was a given. We were a firm "us" and made choices together. Such as planning my move to Manhattan. I'd keep my house, but with the new restaurant location, a permanent relocation was only logical. Right now, it was undeniable that the career action for both of us was in New York.

Brock gestured to the photographer he'd hired to capture candid construction shots. My agent was also hard at work building buzz for the restaurant and pitching me to culinary shows as a guest panelist.

"Okay, we're ready," he called over. "Stand by those blueprints and hold them up like you're looking at them."

I did as he asked while the photographer snapped away. Then I unboxed pots and reviewed the long-since decided paint samples. Ruben would die laughing when he saw these. I left most of the interior design to him and the experts once we approved the digital mock-ups. Provided the restaurant looked like their proposal, I was good.

"Hello, hello!" Ruben shouted over the din of sawing, drilling, and nail guns as he entered the kitchen with his partner.

Steve swept the room with his eyes. "It's coming together. Won't be long now."

"We'll be ready for the launch party. No worries." I answered Steve's unspoken question. The pace of construction had left us behind schedule until a spike in the number of workers over the last few days got work back on track.

"Perfect. We have top food industry influencers coming," Steve said. "We've also invited some politicos and local celebrities. The permit came through for the red carpet outside, and Brock's client list will ensure we get lots of media coverage."

Ruben moved close to whisper. "Maybe Brock's not all bad."

"Yeah, he's growing on me too."

"Good. Because we're going to have you doing a lot of press for this opening. We'll funnel all the requests through him."

"As long as none conflict with my appearance on *Chopped*. Brock landed me a guest judge gig, and I'm fanboying big-time over that one."

Ruben squeezed my shoulder. "Get used to it. All this? You deserve it, and more. Be right back."

Ruben walked across the kitchen to Steve, and the pair left in search of the general contractor.

I shook my head, imagining young me, an orphan with dreams. What would he think of my life now? Grown, with two restaurants, a red-carpet event, and a woman I loved. It was more than I had a right to dream of. But here I was.

A flashbulb startled me back to the present.

"That'll be a good one," the photographer said. "You were lost in thought."

"Probably dreaming of that woman of his. Do you need me to get a stage pass for Leslie's spot on *The Kaelen Reed Show*?" Brock asked.

"Thanks, no. Leslie has it handled. I think I'm more nervous than she is."

Leslie had been relentlessly preparing, digging deep into Reed's past. That approach surprised me. I couldn't tell if it was a Sun Tzu tactic to know thy enemy, or whether she planned to take this debate in a different direction.

With the face-off scheduled for tomorrow, I'd finally find out.

Chapter 43

LESLIE

The last time I stood in this dressing room, I hugged a devastated Victoria Cooper Rawley, who had just been told she had a neck like a goiter. Tonight would be my chance to make a bully pay for his stinging abuse. Kaelen would likely zing insults my way off-camera, but never on. It's partially why I tapped my friends at B'Cause for a new outfit he'd no doubt appreciate.

A snug black dress that dipped temptingly low. A gold and onyx teardrop pendant nestled at the nape of my throat, pointing to my now-fuller cleavage. Eyes smoky, lips full and red, courtesy of the show's makeup team. It was sweet to hear they were all on my side, and it reminded me how much I missed my regular contact with the crew. Being back after so many months away revived my love of being on television.

One thing that didn't concern me was where I'd work. After debating whether to wait until after my showdown with Kaelen, I signed an offer letter this morning with another network. Instead of hosting a weekend show, I'd headline a half-hour Thursday evening interview show that rotated a lineup of different hosts each weeknight at 9:00 p.m. Some were journalists like me, others were social media sensations. The success of my YouTube channel positioned me as a delicious mix of the two. Hopefully, tonight's fireworks wouldn't send them tripping over themselves to cancel my contract. Twice in the same month would be too much to bear.

I fussed with my curls, which the stylist arranged into a cascade over my shoulders. I'd been growing them out, and they looked healthier than I could remember. Luxe and shiny, my hair only added to the slew of physical changes that continued to unfurl the longer I nourished my body. If I ever needed to show up strong, tonight was the night. I secretly feared I'd get triggered, shut down, and be left blinking wordlessly into the studio's cameras.

I blew out a cleansing breath.

I can do this. But a nugget of doubt lodged in the pit of my stomach. How would this mainstream conversation about body acceptance impact my reputation? I'd been on YouTube for weeks, but this was different. This was a prime time cable news event that was advertised ten ways till Sunday to attract viewers.

Counterarguments to the thin ideal were so easily shot down by the "experts" that I feared appearing like a crackpot. Making a fool of myself would seriously hamper my career, just as I readied to launch higher.

My diet coverage had garnered a lot of attention, but it could also be the story that buried me for good.

A bit late to lose my shit over this.

Alone in my dressing room, silence rang in my ears. Risto wasn't allowed backstage, forced to watch from the control booth. It was an odd request from Reed's team and one of the many terms we negotiated for this broadcast special. Given all the promotion online, on-air, and in buses and on billboards all over the country, the network had spared no expense.

My generous pay was also a surprise.

As I sat here, my reporter antennae shot up.

Why had they agreed to do it?

They hated me and canceled my contract. Why invest so much buzz in a person they no longer wanted?

Enticing me back wasn't the answer.

Was I walking into an ambush?

An elaborate takedown, planned as revenge for embarrassing them with my protest?

My instincts never failed me, and right now they were sounding the alarm that something fishy was about to go down. I just didn't know what and was running out of time.

Say what you wanted. Reed was still a journalist. Given his competitive nature, I wouldn't put it past him to try underhanded tactics to get me off-kilter. Maybe he even dove into my background as much as I dug into his?

What would he find?

The eyes staring back at me in the mirror showed the one thing I least expected.

Fear.

Pounding on my dressing room door spiked my heart rate to throbbing.

"Allen! We're ready for you on set."

Never had I headed into a broadcast feeling so rattled. Perspiration flushed my skin as images of me getting verbally eviscerated clanged around my brain. Reed mocking me, leaning back in his chair with a smug expression, waiting for me to step in it.

That must not happen.

Too many people were counting on me to be their champion. To set the record straight and tell the world to go fuck themselves for making us hate ourselves thin. They wanted me to starve myself sick because they found round, full body shapes ugly.

My empty apartment fridge came to mind. Countless times I stood before the open door, chill washing over my skin, wanting so desperately to feel something besides hunger.

Well, I was starving now.

For justice.

For respect.

For a world where our size didn't matter and we felt safe going to the doctor, to work, to a restaurant, or a family picnic without being harassed.

Where fat people weren't presumed to be lazy, or stupid, or less accomplished.

This was my opportunity to strike a decisive blow for everyone forced into sickness and marginalization.

Steeled with outrage, I swung the door open, sending the stage manager jumping away. I marched past her toward the set.

"Let's do this. Will the graphics I sent be available?"

"Yes, Ms. Allen. I saw to it myself."

I stopped short, and she collided into my back.

"Don't bullshit me. I'll stop mid-show and call you all out. Is that clear?"

"I understand. No worries." She looked too panicked to be deceitful, so I resumed the walk down the hall and entered the stage area.

The graphic from the ads splashed across the digital wall behind a circular platform. Two low-backed armchairs awaited us. My heels clacked on the floor before getting muffled on the red carpeted surface. I sat, leaning against the cream leather arms to get comfortable. The seat was deeper than I liked, so scooted forward and crossed my legs. They'd ask me to sit back, but no dice. Posture mattered, and I had no intention of falling for the rookie trick of getting swallowed whole by my chair.

As Reed stepped onto the set in a navy suit and tie, I stood to shake hands. "Kaelen."

"Allen. Guess it's time to clear the air."

We both sat.

Maureen walked over, looking up at us from floor level. "Let's make this one for the record books, shall we? Two titans having a principled debate about an important cultural issue."

"She's hardly a titan, Mo." Reed snickered.

"Then you should have nothing to worry about," Maureen said.

Concern flashed across his face and was gone in an instant.

But I hadn't imagined it.

Good. He should be nervous.

"One more thing, Allen," Reed said. "Those graphics you emailed are a no-go. People aren't tuning in to see an academic lecture on how awesome it is to be fat. We want lively interaction here."

"You can't do that to me three minutes before we air!"

Maureen stopped. Unsure, she arched her eyebrows for verification.

"Mo, we discussed this. Remember?" Kaelen gave her a stern glance, and she slinked away.

"What's your game here?" I asked him.

"No game, Allen. It's called television. I'm the best at what I do, and what I say goes."

"Is that right?"

"Yes."

I looked toward Maureen, who had retreated into the soundproof booth. Through the window, I watched her soundlessly giving orders to the crew. Behind her stood Risto. Seeing his imposing form stare down Maureen made me chuckle. She snuck by and took her seat.

"Allen!" Reed called, tapping his wrist.

The stage manager started the countdown, so I repositioned myself in my chair and exhaled a cleansing breath.

"Live in three, two..." the stage manager gestured as the white lights of the wall-mounted "On-Air" boxes flashed on across the studio.

"Good evening, and welcome to this special episode of *The Kaelen Reed Show*, tonight with guest Leslie Allen Molina. Ms. Allen became an online sensation with her series of YouTube videos challenging the conventional wisdom that when it comes to weight, we've been told a pack of lies."

The 15-foot digital wall behind us splashed to life with a grainy montage of my YouTube shows, complete with me crying. The video package was clipped to include the most sensational statements, out of context. Those were interspersed with clips from the rally, of me on a bullhorn, and picket signs showing slogans that were never there.

We'll eat your babies.

Kill thin people!

Crush the thin elite.

The montage had a fake quality to it. Ours was a sunny day, and the lighting on the provocative signs was flat and gray. The trees in the background hadn't yet sprouted leaves, though we were now rolling into autumn. Trickery like this was beneath them.

While it aired, I got Kaelen's attention. His face wore a satisfied smirk.

What the hell was going on?

When the package ended, Kaelen resumed the interview. "Tonight, I'm pleased to welcome Leslie Allen Molina. Thank you for being here."

Rather than speak, I sat staring at him.

The dead air made the network brass restless, so I let it linger.

"Am I really welcome?" I asked. "Because that video montage was a travesty."

Reed looked at the pages in his lap, then feebly smiled. "Do you deny holding those opinions? It's why you're here tonight."

"That people deserve respect in whatever body they have? That we can move and eat in ways that honor who we are right now? That CDC and NIH studies show that overweight and obese participants live longer than underweight and normal weight people? I very much hold those opinions. What I object to is—"

"How long have you felt this way?" Reed interrupted. "Until recently, you were a regular panelist on my show. I'd never once heard you mention concerns about weight."

"Hard to be concerned while scraping by on a sub-starvation diet. I was undernourished, underfed, and struggled to function in my daily life. My strength only returned when I began my eating disorder recovery."

Reed chuckled. "Looks like you got good at it."

"I'm larger now, yes. But I feel better than I ever have. I move more, I have more energy, and my health vitals have improved versus when I was at a lower weight. Anorexia nervosa is a condition I struggled with for many years, and I'm glad I left it behind and found a healthier path."

"Some would argue that you're lost on that path and need help to find your way... home."

The screen behind us filled with my mom's face.

I clutched the armrests on my chair to keep from spiraling. What would possess her to ambush me live on television? I was her fucking daughter and she'd sided with the network?

Kaelen swiveled his chair toward the screen to stand and pace over toward Mom's face which spanned the entire wall. "We're pleased to welcome in Diana Allen, Ms. Allen's mother. She reached out to us after being shut out by her famous daughter. She joins us live from her home in Albuquerque, New Mexico. Good evening and thanks for joining us."

One camera pivoted to focus on him, while the other rotated to capture my reactions. Tonight was going far worse than my darkest mind could ever imagine. I had to figure out a way to turn the situation in my favor without looking like an ungrateful daughter.

Reed interviewed my mom, asking her questions about my "erratic" behavior, my withdrawal to rural Pennsylvania, and my refusal to seek responsible treatment. I'd become the discredited lunatic, needing mental health services, as they talked about me like I wasn't even there. Out of the shot, the duo presented an open-and-shut case. But I'd worked too hard to let my career implode in a fiery ball.

I stood and walked over to join Kaelen by the screen, interrupting their conversation.

"I find it interesting that you're more interested in hearing what my mother says than in speaking to me directly. May I?"

Kaelen gestured for me to proceed.

"Mom. How often did we eat when I was growing up?"

She bristled. "You ate every day. What a growing girl should."

"Actually, I've calculated my caloric intake at roughly 900 calories."

The crew gasped, earning a silencing glance from Reed.

"And when I returned each summer from Pennsylvania, having gained weight and feeling well, what did you do to drop me down to what you considered to be an acceptable size?"

She crossed her arms, pressing her lips together.

"I'll answer so the viewers know. My mother restricted my intake to one meal a day. She chose lunch, so my school wouldn't get suspicious and investigate. Smart, Mom. Very smart." I addressed the screen before turning toward the camera.

"When my father attempted to feed me, she became so irate that they eventually divorced. My mother was so disordered in her eating, she was unaware that I'd developed anorexia nervosa. Yet, Kaelen, you mock me for being healthier and happier, and for eating normally. So I ask you, who between us is sick?"

A shocked Kaelen spoke to the camera. "We'll be right back."

I paced to my seat and sat as the show went to a commercial break. My mother's dirty work done, the digital screen once again flashed the special's logo.

Reed returned to his chair, saying nothing.

I leaned forward, barely able to contain my rage. "How dare you ambush me with my mother? Is this fucking *Jerry Springer*? You're resorting to shock tactics and fake videos rather than debate my statements rationally. Is that because you can't?"

"Oh, please." He dismissed with a wave. "Don't flatter yourself."

"You could have done this show without me. Why am I here?"

"To get a dose of your own medicine," he snapped.

Kaelen was not only a pompous ass, he was also being grossly unprofessional. Sure, he had major body issues, but I couldn't be concerned about that. It was him or me, and this wasn't over. Not by a long shot.

He'd fucked with the wrong woman.

Chapter 44

RISTO

Leslie was losing an epic battle. The crew in the booth looked stunned, whispering about how awful it was to treat talent this way. The producer, Maureen, sat visibly tense until she slammed her palm on the control panel.

"What's with all of you? Did you already forget the shitstorm she created for us?! Kaelen is right to push back."

The man next to her leaned over. "That fake protest wasn't even close. No leaves on the trees in those shots. No sun, no shadows. C'mon, what were you thinking?"

She crossed her arms. "I don't know what you're talking about."

Just then, someone yelled, "I found it! It's from that rally in Washington. Same people, but the background was swapped for our plaza, and new text overlaid on the picket signs."

Four staffers crowded around the screen, their disgust speaking volumes.

Maureen whispered into her collar.

A moment later, Reed rose on-set and strode toward the booth, yanking the door open with a bang.

"Is there a problem in here? Hmmm?"

He surveyed the room, and the crew went mumbling back to their seats. "That woman led a mob to our doorstep. She deserves to have her wild accusations challenged." He slammed the door to return to his chair before the commercial ended.

Meanwhile, my mind raged. The team proved the protest footage was faked. But what could I do about it?

"Camera Two," Maureen said, and the shot focused on Reed.

"Those were some serious accusations you leveled at your mother," Reed said.

"Camera One. Slow zoom," Maureen instructed.

The camera centered on Leslie and gradually narrowed from a wide shot to focus on her face. When Leslie got mad, her jaw clenched. But I could see no signs of it.

What are you up to, my love?

"I'm sure you can relate. Having struggled with your size in the past."

Reed stiffened. "Me?"

"When I interviewed staff at your elementary school, I heard how hard you worked with Mr. Marinelli, the gym teacher. And that you return often, going as far as to pay for diet programs and gym memberships for the students. Why is that?"

Reed scratched his eyebrow. "My hope is that all children, regardless of means, can be as healthy as possible."

"Any other reason?"

"I'm not sure what you mean," Kaelen said warily.

"How about to avoid bullying?"

"Yes. Of course. That's tough for everyone."

"If bullying is bad, why do you harass your guests about their weight? I have witnessed you reduce a talented, award-winning journalist to tears on this very set because you believed she was too fat."

"That's not true."

"Aren't you perpetuating the same bullying behavior you experienced as a child? That fat is bad and thin is the only way to exist in this world? That if someone lives on their own terms in a larger body that they're diseased, lazy, and defective?"

"Wait, what?!"

"Isn't this crusade against me a ruse to cover up how much the network profits from diet plans, pharmaceutical diet products, diet foods, and government grants aimed at pushing a thin agenda? All despite the CDC research and thousands of studies around the world showing that dieting doesn't work?"

The two sat in a silent standoff.

Reed looked intrigued. Whether genuine or not was impossible to tell. "Tell us why you say diets don't work."

"I prepared some graphics. If the control room would air them, I'd appreciate it."

The crew looked at Maureen.

"Kaelen said no charts," Maureen spat.

Luckily for Leslie, the guy at the control board ignored her. He clicked a button, and a slide appeared on the screen wall behind them.

"As you can see, dieting works only for a short term. Since it's not sustainable over time, people gain the weight back, plus some. The more people diet, the fatter they get."

"But you said fat was fine," Reed tossed back, obviously pleased with himself.

"The issue isn't how much people weigh. The problem comes from repeated weight loss-weight gain cycles and the disordered beliefs about food and body size. People don't fail diets. Diets fail people by making them less healthy, raising their natural set point weight, boosting stress, and leaving people frustrated, hungry, lost, and for most, heavier than before they dieted. If you want a guaranteed path to misery, I suggest a diet."

A bark of laughter shattered the booth's silence, earning a sharp stare from the boss.

"What?" the crew member asked. "It's funny."

Reed looked puzzled. "If dieting doesn't work, what is the alternative for people needing to lose weight?"

Leslie leaned forward. "Why do people diet?"

"To lose weight."

"Why else?"

"To be healthier."

"But if the data shows that you can be healthy at many sizes—lower blood pressure, stable cholesterol levels, better heart function, etc.—why don't we focus on modifying lifestyle and forget about weight all together? Next slide, please."

The graphic swapped.

"This one shows two groups of participants, before and after the study. Both were the same weight by the end. The first group lost and regained the weight within two years. But the second, non-dieting group had much better health outcomes. They were what you defined as healthy, but they lived in larger bodies. If, ultimately, we're concerned with health and longevity, then our focus on dieting moves us farther away from our goal."

Realization dawned on Reed's face, just as it did in the control booth. All eyes were glued to the screen where Leslie's triumph glowed through the lens. She'd turned the tide. Now the dramatic zoom focused on Reed.

"Well, damn. That makes a lot of sense," a crewmember said.

"I've wasted all this time thinking I needed to drop pounds," another whispered.

"Quiet!" Maureen commanded.

Reed leaned forward. "So we can sit around eating Twinkies and live to be a hundred?"

"Not necessarily. But if you want a Twinkie, please go eat one. If you don't, you'll likely obsess about it for hours, probably consume a lot of unnecessary calories, time, and energy instead of having the damn Twinkie and getting back to your life. The key is to balance that with nutrient-dense foods, movement, and sleep."

"It sounds so simple." Reed laughed.

"Yeah. And free."

"Cut to commercial!" Maureen yelled, pushing out of her chair with such force it collided into me as it toppled over. That's when she noticed me, her eyes bugging wide as I fluttered my fingers *hello*.

"Thank you for inviting me to see what happens behind the scenes," I said. "All the nasty tricks viewers never know about. Someone should tell them, don't you think?"

She blanched, but quickly recovered.

"Security! Security!" Maureen yelled, pushing past me to yank the door open so hard that it bounced against the rubber stop and slammed back closed. She stormed over to the set, where her noiseless pleading with Reed played out in front of us as the screens displayed a muted commercial break.

Leslie joined the argument, sliding herself in between producer and talent. What the hell was going on? Aching to get to Leslie, I strode toward the door, but a security guy appeared, blocking the way.

"Visiting time is over, sir. You need to come with me."

Chapter 45

Leslie

"Why the fuck did they cut to commercial?" Reed glared at the booth, steam shooting out his ears.

He stood to meet Maureen, who came charging over. "He heard everything! Security! Security!"

Risto.

What is Maureen doing? He was an invited guest?

I stepped forward in time to spot Risto getting escorted out by a guard. Seeing me, he blew a kiss, mouthing, *It's okay.* He wore a huge smile, so I refocused on the battle in front of me.

"Stick to the fucking script!" Reed yelled at Maureen, puffing up tall.

"I think we should change the next segment to—"

"We're not changing a goddamned thing!"

I slid in between them. "Kaelen. You need to calm down. We're back live in two minutes and need to make some changes."

"We? There's no we. There's only me."

Maureen interjected. "This is good television. Allen has made a lot of valid points. Why don't we put up her charts so you can look at the data together? We have another ten minutes to—"

"Oh, so now you're the big mastermind?" Reed said to his producer, whose head bowed in penitence like a scolded teenager.

"If anyone should be pissed, it's me after your attempted takedown," I screamed at him.

"Fuck you, Allen. This is my show. Mo, get back in the booth and get ready for the next segment." He pointed off-set without looking at the stage manager, who was wildly waving toward the On-Air signal.

A second later, the On-Air light illuminated. Maureen and I matched gazes as Reed's rant continued.

"I don't work for you, Allen, and you certainly don't work for me."

"Yeah, you saw to that. All over a few extra pounds?" I prodded.

"I can't put you on camera looking like the fatty you are now!"

"So you're still using weight clauses, despite the network statement?"

Reed laughed. "Those suits will never allow our talent to blimp up. No one wants to watch that! They're only saying that to appease the mob you brought to our doorstep!"

"That reminds me. Those fake signs you put in the video were a master stroke."

Reed smiled. "They were. Took us three hours, but was worth it to see your face on live television..."

Realization dawned as his head whipped around toward the "On-Air" sign shining brightly. He stared into the camera, then back at me and Maureen. Tugging his shirt neat, Reed stormed off set.

"Well, that's live TV for you!" I said.

Maureen gestured for us to sit. "Before we continue, I want to apologize to our viewers, and to you, Ms. Allen, for the events of this evening. You were our guest, and we didn't give you the opportunity to present your case fairly. Let's do that now…"

We spent a half hour talking about my transformation from the beginning, extending into the next show's time slot.

The information I'd learned.

The interviews I'd done with health providers and researchers.

And Reed's teachers.

I looked straight into the camera.

"We've all been fed a steady diet of lies. But this conversation can change things. Take what you've heard here tonight. Research it for yourself, then think about whether it's time we all ditch the fear and start living our fullest lives. Thank you for watching."

"And we're out!" The stage manager called, and a bell sounded the all clear. But instead of a burst of side conversations erupting, no one spoke a word. Everyone stayed exactly where they were.

I stood to leave, then it started.

A single person slow-clapped.

Then another, until thunderous applause reverberated across the studio. I sank back into my chair, the relief was so great. I suppressed tears for as long as I could, then let them stream down my face.

Eventually, the makeup artist wrapped me in a tight hug, then released to blot my cheeks. "That was unforgettable."

"Yeah, that's what I'm afraid of." I stepped away, laughing as I wiped my wet eyes.

Tonight was a class A clusterfuck, pinging between incredible highs and unbelievable lows. If viewers shut it off after the ambush, I'd be ruined. Hopefully, the last 37 minutes would grab the headlines.

Where Reed bared his black soul for all to see, and I carried on. Alone. Fitting, really, because only we walked in our bodies. It was up to us to set ourselves free. No one could do it for us. It must have been compelling television, since the network stayed with me live, even after Reed left.

I navigated to the edge of the crowd, where someone grabbed my arm.

It was Kaelen. "Guess I owe you an apology."

I stared down to where his hand held me.

He dropped it but was far from repentant.

"What did you expect me to do? You humiliated me in front of the world. The network demanded I set the record straight."

"The only time you tell the truth is when you think the camera's off," I said.

"I was supposed to welcome you with open arms after that stunt you pulled with the protest?"

"I expected you to be a professional. The way I see it, I should get half of whatever outrageous amount they're paying you, since you bailed in the middle of the show. While you cowered in a dressing room, I stayed on-set, telling the world the truth. It's up to them now to live their lives. You can go crawl into the backward hole you came from. I'm done with this fucking network. You don't deserve me."

I walked away, but he called after me.

"A birdie told me about your contract with FlashNews."

A smile crept across my face as I turned back. "How?"

"I have my ways. Who knows? If I get canned, you and I should partner. We're a good pair."

"No way."

He covered his heart as if pierced.

"Why, Mr. Reed, are you flirting with me?"

"That cleavage does look marvelous."

"Pig."

"Always. See ya around, Allen."

He strode across the set in the opposite direction, whistling, of all things.

I shook my head in disbelief. He was either a sly fox or poised for a new beginning of his own. Kaelen Reed would land on his feet.

And so would I.

I entered my dressing room to find Risto and the security guy laughing over a bag of takeout.

They both stood.

"Umm," the young man said, wiping his mouth. "I better go."

Risto fizzed with excitement. "He's studying to be a chef. We've been talking food. What happened after I left?"

After two days of ignoring my mother's calls, I decided to answer. But I refused to speak first. It took every bit of yoga calmness I could summon and sat on my bed for the dreaded conversation.

"Finally! I swear, I have to appear on television to get my daughter's attention."

"That was despicable. What possessed you to do that? And for what? To humiliate me and ruin my career?"

She snickered. "Oh, you're doing that quite well on your own. You've been unraveling for months. What was I supposed to do? You won't take my calls or texts and ran off when I came in person. Did you get any of the letters I sent to Risto's in Pennslyvania?"

Risto and I hadn't been back to the house in a while. He did quick day trips to check on Boricua, but he hadn't mentioned any mail.

"You know nothing about me or my life, yet you presume to lecture me about what's best. I'm an adult and it's time for you to stop."

"I don't care how old you are. You're my daughter, and I'll fight for you even when you won't."

Risto splashed merrily in the shower, so I shifted my heated call to the living room to avoid disturbing him. My man had a big night ahead with the restaurant opening. And I had no intention of letting my mother's tantrum ruin it. While she ranted, my attention drifted toward my laptop.

I was expecting an email from Barbara about my imploding contract at FlashNews. Their execs had shut off the *Kaelen* special after the first 20 minutes and began terminating my deal. Their cowardice made it clear my time there would have ended badly, so we parted ways. I also waved off offers from the other networks, including from NewsOne. Reed shot me a text offering my original Saturday job back, without the weight clause. But I soured on network news, media manipulation, and city buses wearing my face. I'd built a career by telling stories on my own terms, and that suited me just fine.

I would still investigate corruption and bring information forward to challenge what we thought we knew, especially about entrenched institutions. If people wanted to see me, they could catch me on my weekly YouTube reports, always done with me fully clothed and well-fed, then posted to podcast platforms. A syndication offer rolled in from a satellite radio network, and I was seriously considering it.

"Are you listening?" Mom shouted at me.

"No. And we should take time off from each other for the foreseeable future. Not like before, where you texted me nasty messages. A real break."

"You don't mean that." Panic laced Mom's trembling voice.

"Until you can accept me as-is and stop pressuring me to adopt your destructive behavior, it's best we sever our relationship."

"I love you. This isn't what I want," Mom whimpered.

"If that's true, then take some time to think. There's a toxic mess between us, and it centers on disordered behaviors and beliefs about food. I hope you find help or at least treat me respectfully, even if you don't approve of my choices. If you can, I'll be here to support you as you rebuild your life and our relationship. If not, then it's best we go our own ways and try again when we're both in a healthier place."

I hung up, pained that my mom's obsession with weight overshadowed her love for me. She refused to accept me as a human in a larger body. It was too much. I was too much.

But that was a her problem, not a me problem.

I had never felt better and was eager to embrace whatever craziness Risto and I would cook up next. Literally.

"Hey, it's over," I said to Risto through the closed bathroom door. "I'm free."

He cracked it open, and steam billowed moist heat into my face. I stepped back to prevent the humidity from frizzing my freshly styled hair.

"So that's it then?" Risto toweled off his head. Bare butt flexing as his torso showed signs of renewed health. While I wanted to share everything with Risto, my past food obsession wasn't one of them. I was so relieved we'd both moved on.

"Yeah. It's for the best. Maybe someday Mom and I will be able to reconnect."

Risto paced into the bedroom and slipped on his underwear. "Whatever happened with that offer from the professor?"

What started as joke emails between me and Professor Hawley after she saw my special with Kaelen Reed congealed into an intriguing idea. She'd gone to the department chair of the journalism school with a proposal to bring me in as an adjunct to teach a course about journalistic integrity and the need to expose institutional corruption. I had an arsenal of experiences to draw on, and it would help me inspire the next generation of investigative reporters. With newsroom budget cuts, too few of us remained dedicated to pounding the pavement and doing the hard work needed to shed light on uncomfortable truths.

The more I thought about it, the more thrilled I became about the opportunity. I just had to put a course curriculum together for the school to approve.

"You've got that look..." Risto said, kissing the top of my head as he passed by me to select his clothes.

He stood in front of his dresser. I hugged him from behind, his furnace of a body drying all lingering dampness from his skin.

God, I loved this man.

He moved about our apartment like he'd been here forever. Our lives melded so completely I could no longer remember who I'd been before. Old me was unrecognizable.

Alone.

Angry.

Afraid.

And very, very hungry.

Risto rotated in my arms to hug me back. "You okay?"

"Yeah. I have everything I need right here." I kissed his chest.

"So no dinner, then?"

I gave him the stink eye. "That's not even funny. Now get dressed. You're the featured attraction at an event in your honor. Boricua 2 awaits its famous chef!"

Chapter 46

Risto

As Leslie and I approached Boricua 2, the red carpet glowed brightly against the Manhattan sidewalk. Red velvet ropes blocked off the space leading up to a selfie wall in the foyer, complete with our new restaurant logo. Flashbulbs crackled and guests queued up for their moment in the spotlight.

Instead of ordering an Uber, we jumped on the subway, where her black dress and my tuxedo barely raised an eyebrow.

I love New York.

Living here these past months was only topped by finding a home and life with Leslie. Sharing this night together, the biggest of my career, filled my heart to near-bursting.

"There he is!" someone yelled as we approached the scene, walking hand in hand.

Ruben stepped forward to greet us.

"You walked?" he asked, eyeing our attire.

"Subway," I replied with a grin.

He kissed Leslie's cheek. "Hardly the grand entrance you deserve. We'll need to work on that. For now, it's time to shine!"

Urgent cries from reporters stopped Leslie and me nearly every step. We posed, pivoting to show different angles, following photographers' requests. Some shots with us close, me alone, and the two of us hugging. By the time we made it past the selfie wall, I was exhausted and glad not to be cooking tonight.

In the kitchen, my new staff fired on all cylinders. We'd rehearsed dinner service from start to finish on multiple occasions since the construction ended. There were a few kinks, and we'd luckily caught a few missing ingredients that would've been a disaster. The team was as prepared as they could be.

The servers knew the menu.

The chefs were ready.

Boricua 2 was here and officially open.

Staff navigated the capacity crowd, passing appetizers on silver trays. Each diner's nod of approval sent chills of delight rippling down my back.

Leslie took my hand and pulled me close. "You did it. This is all yours, and I couldn't be more proud. Your family is looking down and smiling. You feel it, don't you?"

I did.

Wherever my parents and grandparents were, I knew they were happy for me. Their struggle and sacrifice made me who I was, giving me the confidence to reach this moment. But this night belonged to others as well.

"There you are!" Jose yelled before pulling me into a hug. "This is a dream!"

Freddie stood back, sheepish, so I offered my hand. "This is yours too. Be proud. Both of you. You are as much the heart of Boricua as I am. We did this together, and it's only the beginning."

I pulled them aside, freeing Leslie to greet Dot and Gabby.

"Listen," I said. "Boricua 2 wouldn't be possible without you both running the restaurant back in Pennsylvania. This may not be the right time, but I'm having papers drawn up to make you each part owners in Boricua. If you don't want it, I understand. But you should have a financial stake and benefit from all your hard work."

"For real?" Jose said, his shock apparent.

"I don't even own my car outright. Now I'll be an owner in Boricua?" Freddie looked stunned.

"Did the investors agree to this?" Jose asked.

"Boricua is all mine, and now all ours—with Dot, of course. Boricua 2 is a separate business. I made sure of that. You in?"

"Yes. Thank you!" Jose hugged me in, tears glistening in his eyes. "Now there's an extra reason to celebrate! Come on!"

Jose led the three of us to the bar where we accepted flutes of champagne from the special bottle I'd hidden for this purpose.

"To Boricua!" I cried. "May we always dream big!"

Chapter 47

LESLIE

The night was a phenomenal success. The plates of food were exquisite and the space a wonder. Even more so now that it stood empty. I sat, shoes off, on a magical veranda under an indoor blanket of stars. The effect mesmerized. Tall lines, impossibly high ceilings, with solid stonework and golden lighting. Video panel windows showed palm trees, lit from below, fronds blowing in the breeze. Dining here was an experience, and the world would soon dig into the talents of the man I loved.

Puerto Rican love songs played faintly while fresh memories swirled around me.

Clinking glasses.

Delighted diners.

Well-wishes from our friends and family, overjoyed at our recent success.

It was too much and just right, and I savored every moment.

The kitchen doors swung open and Risto strolled across the space.

God, he's sexy.

And mine.

I smiled so often tonight my cheeks hurt but flashed him another wide one, earning a disbelieving grin in return.

"Yeah, I know. All this?" He gestured to the room.

"Maybe I'm happy about something else?"

He kneeled at my side. "What might that be?"

I opened my mouth to speak, but no words came.

There were too many blessings to count.

I was grateful for my life with Risto. That'd we'd found each other at last and forever.

I was grateful to be well, something that never would have happened without Dot first opening my eyes.

I was grateful to have a career where I could make a difference in the world.

And I was grateful to be me. I battled with myself for so long that having peace left me optimistic about the future.

But that was too much to squeeze into this moment.

Sometimes, silence spoke louder.

I leaned forward to accept Risto's tender kiss.

"Time to go home," I said. "But let's grab a cab. I'm done walking the streets at night."

Thank you for reading *What We Give Away*! If you enjoyed the book, leave a brief review to let other readers know it's worth their time.

Even a one-click rating on Amazon would mean the world. Thanks in advance!

Acknowledgements

Thank you my many friends, family, and peers for your continued support and interest in my writing journey.

- To my health and body size experts, Sydney Gatward, MS RDLDN, who once guided my own intuitive eating journey, and Jaimie (OJ) Bushell from MEDA Inc., a Multi-Service Eating Disorder Association. Thank you for your wisdom, experience, and fearless advocacy for those seeking to love their bodies.

- To my editor, Miranda Darrow. Thank you for your collaboration and 14-page reports. I hope to never write without you.

- To my talented cover designer, Rena Violet of Covers by Violet. Girl, you've done it again! #gorgeouscover.

- To my proofreader and author friend, Nanette Littlestone, for giving What We Give Away her professional eye.

- To Emma Junghans, for her keen expertise and insights about professional kitchens. Sorry about the fast turnaround. :)

- To my sister, Roxanne Media, for your endless love and support. Your encouragement means the world to me.

- To my daughter, Veronika Stout, whose frank thoughts made

the book you just read even better. I love you, sweetie!

- To Laura Henry, your passion and early feedback for my books is such a blessing. Thank you!

- To my dear friends Amy D'Alessio and Maureen Shirley. Your strength and unwavering love are a treasure.

- To Lainey Cameron, my podcast co-host and true writer friend. Your support means the world. I'm excited to see where life takes us.

- To Kelly Elizabeth Huston, Heidi McIntyre, and the members of the Women's Fiction – Indie Author Support Group. You have become steadfast supporters and collaborators in all things literary, and I'm very grateful.

- To the members of WFWA who provide frequent doses of writer friendship. Thank you for your support.

- To my son, Max, whose enthusiasm for my work never fails to buffer me in doubting moments.

- To Markus, my husband of now 30 years. The life we've built together leaves me free to create. I love you.

- And most of all, to the many readers enjoying my books around the world. Thank you for giving my stories a chance.

Hungry After Reading?

Claim your free download of ***Recipes From What We Give Away***! It's a sampling of dishes with simple ingredients that even beginner cooks can make.

Get yours FREE at: https://BookHip.com/DDHNVQF

Resources & Additional Reading

Books

- *The F*ck It Diet* by Caroline Dooner

- *Fearing the Black Body: The Racial Origins of Fat Phobia* by Sabrina Strings

- *Intuitive Eating: A Revolutionary Anti-Diet Approach* by Evelyn Tribole and Elyse Resch

- *Health at Every Size: The Surprising Truth About Your Weight* by Linda Bacon; Lindo Bacon

- *Life Hurts: A Doctor's Personal Journey Through Anorexia* by Dr. Elizabeth McNaught

Minnesota Starvation Experiment

- What We Can Learn From the Minnesota Starvation Experiment , Psychology Today, August 10, 2021

- Starvation Experiment of Dr. Ancel Keys, 1944-1045 , MNOPEDIA

Harmful Effects of Dieting

- Have Our Attempts to Curb Obesity Done More Harm Than Good? California Institute of Behavioral Neurosciences and Psychology, Memon A N, Gowda A S, Rallabhandi B, et al. (September 06, 2020)

- "What Happens to Your Body When You Go On An Extreme Diet," US News and World Report, August 3, 2021 by K. Aleisha Fetters, MS, CSCS

- "Metabolism to Mental Health: 7 Ways Losing Weight Too Fast Will Backfire," Undated, Healthline, Gabrielle Kassel.

Weight and Longevity Studies

- "Overweight" People Actually Tend to Live Longer Than "Normal" Weight Individuals," The Science Explorer, May 16, 2016

- "Fat Can Be Healthy: Some Obese People Live Long Lives," LiveScience, August 15, 2011

- Flegal, Katherine M., et al., "Excess Deaths Associated with Underweight, Overweight, and Obesity," Journal of the American Medical Association 293, no. 15 (2005) 1861-67. *What It Shows: The CDC revised computational errors and found the death risk of obesity and overweight fell by 15x using the corrected data. The new analysis showed "overweight" people lived longer than "normal" weight people. Most obesity death risk fell at the highest end of the BMI range where few Americans fell. The CDC did not publicize the revised findings nor change the policies based on the original, faulty data.*

- Gibbs, W., "Obesity: An Overblown Epidemic?" Scientific American. Vol June, 2005.

- Waaler, Hans T., "Height and Weight and Mortality: The Norwegian Experience," Acta Medica Scandinavica Supplemantum 679 (1084): 1-56.
  What It Shows: A study of 1.7 million people in Norway found that those categorized as overweight lived longest and those categorized as underweight had the shortest life expectancy.

- McGee, Daniel L., "Body Mass Index and Mortality: A Meta-Analysis Based on Person-Level Data from Twenty-Six Observational Studies," Annals of Epidemiology 15, no. 2 (2005): 87-97.

- "Clinical Guidelines on the Identification, Evaluation, and Treatment of Overweight and Obesity in Adults," Bethesda (MD): National Heart, Lung, and Blood Institute; 1998 Sep. Report No.: 98-4083
  What It Shows: The report is heavily supportive of viewing obesity as a health risk. Yet its own data shows the lowest

deathrate is among those with a BMI considerably over 25, which falls in the overweight range.

Problems with the BMI Scale

- "Is BMI Accurate? New Evidence Says No,"University of Rochester Medical Center, January 8, 2024

- "BMI is trash': Why so many doctors say it's time to ditch body mass index," The Montreal Gazette, October 24, 2022.

- "Don't use body mass index to determine whether people are healthy, UCLA-led study says," UCLA Health, February 4, 2016

- Gibbs, W., "Obesity: An Overblown Epidemic?" Scientific American. Vol June, 2005.

- "BMI Is a Terrible Measure of Health But We Keep Using It Anyway," FiveThirtyEight - Science, February 25, 2016

USDA Guidelines

- USDA 2020-2025 Dietary Guidelines – Executive Summary

- USDA Guidelines 2015-2020 Page 18: Healthy 2,000 calorie per day diet; Page 20:

What It Says:"1,200 to 1,500 calories each day can help most women lose weight safely."

Body Positive Yoga

- BodyPositiveYoga.com Blog: Pose Modifications

- DianneBondy.com: Resources for Yoga Students and Instructors

Recovering from Anorexia Nervosa

- "Unlocking a Healthy Mindset: The Road to Recovery from Anorexia Nervosa," Johns Hopkins Medicine

- "The Things No One Tells You about Anorexia and Recovery," Psychology Today, May 16, 2019

- "3 Tips for Lasting Recovery From Anorexia Nervosa," Psychology Today, February 15, 2021

Post a Review

If this book meant anything to you, please take a moment to leave a review. Like you might skip eating at an empty restaurant, the same applies to books! Thanks for letting readers know my book is worthwhile.

Or visit: paulettestout.com/review

Keep Reading

Turn the page to read Chapter One of Bold Journeys Book One: Love, Only Better! It's Rebecca's empowering story and it's where she first meets Kyle.

It's spicy, but don't we all need spice in our lives?

$$\text{L{\small OVE}, O{\small NLY}}$$
$$\text{B{\small ETTER}}$$

Chapter One

I t wasn't as if the words were unexpected. Hell, Rebecca said them to herself a thousand times over. Only, this was different. Hearing someone else say them—someone she loved. Someone who shared her life and her bed for three years—somehow made them true. And to have Ethan say them. For him to let them free that way. Now, they were alive to reverberate through the universe and rebound on her in unforgiving ways. And he'd no longer be around to save her.

Frigid. Ice queen.

Who calls someone they love an ice queen? Rebecca wondered.

That's the ticket. Ethan didn't love her. Had he ever? Or was she just a bad lay; a notch on his belt. Not even a trophy. A third-place yellow ribbon no one wanted, abandoned in the bottom of a drawer.

A wisp of spiderweb dangling from her headboard above fluttered in time with her cleansing breaths. Dust covered. Abandoned. Even the stupid spider hadn't stuck around.

Frigid. Ice queen.

She flipped up her covers to snatch a tissue from across the room, wiping her eyes and nose before tossing it into the wastebasket under her old desk. The desk in name only. Even bac k in high school, she did her homework on her bed. The desk chair, like now, was a glorified staging area for clothes somewhere between clean and dirty.

Did she still have it?

She yanked the center drawer open, pawing the time capsule within. Old lipstick, diaries, hair elastics, the wallet-sized card reproduction of her university diploma, tarot cards, and there it was: her third-place ribbon. She won it at summer camp for archery. She'd never held a bow before then, or since. But there it was; evidence that she was once good enough at something to warrant recognition.

The silky cord slid between her fingers until hitting the tassel knot.

So fitting. Third place. Rebecca was third place in her own life, too. She was certainly last place to Ethan. He was probably off finding himself a blue-ribbon sex machine worthy of His Majesty. Even at this hour. New York City never sleeps, after all.

Growing up in the belly of Manhattan, the buzz of life at all hours was as natural as air. The humming streetlights, the shadows, everything held a pulse. Teeming.

Except for her. Rebecca was the one spot of lifelessness in the whole city.

Frigid. Ice queen.

She dropped the ribbon in the drawer and slammed it shut, then quickly froze. Alert, she listened for sounds of stirring. Barbara, her roommate and best friend, was fast asleep in the next room. A lawyer with a big day in court ahead.

Rebecca released her breath, then strode back to bed, flopping on top of her navy down comforter and making herself a burrito with its folded edges. It was as close as she would get to an embrace for who knows how long.

Wiggling for her night table, she switched off the light. Shadows formed at familiar angles on her ceiling. The ceiling she'd pondered for twenty-eight years. Framed pictures of Salvador Dali and Kandinsky hung over her low, long dresser, once filled with frilly pink play clothes, now stuffed with T-shirts and leggings in mismatched shades of black. Her collection of discount designer shoes spilled out of the closet, distractions for the shortcomings of her noir wardrobe.

Her eyes drifted closed.

Ethan's contorted, red face jolted her awake.

Would she ever sleep again?

Would she ever love again?

Would anyone ever love her?

Was she even worthy of being loved?

She wasn't sure.

On cue, her nemesis, the mourning dove, made a fluttery landing on the air-conditioning unit blocking half of her window. The distinctive coo was maddening. Was that how Ethan felt when she was unable to climax in bed? A fury of frustration without an outlet?

Rebecca abandoned covers and leaped to battle stations. The vinyl shade creaked its objection as she bent it up to spy on the enemy. The pink towel she put out to dull the air-conditioner drips from upstairs had become a bird magnet. Twigs, leaves, tinsel? Where did they find tinsel in June?

"Shoo! Shoo!" Rebecca whisper screamed, banging on the glass with her fist.

The dusty bird settled in.

"Go on. *Go.*"

"Becca! Are you fucking kidding? It's 4:00 a.m.!" Barbara shouted through the wall.

"Sorry!" Rebecca hollered back, watching the bird tuck its wings for sleep. There was a beat of silence.

"Shit," Barbara muttered. Rebecca heard her feet hit the floor and storm down the parquet hallway, a staple of 1950s' NYC apartments. The bathroom door closed.

Rebecca dropped the shade and collapsed into the cup of her papasan chair under the window, drawing a branded fleece blanket over her. It was one of the many freebies she got working in advertising; this one was from her hotel client.

After the flush and wash, Barbara exited then walked through Rebecca's perennially open bedroom door and switched the light on.

Her hand shielded her eyes from the sudden brightness.

Barbara stood in a pink satin Victoria Secret nightie, a matching sleep mask holding up her long, dark locks—a top-shelf weave and proudly not hers—flowing over ebony shoulders.

"What the hell are you doing up?"

"I'm so sorry—"

"Jesus, what happened?"

"What do you mean?"

"You look like a clown on acid."

Rebecca crawled out of the saucer and stood in front of the mirror.

"Yeah, not my best look."

Black mascara streaked down her face from the blotchy eyes she had been rubbing for hours.

"Where's Ethan? I thought he was staying over?"

"Gone."

"Gone home?"

"No. Just gone. We're done. Well, actually, he was done with me."

"Wow. I'm so sorry. But... not as sorry as you should be for waking me up..." Barbara said, launching herself to Rebecca's bed and sliding her sleep mask down over her eyes.

"That's it? That's all the consoling I get? I have a blowout with my boyfriend who calls me a 'frigid ice queen' and leaves, and..."

"He didn't," Barbara said, lifting up on her elbow and raising her mask.

"Oh yes he did."

"You're not an ice queen. You know that."

"Counselor, the evidence is overwhelming."

"He's a jackass. I've always thought so."

"Oh, he's not that bad..."

Barbara raised an eyebrow.

"Come on!"

"I won't lie to you and say I'm disappointed he's gone."

"But... I am," Rebecca whispered.

"All I mean is he didn't treat you right. You can absolutely do better."

Barbara patted the bed next to her. Rebecca folded her arms and looked away.

"You CAN do better. Ethan will regret losing you, and you'll look back and NOT regret losing him."

Rebecca pouted her bottom lip.

"Suit yourself. I must sleep more, though." Barbara left the bed, popped a squeaky kiss on Rebecca's forehead.

"Leave that damn bird alone, will you?" she said before leaving.

"You left the light on!" Rebecca called after her, but Barbara's bedroom door closed with a click.

Sighing, Rebecca crawled out of the chair and crossed the room to switch off the light. Dawn's blueness was already invading. She looked at her bed, but instead returned to sit under her fleece blanket, gathering it about her.

Maybe she could sleep if she was out of bed, away from his smell. She'd have to change the sheets later. She wanted to change everything; beginning with herself.

To keep reading, buy your copy of Love, Only Better at this web link or visit: paulettestout.com/buy-books

About the Author

Paulette Stout is the fearless author of empowering stories about women finding their voices, being heard, and embracing love.

Read in 43 countries and counting, her 17 book award recognitions span her novels, *Love, Only Better. What We Never Say*, and *What Eyes Can't See*—adding to her three media industry awards, including a MediaWeek All-Star. *What We Give Away* is Paulette's fourth novel.

Raised by a single dad in Manhattan, you can now find Paulette rearranging words into pleasing patterns at her home in Acton, Massachusetts.

Connect with Paulette on her website at paulettestout.com, on Instagram, Facebook or TikTok @paulettestoutauthor.

And don't forget to **join Paulette's monthly newsletter** for free reads, news, book recommendations, and to learn what's she's up to next.